Atlas Died

Michelle N. Onuorah

Atlas Died
Published by MNO Media, LLC
Printed in the U.S.A.

ISBN-13: 978-0996627108
ISBN-10: 0996627103

This is a work of fiction. The characters, incidents, and
dialogues are products of the author's imagination and are not to
be construed as real. Any resemblance or references to actual
events, places or persons living or dead, is entirely coincidental
or fictitious.

**Please note that there are instances of profanity, mild violence,
and unapologetic themes of religion, politics and spirituality
within this work of fiction. Reader discretion is advised.**

Formatting by Polgarus Studio.

Scripture is taken from the King James Version
of the Bible. (Public Domain)

Other Titles by Michelle N. Onuorah

Type N
Taking Names
Remember Me
Jane

Atlas Died

USA: A RELIC OF LIBERTY
An Exploratory Piece by Natalie Rummel
South African Times
July 4, 2626

Today marks the 850 year anniversary of what used to be the United States of America's Independence Day. The country, now only known as USA, reportedly no longer celebrates the holiday or any other commemorating the

American Revolution. The United States of America once held great influence and power across the globe, and was celebrated for its ideals of life, liberty, and opportunity for all willing to work hard. Now regarded as one of the most hostile nations in the world, USA has been in a self-imposed isolation from all foreign nations since 2600, when the nation's president initiated what is now known as the "steel wall." No communication from the nation, outside of aggressive military defense, has been heard since. The map shown above is the last known geographic layout of the country.

Originally founded on the ideals of democracy, freedom, and justice for all, USA experienced a rapid social, political and economic decline in the 21st and 22nd centuries. After which, numerous legislative measures stripped the nation's citizens of the rights the country was once renowned for. After a devastating plague wiped USA of nearly all its population, a new regime rose to power that many believe was even worse than the government that initially caused the decline.

At the time of the steel wall's formation, USA had not celebrated Independence Day in over two-hundred years. In light of what it has now become, one can only wonder if there is anything left to celebrate. USA was once the land of the free and the home of the brave. Now the question remains: is there still life, liberty, and the pursuit of happiness on its shores?

"The tree of liberty must be refreshed from time to time with the blood of patriots and tyrants. It is its natural manure."
-Thomas Jefferson

CHAPTER ONE

September 2628

The alarm blares obnoxiously near my ear. I open my eyes slowly, peeling one lid open after the other, as if the slow movement will ease the sudden pounding in my head.

It doesn't.

I reach over to shut the annoying contraption off. Wiping a heavy hand across my brow, I yawn and give myself five seconds to lie in bed. Pretend I don't have to get up. Don't have to face the day ahead. As I rise slowly, painfully really, it dawns on me that I can't remember the last time I woke up happy to be alive. The last time I woke up, looking forward to the day ahead.

Maybe when I was a child.

In elementary school.

During the last vacation I'd ever take.

Before the country came to complete shit.

Now everything is a duty, all the way down to swinging my legs over the bed. In fact, now that I think about it, the only thing I actually look forward to is going back to bed at the end of the day.

Why can't I just sleep and stay that way? I think. *Indefinitely.*

I move on autopilot, barely aware of the small, cramped surface area that defines my surrounding. Even though it's morning, my room is perpetually dark, curtains drawn at all hours of the day. I don't spend much time here, except to sleep so there's no point in bringing in light. I use the bathroom, careful not to knock over any of her bottles and knick knacks. I don't know why I allow her to put her excess stuff in my bathroom when she has plenty of room in her own. Well that's not true. Neither bathrooms are particularly spacious but still... How many things does a woman really need to get ready for the day? Particularly a woman who doesn't leave the house except on the rare occasion? Emerging from my room showered, changed, and ready to go, I smell the coffee before I see it in my favorite mug. I give a slight smile. The toast sitting beside it is more inviting. My mom tries, she really does. But nothing she does can make me forget the coffee is several days old. Yet another reminder I needed my check yesterday.

I make my way around the tiny kitchen, my large body deftly avoiding the familiar edges of the tight space. Our apartment can only be described as neat and small, with two rooms, two bathrooms, and a living space that is forced to accommodate the kitchen, dining area, and living room in a twenty by twenty foot space. Tiny and tidy. It has to be for two people to fit in something so small. I scan the room, my eyes barely taking in the old frayed arm chairs, worn wooden tables, and dilapidated sofa cushions. The same furniture my grandparents used when they were alive. The same furniture they purchased as newlyweds right before one of the most severe inflations hit the nation sixty years ago. Furniture shopping now days is a pipe dream. Only Atlas people have the money for that. I've spent more hours than I care to recall patching up these fixtures to keep them stable. Usable. Still, it's more than what most families on Commons have. I turn back to the counter and pick up the mug, swirling the stale black contents inside. I peek around the corner and see my mother perched at her desk in her room, her small body slumping over the severely outdated laptop.

How many times have I told her not to slump like that? And then she complains of back pain.

I shake my head, turn on the faucet and quickly pour the coffee down the drain.

"You know if you didn't want it, you could have given it to me."

I groan at the chastising tone and turn off the faucet. Taking the saucer, I bring it into her room.

"Do mothers have eyes in the back of their heads or something?" I ask, leaning down to kiss the top of her head. I hear the smile in her voice as she taps my cheek affectionately.

"You can't hide anything from me."

"Don't I know it." I gripe jokingly. My smile, and the

good mood with it, freezes in its place as I look past her head. On her computer screen, above a video, the headline blares: "SIX STEPS TO REAL ESTATE FORTUNE!" Never mind that real estate on Commons has been gridlocked since 2522. Where is she planning to accrue real estate fortune? On Atlas? It takes everything in me to withhold from rolling my eyes right in front of her. I keep silent and re-focus my gaze on the lady of my life. Small and petite with an upturned nose, Mom looks like a doll to be handled with the utmost care. She has the kindest eyes I've ever seen. They're small, dark and slightly slanted, one of the few traits I inherited from her. That and her dark hair. Nothing else in my features would give away that I have a mother of Korean descent. The rest of my features resemble my father.

I hand her the saucer.

She shakes her head. "I already ate."

Liar.

"There were only two slices left yesterday, Mom. I checked."

I shove the plate in her hand insistently.

"Don't worry about me," I continue. "I'll get some at work."

If there's anything left. I'll be lucky if I can get something for myself, let alone the both of us. My check won't come in for two days. Will she have enough to tie her over until then? Will I? There has to be a couple of cans of *anything* left in the house. On days like this, I wish we would just cave in and get the junk genetically modified "food" everyone else on Commons eats to stay afloat. But my mother would rather starve to death than eat something so toxic. She raised me on real food, insists on real food. Only problem is real food costs real money. More money than most Commoners can pay. Atlas taste on a Commons budget. Which is why my entire check goes right back out every time I get paid. I don't want her to see my concern, my thoughts still fixed on food.

I kiss the top of her head again and turn to pull on my holster. I feel her eyes on me like they always are whenever I do this. Sometimes she speaks, telling me to be careful. Other times, like now, she just looks, as though trying to assure herself I'll be fine. After fourteen years, I thought she'd get used to my job. I keep my back to her as I check my rounds. I haven't had to use my weapons in months so a trip to the armory isn't necessary. I shrug on my jacket, effectively covering my gear. Keys in hand, I check the barricade beams surrounding the entrance.

"I'm heading out now," I tell her. "The gun is under the floorboard, remember?"

"Everything's under the floorboard," she mutters, her eyes back on the screen. "Ever since you were a child, everything important," she makes a cupping gesture with her hand. "Under the floorboard."

"Mom, pay attention. You need to remember that in case-"

"In case what?" she looks away from the screen, exasperated. When she sees my expression, her eyes soften. "Honey, we live in the Police Quarter. I never need it. I never will. Besides," she continues before I can protest, "no one comes here. Except Caden."

I sigh, frustrated with her cavalier attitude. "I know, but just in case-"

"Yeah, yeah. Have a good day, sweetie. I love you."

This time, I don't refrain from rolling my eyes. "Love you, too."

I cross the threshold and immediately feel the change. I stiffen my spine, roll my shoulders back, and take on the most passive expression I can. My expression is passive but my awareness of my surroundings has skyrocketed. I'm no longer comfortable. No longer relaxed. I can't afford to be. The minute I leave my place, I'm in work mode. And I'll stay in that mode until I re-enter my home at the end of the day.

I exit my building and immediately feel the thick, grimy filth on the bottom of my thick-soled boots. The Police Quarter is cleaner than most other quarters in Commons but it's still incredibly dirty, with severely limited funds to support infrastructure, much less the cleanliness of the island. Even worse than the filth literally sticking to my shoes is the rancid smell that permeates all of Commons. Urine, dirt, and stale gas. Living in a clean home with a neat freak mother, I sometimes forget that our apartment is stationed in the middle of a virtual stink hole. I cough and force myself to deal with the stench. I walk past people, seen and unseen, familiar and unfamiliar. No one says a word. No one greets one another. I glance up and start counting.

One…two…three…four…five security cameras in less than a block, attached to every street light, street sign, and corner of every building, private or commercial. There are forty-two between my building and the five minute walk to the train. I count them almost every morning. The closer I get to the train, the more mixed the crowd becomes. Other Commoners from other quarters stream through the Police Quarter to catch the Atlas Express for work. My mother feels safe in this quarter because it's mostly inhabited by police officers. She often fails to remember that every other Commoner, save the factory workers, walk through the quarter on their way to and from work. It's not safe. No quarter on Commons is truly safe.

No matter how many cameras they install.

"Welcome to Atlas Express." The automated voice reminds passengers that the train is set to leave in exactly four minutes. Updated four years ago to better accommodate the growing population, the station is sleek, modern, and completely white. So bright it almost hurts the eyes to stand here too long. A perfect juxtaposition to the dark clothed people trying to board its trains. I wade through the jostling crowd and steadily make my way to the front of the line. I recognize the guard manning the security consul. With a nod at Wallace Jackson and the flash of my badge, I clear the long line, and find my way to the security section of the train. Officers get immediate access

to the trains as our position is considered most important to the safety of Atlas civilians, or Atlans, as they're called.

Not that Commoners care to hear that.

"Cops," a waiting passenger jeers behind me. "Pretentious pricks. Always looking out for their own."

I ignore the dig and move forward.

"What was that?" Jackson asks the passenger. My eyes flick to Jackson's flushed face and I glance back in time to see the passenger's face turn from angry to cautious as he looked between myself and the guard. I can almost see the war on his face: speak his mind or stay out of trouble? I shake my head at him slightly. Warningly.

Don't be a fool.

He chooses the former.

"All of you - pricks. You treat us like dirt and skip to the front every damn day. Doesn't matter how long *we've* been waiting here!" The passengers around him murmur in agreement, though not loud enough to be confronted themselves. Jackson gets up and approaches the man. The man freezes as his expression gives way to sheer fear. He glances at me and even though he called me a prick just seconds ago, I feel an uneasiness rise in my gut. A desire to help him.

"Jackson."

Jackson glances at me, a small cruel upturn on his lips. "Have a good day, Channing."

Discussion closed. He's going to do what he wants to do and I need to stay out of it. I turn, not willing to see the ramifications of the man's reckless speech. I stride to board the train, but not before hearing the crack of a baton and the unwanted sound of the man groaning in pain. Glancing back, I see him buckle to his knees, Jackson walking away with his baton still drawn. The other passengers circle around the guy and I can only hope Jackson didn't break a bone. There's no such thing as days off or worker's compensation for Commoners. And a trip to any hospital or doctor outside of a field nurse at work, is as expensive as reserving a stay on McKenzie Isles. No Commoner can afford health care. Even police officers like me, who have a decent doctor on staff, can only get so much assistance for injuries or illness. If it can't be solved with a quick pill or a few minutes lying down, you're shit out of luck. I turn and take a seat, ignoring the turmoil in my gut. I pull out the small pamphlet from my jacket and read.

"Two minutes 'till departure," the voice rings again.

"Morning, Decker," a familiar voice says. I feel him sit next to me before I look up.

"Morning, Adams."

Joseph Adams is a medium height, medium built man with a buzz cut and cheerful blue eyes. Outside of my mother, I can't recall meeting someone with such open kindness. Not on Commons at least. He's been in the Force as long as I have but the fourteen years of service don't seem to have jaded him like they have me. He's the only guy on the Force I truly trust...well, the only guy since Jenner's dismissal.

"Think we'll make it in time for Yang's address?"

"It's just a meeting," I remind him.

He shakes his head. "With Yang, it's never 'just a meeting.'"

I smile and nod. The new Chief of Police is already establishing a reputation for his long winded, self-important speeches in what are supposed to be routine meetings. He's already a favorite of most men on the Force - and by favorite, I really mean a bad taste in all our mouths.

Adams points to the pamphlet in my hand. "What you reading?"

"*Common Sense.*"

He frowns questioningly.

"*Common Sense,*" I repeat. "By Thomas Paine. Founding father. Published in 1776."

"You and ancient literature, I swear." Adams shakes his head. "How can you even make heads or tails of whatever the hell they're saying in it?" He flicks his fingers at the small pamphlet. "And on paper? Who reads paper anymore?"

"I do," I answer, used to his good-natured ribbing.

"You see the commotion back there?" He gestures to the loading dock where massive crowds still wait.

I nod, my expression veiled. "Jackson's on duty. Enough said."

Adams nods.

Jackson is one of the most brutal patrol guards assigned to Atlas Express. He's never caused me trouble but I know it's only because I'm an officer too. Men like Jackson firmly establish the "Us vs. Them" mentality on Commons. Cops vs. Civilians. Police Quarter - the quarter of traitors. The rest of Commons generally hates us and I can't say I blame them. I'd feel the same way if I were in any other quarter, any other field.

Adams reads what must be a troubled look on my face, gesturing to the crowd outside. "You have anything to do with it?"

I shrug. "Not really."

Most officers would have considered what Jackson did a favor to them. But I know he didn't do it to defend me or be friendly. He did it because he's on a power trip and enjoys the role way too much.

Adams reads my face. "It's wrong. We both know that. But he's well within his rights to do whatever he wants while on patrol. We can't interfere."

I nod. "I know."

That doesn't mean I have to like it.

"Now arriving at Security Headquarters. Please watch your step."

We get off the train and take the short elevator ride up to the main level of the police station on Atlas. The police station, officially known as Security Headquarters, is a lot like the train station for Atlas Express. White, modern, with clean lines and efficient cameras parked in every nook and cranny of the building. All the halls and turns look the same and many a rookie gets lost in the complicated layout of this state of the art facility. Adams and I take the turns expertly and manage to find seats near the back of the room, just in time to hear Chief Yang speak. Stan Yang is a short, well-built man with no hair and small dark eyes that almost resemble my mother's. Only they lack the kindness hers hold.

There's nothing kind about the man. Nothing kind about him at all.

"Okay," he starts, his beady eyes scanning the room. Silence immediately falls across the room as a hundred or so men fix their eyes on him.

"We've just received news that Security Bill 91575 has been passed by Congress. In case you've been living under a rock these past few months, this law, when signed by President Hamilton tomorrow, gives us much greater leeway in discipline and maintaining order."

I shift in my seat uncomfortably. The sight of that man buckled over isn't far from my memory.

"In addition to the rights you already have - batons, tasers, unmirandized arrests; you now have the authority to draft and draw search warrants on the spot, interrogate suspects without supervision, and protect the Atlas families you serve at all costs..." he pauses as his small eyes scan around the room once more. "This includes the use of lethal force should you deem it necessary. No questions asked."

Adams draws a sharp breath with some of the others. My gut wrenches uncomfortably.

"The Commoners will not respond well to this new

legislature. They will murmur and complain of 'oppression' or 'discrimination.'" He flicks his hand dismissively like flicking at a pesky fly. "Let us remember who the Atlas Police Force is designed to serve: Atlans. Your loyalty is to the families on Atlas who pay us to protect them against the violent outbursts of Commoners. I have personally spoken with President Hamilton, who has the utmost confidence that we will use this new breadth of authority safely and responsibly for the benefit of all - including the Commoners."

Oh really?

Yang continues, "So long as they are respectful and not a threat to Atlans, there will be no disruption to their lives. President Hamilton is trusting us with a great deal. Do not disappoint him. Do not disappoint me."

The short, stern man nods as a way of dismissal, surprising us all by the brevity of his talk. I immediately stand to exit. Adams silently walks beside me until we reach the locker room.

"What do you think?" he asks.

I shake my head and glance at the ceiling. Adams follows my eyes to the camera built into the ceiling light. He nods. I'm not about to state my true opinion on the bill. Not in this building.

So I shrug and simply say, "I think I'll keep doing my job and defend the families I'm assigned to."

I've never needed the new measures and I don't need them now.

Adams nods in agreement. "What would I pay to see

Jenner's reaction to this."

I smirk and shake my head. "Who knows what he would have done?"

Caden Jenner's been off the Force for more than a year now. The more I think about it, the gladder I am he left when he did. As impulsive and headstrong as he was, he would have run amok with Yang in a matter of days and Yang would not have been as forgiving as retired Chief of Police, Harry Stanton, was.

"Jenner was lucky not to get thrown on The Gauntlet," I murmur. Adams shudders involuntarily, as most people do when they consider the no man's land of USA, uninhabitable after years of toxic chemical poisoning and radiation strong enough to kill someone in 48 hours. It's a painful, torturous death worse than immediate execution on Atlas or Commons. The minute Jenner mouthed off to his Atlas superior, refusing to sail along the edge of Commons in a move that would have endangered them all, his days as an officer were over. The severity of his punishment was in Stanton's hands and Stanton had been merciful, more benevolent towards the end of his thirty-five year tenure as Chief of Police. He could have done more than discharge Jenner dishonorably but he didn't - he left it at that. And now Jenner is like every other Commons civilian.

"He still working on Danielton?" Adams asks.

I nod. "Moved to Factory Quarter four months ago."

I refrain from telling Adams how much he hates it. All Jenner does now days is complain about how miserable his job is. But work is work. We all have to do something to eat. To survive.

Well, not all of us.

Atlas is the island that was once known as Manhattan when the country had states and cities. According to historical records, there was a time when it was considered "the City" of New York City, the most well-known of the five boroughs that made up what was once New York City in what was once New York State. Sometimes it blows my mind to imagine how much land USA used to inhabit. We now occupy only one one-hundredth of the land we used to and our population has diminished by about the same amount.

I read in a book once that Manhattan was a city of multiple cultures, ethnicities, and socioeconomic backgrounds. That the rich and elite lived on something called the Upper East Side of the island and the poorer lived around a place called Harlem. There were even housing projects, similar to the ones all over Commons.

There are no housing projects on Atlas.

If the Upper East Side was the best of the best in Manhattan, then I would say the whole island has transformed into the Upper East Side now. The streets are clean, the sidewalks are perfectly paved, swept, and hosed down every night. There's an abundance of parks, museums, and recreational sites for the residents. No one walks in fear and there's plenty of room to breathe. And the air is always fresh. Working on Atlas is like working on an oasis, a paradise of a city that you can serve but never enjoy. Anyone who *lives* on Atlas makes a minimum of three million dollars per year while the average income of Commoners is $25,000. And if the socioeconomic disparity isn't enough, the inflation has kept up with Atlas income, driving Commoners into survival mode. Genetic "food," poor housing, and increased crime. The results of an endangered middle class.

Pretty much extinct middle class.

"Yoo hoo? Hello? Earth to guard!" I look up in time to see a perfectly manicured hand snap impatiently in my direction. Abigail Dodson is pretty, blond, and utterly pretentious. The partner of Lewis Trenton, a technology tycoon, they've been under my guard for nearly a year, mostly during day shifts.

I swallow down the temptation to retort, *"What?"* and calmly raise my eyebrows at her as she gestures to the basket two feet away from her, and only a foot away from her partner. "Be a doll and fetch that for me, won't you, Mr. Guard?"

Nearly a year and she still hasn't taken the time to get my name.

Apparently it takes a good three years for her to bother.

We're in the middle of Atlas Park. Sprawling grass and plenty of trees for shade as their kids run around and play a game of tag. I move from the tree I was stationed at and cross the four yards to deliver her picnic basket. The Trenton-Dodsons are easy enough, less demanding than families I've guarded in the past, but Ms. Dodson has a habit of treating everyone like a servant, her partner and children excluded.

One of them, 10-year-old Timmy, runs up beside her and sticks his dirty hand in the basket.

"Timmy!" she exclaims.

He ignores her protests and pops a cluster of grapes in his mouth, chewing and speaking simultaneously. "Mom, this summer, can we go abroad? I'm tired of McKenzie Isles."

Mr. Trenton lowers his tablet for the first time since arriving and meets her eyes. He quickly looks at their son and says, "We always have fun at McKenzie, Tim. Why would you want to go anywhere else?"

"We go there *all the time*," the child whines. "I want to go to one of the places I read about in your encyclopedia. France or Spain. Maybe England."

I smirk and turn a watchful eye to their daughters Abigail Junior and Sofia. Their blond curls bounce around their bobbing heads as they chase each other across the park, giggles filling the mostly quiet space. I focus on their innocent laughter while their parents spin their older brother whatever rubbish they want about why they're not going abroad. He'll learn when he's older that they don't actually have a choice.

The one thing Atlans and Commoners have in common: no one can leave USA and no one can come in.

"Timmy!" I turn to see him bolt up and storm towards me, eyes blazing as he swings his foot back and kicks at the tree I'm standing next to.

His mother stands up to follow him but he turns and yells at her crossly, "Leave me alone! I want to be left *alone!*"

Mr.   Trenton   gestures   to   his partner…girlfriend…partner. Oh what I would give for the days people actually married before starting families. I never quite know how to refer to women who, a few generations back would have been wives and men who would have been husbands. Now they just move in, have sex, make kids, and give said kids both of their names for the sake of equality. Almost everyone on Atlas and Commons has hyphenated names. They just go by the first for the sake of ease. Mine is a rare exception.

Mr. Trenton tells Ms. Dodson, "Leave it, dear. He'll calm down."

She hesitates, glancing at me in slight embarrassment before sitting back down. She snaps her fingers at a nearby maid, "Um, Maid…" and busies herself with the food.

I look down at the kid next to me. He's spoiled and immature. But when he's in a better mood, he's a nice enough child to be around.

"You alright?" I ask him casually.

He sulks, glancing up at me. "I will be. I just hate it when they lie to me."

I raise an eyebrow in surprise. Then again, I shouldn't be surprised. Kids are a lot smarter than we give them credit for. Maybe I forgot because we don't have many kids on Commons. The Population Control Act of 2400 helped with that. And now most Commoner women inject themselves with conception-proof serums when they reach the age of sixteen. If there are any kids, most will be found on Maids Quarter, where the women raise them single-handedly and their useless fathers live and work in the other four quarters. Only the wealthy *try* to have kids.

"If you had to pick, where would you go first?"

Timmy thinks about it, his 10-year-old face scrunching up in deep thought. "France. I want to see the Eiffel Tower."

I nod. "Good choice."

I've only ever seen the monument in pictures. It's probably still standing, though we'd have no way of knowing.

"Do you know why we can't go abroad?" Timmy asks.

I'm tempted to tell him. I really am. Spill the beans about the U.N. Fracture - what happened when USA left the United Nations and rescinded their loyalty to every foreign power. Under President Eilenwich thirty years ago, the nation decided it no longer needed foreign resources or supplies. His administration campaigned that having a global stance was a threat to the prosperity and survival of the nation. Rather than giving aid, we needed to centralize and maintain our wealth and stop getting involved in the mess other countries made for themselves. It was a strong, convincing argument but one that veiled the intention of absolutely no friendly relations with *any* nations, something George Washington himself encouraged during his exit speech. We withdrew our foreign aid, support, and military presence in all nations, adopting a rather hostile foreign policy. When foreign powers attempted to fight Eilenwich's policies, he ordered a nuclear strike on several nations, obliterating them completely, terrifying the others into submission. He single-handedly secured USA's isolationist stance. Victor Hamilton took office two years later and continued the same policy. If I could sum it up in a simple phrase, USA's message to the rest of the world is: "don't bother us and we won't obliterate you."

Naturally, this prohibits international travel. If anyone manages to leave, they do so at the guarantee of no re-entry. Immigration officially ended before I was old enough to go to school, when Hamilton instituted the "steel wall."

But I can't tell all this to a 10-year-old kid. And I'm not willing to lose my job.

I shake my head. "Sorry, buddy." I lie. "I have no idea why we can't."

LOBBY BAN FAILS TO CARRY IN CONGRESS

Corey Tenner
Washington Post
November 7, 2050

The United States government has failed to pass Bill 91248, a law that would have made it illegal to lobby any elected official. The controversial bill was supported by a startling majority of citizens. Up to 84% of men and women polled said they approved of the law and saw it as a means of reducing political corruption. While the bill passed the House of Representatives by a slim two vote margin, the Senate failed to pass it by just five votes.

Political experts had hoped the passage of this bill would help minimize the level of political bargaining and special interest voting that has become rampant in the United States government over the years. Dr. Joaquin Voto, political science professor at Princeton University, says, "Our Congress fails to get any work done partly because of their gridlocked positions. Concessions are next to impossible when the lobbyist funding you refuses to compromise." Political columnist Sarah Green adds, "Career politicians are the worst poison to the democracy of this nation. When you care more about keeping your seat and getting re-elected than you do writing and passing laws, even unpopular ones that benefit the people, you are no longer worthy of representing the people." Popular American pastor, Reverend Rick Maner, proposed a call for prayer at the Capitol but his request was denied.

Today, Congress only manages to pass up to 200 bills per year, well below the 758 bills passed on average by previous congressional sessions. The embattled branch typically triggers at least four government shut downs a year. Though not as severe as 2035, when it experienced an unprecedented 14 government shut downs, citizens point out that there was a time when Congress could function without *any* shut downs at all.

"It's a major problem," Voto says. "Because politics can only become so partisan and so divisive. If it continues in this pattern, there may not *be* a *United* States of America.

"The wise and the good never form the majority of any large society and it seldom happens that their measures are uniformly adopted."

-John Jay

CHAPTER TWO

"Kids, it's time for dinner!"

I'm exhausted by the time I arrive at my last shift. I'm guarding the Washingtons from seven to ten tonight but in spite of my exhaustion, I can't help but smile as I walk in the door.

"Decker!" Grace Washington exclaims with her patented smile. A short woman in her mid-fifties, she's strikingly beautiful for her age, her Mediterranean features prominent on her olive-toned face. She rushes to the door and gives me a warm hug and kiss on the cheek.

"Hey, Decker!" her husband, Tobias Washington, greets me as he emerges from his study. "You're right on time for dinner."

I shake my head. "It's against protocol."

Mrs. Washington rolls her eyes. "Oh, for Heaven's sake."

"You've been saying the same thing for fourteen years and we always convince you to eat," Mr. Washington reminds me patiently. "Who's going to find out? Big

Brother? Sit, sit!"

This family makes the job worth it.

I've been guarding the Washingtons for fourteen years, ever since I joined the Force at eighteen. They're unlike any other family on Atlas I've ever encountered. For one thing, their parents actually bothered marrying before having kids. For another, they're generous, warm, friendly and kind. After so many hours of blending in the background, rarely acknowledged and if so, mostly by children, it's refreshing to serve a family that actually looks me in the eyes and smiles.

They treat me like I matter.

Not many people on Atlas do.

The Washingtons live on the northern end of Atlas. The entire island reeks of money and prestige. There's no difference in safety, structure, or appearance on this end of the town but for some reason, most of the surviving "middle class" live here. There's an invisible line at which the income level drops from $50-100 million to single-digit millions. Perhaps because this section of Atlas was once known as Harlem. And Harlem once held lower income families, much like the ones on Commons. Several centuries of gentrification later and Harlem matched the Upper East Side before the entire island blended into Atlas. This apartment easily matches the quality of all the other ones I've protected further south. The marble-encrusted lobby below is fit with a doorman, concierge, and twenty-four hour security personnel from the Force. But I guess there's more prestige in living in a *historically* wealthy area.

I refrain from rolling my eyes.

I obediently follow Mrs. Washington into the dining area and barely take in the richly decorated, opulent space they call home. I've grown used to the polished hardwood floors covering every inch of the landing. The heavy Persian rugs. The square footage alone can fit twenty of my apartments in here. Everything is gold: from the chandeliers to the wall paper, all the way down to the gold-encrusted frames hanging artwork that probably matches my yearly wage ten times over. But it's still warm and inviting, open with a semi partition between the living room, kitchen, and dining area. There's a stunning backdrop of the city skyline in floor to ceiling windows. And despite the grand luxury of the modern, state of the art home, I never feel beneath them. The home shows off Mrs. Washington's good taste, not any pretension or pride.

I'm hit with the mouth-watering smells of well-seasoned meat, vegetables, and whatever else the family matriarch has been cooking. Something else I like about her - she cooks for her family - doesn't just shrug it off to a private chef. And boy, is she a good cook.

"Hi, Decker!"

"Hey, Tommy." I reach up and fist bump 14-year-old Thomas, their youngest child. His sister Karen sits next to him and gives me a quick smile.

"Hi, Decker." she says quietly. Blond with blue eyes, Karen looks nothing like the rest of her family. She got the eyes from her dad but he has dark hair. She's also the quietest of the group, more content to observe than participate in their lively conversations. She'll be going to college soon and has yet to declare her major. Her older brother, Tobias Jr., comes in.

"Decker," he nods, shaking my hand. He just graduated college and will be working in solar engineering with his dad. Tobias Sr. owns the top solar engineering firm in the country. A pioneer in the industry, his solar technology is utilized in nearly 80% of the machinery produced on Danielton, USA's factory capital.

We all sit and waste no time digging in. It isn't until I put the first bite of tender, melt-off-the-bone roast beef in my mouth, that I realize this is my first meal all day. The complimentary muffins and fruit at the station were completely gone by the time Adams and I arrived and I didn't have the time or money to grab something to eat. Purchasing a bite on Atlas is tantamount to spending an entire grocery budget on a donut. I went hungry instead.

Conversation swirls around me as I eat and allow my gnawing belly to relax. By the time I look up from my plate, I remember a family member's missing.

"Is Nicole at work tonight?"

Mrs. Washington nods slowly, a frown marring her pretty features. I wonder what's bothering her until her eyes travel down to my empty plate. She quickly stands, grabs the plate, and puts another heaping serving on it. I open my mouth to protest, knowing it was rude of me to finish so quickly.

"Not a word," she cuts me off. She hands me my re-filled plate with a stern brow raised. "Eat."

She doesn't have to tell me twice.

The second helping does the trick and I want nothing more than to lean back and let the food settle. But I can't. I'm not here visiting with friends. I'm on the clock and I've already broken a cardinal rule of work.

"Thank you so much for the meal, Mrs. Washington." I nod at her husband. "Mr. Washington."

I stand and ignore her protests as I take the plate to the kitchen and wash the dish myself, placing it on the dish rack beside the sink. I walk past the dining room and point to the terrace. "I'll be at my normal post if you need me."

Mr. Washington nods, "Thank you, son."

The Washingtons' terrace really is a large garden on an enormous balcony overlooking the city. Like most nights, every night really, it's dead silent. Save for a few laughing families in neighboring buildings, there's not much to patrol. I can see with my naked eye a handful of other officers patrolling their own terraces a few buildings over. We nod at each other in acknowledgment but keep to ourselves after that. We're not here to chat. We're here to watch. Even if there's nothing to watch.

Fifty minutes in, I bite back a yawn.

"The food's getting to you, isn't it?"

I turn at the sound of her voice, completely calm. "It never ceases to amaze me how quiet you can be."

I didn't even hear a footstep and my ears are sharp as

knives.

Nicole smiles. "And it never ceases to amaze me how unruffled you are, even when I sneak up on you."

"I said you were quiet. I didn't say you snuck up on me."

"Oh, okay." She nods, though I can tell she doesn't believe me.

Nicole Washington is the oldest of the Washington children. Twenty-nine, she's a younger, taller version of her mother and just as beautiful. Her long thick dark hair falls straight to the middle of her back - so dark, it's almost black. Her eyes are a lighter shade of brown, framed by long thick lashes. Slightly fairer than her mother, her skin has a healthy tan and flush to her feminine, angular cheeks. She's a pretty girl, even more pretty because of her optimistic personality. We like to give each other a hard time, but if I have a single friend on Atlas, she's it.

"How was work?" I ask, scanning the cityscape once more.

I can imagine her standard shrug and nod as she answers. "Good. Same old, same old. After the first year, PR work really isn't as glamorous as you think it would be."

She's been working as a public relations specialist at Atlas Network News, or ANN, for five years. She initially wanted to be a reporter and went to school for journalism but changed her mind two years in. As always, her parents supported her one-hundred percent and she seems to enjoy what she does now.

"So what are you reading this week?" she asks. I glance and catch the faint smirk on her lips. Like Adams, she knows how much I like to read.

"*Common Sense*," I answer.

"By Thomas Paine?" she asks, a surprised brow lifted. I nod. "Wow. That's an oldie but a goodie. Have you read it before?"

I nod. "In middle school."

It was one of the last books I read before leaving for Academy training.

"*Middle school?* That's college level reading. How did you get your hands on it in middle school?"

I roll my eyes. "There's this really big, ornate building called *the library*. It holds a lot of books, you know?" She punches my shoulder with an unspectacular thump as I laugh. "My mom picked it up for me when I asked."

She nods. "Before the Education Reformation Act?"

I stiffen and nod quickly. She must sense my immediate change in demeanor because she follows with, "You were at the cutoff point, weren't you? The first class to be shifted."

My breathing turns shallow and I clear my throat. "Yeah."

In 2610, President Hamilton and his pathetic excuse of a government implemented a sweeping educational reform that ruined the futures of Commoners, starting with the children in my age group. For centuries, public education lasted until a child's twelfth year in school. And up until 2600, Commoner children still had a chance to attend college if they were deemed remarkably intelligent. In 2610, Hamilton and Congress passed the Educational Reformation Act which scaled a USA child's right to a free education back from grade 12 to grade 8. After which, parents of the child would be required to pay for their child's education all the way through college. This, of course, was no problem for Atlans - they were already funding their children's education from pre-K on. But high school was no longer free and for every Commoner child, myself included, that meant high school was no longer an option.

Congress decided to initiate the reform with my class year. At the end of eighth grade, instead of going to high school like the class ahead of me, we were thrown into aptitude testing units. The only problem with the tests was that they tested for a limited range of aptitude possibilities: security and defense; mechanical trade; repair work; hospitality and maintenance; and assembly, i.e. factory work. There were no options for creative fields like the arts, media, law or, my personal preference, history. Those fields are now dominated by the people whose parents could afford to educate them in those areas. Only those with exceptionally brilliant mathematical and scientific potential were given the opportunity to attend privately funded high schools on a scholarship with a guaranteed track to college.

The rest of us had to choose between two career fields based on the results of our tests. My choices were security and defense or mechanical trade. Hopeful that I could have some chance at a purposeful career, I chose the former. Little did I know that the police, like every other career available to Commoners, are only meant to serve those on Atlas. Nothing more.

I don't know how long I'm silent but I know my sober demeanor has affected Nicole.

"I'm so sorry, Decker."

I look at her sharply. "For what?"

She shrugs. "For everything. For…" She shrugs again. "It sucks."

I nod. It does suck.

We don't say anything else the rest of the night. She silently keeps me company for the rest of my shift and I'm relieved when it's time to go home. The sooner I get to my bed, the better. When asleep, I don't have regrets. I don't long for more. I don't feel angry or tired or defeated. Sometimes I even have dreams. Nice ones. And they don't get squashed until I wake up the next morning.

I step back into the apartment, intent on making my goodbyes quick. As I cross the living room, I see Mr. and Mrs. Washington standing near the island of the kitchen. They're holding hands and their heads are lowered, eyes closed as Mr. Washington speaks in a low tone. I blink in surprise.

Are they *praying?*

In all my years of guarding them, I've only seen them do this twice before but I've kept silent, unsure of what to say. USA citizens, Atlan or Commoner, don't pray. And to suggest that someone might is tantamount to threatening their lives. The Washingtons can do whatever they want in the privacy of their homes but I'd rather not be privy to it.

Suddenly, as if aware of my presence, Mr. Washington lifts his head and quickly gives his wife a peck on the head. He turns to me and smiles; as if it's the most natural thing in the world to see him…doing whatever he was just doing with her.

I'll follow his lead and start walking towards the door. "Good night, sir."

"Wait, Decker, before you go…" he pulls me aside. He reaches into his pocket and folds a wad of cash into my hands. I immediately shake my head and try to press it back into his palm.

"Mr. Washington-"

"I insist."

"I can't accept."

"Listen, I know you're a grown man and you work hard for a living. I'm not trying to insult you. It's not for you, really. Consider it for your mom. If you were just taking care of yourself like most officers, you wouldn't have as much of a strain."

He's half right. Most officers on the Force are single and the pay is far better than any other career on Commons. But everyone on Commons, officer or not, has to make concessions. The outrageous inflation and stagnant income has made decent living virtually impossible for Commons. The single officers eat crap like every other quarter to keep afloat. Some room with other officers. The few with families of their own get a slightly higher pay rate but it's never enough. And a disabled mother doesn't qualify for that rate. I'm earning the pay of a single male with the expense of an additional adult.

Mr. Washington must read my concern. "Tell me the truth. How are you doing? You and your mom?"

I meet his clear blue eyes. He's not being nosy or rude. He's genuinely concerned. This isn't the first time he's tried to help my mother and me. And yet it feels so strange to talk about my next-to-nothing finances with someone so exceedingly wealthy. Even though it shouldn't, my pride kicks into overdrive.

"We're alive," I reply. He straightens at the edge in my tone.

"I'm sorry," he says quickly. "I didn't mean to pry."

I shake my head, already feeling guilty. "You're not prying. I know you're trying to help and I appreciate it. I really do. But I can't accept your money." He opens his mouth to protest but I surge on. "They'll find out if I do. They do regular searches at the station and at Atlas Express. If they discover me with a wad of cash on my person, I'll be without a job permanently. I can't risk that, Mr. Washington."

He nods soberly, finally understanding. As much as it pains me, I fold the money back into his hands, knowing I just gave away my mother's chance at a decent meal. Maybe even a chance at a new chair or sweater. We haven't purchased anything outside of food in years - not since the last inflation spike early in my career.

"Thanks again for dinner," I say, my calm demeanor

belying my inner turmoil. "Have a good night."

I turn only to find Mrs. Washington standing with an aluminum tray of foil-covered food in her hands.

"You're allowed to accept food. I checked the Atlas Police Decorum Guide of 2602. The latest edition. If they try to give you a hard time about this, let me know and I will *personally* have a discussion with the Chief of Police."

I blink at her blatant threat. Her no-nonsense expression all but forces me to take the warm tray out of her hands. Though covered, I can already smell the delicious leftovers from tonight's dinner inside.

"Thank you, Mrs. Washington."

She gives me a brilliant smile that starts to turn watery. Leaning on her tip toes, she kisses my cheek and sends me off. "Tell your mother I said hello. We're long overdue for a visit. Be careful on your way back, please."

"I will," I nod. I cross the threshold and make my way to the elevator. I don't hear the door close until I get on.

To my relief, the ride home is uneventful. The other officers heading back are too tired to mention my bounty though many of them eye it jealously. It's on one of these nights that I'm grateful I live in the Police Quarter. If I were walking around any other quarter with piping hot real food, I'd have to bare my gun and badge to keep desperate Commoners off me. I unlock the door to my place and am surprised to see the lights still on. I walk in and discover Mom leaning against the counter, her laughter carrying across the kitchen. Sitting at the dining table is none other than our most frequent guest.

"Hey, Jenner."

Caden Jenner turns and smiles, his light blue eyes already cheerful. "Decker, hey!"

Four years younger than me, Caden Jenner is one of my best friends from the Force. He has light blond hair, cut close to his scalp, light blue eyes, and stands a few inches shorter than me. He's been out of the Force for a while but is still strong with a medium, muscular build. No one would call him particularly handsome or ugly. Unless you know him, he has the sort of face that blends in with the crowd.

I'm glad I know him.

Mom meets me halfway and greets me with a peck on the cheek. "Sit down, sweetheart. You must be exhausted."

She doesn't say anything but she doesn't need to. I can see the relief that I'm safe clear on her face.

"I brought some grub," I hand her the tray. "Mrs. Washington says hi."

Mom gasps and opens the top. "Oh, what a lovely woman. You be sure to thank her for me."

"You really hit the jackpot when they hired you, man. I'm telling you." Jenner says, shaking his head in wonder. I look at him and gesture at the tray.

"You eat yet?"

He shakes his head. "It's late, though. Don't worry about me."

I don't even have to ask Mom. She starts fixing him a

plate, wordlessly ignoring his protests. He glances at me and smiles weakly. "Thanks, man. You know I'll bring something when I can."

I nod, knowing he will. We always help each other when food is low.

I lean back in my seat, my mood already lifting. "So, what were you two laughing about earlier? You hitting on my mom again, Jenner? I told you - she's single but not available."

Mom swats me on the shoulder while Jenner laughs, standing up to briefly kiss her cheek. "You know, if I were born a few years earlier, we could have had some nice looking kids-"

She gasps at his flirting but he continues on, unfazed. "Even better looking than you."

I roll my eyes while Mom serves him his plate. She looks at me. "Want some, sweetie?"

I shake my head. "I ate there. Go ahead and eat."

She shakes her head. "It's too late. When you young ones eat late at night, you don't find it on your hips the next morning. People my age aren't so lucky. I'll try it out tomorrow."

She puts a hand at the small of her back, her face tensing up at the touch.

"Did you stretch today?" I ask, concerned.

"I'm fine. Just hunched over a little too much."

"I could have told you that," I reply, still worried. "Do you want a massage?"

Ever since she threw out her back my senior year at

Academy, Mom has suffered chronic back pain. When she first injured it, it was so bad she was bedridden for weeks and immediately lost her job. She's made somewhat of a recovery but not enough to do any kind of work Commoners are limited to.

"I'm okay, sweetie. Besides, you must be tired." She leans down and kisses my forehead. "I'm going to bed. Love you."

"Night," I reply. "Love you, too."

"Night, Ms. K."

We're both silent the first few minutes. Jenner scarfs down his food and cleans the plate as quickly as I did the first round. I offer him some more but he's careful not to take too much. He takes a couple of bites before pushing the plate aside. Leftovers to take home.

"How's work?" he asks. He always asks. It's been fourteen months since he was discharged but his curiosity hasn't abated a bit.

"Same as when you left it, only worse." I reply. "More freedom to brutalize Commoners, less freedom to make our own decisions about patrols. More leeway to terrorize innocent people, less leeway to speak openly with our superiors. Yang is convinced he's making the Force better. Two months in and he's on a full scale power trip."

"Asshole," Jenner sneers.

I nod. "It'll only get worse."

"Because of Bill 91575?" he asks. "I heard through the grapevine it's been passed."

Grapevine being Adams. I nod. "All of Commons will

43

know in a matter of days. Maybe hours. Hamilton's set to sign it tomorrow."

He sucks his teeth. "Bullshit. We don't need a bill to stand up to Commoners. We need a bill to stand up to Atlan tyrants."

I smile slightly, noting how he referred to himself as part of the Force.

"You miss it," I observe.

He stiffens and for a brief second I see the pain in his light blue eyes. Getting discharged didn't just rob Jenner of his career, his pay, his privilege. It robbed him of his dignity. His sense of purpose. It pains me to see him so down.

"I hate Danielton," he says in a near whisper. "Every day the same old shit. Put part A to part B, part F to part G. Do it again and repeat. Over and over and over again."

When a person gets fired from the Force, it's next to impossible to do anything outside of their training. Factory work on Danielton is the only option for most injured or discharged officers. The factory workers make up fifty percent of the population on Commons, most of them testing directly into the field during their aptitude tests. Instead of taking Atlas Express, they board several ferries to Danielton, an island formerly known as "Staten Island." Developed in 2268 by business tycoon Daniel Sorronto, the island is now completely covered in factory buildings and concrete, making the land uninhabitable. So the workers sail in every morning and ship out every night, Jenner now among their ranks.

"You know what I miss most about being a cop?" he asks.

"What?" It doesn't escape me that he's slipped into the pejorative term for the role.

"The illusion of control. We were watched all the time. Constantly ordered by Stanton, our supervisors and the Atlan dicks we served. But every now and then, I could fool myself into thinking I had some authority. That I had some control."

I see what he's saying but I don't agree. Maybe it's been too long since he last worked on the Force but we've never had a say in anything.

"Well," I sigh, leaning back. "You're not missing much now. That's for sure."

Jenner peers at me, his expression thoughtful. "Why don't you go back to Academy training? You were the best they ever had. Kicked all our asses into shape. You graduated first in your class, too."

I'm shaking my head before he even finishes. Jenner was in the second class I trained at the Academy. Two classes later, I quickly lost my taste for the job. Why would I find it fulfilling to bring people into a job that ultimately oppresses others?

"I'm good," I tell him.

He shrugs. "Okay." Seconds later, a mischievous smirk crosses his lips. "You know, if this cop thing doesn't work out, at least you have the looks to be an escort."

"Shut up!" I reply as he chuckles at his stupid joke. The thought of it literally turns my stomach. In 2300, the

Supreme Court ruled to legalize prostitution. Over the years, the laws have changed to regulate it. I don't know why, when it's been legal my whole life, but it makes me sick to think that attractive Commoner women, and men, actually make a legal living selling their bodies to wealthy Atlas clients. No one seems to think twice about it in USA but for some reason, it makes my skin crawl.

I may have "the looks" but I'd rather swim the channel to The Gauntlet before *ever* taking that route.

RELIGION AND MENTAL HEALTH: SOME SAY THE TWO DON'T MIX

Celia Danning
The New York Times
February 4, 2104

A whirlwind of controversy surrounds the American Psychological Association on the heels of a groundbreaking article they've released in their latest journal. Harvard University researcher Dr. Gwendolyn Newby wrote the article, claiming to have found scientific support that shows the harmful effects of religion on the human psyche. Newby claims that all religious conviction should be equated to "religious paranoia" because it "deadens an individual's ability to face the realities of life without the context of make believe spirits, persons, and stories that historically never happened." She claims that treatment should be offered to empower individuals to succeed in life without resorting to religion, a "dangerous coping mechanism."

The article has faced severe backlash from religious bodies and organizations but Newby, and the American Psychological Association, stand firm behind their decision to publish their findings. "I think we've all been petrified of offending the religious," Dan Wallaby, APA publishing coordinator states. "But the American Psychological Association is less interested in soothing the sensibilities of the easily offended, as we are in helping those who need psychological help. Dr. Newby's research shows there may very well be a strong correlation between insanity and religious conviction."

This article comes only two years after the release of

Maryland University sociologist, Dr. Wallace Kronisky's controversial research, which condemned religion as a "toxic and divisive tool against the progress of society." Kronisky pointed to defeated terror groups like ISIS and other religious extremists that have killed countless people. Recent polls show that the majority of Americans agree with Kronisky and Newby's conclusions, with nearly 85% voting for the removal of public references to religion, especially Christianity.

President Jared Witlow, the nation's first openly atheist president, has declined to comment on the research or the controversy surrounding it.

"A patriot without religion in my estimation is as great a paradox as an honest man without the fear of God."

-Abigail Adams

CHAPTER THREE

Two Weeks Later:

"I haven't had a day off in two years and *now* is when you're asking me to fill in for you?" I gripe on the phone.

"Decker, please." Adams - or at least that's who he claims to be - rasps across the phone, his voice unrecognizable. "I would do this sick if I could but I can't stand for longer than a few minutes without getting dizzy. Please. I'll give you my next day off. I get one in six weeks."

Six weeks! I inwardly groan.

"*Please*," he repeats, as if he can read my mind. "I don't want to lose my job over this."

He's not exaggerating. If he doesn't find someone to cover him or go in himself and keep his shit together, he won't get thrown to The Gauntlet, but he can kiss his badge and his livelihood goodbye. I glance at my watch. It's mid-morning and Adams' shift starts at noon. If I leave now, I can make it in time.

"Okay!" I tell him. "I'll go."

I know he would do the same for me.

"Thank you, Decker. Really. Thank-" he hacks another heavy cough into the phone.

"Get some rest," I tell him over his hacking. "I can't cover you tomorrow. You'll need to recover fast."

I hang up, quickly dress, and tell Mom goodbye.

On Atlas Express, I switch things up and actually decide to watch the news playing on the overhead holographs.

"It's been two weeks since President Hamilton signed Security Bill 91575. Congress calls this law 'groundbreaking legislation that will ensure the safety of Atlans and the accountability of Commoners.' The Bill empowers Atlas authorities to more efficiently identify and detain suspects, defend working citizens, and protect countless lives."

All the while terrorizing citizens.

What the pretty ANN anchor fails to mention is that what once would be considered "police brutality" has now skyrocketed since the new law legalized it. Atlans may feel safe. But they're the only ones who do. All of Commons has been on edge since Hamilton signed on the dotted line.

The footage cuts to the unpopular president - well, unpopular to Commoners. He's a middle-aged man, nearing his late fifties with salt and pepper hair, green eyes, and a calm, stately demeanor. He's still handsome and has a rather charming smile. It's no surprise to me that he won his first election in a landslide all those years ago. I imagine his charm and good looks kept him in office a few more terms before his corrupt character and willingness to be bought, kept him in office beyond that. Though unruffled in appearance and charming to the eye, President Hamilton is very passionate about one thing.

Keeping his power.

He stands in front of several cameras in the holograph and addresses the media. "Having spoken to Chief of Police Stan Yang, I am very pleased with the results of Security Bill 91575. Congress has worked tirelessly alongside the Atlas Police Force to maintain the safety and stability of USA."

I close my eyes and lean back in my seat, refusing to pay further attention to this moron. He's been in denial about the state of this nation since he first got elected when I was a child. Never mind the fact that he has no business remaining president of this nation after so many years.

I take the train directly into the Financial Peninsula of Atlas. Officer Canenbreg, Adams' direct supervisor, sent me the details of the family I'm guarding. I'm vaguely familiar with this part of town. I once guarded a young family here two years into my tenure as an officer. The assignment only lasted two years in all when the couple split and the female partner took their two young kids to McKenzie Isle as a part of their separation deal. Newly single, the businessman didn't find security detail as necessary and I got re-assigned elsewhere.

Police work on Atlas is like a revolving door. Family situations change, preferences change, and we as guards have to change with them. But if you're good enough and graduated Academy with a high enough rank, the Force always finds a new family or client to protect. Adams just got assigned to this family less than a week ago. But from everything he's told me, they're not particularly high maintenance.

I step out of the station and quickly cross the street to the shopping complex where I'm supposed to meet them. Adam Stafford and his teen daughters, Rosalie and Raphaelle. I stand at the entrance of the overpriced mall and wait. A good twenty minutes pass before I hear the tell tale giggles of two girls. I turn around and there they are: Tall Blond One and Tall Blond Two. They're pretty girls with more make up than they need and clothes I would never allow my own daughters to wear if I had any. I step forward to introduce myself but am taken aback by the look they give me. In slow sweeping motion, their twin green eyes rake over me from the crown of my head to the soles of my feet and back up, lingering on the area just below my abdomen. I feel heat rush to my face as I look down to make sure my fly is zipped. It is. When I look back up, they stare at me with suggestive brows before glancing at each other and bursting out in another annoying fit of giggles.

I've never had this happen to me before. Well, not *never* exactly. I'm tall, well-built, and strong. I have my mother's dark eyes and thick, dark hair but the rest of my features resemble my dad's, who, in his day, was really good-looking: straight nose, full lips, strong jaw, angled cheeks. I'm not blind when I look in the mirror but I'm not vain enough to look for long. I've had *women* hit on me before. But they were grown women, not two underage girls. I've just been objectified by two teenagers and the heat is growing redder on my face.

I'm tempted to get angry. I've never been so embarrassed and uncomfortable on the job and I shouldn't be made to feel this way. I'm here to protect them, not serve as their amusement. I swallow, take a deep breath, and extend my hand to them.

"Rosalie? Raphaelle? I'm Officer Channing. I'm filling in for Officer Adams today."

"Can you fill in every day?" one of them asks. They glance at each other and burst into another fit of giggles.

For goodness sake.

"Where's your dad?" I ask them coolly.

They must sense my slight irritation because they calm down and quickly answer. "His meeting got delayed so he'll meet us here as soon as he's done. That can be in an hour or by the time we go home."

I nod. Sounds like a workaholic father compensating by spoiling his teenage daughters.

"Well, I'm here to watch and guard you guys. Go wherever you want to go and I'll follow quietly. Consider me a fly on the wall."

The other twin, Rosalie, nods. "We know the drill. And don't worry, we won't cause you any trouble."

That last sentence surprises me. Maybe they aren't as bad as I thought. Adams did say they were low maintenance. We walk into the mall and within minutes, they set me at ease. It's a straightforward shift as I patrol and keep watch while they shop and spend egregious amounts of their father's money. To their credit, they stop their annoying giggles, limit their gossip to other members of the opposite sex, and wrap up their shopping excursion in under two hours. We leave the last store they wanted to visit when they suddenly run ahead of me.

"Daddy!"

With all the fanfare of two little girls, the young women launch themselves into their father's arms at the same time. A tall, dark haired man in an impeccably tailored suit manages to catch them, though I can tell their combined weight throws him slightly off-balance.

"So sorry I'm late, sweethearts," he says warmly. He kisses both their foreheads before looking past them to me. He untangles himself as his expression cools from doting father to authoritative business man. His patronizing tone of voice matches the veneer.

"You must be Adams' fill-in for today."

I nod and extend a polite hand. "Officer Decker Channing. Nice to meet you, sir."

He looks at my hand but doesn't offer his in return.

"Any trouble today?" he asks in the same frosty tone.

I lower my hand, my back stiffening. I should have known better than to think an Atlan man would shake my hand. Probably too riddled with calluses for him.

"Not at all," I reply, working to keep my tone respectful.

"Excellent," he says, dismissing me with his eyes. A happy smile fills his face as he looks down at his daughters. "Well, what do you say we get some ice cream before we go home?"

The girls gasp and clap like excited toddlers.

"Only don't tell Mom," he adds.

I follow them dutifully to the ice cream parlor and watch them select from a mouthwatering array of colorful choices. I stand invisible as they eat, joke and chatter, wondering how long it will take before Rosalie and Raphaelle adopt their father's pretentious attitude toward Commoners. Or maybe he's just in a bad mood and has reserved the brunt of his rudeness for me in particular. It's almost hard to believe that the man who raised such friendly girls is the same man treating me so coldly. Then again, Atlan children are known for being kind before switching into selfish, cold Atlan adults. The Washington children are the only exceptions I've met.

Half an hour later, we all head to the entrance in time to meet their car service.

The girls continue chatting as they enter the car with all their shopping bags and nary a backward glance. With daddy around, they've all but forgotten my presence.

Their father walks over to me, a flat expression on his haughty face. He reaches into his pocket and hands me a crisp, folded bill. I'm surprised.

"Oh, thank you but I can't-"

"I'm not impressed with an officer who cuts off in the middle of the week. Let Adams know his assignment with me is hanging by a thread. You survived my girls - maybe you can do the job instead."

"But-"

He doesn't wait to hear my reply. Simply turns on his heel as if I didn't say a word and enters the car with his girls, the driver immediately taking off.

What an asshole.

I turn and walk in the opposite direction, feeling sorry for Adams. I've worked with a fine number of Atlas jerks but there's nothing you can do, save gritting your teeth and bearing it until you move on to something new. Now I'm stuck wondering how I'm going to unload this bill before boarding Atlas Express. The Force is very strict about officers caught accepting tips or monetary favors. As outrageously low as the pay is for protecting these people, our superiors refuse to allow us a chance to make any extra money on the side. There's no chance of me sneaking this money home anyway. I have to check in at the police station before going back to Commons and there are thorough security checks at every entrance. Canenbreg will want a full report on how my fill-in went. I'm yards away from the train station. Just as I begin to contemplate the horror of possibly throwing this money away, I hear commotion in front of one of the buildings I'm about to pass.

"No loitering and no soliciting! How many times do you have to be told?" an officer yells. Baton already raised, he strikes the shabbily dressed man near the head. The homeless man's instinctive crouch and raised hands are the only thing that protect his skull from being shattered.

"Ahh! Please!"

"Please what?" A man wearing a tailored suit stands nearby. He must be the client the officer is "guarding." The woman standing next to him sneers in disgust - but not at the brutality. Disgust at the poor man's presence there.

"Disgusting creature," she says snidely. "He comes here every other day *begging* for money to buy food. Probably wastes it on drugs."

"I don't care what he does with it," her partner replies. "What I want to know is why doesn't he get up off his ass and *work* like the rest of productive society?"

The officer, fueled by their commentary, draws back a foot and kicks the man squarely in his ribs.

"Ahh!" he flies back, clutching his torso.

"You've been warned before. You knew this was coming, idiot!" the officer yells. I don't recognize him. I haven't worked on this part of town in years but any other officer I know would have dropped it by now. A small crowd is forming but rather than wrapping up his self-determined "punishment," the officer seems to relish the attention and plants more kicks, punches, and baton strikes to the man old enough to be my father.

Finally, the woman glances at her watch and addresses the officer. "Why are you wasting any more time with this? He shouldn't be here. Even after this, he'll just come crawling back in a few days."

"Yeah," her partner agrees. "Hamilton signed that bill for you men. Why don't you *finish* him?"

He can't be serious. The other officer immediately gets what he's saying. He glances at the small crowd and hesitantly reaches into his holster. He looks back at his clients, who nod and urge him to continue. Bolstered by their orders, he wraps his hand around his gun and starts to withdraw it. I can't allow this. I don't know what it is that propels me to do what I do but I can't allow an innocent man to just die.

I push through the crowd. "Wait!"

All eyes turn to me as I help the man up.

"Hey!" I feel the officer's hand shove my shoulder. I shove him back and flash my badge. He blinks and steps back, unsure of what to do. I turn to the man and quickly stuff the bill in his hand.

"Run," I tell him. "Don't come back here again. *Ever*."

The man looks at me, blood streaming down the side of his face, his gray eyes haunted. Haunted but grateful.

"Thank you," he whispers. He glances at the officer and the officer's clients before bolting down to the station.

"He's going back to Commons," I tell the officer. "He won't come here again."

The officer looks mollified, as though embarrassed to have done that in front of another man on the Force. But the business man behind him looks outraged.

"Why did you interfere?" he yells. "You're encouraging this type of behavior!"

"And that behavior warranted him being killed?" I ask in reply. The voices murmuring around me seem to agree. I level my eyes at the man and his girlfriend. "I'm sorry for interfering," I lie. "I didn't mean any disrespect. But I thought there was another way to make him disappear without killing him."

I hold my tongue before I say anything they could perceive as disrespectful. As I walk away the murmurs get louder but I tune them all out. I board the next train to the station and get off in time to meet with Canenbreg.

"So overall it was a routine shift?" he confirms.

I nod. "Smooth sailing all around."

Canenbreg stands and shakes my hand. "Excellent. Not that I expected anything less from you, Channing. You're as sharp as when you first joined the Force."

I smile, pleased with the compliment. "Thank you, sir."

Officer Wylie Canenbreg is one of the few supervisors I respect. Fair, friendly - he helped make the transition from Academy into the Force a lot easier when I first came on. It's only fitting he works closely with Adams, the other friendly officer in the ranks.

I leave his office and stride down the maze of the station, ready to board the train and call it a night when I hear a different voice call me. "Officer Channing!"

I turn and see Officer Kirby at the opposite end of the hall. He gestures to me and turns. I quickly follow and make my way through the door he holds open for me. Within seconds, I realize where I am.

Chief Yang's office.

The man himself sits behind his desk, his small beady eyes sweeping over me.

"Officer Channing," he says calmly. He nods politely.

"Chief Yang." I nod back, follow Kirby's lead and take a seat.

Kirby speaks first. "Officer Channing, is it true you were guarding a family on the Financial Peninsula this afternoon?"

I nod, suddenly feeling nervous. "I did. Adam Stafford and his two girls."

"Did you go directly to Atlas Express upon the completion of your shift?"

My stomach drops. "I walked that way as soon as we parted, yes."

"Without interruption?" Kirby asks.

My stomach drops.

I look between the two men.

"What's going on?" I ask.

Yang speaks. "We received a complaint today from an Atlan by the name of Ryan Dulexio - a powerful business magnate who owns nearly thirty percent of the real estate on the Financial Peninsula. He and his partner, Helena Worthington were being harassed by a homeless Commoner that their assigned officer, Dylan Helming, was taking care of. Mr. Dulexio informed us that you interfered in Helming's duty and rewarded the degenerate solicitor by giving him money and letting him go."

I ignore the burning in my chest and the fear rising in my gut.

"Sir," I respond. "Officer Helming was being pressured to kill the man for simply asking for-"

"Code 436 of Security Bill 91575 states that an officer now has the right to implement lethal force according to his better judgment."

"He was going to murder the man, sir-"

"Officer Channing, you are officially relieved of your duties and discharged as an officer of the law under dishonorable circumstances. Hand me your badge and relieve yourself of your weapons at once."

The air that escapes my lungs can't seem to find its way back in.

"Wh-what?" I stutter.

"You are no longer an Atlas officer. Disarm yourself immediately and hand me your badge."

He sticks out his hand, expectantly.

I turn to Kirby. The man isn't kind or particularly fair. But he's known me just as long as Canenbreg. Something tells me he has a more sympathetic ear.

"Don't I get a hearing? A-a trial?"

Kirby shakes his head stiffly, his brown eyes sober. "No, son."

Yang stands, impatient. "That was under Stanton. There's a new chief in town." He stands right above me and holds out his hand once more. "Badge. Guns. Now."

I'm in shock. I go through the motions and ignore everyone around me. I don't know if anyone notices Kirby walking me to the train. Or the fact that my badge and holster are noticeably gone. The ride home is quiet and I leave the police car of the train, knowing I will never enter it again.

Fourteen years.

I diligently worked and served the Atlas Police Force for fourteen years. And it's all flushed away. Over the words of a spoiled Atlas man and a psychotic new chief. I turn the key into my apartment. Everything looks the same but everything has changed.

"Hi, sweetheart!" Mom calls from her room.

I don't know how but I manage a cheerful, "Hey, Mom!"

I quickly stride to my room and shut the door. I can't tell her. Not yet. Not only because I don't know what the hell I'm going to do but also because I can't bear to say it aloud. I've been fired. Fired for the worst reason possible. My room is cloaked in darkness. It matches my sullen mood. I don't bother to take off my jacket, my shoes, anything. I lie back in bed, close my eyes, and will my body to give my mind a break. When I sleep, the problems are gone. Nothing's there to catch me but my dreams.

The problem with sleep is...it can end whenever it wants to. I wake up hours later, knowing that it's well past midnight. I shake off my boots, my clothes and change into something more comfortable. Rather than going back to bed, I listen to my gurgling stomach and go into the kitchen. Mom's asleep by now. The living area is cast in silence. I open the fridge and pull out a small block of cheddar. When I was young, Mom used to call me her little mouse. *"Always chomping on a block of cheese!"*

Suddenly, out of nowhere, the fear grabs my sides with a vice like grip. What am I going to do? How are we going to eat? How long can we keep this apartment? How are we going to survive? I was struggling on a police officer's salary. How am I going to make it and take care of my mother on any other job in Commons?

I'm all by myself. No one's here to see me. I allow that reality to sink in and it gives me the space I need to put my head in my hands and just cry. A rivulet of silent tears washes down my cheeks as I grapple with the sudden loss. Loss of income. Loss of security. And loss of the job that defined and shaped nearly half of my existence on this earth.

Why does it have to be this way?! I cry out inside. I don't know to whom but I cry out. And in place of the fear, the sadness, the tears, something far more dangerous takes shape inside.

Anger.

Hot, piercing, boiling anger.

I'm angry at Dulexio. I'm angry at Yang. I'm angry that I don't even have a penny saved because all of my money has gone right back into the pockets of wealthy Atlan monopoly owners. But even more so, I'm angry at this nation and the piece of shit it has devolved into. This is nothing like what I read in Common Sense, the

Constitution, or the Declaration of Independence and no one seems to notice the disparity except me. This nation, this economy, this inequality is the very thing the founding fathers of USA - once called the United States of America - risked their lives to overcome. Fueled by a surge of righteous indignation, I walk to my mother's closed door with deft, light steps. I crack it open and retrieve the laptop from her desk. I come back out, turn the computer on, and open the Word document, blank screen waiting for me to type.

I make the title simple and quickly type out: *American Sense - a Plea for True Freedom.*

IT'S OFFICIAL: THE UNITED STATES HAS NO RELIGIOUS AFFILIATION

Chad Thenstead
The Washington Times
June 26, 2148

Citizens nationwide are celebrating Congress's landmark decision to officially renounce all claims that the United States is, or was ever, a Judeo-Christian nation. Voting unanimously in favor of the measure, both the House and the Senate have laid the contentious religious and political debate to rest, releasing the following statement:

The United States of America is a secular nation with no religious affiliation. Though founded by potentially religious men, the nation has evolved to the degree that any civic religious loyalty, particularly Judeo-Christian loyalty, would prove a dishonest representation of the 700 million citizens that call this nation home.

The statement, though brief, finally affirms the convictions of the majority of American citizens who, polls show, are tired of the dwindling religious right's attempts to influence politics and legislature. "It really draws a line in the sand," political scientist, Brennan Sanders says. "For centuries, there has been a very loud and vocal minority of citizens claiming this nation was founded on Christian principles. But the people, and Congress, have landed on the opposite conclusion."

Sanders claims this statement will make it easier for Congress to pass measures that have been previously blockaded by religious citizens. He also claims it will give room for the Supreme Court to give objective rulings fair for *all* citizens, such as last year's ruling to once again redefine marriage - this time between any consenting adults - no limitations to gender, number, or relation.

"We're making progress," he concludes. "Just a few centuries ago, this declaration would have been unfathomable. But we're moving forward to the point where every voice matters...well, at least every voice that's reasonable."

"Our Constitution was made only for a moral and religious people. It is wholly inadequate to the government of any other."

-John Adams

CHAPTER FOUR

The next morning I slowly rise out of bed. The sun is fighting to stream in through my closed blinds, which tells me it's far later in the morning than I'm used to being here. I brush my teeth and rinse my face, holding the cool water to my sore eyelids. I don't know how long I stayed up last night but however long it was, my body sure feels it now.

I shuffle into the kitchen and find Mom at the rickety dining table, eating some toast and an egg.

I kiss her forehead. "Morning, Beautiful."

She jumps as if startled. "You're still here? What are you doing here this time of morning?"

It's disturbing how easily the lie slips out of me. "I got today off since I covered for Adams yesterday."

"Oh, that's nice. Good. You need a break."

I need a job.

I turn to the stove and make myself a quick bite. Mom finishes her food and heads to her room. She pauses at the threshold and looks back at me, smiling.

"What?" I ask.

She shakes her head. "Nothing. I just...I love you."

I blink at her burst of sentimentality, trying to ignore its effect on me.

"Love you, too." I reply. She closes the door and goes back to the laptop she has no idea I borrowed the night before. With her gone, I can finally focus on the day ahead.

I need a job. And fast.

Between the four other quarters, I'm only remotely qualified to work in two: Mechanics or on Danielton. I'd rather chew glass than assemble parts on Danielton all day so I quickly come up with a plan to find work in Mechanics Quarter. I down the last of my coffee and stand, ready to get dressed and head out. Someone knocks on the door as I put the dishes away.

"I got it!" I yell, crossing over to the door. I peek through the peep hole and immediately open it, turning back towards the kitchen as soon as I do. "Hey, I can't talk long."

Jenner closes the door behind him and looks around. "Your mom here?"

I face him and nod my head towards her closed door. He nods and lowers his voice. "I have an afternoon shift so I thought I'd check in. Does she know?"

I shake my head. "But it sounds like you do. Who told you?"

"Adams," he says. "Decker, he's been trying to call you-"

"I haven't been taking any calls." I turn and head towards my room. Jenner follows, hesitating at the threshold. He's never been in my room. Has had no reason to. I look at him and shrug, gesturing to the bathroom. "I've got to change and get ready. I can still hear you while I'm in there."

Jenner nods, walks in and sits at the edge of my bed. I close the bathroom door behind me right as he asks, "What happened?"

"What did Adams tell you?" I call back.

His voice is slightly muffled behind the door. "Only that Yang discharged you on the spot. No hearing, no trial, no chance to defend yourself. Stanton was a bit of a shit when he let me go but at least an entire committee decided to. What the hell kind of power trip is Yang on?"

"A reckless one," I mutter to myself. I turn on the shower and quickly step in.

"So what exactly happened?" I barely hear Jenner repeat.

I sigh and re-tell the story, yelling over the water and keeping it as short as possible. By the time I'm done narrating, I'm out and pulling on my jeans and a shirt. Jenner's been quiet the past few minutes. I open the door, half expecting him to have bailed. To my surprise, he's not only still sitting at my bed, he's sitting there holding a sheet, his eyes transfixed on the paper.

He looks up at me, his blue eyes slightly glassy. "Where did you find this?"

I look over his shoulder. "Oh, that. I wrote it. Woke

up in the middle of the night all pissed."

Jenner gasps, as if shocked. "You *wrote* this? All by yourself?"

"Yeah, last night." I frown at him. "Are you okay? You look…I don't know. Wired."

I find my jacket and pull it on. Check for my keys and grab my boots before heading for the door. "I got to go."

I look back and see no trace of him. "Jenner?"

Jenner appears at the door of my room, with the same shell shocked expression.

"Jenner," I repeat, this time impatient. "I've got to go. Come on!"

He snaps out of it and looks at me, a serious look overtaking his face. "Have you thought of spreading this?"

"Spreading what?" I ask exasperatedly.

"This!" Jenner waves the paper at me. "This document. This…declaration of equality. Have you thought of showing others?"

I look at him like he's insane. "No! Of course not. Why would I spread something I wrote in the middle of the night in the heat of my anger? For what? I don't need to spread anything, Jenner. I don't need to start anything. I need to find a *job*."

Suddenly, the door to my right opens and out walks Mom. My heart skips, hoping I didn't speak too loudly. Jenner quickly folds the paper out of view.

"Caden! How are you, sweetheart?" she kisses his cheek.

"Doing good, Ms. K. How are you?" He glances at me,

his eyes wary.

"You weren't leaving, were you?"

"Well, I-"

"Sit! Sit! I'll make you some breakfast."

Any other day I wouldn't have minded her generous offer. But hearing my mother offer our limited, much-needed food to someone outside of our home reminds me all the more how soon I need to land another job. Either that, or tell her immediately so she doesn't give us out of house and kitchen.

To his credit, Jenner immediately declines. "Thank you, Ms. K, but I've already had breakfast. I gotta get going along with Decker. My shift on Danielton starts soon."

"Oh," she says, slightly disappointed. "Okay. You boys be careful."

She looks at me. "Sweetie, when will you be back?"

"I'm not sure," I answer. "Before evening probably."

She nods. "Okay."

I kiss her cheek once more and turn, Jenner following behind.

We go down the stairs, pass the lobby, and exit the building.

"So where are you looking for work?" Jenner asks.

"Mechanics Quarter. I still remember some stuff from before. Hopefully someone will take me on."

"Will be tough without trade school. You have a connection you can tap into?"

"Yeah," I reply. "My dad."

Mechanics Quarter is the greasy, smelly, grimy abyss of Commons. A quarter entirely dedicated to repairing vehicles and transportation machinery, it's hard to believe the men who work in these conditions also live in them. My dad works in a shop on the far east of town, overlooking the Atlantic.

I walk into the enormous rusted metal workshop and scan the area for him. It doesn't take me long to find him, hunched over the hood of a fancy Atlas Lexley. The years of hard labor have slightly slumped his back and added a small pouch to his belly but Dad is still tall, strong, and memorable with a handsome mug, light blue eyes and dark blond hair. His hair, like his face, is smudged with grease and sweat. He doesn't notice me when I first walk up.

"Hey, Dad."

He straightens immediately and blinks at my sudden appearance. "Decker? What are you doing here, son?"

"I, uh, I need some help."

He frowns. "You okay? Is it your mother?"

I don't know why but it pleases me whenever he thinks to ask about her. My parents actually took the trouble to get married when they fell in love. They had me two short years later and for a while, were very happy together. Both from the dwindling middle class, they had every reason to believe they had a bright future, as well as their young child. But they found themselves unable to keep up with the frequent inflation crises racking USA at the time. My father, an aspiring businessman, poured all of their savings into an investment my mother found - one that turned out to be part of the largest Ponzi scheme to impact the nation. Wealthy Atlas investors survived the loss - it was an annoying bite out of their vast financial reserves. But the scheme effectively killed the dwindling percentage of middle class families, my parents included. They lost everything - save the home my maternal grandparents owned - the apartment I now live in. It destroyed their marriage as they dissolved into the blame game: Mom blaming Dad for putting it all in one pot, Dad blaming Mom for urging him to invest in the first place. He never fully recovered from the defeat and she never fully forgave him for leaving.

I snap out of the memories to find him looking at me, his frown deepening. "Son, what is it? What's happened?"

"I lost my job," I blurt out. There's no point in mincing words. Thankfully, his co-workers are well out of ear shot. I keep my story brief and get to why I'm here. "It's either this or Danielton. Do you know of any leads in Mechanics?"

He doesn't ask any questions. Just looks me over before stepping back from the car. He opens an arm and heads towards a set of stairs. "Come on. Let me introduce you to Tony. He may be able to give you something temporary. Tide you over 'till we can find something permanent."

Two hours later, I'm re-entering the Police Quarter, encouraged and relieved. Dad put in a good word with his boss, Tony, and Tony's taking me on for some temp work he needs on the floor. Like every business on Commons, the shop is owned by an Atlas monopoly but Tony has hiring and firing power. I almost smile as I make my way to my building. It's not permanent but I'm relieved we won't starve in the next few weeks. It's something for now and if I'm smart and play my cards right, this may even turn into something permanent. Maybe we *can* stay afloat. Maybe I *can* tell Mom what's happened now. Maybe-

"Decker Channing?"

I turn in time to see two officers approach me. I recognize their stance and immediately know the words they're about to say next.

"Decker Channing, you're under arrest. Hands behind your back, *now*."

Never.

Never in a million years did I think I'd walk these halls with cuffs on my hands. I feel like dying from the humiliation as Carter and Gene pull me down the dark, sterile hall, past my former colleagues, into an old fashioned interrogation room. My only reprieve is that I'm at the station in Commons, not Atlas. Less officers are based at this station. That doesn't mean word won't get around I've been arrested.

My hips barely hit the seat when Yang himself strides into the room. I look up, surprised.

Doesn't he have better things to do than question me?

Didn't that stupid law give these officers the right to interrogate me on their own?

"You're frowning," Yang says casually. I look at him questioningly. He repeats, "You're frowning. Something wrong?"

Is he joking?

Yang chuckles and turns his back to me. He asks in a sudden, booming voice, "How long have you been trying to start an insurrection?"

"What?" I ask in disbelief. What on earth is he talking about?

Carter and Gene snicker at my response but Yang remains steady.

"You can drop the act, Officer Channing. Or I should say, *former* Officer Channing."

The dig hurts. But not as much as I would expect it to.

He continues, "You were once the finest officer on the Force. Graduated first in your Academy class. How far have you fallen?"

Okay. *That* hurts.

Yang gestures to Gene and Gene pulls out an old remote. Unlike Atlas, the station on Commons only has antiquated technology. I can still remember which buttons to push as they pull the screen down in front of us all. Seconds later, an image appears from one of the surveillance cameras. I glance at the date stamped on the corner of the footage. It was earlier today. Early afternoon. Location: Danielton. Jenner appears on screen, showing a piece of paper to his friends in one of the factories. My stomach drops. The paper looks all-too-familiar. Yang turns up the volume and we hear them speaking.

"It's incredible, man." Jenner's voice is awe-struck. "It's like he took the thoughts out of our heads and put it on paper for us all to see."

"Who wrote this?" a friend asks.

"Decker. Decker Channing. He's an Atlas officer."

"An *officer*?" another friend sneers, half in disbelief, half in disgust.

"Well, he was. They canned him the other day. Assholes."

The sneering friend continues, "I can't believe an officer wrote this."

Jenner's head whips up. "Hey, I was one too, remember? Some cops are real shits but Decker…Decker's the real deal. He was always looking out for others, Commoners too."

Friend One says, "He sounds like a good guy. Why was he sacked?"

"It's a long story but basically he was trying to keep a homeless Commoner from getting killed. By another officer."

The friends murmur admiringly. Yang glances at me, trying to read my reaction. I keep my poker face on and nearly smile when he rolls his eyes in frustration before turning back to the screen.

Jenner continues, "The point is, what he says is right. This country isn't what it was meant to be. The founding fathers…Washington, Jefferson, Adams, and…whoever else…they'd be rolling in their graves if they saw how it is now."

"I like what it says," Friend Two says. "But what does it mean for us?"

"It means we have a reason to fight for our freedom. A right to."

My heart pounds at those words. Without knowing it, my best friend has just put my life in danger. And probably his.

Yang stops the video there and turns back to me, his beady eyes blazing.

"What was that?" he asks, calmly.

I look up at him, expression still passive. I can't afford to let him see a hint of what I'm thinking or feeling. "I don't know."

"What exactly did you write on those papers?" Gene asks me. Yang glances at him and I immediately sense he's annoyed. Apparently he likes to interrogate alone.

"I wrote that this country was founded on ideals. Ideals which included life, liberty and the pursuit of happiness. I wrote that it was intended to be a country for anyone willing to work hard to achieve their dreams."

"And you don't believe that's what the country is now?" Carter asks. I keep silent and look at him. Surely he must be joking? Even *he* doesn't like his job. He blinks at my candid stare and backs off. Yang frowns at him and looks back at me.

"Did you mention anything about fighting for freedom? About rebelling?"

I meet Yang's eyes and lie. "No."

"No?"

I shake my head. "No. The pamphlet was just a summary of what I studied about American history, about the ideals the founding fathers espoused. Nowhere did I say anyone should rebel, up rise, or try to usurp authority in anyway." Yang leans back on his heels and I know he's trying to decide if he trusts my word. He did, after all, just fire me. And because I am lying, I lean forward in my seat, determined to convince him. "Chief Yang, I'm not trying to start anything. I wrote that paper in the heat of the moment when I was upset about…" I glance at the other two officers, my former colleagues. "I had no idea Jenner would steal the papers from my house and spread it to friends."

Yang nods, not really listening to me anymore. He looks at Gene. "Jenner. What can we do about him?"

My heart pounds harder. As pissed as I am at Jenner, I don't want him or anyone else to suffer, possibly die, because of something I wrote. To my relief, Carter speaks up.

"Sir, it might not be necessary to handle him."

"Why?" Yang asks sharply.

Carter glances at me. "Well…from what I can remember about Jenner, he's all talk and no action. He spouts off shit all the time and forgets about it the next day."

Gene nods. "But if we go to him and make an issue about this, we'd be adding fuel to the fire. Proving he's right to his little friends that he has something. That's the last thing we want."

Yang folds his arms and rubs his chin between his thumb and index finger, mulling it over. After what seems like an eternity, he straightens, puts his arms down and looks me squarely in the eye.

"Tell your friend to zip it. Before I zip it for him permanently. That paper he has…"

I nod.

"Ensure that it's burned and never sees the light of day."

"I will." I nod.

Yang nods at Gene and Gene moves to uncuff me. I rub my wrists as Yang walks to the door.

"Lastly," he says. "You're now on the list of suspected rebels."

My stomach drops.

"As you know, this limits your freedom of transport to and from Atlas. Removal is subject to monitoring."

I glance at Carter, who frowns. "Sir, he was one of our own."

Yang looks sharply at him. "Would you like to be relieved too, Carter?"

Carter looks down.

"Jenner was one of our own too and look what a shit he's turned out to be." Yang looks at me again. "I'm taking your word for it this time, Channing. Not because I like you or because of these officers. But because of your track record. Prior to the incident on Atlas, you were one of the most respected officers on the Force. Stanton himself admired you. Keep your nose out of Atlas affairs and hopefully I'll never see you again."

I nod, my eyes fixed on the table. "Yes, sir."

It kills me to say those two words. Words of respect. Words of appreciation. Words that I would rather give to any other man than the one standing in front of me. But he's spared my life and given me a chance to walk free. Tonight could have ended much differently than it has.

"Hey, Decker!"

Nothing could have prepared either of us for the rage that floods my senses when he says my name. My fist plants itself in the side of Jenner's nose before either of us can register what's happened.

"What the-? Hey!"

I watch Jenner fall to the ground, blood exploding across his face. He looks up at me, confusion marring his already bloodied features.

"I told you I didn't want any trouble." I growl in fury. "You stole that paper from my house and spread it around!"

Jenner scrambles to his feet and holds his hands in front of him, pleadingly. He could try to hit me back, physically defend himself - we both know that. But I'm the one who trained him in Academy. He might survive if he fights, but he will not win. "Look, Decker, I'm sorry. I shouldn't have taken it. You're right. I just wanted to-"

"Wanted to what?" I cut him off. "Get my ass sent to The Gauntlet? Get me in even deeper shit with Yang?"

Understanding dawns on Jenner's face. "The cameras. They saw me through the cameras."

"No shit, Sherlock." Has he been out of the Force so long he can't remember surveillance mechanisms? "They heard you too as you repeated my name - *my name* - over and over and over again! You could have gotten me killed!" my voice explodes as my rage picks up fresh steam.

"Decker, I'm sorry." Jenner doesn't even try to defend himself. He can't. I turn on my heel and stride into my building. I can hear him following me as I take the stairwell up. Maybe the trip will cool me off.

"Stop following me," I bite out over my shoulder. "You are no longer welcome in my home. Stay away from me and stay away from my mother."

"Decker, I know you're upset but please, will you hear me out? Once you calm down, maybe you'll see what I was saying. We have something here-" he cuts off when I unexpectedly wheel around.

"Are you hard of hearing?" I ask him incredulously. I glance at the camera fixed on the corner of the stairwell and say this loud enough for it to pick up. "How many different ways can I reiterate that I don't want any trouble?" I point a finger at the other man's sternum. Hard. "You burn that paper, Jenner. You burn it immediately. If I catch you using *my name* or anything from my house to stir up trouble again, I will end it. *Personally.*"

I don't wait to see what he says. One glance at his face, and I know my warning is heard loud and clear. I turn on my heel and march the rest of the way up to my place. Jenner doesn't follow behind. By the time I reach my door, the rage has evaporated.

But in its place, guilt finds a home.

PRESIDENT TO ADDRESS SOCIETAL CONCERNS IN STATE OF UNION

Celia Hall
Los Angeles Times
January 9, 2202

President Aiden Tate is scheduled to give his State of the Union address in two days and political experts claim this may very well be one of the most anticipated presidential addresses in the last century. He is expected to address a plethora of concerns, chief among them the unprecedented rate of overpopulation in the nation.

Five months ago, the United States crossed the two billion citizen threshold and this number does not include the millions of illegal immigrants occupying limited American soil. The rapid increase in population has also resulted in the rapid increase of crime with homicides more than doubling in the past four years alone. Rape and other instances of sexual assault have increased by 24% in the last year. Theft and burglary have also skyrocketed from east to west. Several governors across the country have declared states of emergency in the face of rampant looting. Police believe much of the crime points to national unemployment reaching a staggering 31%.

In addition to the crime, a panel of more than 450 sociologists has expressed their concern about the deteriorating fabric of the American family. More than 70% of children are reportedly fatherless and more than 90% of American adults are no longer marrying. The panel claims that the deterioration of the family unit may have informed the lack of education, progress, and civil responsibility in citizens.

New York University historian Jamie Milstein observes, "Historically, nations with higher rates of broken homes suffer economically and socially. When a mother or father are absent from the home, the child is less likely to succeed in school and their resulting career thereafter." She criticizes the anti-religious research of the American Psychological Association. "What the late Dr. Newby and other biased researchers of the past failed to note is that religion and other cultural constructs founded on absolute morality historically assisted in the stability of a family unit. And stable family units historically resulted in societal flourishing."

When asked if America has a chance of returning to such stability, Milstein was rather pessimistic.

"I'm afraid we've opened Pandora's Box and it may now be too late to close."

"Among the strange things of this world, nothing seems more strange than that men pursuing happiness should knowingly quit the right and take a wrong road, and frequently do what their judgments neither approve nor prefer."

-John Jay

CHAPTER FIVE

Mechanics Quarter.

I make my way down the dirty, grungy streets and notice that everything is ten times grayer than what I'm used to. The Police Quarter is dirty but at least the sky is still blue. Here, there's a perpetual fog of smoke, gasoline, and exhaust permeating the air. I wonder just how many people here die of lung cancer.

And my father lives in this junkyard.

It takes me twice as long to get to the shop as it would have to Atlas for work. But I'd better get used to it now. This is my new job. And it may turn permanent. The thought of that wrenches knives in my gut.

I walk through the main entrance and make my way to Tony's office. Right before I reach the door, I hear my name.

"Decker!" I turn and find my dad striding over to me. We shake hands. "Ready for your first day?"

I nod silently. He leads me down a flight of stairs, past two winding hallways and deeper into the back of the shop. I make note of the turns we make. I know I won't be able to use him as my guide much longer. We end up at the work site, a huge warehouse with dozens of vehicles being worked on simultaneously. Some men work on parts alone, others work on vehicles in groups. Dad takes me to a small work station with a part I immediately recognize.

"A hover craft engine?"

He nods and smiles, clearly proud. "You remember."

Of course I remember. It was one of the coolest engines he'd ever shown me. New at the time, it was the talk of USA because it had the horsepower required to elevate a vehicle off the ground for the first time without the assistance of a battery. The solar film inside it, harnessed the energy needed to function. It's been re-worked and improved over the years but is now the standard engine for most cars on Atlas. The part is still too expensive for Commoners and will be for centuries to come.

Dad taps at it. "The rotary is..." he trails off. "Actually, I think I'll let you figure it out."

I nod. "What do I do when I'm done?"

He raises a brow. "You mean what do you do *if* you're done by the end of today. Four teams have tried figuring this thing out. I doubt you'll be done in time to do anything else today."

I frown. "Then why'd you assign it to me?"

He shrugs. "You're gonna get assigned to it eventually. Why not start with it and move on to something else later?"

I blink. That makes no sense but something tells me my dad put me here for a different reason than what he's sharing. Whatever. It's a job. It's money. It'll put food in my mouth and my mother's.

"See you at lunch," Dad says. I nod and shake his hand once more.

As soon as he leaves, I hear them. The snickers. I look from the door to the table across from me. A group of men, streaked with engine oil and machinery grease smirk at me. One of them tilts his chin at me and says, "You Channing's kid?"

I nod silently.

"When'd you leave trade school? You look old to be new."

I look at him. He's making small talk but I don't know why. Is it to be friendly or to set me up for another joke. *Can't I just work?*

I shrug off my jacket, sit on the stool behind me and roll up my sleeves. Eyes fixed on the engine before me, I answer briefly. "I never went to trade school. I'm temporary right now."

I hear them murmur amongst themselves but keep my eyes fixed on the engine, the intricate curves, spindles, and grooves of the machine. Dad wouldn't even tell me what's wrong with it. And I'm supposed to fix it.

"Hey, uh…why'd Tony hire you then? You don't have no experience. He never hires nobody but the best."

And apparently passing English isn't necessary to be the best.

I glance up at him and realize he's serious. What does he want me to do? Whip out my mechanics' resume?

I shrug and focus on the part again.

"Oh, you're too good to answer me now?" Loud Mouth continues. "Look, just 'cause you're Channing's kid don't make you no better than me." I feel a liquid heat stir in my chest. It's the same feeling I get whenever someone tries to initiate conflict. Loud Mouth continues, "I heard about you. I remember Channing telling us he had a kid in the Force. What? You got fired?"

I look to the right of the engine and find a long, thin metal piece. It's been years since I worked on a car with Dad. I have no idea what this tool is called, but it allows me to reach into the heart of the engine and peel back the thin layer of solar-catching film. The piece folded back, I attempt to turn the engine on. It makes a painful, grinding noise. I turn it off and continue to observe. That's when I realize Loud Mouth is still talking.

"Do you know anything about vehicles? What? Daddy got you a job and now you're gonna screw up Tony's entire shop because you don't know what the hell you're-"

I finally look up and speak. "Look, is there something you want from me? Because if there isn't, stop wasting my time, wasting your breath and wasting Tony's money talking shit when you should be working."

Silence.

I didn't speak very loudly but silence falls over the entire shop. I look around and see a variety of expressions from grudging respect to bemusement to outrage that I would dare speak to a veteran mechanic this way.

"You looking to get your ass kicked, buddy?" Loud Mouth seethes.

I can't help myself. I laugh. I laugh hard - so hard, I have to drop the tool to steady myself. I look around and see the growing hostility on my new co-workers' face. Finally I get it. It's human nature - or at least male nature. They're challenging me and testing my boundaries. Why didn't I see it before? The guys at the Academy pulled the same stunt when I first joined. And they do it every year to new recruits on the Force. This place is no different.

I throw down the gauntlet.

"You're welcome to try, Loud Mouth." He and the other men gasp at the nickname I've given him. "But just keep in mind that even though I didn't go to trade school, I went to the Academy and I graduated first in my class. Meaning, that while I'm not formally trained to repair vehicles, I am formally trained to kick your ass, your friends' asses, and everyone in this room's ass all at the same time without breaking a sweat. You…" I look around the room. "And anyone else in this shop are welcome to test me. But I'm not responsible for whatever injury I give you and whether or not you'll be able to work after I give it to you." My eyes land on him again and I raise a brow.

What do you want to do?

Loud Mouth swallows hard and I see the war waging in his mud brown eyes. It's the same war I saw weeks ago on the train passenger's face: whether or not to be foolish and angry or smart and submissive. This time, the latter wins. The fear dissolves into a petty sneer as he twists his mouth and spits to his side. I note that he's very careful not to make it land near me. He rolls his eyes and turns back to his work. His friends follow suit. I look around and see the other men. They've turned back to their projects too but whispers abound as they glance at me. I could almost laugh again. They're acting like gossiping teenage girls and I'm their target subject.

Great.

I've alienated myself by scaring them off. But I don't really care if they like me or not. Finally, I get the peace I need to figure out this damn engine. I pick up the tool and focus on the part in front of me.

I've wasted enough time focusing on something else.

Just one more piece…

Clink. My head snaps up at the sound of a bag hitting the table beside me. I look up and see Dad, standing with an indiscernible expression on his face. The shop is empty. It's just the two of us as everyone else has gone to lunch. I glance inside the paper bag. A sandwich, some chips, and an apple. He hands me a can of Coke.

I frown. "I was going to get something when I get home."

"You need your energy."

"And you need your lunch."

"We'll split it."

I shake my head. "Dad-"

"We'll split it, son," he says with finality.

I look at his stubborn expression and cave. "Thanks, Dad."

He nods, pulls a stool and sits next to me. He takes out the sandwich first. Tears it clean in two and hands me my half. He bites into his and speaks around his food. "Heard you caused quite a stir earlier today."

"You mean they're *still* talking about me?" I ask. I bite into the sandwich and almost roll my eyes to the back of my head, it's so good. I see one thing from Mom has rubbed off on Dad. He still eats real food. The ham, lettuce and tomato sandwich hits the spot.

"You're new," he reminds me. "We don't see much action around here so everyone's entertained by you. Especially your ass-kicking speech."

I sigh. "I'm sorry. I don't want to make trouble for you-"

"What trouble? I earned my stripes a long time ago. Nothing you say or do can mess things up for me here. Tony knows you're your own man. And I know you won't do anything to make me regret vouching for you."

I nod.

"I'm proud of you," he continues. "You made it clear that you can hold your own. That you don't need 'daddy' to defend you. And whether they say it or not, they respect you for that. Just do your work and ignore idiots like Watson."

"Is that his name?"

MICHELLE N. ONUORAH

Dad chuckles. "Yeah, I heard you gave him a new nickname though. Several guys are already calling him Loud Mouth now."

I chuckle too. I can't say I feel bad for him.

I finish my last bite and shake my head when Dad offers me some chips. I swipe my hands across my lap and turn back to the engine.

"I told you, son, you have all afternoon to work on this."

I glance at him and raise a brow. "Why work all afternoon on this when…" I flick the switch on. "I could have it done by the end of lunch?"

The engine whirs up. I down the rest of my Coke and put the empty bottle on top of the engine. Right before our eyes, it lifts, the can balancing perfectly on top.

"What do you think?" I ask, my eyes fixed on the engine. "I think the sound can be cleaner but there may just be some exhaust particles in the filament chutes."

I look over at him but he's not there. I turn off the engine and the can clinks to the floor.

"Dad?" I call, looking around. "Dad?"

The doors open and in walks the herd of men. I turn away and start to clear the mess we made. Sure enough, as I stand and throw some of the trash aside, I can hear Loud Mouth Watson murmuring to his buddies. His voice is just one of many whispering about me. I pick up bits and pieces from them in their work stations as I clear mine, their voices competing with the noise of tools back at work.

"Prick."

"Why'd Tony pick him?"

"He's been working on that engine all during lunch. A real mechanic would know it's ready for the scrap heap."

"He's been working on it all lunch because he know don't nobody like him."

"Where was Senior during lunch?"

"Eatin' with his sorry ass kid."

My station is spotless. I don't know what else to do and I don't know where Dad is. I'm sure as hell not about to ask these jerks where to go. I glance at my watch and look at the door.

"Hey Junior, already looking to go?" Loud Mouth jeers. His friends laugh. "The pigs on the Police Force don't work as hard as us real men. No wonder you're sleepy."

Apparently a sandwich and some Coke has re-fueled this guy's ego. Or dulled his memory. I stand up contemplating if kicking his ass will get me fired. It probably will so I turn and head to the door. I'll find Tony myself. This greatly excites my new friend.

"Going so soon buddy?" he yells at a decibel well above the whirring machinery. "One little engine sent you running to Daddy."

Before I reach the doors, they burst open and in walks Tony himself. Dad is right beside him. The voices die down but the tools still whir. Bosses don't like to see anything but work being done.

Tony's steel gray eyes immediately land on me. "Is it

true?"

I look between him and my dad, whose eyes are bouncing with excitement.

"Is what true?"

"Hey, yo, Boss!" Watson yells. "It was nice of you to give Channing's kid a shot but he ain't worth shit!"

"Watch your mouth about my son, Watson!" Dad bites out.

Watson shuts up but nods with a nasty grin. Tony ignores the exchange and passes me, going straight to my station. All eyes are on him as he looks around the spotless area, touches the engine and flicks the switch on. Like clockwork it fires up and hovers over the table.

The other tools stop. Complete silence washes over the room and the only thing heard is the little hover engine working its magic. I glance at Watson, whose face has blanched to a sickly white. I don't respond to idiots but my dad can't resist a dig.

"You were saying, Watson?"

The older man looks between my father and I then back to the engine. I look back at Tony and see him rise slowly to his feet, his eyes transfixed on the engine. "How did you do it?" he asks.

I flick the switch off, pull the tiny tool I used and show him what the problem was.

"The conductor wire." his voice hitches in disbelief. "All you had to do was untangle the conductor wire?" I nod and he looks around at his men. "How is it that several of you took this thing apart for weeks and couldn't figure it out but this 'newbie' fixed the conductor wire over lunch?"

His eyes land on Watson and turn to pure steel. "Keep talking, Loud Mouth." Watson literally deflates at Tony's use of my nickname for him. A couple men whistle at the insult. "But Decker Channing may end up replacing you if he keeps up this level of work. And it won't be because he's Channing's kid."

He looks at me and pats my shoulder."Excellent work. I have a new order in I want you to look at. Your old man will show you." With that, he turns to the other men. "What are you all gawking at? Get back to work!"

The tools fire up immediately and voices start to rise.

Tony nods at Dad and goes back to his office.

As I follow Dad to the new project, I hear the voices still mentioning me. But there's admiration this time around. And more talk about what a fool Watson showed himself to be.

By the time I get home, it's well past dinner time. My stomach is growling and my back feels like a hundred knives have sawed through it. For a pretty entertaining start to the day, it ended on an abysmally boring note. After Watson got chewed out, Dad brought me to a new car. The fix was easy and I quickly moved to another one. Within an hour, Dad and Tony realized just how fast I could work. So they put me on a line of vehicles that were past due for repair and return. I got the work done. But my hands, back, legs, and neck are screaming for relief.

So is my brain.

As I walked down the dangerous, grungy streets of Mechanics Quarter, I faced the horrifying reality that this could be my life for the next forty years. If this job works out. If I stay and become permanent, like Tony suggested again before quitting time, I could turn into my father. Fixing cars and wiping grease until I'm too crippled to move.

That's not what I want.

I open the door to my apartment and immediately smell my favorite dish. Mini meatloaf.

I groan. Unable to contain myself, my hand immediately reaches for a bite. "Mom, thank you!"

I hear her come out from the other room. I don't know how she moves so fast but she manages to slap the top of my hand before I can get my dirty fingers on the food.

"You know better than that!"

I sigh, move to the sink and watch the filth pour off my hands into the metal below.

"I thought you'd be here a little earlier. Thursdays are your early days, aren't they?" she asks.

I stare at my hands under the water, wondering why I didn't just tell her earlier. Better late than never, I guess. "Mom," I turn off the faucet and face her. "I'm no longer with the Force. I made a switch and now work at a shop in Mechanics."

She gasps. "No wonder you're so filthy. What happened with the Force? When were you going to tell me?"

I put up two hands to stop the avalanche of questions. Whenever she's confused, she shoots out a ton of questions like a battalion at war. I pull a plate from the cabinet and take a whopping size of the meat. Sitting down, I stuff a hot, savory piece in my mouth and groan again.

"So good!" I exclaim. She smiles slightly but I see the worry in her eyes. I gesture to the seat beside me and she sits. Around bites of my dinner, I tell her what happened. To her credit, she doesn't ask questions and she doesn't interrupt. Just listens as I recount how I got fired, why, and what I did next. She blinks but doesn't say anything when I mention how dad hooked me up.

By the time I finish talking, my plate is also clean. She leans back, takes a deep breath and tries to process all I've told her. I get up and take a second helping. This time, I make it small. I should have rationed it the first time. This meat has to stretch us a few days at least.

When I sit back down, she's ready to ask, "There's nothing you can do to appeal the discharge?"

I shake my head, fork already near my mouth. "Who can I appeal it to? The buck stops with Yang. Maybe if the Department of Justice still existed, I'd have a say, but they closed that department before I was born."

She nods. "I remember."

She rubs her forehead, still very troubled.

"I'm sorry I didn't say anything earlier," I add. "I just...I didn't want you to worry. I didn't want you to know until I had something else lined up. And now I do."

She nods. "This is permanent?"

I hedge, "It will be."

She peers at me while I chew. It scares me when she does that. For a woman who's gullible to get-rich-quick scams, kind to complete strangers, and naive about my everyday business, sometimes I feel like she can look into my very soul when she really wants to.

"How is it?" she asks, her voice eerily calm.

I look away. It's only been a day and she's already touched on a really raw nerve. Is it that obvious that I hate the job already? That I dread the idea of doing this permanently?

I focus on my empty plate and shrug.

"You hate it."

I look up and meet her gentle dark eyes, eyes that match my own.

"It's money," I reply.

"What if we could get money some other way?"

I stiffen involuntarily. "How?"

"Well…" she stands up and shuffles to her room, emerging seconds later with a flyer. "What if we could make all the money we need without you working some dead end job, like your father."

There it is. The dig I was waiting for. They've been divorced for nearly thirty years but she still can't resist putting him down. I ignore the comment like I always do and focus on the more troubling thing - her hawking yet another scheme at me.

"I'm not interested, Mom." I say, rising to wash my plate.

"Oh, come on! You always do that!" She continues talking while I scrub the dishes. "You know I don't just sit here twiddling my thumbs all day. I've been watching this guy's stuff. Marcus Zerelio. He's a social media magnate who made his fortune advertising real estate deals to Atlans."

I frown. Does she even *realize* how stupid that sounds? "Why would Atlans need real estate deals? They're rich. And who uses social media anymore. Mom, Facebook went under during the Cyrian epidemic!"

"Other platforms have come up!" she exclaims, undeterred by my objections. "Marcus Zerelio says-"

"Mom, please. It's been a long day and I'm not interested in whatever it is Marcus Zerelio says." I put the dishes on the rack and dry my hands.

"Why not?"

I turn to face her. "Because it'll be as useless as what Flora Lioni said. Tatum Ritzer said. Lawrence Filburn, Cara Soro, and all the other useless get-rich-quick Commoner scammers you've ever listened to before!"

I watch her face tighten right before my eyes. Her dark eyes narrow into near slits and her mouth purses the way it does whenever she's about to tell someone off. "You never gave them a chance. None of those programs worked because you refused to let me invest in them."

"And I won't be helping you invest in this. And do you know why?" I charge on, trying to keep my voice down.

"Because I can still remember the small fortune we lost on all the other scams we invested in before. Peruvio Lanari, Cecily Jenkins, Gordon Dyson, Patrick Hudson…Mom, we could have purchased a whole new sofa set with all the money we wasted on those 'programs!'"

She shakes her head, refusing to listen. "They were bad deals. You can't dismiss them all because of a few bad apples."

"Yes, I can. And I have. No more scams, Mom. I'm done."

"Why won't you listen to me on this?" Her voice starts to rise. "Do you really want to spend the rest of your life washing grease from your hands?"

The question strikes me like a blow to the chest. She's fighting hard.

"I kept silent because when you were an officer, you seemed somewhat okay. You had Jenner and Adams and you were respected. Clearly I was wrong if they were willing to toss you aside after *fourteen years* of service."

"Mom…" I say warningly. I can feel heat rising in my chest, traveling to my face.

"Decker, you're still young. You can still do something useful with your life instead of spending the rest of it poring over cars for rich, selfish Atlas people who will never have to work nearly as hard as you do. Do you really want to become your father?"

"*Mom.*" She's struck again.

"Because that's who you're turning into! He took one bad risk and let it scare him into spending the rest of his life working with the rest of the other losers in Mechanics Quarter-"

"That's enough!" I yell. She gasps and immediately falls silent. I clench and unclench my fist, the heat stifling my collar. I fix my gaze on the window past her head. I know without looking at her that tears are falling from her small, dark eyes. I've never yelled at my mother before.

Ever.

I clear my throat and take a deep breath. I can't end this evening this way. "I'm sorry," I say quietly. "I shouldn't have yelled at you. I should have said it calmly. You're my mother and I will never disrespect you like that again. I'm sorry." I still can't look at her, I'm so angry. "I don't know why you still have so much bitterness against my father-"

"Decker-"

I hold up a hand and keep talking, "But every time you speak against him, you hurt me. Whether you know it or not, it hurts. He's not perfect - I already know that from experience - but he was there for me when I lost this job and 'loser mechanic' or not, he's a hard working man. Which is more than I can say for the dozens of scammers who have pulled the wool over your eyes."

She exhales in exasperation but I keep my eyes steady on the window.

"You may think Dad has wasted his life working as a mechanic but you have wasted fourteen years listening to people who only want your hard earned money - *my* hard earned money. I can't force you to stop listening to them, even though it kills me to see you do it. But I'll be damned if I give a single dime to any of these worthless, lying, sniveling charlatans ever again. I'm *done*." With that, I grab my keys and shrug my jacket back on. "I'm going out. Clear my head."

I walk blindly, ignoring the people, streets, signs, and cameras around me. My feet move on autopilot and before I know it, I'm on Atlas Express going into town. By the time I make it to the library, most patrons have left and librarians are clearing up books. Any other day, I would have found a corner of the building and just lounged here. Most people, Atlans or Commoners, don't particularly use the library for fun. They use it mostly for research. Though open to Atlans and Commoners, it's predominately occupied by Atlans - Atlas kids who can afford to stay in school past fourteen and who go on to college after that.

Sometimes I wonder if I'm the only person here who reads these books for fun.

I go to my usual section and pick up several books on Ancient American history from the founding of the nation to President Obama's first term in office; what most scholars call The Great Shift. With two months to keep them checked out, I figure I'll stock up and have something interesting to do when I'm not working. Maybe exercising my mind will make my job more bearable. I go to the automated checkout machine and insert my books:

the third volume of John Adams' autobiography, George Washington's *Rules of Civility and Decent Behaviour*, and a couple other history books.

I exit the building just as the staff announces they're closing in five minutes. I run down the stairs towards Atlas Express. I can make it in time if I hurry.

"Decker!"

"Nicole?" To my surprise, she's running down the stairs after me, two books and a library slip in her hand. She reaches up and gives me a hug and I stiffen involuntarily. Most Commoners don't share affectionate gestures with Atlans. If she notices my reaction, she doesn't show it.

"Decker, we've been worried sick about you! What happened? One day you were guarding us like always and the next, we get a new officer in your place."

I shrug and quickly say, "I'm no longer an officer."

She nods. "Yeah, Dad found out you were...discharged," she says hesitantly. "But why? You're an excellent officer. Graduated first in your Academy - it's why Dad went to so much trouble to have you assigned to our family."

Suddenly, I hear the blow horn for Atlas Express. I glance at my watch and begin to blanch.

"Listen, Nicole. I'm sorry but I don't have time to explain what happened right now. I have to catch the train. It's the last one out of Atlas."

She frowns. "I can take you home. Or you can sleep over at our place, if you want."

I shake my head. "Thanks, but no. I have work tomorrow morning and I don't want to inconvenience you."

"It's no inconvenience," she says, totally relaxed. "My car-"

"Thanks but I really gotta go." I start taking off towards the station. "Give your folks my regard!"

I run, leaving her standing on the steps with a bewildered look on her pretty face. I feel bad that I have to run off but relieved for two reasons: first, I catch the train just seconds before it leaves the platform and second, my quick escape spares me the burden of having to tell yet *another* person why I got fired. I've told the story at least three times. I don't want to have to tell it again.

The ride home is a short one and the walk will be even shorter. But I manage to squeeze a couple chapters of Adams' autobiography before I get off the train. I blink at one portion of the book:

"Suppose a nation in some distant Region should take the Bible for their only law Book, and every member should regulate his conduct by the precepts there exhibited! Every member would be obliged in conscience, to temperance, frugality, and industry; to justice, kindness, and charity towards his fellow men; and to piety, love, and reverence toward Almighty God ... What a Eutopia, what a Paradise would this region be."

If I've learned anything in reading the documents of the past, it is that men of his day were very religious. I can't imagine saying, much less writing, such a bold declaration about religion. It makes me curious. About what the country was like before religious expression was banned. And what it is about Christianity that inspired such devotion on the part of these men.

My head is mulling over his words as I walk home, taking sure steps towards my building.

"Hey, Channing."

I turn only to find my face connect with the end of a heavy fist. Pain explodes through my nose and travels to the back of my head as I completely lose my balance and fall to the filthy ground below. Before I can catch my bearing, a heavy boot strikes the center of my torso repeatedly.

"Ahh!" The air rushes out of my lungs. I feel another kick. This one to my back. The pain is blinding. I twist, trying to defend my body but it's no use. The kicks and punches come at all angles and I quickly realize there are multiple men on me.

I grab the next fist to strike and pull hard. "Whoa!" The man lurches forward and I manage to connect my knee to his nose.

"Ahh!"

He reels back in pain. I catch a swinging foot and roll, holding it under my arm. The man falls with a loud thud to the ground. I use the momentum and stand to my feet but I don't stay up for long.

Suddenly I hear the crack of a baton, striking me right behind my knee.

"*AHH!*" The pain explodes from the back of my knee

and radiates up my femur. I immediately fall to the ground.

"Stay down, Decker. I don't want to hurt you worse." I recognize that voice.

"Carter?" I gasp out.

"Zip it." I feel another kick to my torso. This one avoids my ribs. Suddenly, I get it. This isn't an attempt at mugging. Muggings rarely happen in the *Police* Quarter. The men jumping me *are* police officers. And Carter is trying to hurt me without seriously hurting me. By the time the two minions recover, Carter and another officer have gotten in a few more licks. I could fight back. I could probably take them down. But these men aren't the men in Mechanics Quarter. These men are also trained to kick ass. I risk serious injury if I fight back and lose. I risk a good chance at death if I fight back and win. If I get injured, I can't work. If I die, my mother starves. The other two officers are pissed. Their punches are harder, their kicks stronger - especially now that I'm not fighting back. The pain goes from sharp to numbing and by the time they finish, silent rivulets of blood flow freely from my mouth and nose. I have what will be a shiner of a black eye by tomorrow morning. I spit out blood and can only hope my ribs haven't been broken.

I hear the footsteps of the officers leave. Suddenly, I see a pair of legs crouch in front of me. I recognize the boots as Carter's. He leans close to my ear and whispers. "Suspected rebels shouldn't act suspicious. You *know* they're watching you. Leave for Atlas this late again and you'll be taken back in. You...you know what they do to repeat offenders." He stands. "Be careful, Channing."

His footsteps retreat and I know they're all gone. But something keeps me glued to my spot on the ground. It's not the pain. Though searing, I can still move all my joints. It's what he said. His warning.

All of this over a library *visit?*

In my haste and hazy mind, I completely forgot that my freedom to go to Atlas "after hours" had been revoked. I vaguely remember the rules for suspected rebels. In addition to careful monitoring, Atlas visits, unless necessary, are frowned upon. I can remember the policies. What I don't remember are suspects ever getting beaten to a pulp for a late night trip. Stanton would never order such a thing. But why am I surprised Yang would?

The bastard is halfway psychotic.

I stand slowly and check my ribs for fractures. Nothing is broken but they are beyond sore and they'll bruise up nicely right along with my left eye. It hurts me just to stiffly bend and pick up the books that are now filthy from the ground. I don't have the money to pay for the damage. The thought of taking any funds to cover the mess *they* made hurts almost as much as the back of my knee. And yet I'm grateful Carter struck me there. If Yang assigned any other officer - like Jackson - that baton could have relegated me to a wheelchair. He chose the least damaging spot to hit me with it. I never thought I'd feel gratitude to a man who just beat me up.

The remaining two minute journey takes an extra ten

as I slowly and painfully walk my way back to the apartment. I'm relieved to find all the lights out. Mom is asleep. I hadn't even thought of a way to explain my appearance to her. I shuffle into my room, drop my stuff and peel out of my mud-soaked clothes, wincing at every wrong jerk. I lean heavy on the shower tile as the hot water cascades over my sore muscles. A sharp sting of pain radiates across my skin every time the water hits an open wound. But I need to wash everything. I can't risk an infected wound. I dry off, change, and find an old tube of Mom's antibacterial ointment in the medicine cabinet.

Light on, I apply it to every cut, scrape, and abrasion on my face and torso. I can already see a purple splotch form where my ribs are supposed to be. I creep into the kitchen, determined not to wake her up, and open the fridge. To my relief, there's some left. Growing up, I used to scoff at my mother's insistence on keeping fresh aloe vera leaves in the fridge. I argued it was a waste of money. But from skinned knees to bloodied Academy noses, the gel in the leaf was her go-to remedy for wounds. I take one of the leaves out of the plastic wrap and hurry back to my bathroom. Squeezing the gel out of the leaf, I apply it to my throbbing left eye and re-dress all my other cuts. I find a bottle of pain reliever on my dresser and dry swallow three pills.

My body is aching to go to bed. But there's just one more thing I need to do before I give it the rest it needs. I pick up my phone and dial the number. It rings four times before he finally picks up.

Jenner's groggy voice answers, "Hello?"

"Meet me here tomorrow afternoon," I tell him.

"Decker?"

"I'm in."

BREAKING NEWS: UNITED STATES' FIRST AMENDEMENTALTERED FOR THE FIRST TIME IN OVER 400 YEARS

Zoe York
Daily Mail UK
14 July 2242

Shock has rippled across numerous democratic nations around the globe in response to the United States of America's recent passage of the Thirty-Fourth Amendment. The stunning legislature, passed by U.S. Congress this morning abolishes public religious expression, limits the rights of the press, and imposes new consequences for "reckless speech." In addition to these measures, the right to assemble and petition the government has now been abolished following the public attack on the White House and other landmark government properties on July 8th.

More than five million citizens were arrested that evening, when what started as a peaceful protest over the economic and social state of the nation, erupted into a violent attack on the White House, Capitol Hill, and even the Pentagon. More than 86,000 people lost their lives - both those protesting and those defending the capital. Millions of dollars worth of damage and vandalism have disfigured the nation's capital. President Willis Soto had to evacuate the White House and fly to a secure and confidential location out of fear for his life. Congress, which quickly reconvened at a safer, mobile site, immediately drafted and passed Amendment Thirty-Four in response to the deadly incident six days earlier.

The First Amendment, drafted by founding father and fourth American president, James Madison in 1789, states: *"Congress shall make no law respecting an establishment of religion, or prohibiting the free exercise thereof; or abridging the freedom of speech, or of the press; or the right of the people peaceably to assemble, and to petition the Government for a redress of grievances."* The Thirty-Fourth Amendment has essentially overridden this law.

Passed by a slim majority, it is the first measure to ever alter the nation's First Amendment in over 400 years. American citizens are still reeling from the events of July 8th. We have yet to see how they will respond to this new development.

"Resistance to tyranny becomes the Christian and social duty of each individual. ... Continue steadfast and, with a proper sense of your dependence on God, nobly defend those rights which heaven gave, and no man ought to take from us."

-John Hancock

CHAPTER SIX

I wake up the next morning to a throbbing headache. My spine feels like it's been twisted into a pretzel and the muscles in my back clench painfully. My ribs are sore and my left eye's swollen. As shitty as my body feels, I know I probably look worse. And yet, in spite of all the pain, for the first time in *years* - since I was a child, really - I wake up actually feeling excited.

Like I have a purpose. A mission. A goal.

Jenner and I both have morning shifts today. As eager as I am to see him, I'll have to curb my enthusiasm until then. I rise out of bed slowly, cautiously, and successfully change into my work clothes. Looking in the mirror, it's just what I suspected. My left eye is black and just about swollen shut. The other cuts are visible but I can already see the aloe vera gel taking effect. They should disappear in a few days. The black eye will take a little longer. I learned early on in Academy that I had thick skin, literally, but no matter how many cuts to the nose or jaw I avoided, if I got a shiner, it would last a good week or two. I wonder what the men at the shop will think when they see me. It doesn't escape me that just yesterday I threatened to kick everyone's ass. And now it's clear *my* ass was kicked. I'll need to come up with a good lie between here and that garage. What I can't come up with is a good lie between here and my mother just a few feet away. Though I feel bad about leaving before making up with her, I peek out the door and the minute the coast is clear, make my escape before she can see her only child's black eye. I'll make up with her soon enough.

By the time I get to work, my body is screaming for a place to sit. But I don't relax yet. I straighten my back and force myself to stride through the garage, ignoring the painful steps, willing my face to give an air of complete ease.

"Whoa!" one of the guys sees me. "What the hell happened to you?"

"Fight night," I reply.

They look at me, clearly confused.

"Fight night," I repeat. "Police tradition. Keep up your training by practicing on each other. No pads. No mercy."

"You look like shit," Watson says. His tone is different today. Not jeering or antagonistic but rather mellow.

I look at him and nod. "You should see how the other guy looks."

The guys laugh and turn back to their work. They've bought it - hook, line and sinker. They have no idea there's no such thing as a fight night and that when training, officers do it at the station gym, completely padded up. Whatever. I doubt they'll ever find out and by the time they do, I'll be gone, dead or alive.

As I work my shift and fix my hands on the machinery, my mind is miles away. All I can think about is meeting with Jenner now. What did he have in mind when he first suggested spreading *American Sense*? How will we do it? My mind racks over all the possibilities but I can't think of a safe, effective way to do it. Which is why I need to find out what he's thinking. I function on autopilot and the work goes by in a blur.

Come quitting time, I'm one of the first to head out.

"Decker?" I stop and see Dad walk over to me. He looks at my face. "What happened to you? The guys said you were in some-"

"Fight night," I tell him, glancing at the entrance. I'm ready to go.

"What 'fight night'? When did that start? And why would the Force allow you to participate if they discharged-"

"Dad, please." I interrupt. He would be the one to think right through my lie. "I'm fine. I had a run in-"

"A run in!"

"Shh." I look around. "I'm fine. Will you please drop it?"

He levels his blue eyes at me, very concerned. "Decker, what's going on?"

"Nothing," I tell him. "It was a misunderstanding that's completely cleared up now. I'm fine. I *promise* you."

He looks as if he doesn't believe and is about to say

something else until he stops himself. Suddenly, as if remembering that I'm a grown man now, he steps back and reluctantly nods.

"Okay," he says. "I'll take your word for it. You're a good kid. Always were."

I nod, slowly. "Thanks for the concern."

"I'll always be concerned. You're my son."

I give him a slight smile and wave goodbye.

The run-in with him makes me realize I'd better come up with a better story for Mom. If Dad could see right through that bullshit, she'll demolish it in five seconds flat.

"Oh my goodness! What happened to you?"

The chair legs scrape against the floor as she rushes to her feet, hands flying to my face.

"I'm fine, Mom-"

"What happened?" She's not asking. She's demanding an explanation.

"Work scuffle. I tried to break up a fight and ended up taking a couple hits. I'm okay."

She gasps. "What kind of place is this? And your father works there? Why would he allow you to-"

Her words die as she feels me noticeably stiffen under her berating words regarding my father. And there the elephant is again. I look at her and take the bullet.

"Mom, I'm sorry for yesterday. I shouldn't have yelled at you like that and I shouldn't have stormed off."

She shakes her head immediately. "*I'm sorry.*"

She gestures to the living room and we move to it. I sit on the couch next to her.

Eyes fixed on the faded flower patterns in the ancient fabric, she continues, "I feel terrible about what I said last night. I was out of line talking about your father the way I did. Whatever issues I have with him, I had no right to drag you into it. He's your dad and he loves you. I know this wasn't the first time I've bad mouthed him in front of you but I'll do my best to make sure it's the last."

"Thank you," I say quietly.

She nods, adding, "I was also wrong for trying to pressure you into doing something you don't want to do. You've made it clear so many times you're not interested in my business opportunities. I don't know why I keep bringing it up. Pressuring your father was the same thing that put our family in the financial mess to start with."

I look at her in surprise. I've never heard her admit to any fault in the bad investment that destroyed their financial security…and ultimately their marriage.

"Did you love him?" the question pops out of my mouth before I can remember thinking it.

She looks at me, her eyes thoughtful, haunted.

"I did." She looks down at her hands, her mind a world away. "We made a lot of mistakes and hurt ourselves terribly. Hurt you, too."

I frown at that. "I'm okay, Mom."

To my horror, she looks up at me, tears welling in her eyes.

"Mom?" I ask, alarmed. "What is it? What's wrong?"

She shakes her head, the tears falling. I feel helpless, trapped almost, as I watch her cry. For the first time in years, I see just how unhappy she truly is. I haven't seen my mother cry since I was a child, just months after my father moved out. I instinctively pull her into my arms and hold her. She's crying over things that took place years ago. Things that can't be undone.

"I'm sorry, Mom. Things will get better."

She pulls out of my arms and shakes her head. "Oh, sweetheart, don't you see? I'm not upset about me. I'm upset for *you*." I frown, making it clear I don't get it. She laughs tremulously. "You're so strong. You always were. I love you so much. All I wanted was to give you so much more. And all I've done is the opposite."

Finally, I understand.

"Mom, don't. I love you, too. And I'm alright. I'm fine." I pull her into my arms and feel her small slender arms hold me in return.

I'm fine. I've never said that phrase so many times - and to both parents on the same day. It's bizarre. We pull apart and smile at each other, the emotional weight gone. She wipes her tears and cocks her head to the side, her eyes suddenly mischievous.

"What?" I ask, suddenly concerned.

"If you're working in Mechanics now, how are you ever going to find a girl?"

Oh no.

I roll my eyes. "Mom, we've had this conversation before."

She steamrolls past me like I haven't spoken. "I always thought you'd get with that lovely girl, Nicole."

"*Nicole Washington*?" I exclaim. "Mom, she's an Atlan."

"So what?" my mother scoffs. "Does that make her royalty? And even if she was, she'd still be the luckiest girl in the world to marry *my* son."

Her words, though ridiculous, warm my heart. "No one marries in USA anymore, Mom."

She snorts. "Don't remind me. Just shack up, pop out children, and then shack up with someone new. Disgusting."

I keep silent but I can't say I disagree. Ever since the Supreme Court defined marriage as a legal union between any consenting adults, no limitations allowed, people stopped valuing the institution of marriage as a whole. If a man could legally marry his sister, or a woman marry both of her boyfriends, what was the point of making a relationship official? People found ways to start families without a "piece of paper" and less than ten percent of couples marry in USA now.

"No," Mom continues. "When you meet that special lady, I want you to marry her."

I sigh, once again silent. I think in the midst of our heart-to-heart, she's forgotten how much I dislike talking about this topic. The reality is, between Academy and work, I haven't dated anyone in years. Sex isn't an issue. Building a life with someone is.

Mom must see my wary expression because she then

reminds me, "Honey, you can't keep putting off your love life, you know? You're still young but *I'm* getting old. I want to see my grandchildren before I die."

And that's enough.

I stand up and kiss her forehead. "I'm going to change now. Good talk, Mom."

By the time I come back out, showered and changed, Jenner stands in the kitchen, a wary expression on *his* face. Mom is buzzing around the stove, talking over her shoulder. "Caden, sweetheart, sit down. Why are you so skittish today?"

He laughs nervously. "I'm not skittish, Ms. K."

I frown at him and shake my head. This guy was once on the Force, privy to top secret info and various operations and he can't keep his shit together in front of my mother? I walk out and save him before he spills our entire plan to her.

"You ready?" I ask him.

He nods, glancing at Mom again. She turns from the stove.

"Where are you going?" she asks.

"Out." I kiss her forehead. "I'll be back soon."

The Police Quarter is surrounded by three other quarters: Maids, Mechanics, and Factory. When Jenner hires a Commons cab, I know he's taking me somewhere significantly far. We drive out to the eastern edge of Factory, and get out by the pier. From this place on the island, I can see The Gauntlet. Jenner and I have a very good chance of ending up there if we don't do this thing right.

We walk down the pier for several minutes before he leads us to an abandoned, boarded up shed on Laurelton Drive. Though the outside doesn't look like much, the interior is rather large, with various shelves, random crates and long abandoned chalk near a portable chalkboard. I briefly wonder if classes were ever held here. The place might have been a school house several centuries ago.

"Okay." Jenner shrugs off his jacket and dusts off the green surface of the board. "Let's plan."

"Who created the problem that is now USA?" he asks me.

I grab a piece of chalk and write various names at the very top.

"The government. In a nutshell, you have the President and his Cabinet, Congress, and the Supreme Court. All of them make the decisions that affect the rest of us Commoners."

Jenner nods. "Right…?"

"Well, did you know that every last politician and judge in office is funded by the three wealthiest men on Atlas?"

Jenner frowns. "No, I didn't. Who?"

Lifting my chalk to the board, I write their names.

"Winston Soch, Brian Wartman, and Elliot Lieberman. Soch owns Atlas Energetics, the plants that supply all of USA's energy and water; Wartman owns Atlas Engineering, the premier civil engineering firm in the country-"

"Doesn't do shit for Commons."

"I know, right? And Lieberman owns ANN."

"The news? He owns the news?"

I nod. "Whatever he wants people to know or think, they post it as news and facts - that's the media for you."

I refrain from telling him how there' s been no competition from rival media outlets, civil engineering firms or energy plants since the reversal of the Supreme Court's ruling on monopolies. Soch, Wartman and Lieberman are the Vanderbilt, Rockefeller, and Carnegie of today.

I look over the board at their names. "It would be one thing if they would just stick with their empires and rack up money quietly. But they each have heavy hands and even heavier wallets in politics."

I go up to each name and write bold figures next to them from memory.

"Soch donated $12 million to Hamilton's campaign the last time he ran. Wartman spent $15 million getting half of Congress in their seats and Lieberman supplied funding for the other half. In exchange for their support, Soch, Wartman and Lieberman's lobby men have full, twenty-four-hour access to Hamilton, his Cabinet and the rest of Congress. They also fund think tanks, drumming up Atlas support for bills that increase Atlan profit margins and steadily strip workers-"

"-Commoners," Jenner interjects.

I nod. "...Of their rights. Stagnant wages, increased

taxes for Commoners, increased tax cuts for Atlas, no worker compensation or sick leave. Dismissal without cause. Right to skyrocket prices out of nowhere. Half the bills they introduce are drafted by Soch's lobby men. The majority of the laws they pass are pushed for by Wartman and Lieberman."

"How is this legal?" Jenner asks. I can tell he's growing agitated.

"Lobbying is a protected right," I explain. "The one thing the Atlas business men ensured would be protected, screw all our other rights."

Jenner frowns. "What do you mean?"

I go back to the board. On the far right side of it, where it's still empty, I write: *"One: Freedom of religion, speech, the press, the right to peaceably assemble and to petition the government for a redress of grievances."*

I look at Jenner and ask, "Which of these rights do we currently possess?"

He frowns at the board. "None. Except maybe the first one."

"Really?" I ask, brow raised. "When's the last time you ever heard anyone talk about their religious beliefs?"

"Never, of course....but you're free to think whatever you want-"

"Of course you are. No one can monitor your *thoughts* yet. But you can't talk about your religion. You can't talk about God. And you damn sure can't talk about anything the government might be doing wrong."

"You're right," he says in a hollow tone. "How many

people have we arrested for 'speaking out of turn' as Stanton would put it?"

On the board, next to the amendment, I write, *"Religion - outward expression abolished in 2242; speech restricted in 2242; effective 2248, peaceable assemblies must now be accompanied by guard for approved purposes. Right to petition abolished 2242."*

I continue to make my list down the line:

The right to bear arms was revoked and limited to police in 2248.

Automatic warrants for search and seizures was legalized in 2540.

Grand jury, double jeopardy, self-incrimination and due process abolished for Commoners in 2508.

The right to a trial with counsel was abolished in 2510.

I say the last one aloud, "Torture is now permitted for Commoner prisoners held without bond and most recently, Atlas Police have the right to execute Commoner civilians on the spot."

My voice is the only one that fills the shed. That and the sound of the chalk scraping along the board. Jenner has been quiet for what seems like an eternity. I turn to look at him and blink in surprise. His face is red all over, his blue eyes blazing with fury. He looks from the last letter I've written to me, his eyes blurry with angry tears.

He points to the untarnished rights on the left. "What were these rights called?"

"The Bill of Rights," I tell him. "Established by the founding fathers in 1791. The first ten amendments listed in the country's Constitution. Never meant to be removed or altered."

"And you mean to tell me that every last one of them has been abolished or restricted in the past three centuries alone?"

I nod. "The only one untouched is the quartering, or housing, of troops in times of peace. That's the only right left untouched by Congress. Everything else has been...changed."

There was a time when USA citizens, rich or poor, had all the same rights and opportunities as anybody else in the nation. A time when immigrants from other nations flocked to this one because anyone, no matter their past could pursue their goals and make a better life for themselves. Those days are gone.

Jenner begins to pace, his whole frame shaking.

I speak to his pacing profile. "I know I said I didn't want to rock the boat or cause trouble. But after last night...I don't know, something in me snapped." I already told him about my run in with Carter. "Something has to change. Something's needed to change for so long but no one has the balls to stand up and fight."

Jenner stops. "I agree. So what's the solution?"

His eyes steady on me, I turn back to the board and pick up the dusted eraser. Blowing off the sheaf of dust, I lift it to the board and one by one, start erasing names. Soch, Wartman and Lieberman all go first. Then the others.

President Hamilton.

Vice President Flemmel.

Secretary of State.

Secretary of Treasury.

Secretary of Defense.

Attorney General.

The President's Cabinet clear, I move on to the "Legislative" branch of the chart. One by one, I erase all seven Senators and all seven House Reps. I then move over to the Supreme Court and erase their five names: Riddick, Mayer, Thompson, Kennedy, and Laurel.

The only thing remaining on the left side of the board is "USA Government."

Jenner and I look at each other. Jenner nods slowly. "A do-over."

"We have to," I add. "Nothing will change if any of them remain in office. They all benefit from the status quo."

"And will guard it jealously."

I nod. Still, as much as I know a complete overhaul is necessary, I feel a prickling in my spine. These are men and women. Fathers and mothers. Sons and daughters. I don't *want* to kill anyone. As shitty as he's been to me, I wouldn't even wish death on Yang, let alone complete strangers - even strangers who have been oppressing me and those I love all my life.

I look at the board and shake my head. "What if there's another way-"

"There isn't," Jenner cuts me off. "There isn't and you know it. If there was, you would have thought of it."

"Maybe we could protest-"

"We'd be killed before we could even make a splash on ANN. There hasn't been a large protest since the one that burned down the White House all those years ago. And all the other once since have resulted in death sentences. Think of all the men and women who've died trying to protest in the past. Peacefully too!"

I nod, trying to drum up another solution. "What about trying to change the laws?"

Jenner shakes his head, insistent on our original plan. "Remember that lawyer from Nigeria? The one who immigrated with his family and was killed?"

I remember. The thought sends a chill down my spine.

Emmanuel something. The man was a brilliant attorney who entered the country right before the borders closed. He and his wife had a daughter and he was successful for many years as a top notch Atlas attorney, handling massive lawsuits between petty Atlas clients. Commoners don't have the money for that shit. But then he started fighting for new legislation...a way to make things more equitable for Commoners across the river.

He didn't stand a chance.

ANN reported that he and his wife lost control of their car on the Mohanan Bridge late one night.

No one has lost control on that bridge since its dedication in 2022.

They left their only child, a teenage girl at the time, an orphan at the age of fourteen.

"We have to do this, Decker." Jenner urges me. "Let's

get rid of them all and start over. New president, new senators. New everything."

He has a point. With them gone, we can restore the Bill of Rights. Along with the whole Constitution. Restore it and strengthen it so that it never again gets repealed. No more lobbying. No more selling. Justice at last.

Justice for all.

But still. These are people's lives. Numerous lives.

"Let me think about it," I tell him warily. "If I can't come up with an alternative by tomorrow, we'll go with wiping them out. If there's another alternative, I want to give it a shot."

Jenner sighs but slowly nods, knowing I'm decided.

"For now, let's focus on getting support. Regardless of what we decide, we can't do it on our own," I reason. "We need supporters. A lot. In fact, we need all of Commons if we even have a shot at doing this. We need to create dissent. Get people angry again - like you and me. Commoners are walking around like robots because they've lost all their fight. We have to piss them off enough to want to join us."

"*How?*" Jenner asks.

I point to the rights listed on the board.

"Tell them the truth."

Jenner's eyes widen and he straightens. "Of course."

Most Commoners don't know what they've lost. No one paid attention as Atlas politicians changed the rights time and time again. Congress hasn't been challenged - really challenged - by the people in three hundred years.

"If the public feels a fraction of what you felt when I showed you this," my knuckles hit the words on the board, "then we've won half the battle."

"You're right." Jenner picks up an eraser and removes every trace of our meeting. He goes to a nearby shelf and shrugs on his jacket, locked and loaded. "Come on. There's someone I want you to meet."

An hour later, we're in the Repair Quarter. I'm surprised by the look of the place. I thought the Police Quarter was the nicest of the five but, while the cleanest, the Repair Quarter has far superior infrastructure and architecture than any other quarter I've seen. It could rival Atlas itself.

Jenner leads the way to a modest but quiet building on the south end of town. He knocks on the door in a specific pattern. Seconds later, the door cracks open.

"You're late," a voice calls out. The door opens fully and we step through. I follow Jenner and immediately take in my surroundings. It's a studio apartment with a tiny kitchenette and an even smaller bathroom. To the left of the room is a full-sized bed and to the right, a makeshift work area fitted with multiple computers, devices, and regular handyman tools. I turn in time to see the resident.

Jenner wastes no time. "Decker, this is Bill Humphrey. Bill, meet Decker Channing."

Bill Humphrey is a thin, lanky man, tall enough to meet my eyes. He has dark, shaggy hair and dark blue eyes, almost the same shade as Adams'.

We shake hands and despite his lean stature, he has a strong, confident grip. I already like him.

"Nice to meet the legend in person," he says.

I frown. "Sorry?"

He smiles. "I read your declaration. *American Sense.* When Jenner showed it to me, I was in - hook, line and sinker. Thank you for writing it."

I can tell he didn't mean to add that last part but it's genuine. I nod, unsure of what to say.

Jenner speaks up. "So, we need your help. Decker just showed me something incredible. If all of Commons knew about it, Atlas would be turned on its ear."

Bill raises an eyebrow and looks at me. "Really? Even more than *American Sense*?"

Jenner grabs a piece of paper and hands it to me. "Write them out again?"

I do. I write the original Bill of Rights from memory and the parallel years they were stripped or altered. Bill stares at the sheet, aghast. "This is true?"

I look at him. "What do you think?"

"We have to get this out immediately." He rushes over to his cramped work station and immediately boots his computer. Over his shoulder, he tells us, "Back in Washington's time, people spread information via the printing press."

I nod but Jenner frowns. "The what?"

"The printing press," I explain quickly. "It's the way people got ink to paper and published books, newspaper and other media. Before technology became digital."

"Exactly," Bill glances at us. "But we *are* digital now. We can't exactly pass out flyers about this. We'd be torn apart from surveillance before we even covered a quarter. But what I *can* do is hack into ADC's mainframe."

"'ADC?'" I ask.

"Atlas Digital Correspondence - the largest digital communications platform in USA." He frowns. "Come to think of it, it's the *only* digital communications platform in USA now. They bought out AT&A last year."

"So what will this do?" Jenner asks impatiently.

"This will get the Bill of Rights onto every personal phone, computer, or imaging device on Atlas, Commons, or both. Whatever you want."

I blink, finally understanding why Jenner brought me here.

"Do you mean to say-"

"They'll be holding our message in the palm of their hands!" Jenner exclaims.

Bill nods. "Exactly."

We won't have to do anything. No hiding. No running. No scrambling to spread the word. With a few strokes of a key, the whole island will know the truth. I only have one question.

"Is this untraceable?"

Jenner glances at me, before looking at Bill.

Bill immediately nods. "One-hundred percent. I cover my tracks well. Remember, if they trace this back to the source, they trace it back to me. And I won't let that happen."

"How do you know for sure?" Jenner asks.

"Because I helped design ADC. I can get around all their firewalls, tracking and backtracking software. I'm the one who installed it."

Holy shit.

"And here I was thinking you were just some whiz kid," Jenner says in awe.

Bill shrugs. "I'm ready whenever you are. All you have to do is tell me what you want to say."

He pulls up ADC's Internet and immediately the headline blares under Atlas News: PRESIDENT HAMILTON SEEKS RE-ELECTION.

"What?" Jenner bellows.

"You cannot be serious," Bill mutters.

"Click on it," I tell Bill.

He does and the website immediately connects to a recording of Hamilton in front of the press. "..I had planned to announce this at a later time, but in light of the upcoming President's Ball and in celebration of the success of our latest Security Bill, I am pleased to announce my intention to seek another term in office. For twenty-eight years, I have led this country in prosperity, peace, and international and domestic security. It would be my honor to continue along the same path of hope, joy, and victory for all."

"Joy?" Jenner exclaims in disbelief. *"Prosperity?"*

"He's delusional," Bill mutters. "He's freakin' delusional."

Twenty-eight years. This man has been president for

twenty-eight years and he *still* wants to be president. It suddenly hits me like a lightning bolt. He won't step down. He won't hand over the reins. And he won't compromise or change anything about his leadership or his regime. Because he doesn't see anything wrong with it. This man plans to live in the Capitol until the day he dies.

And I can't wait that long.

I lock eyes with Jenner and he nods, the same thought in mind.

I don't need to wait until tomorrow to decide. We're putting an end to USA government. And we're putting an end to the man who leads it.

Atlas must die.

CONGRESS PASSES POPULATION CONTROL ACT

Harper Peterson
Australian Times
14 May 2405

Despite numerous illegal protests, petitions, and unpermitted publications expressing public dissent, the United States Congress has passed the controversial Population Control Act. The new law prohibits citizens from conceiving and delivering more than two children per family.

Viewed by many in the nation and abroad as a violation of personal liberty, the U.S. Congress has insisted on the necessity of limiting the growth of its already enormous population. Last year, the populace hit an unprecedented three billion mark. To accommodate the explosion of inhabitants in the past hundred years, urbanization has spread to every region of the United States, including areas that were once only rural farmlands.

In an effort to prevent mass nationwide starvation, scientists have made strides in genetic modification - so much so that farms are now seen as irrelevant sources of food. More than 80% of American farmers in the last century alone have been driven out of business. The economic and social terrain of the country has changed rapidly, along with its geographical make up. Suburban neighborhoods across the nation have been leveled to make room for city infrastructures. "If we can't stretch out," Congressman Steve Foyer of Colorado says, "we must build up." Large stretches of farmland that once held nothing but crops have now been cleared, filled with concrete, and built over o provide homes, businesses, and resources for American society. But the population growth is outpacing the building. And Congress hopes this new measure will slow things down.

"A nation with too many people and not enough resources can result in an absolute catastrophe," President Jennifer Framer stated in a recent address. "While this new measure is unpopular and limiting, it will serve the overall good of the American people. Keeping our reproduction to the rate of replacement will not only stabilize this nation but will serve the environment around us."

"Human law must rest its authority ultimately upon the authority of that law which is divine."

-James Wilson

CHAPTER SEVEN

"Hey, turn that up!" a customer asks the barista.

It's the weekend. We're sitting in a cafe in the Factory Quarter - Atlas owned, of course - and almost everyone and their grandmother is out and about town today. The barista turns up the outdated flat screen TV and the ANN reporter's voice carries across the tiny establishment.

"It's only been two days since a flyer of mysterious origins appeared on every phone, tablet, and holographic device on Atlas and Commons. The flyer simply contains a chart listing the historical Bill of Rights drafted in 1789, alongside the amended rights currently enacted today. The flyer suggests that many original rights of USA citizens have been altered or completely revoked since the amendments were originally ratified more than eight hundred years ago in 1791."

Jenner looks at the screen, shaking his head. "It worked. I can't believe it worked."

"Shh," I warn him, looking around.

He looks at me again and smiles, clearly excited. I can't

help but smile back. He's right. We did it. Or more accurately, Bill did it. Within hours of meeting with us, he put together the rights I wrote on that scrap sheet of paper, designed a rudimentary flyer and had hacked into all the personal devices of USA citizens by the time I got home.

I turned on my phone and found my words staring back at me.

It feels surreal to see and hear everyone talking about it now.

And now one thing's for sure: Pandora's Box has been opened. There's no going back now.

The anchor continues, "The re-distribution of the original rights has had a ripple effect on the conscience of society in recent days. Many citizens, Atlans and Commoners alike, were unaware of the exact nature of the original rights as the nation hasn't reviewed them since 2242. Copies of the original document were never re-displayed after the move of the capital from Washington D.C. to New York City - now Atlas - in 2248. The Bill of Rights has not been included in basic educational curricula since 2109."

Jenner's brows shoot up in surprise. "Even Atlans didn't know." He looks at me and lowers his voice. "How did *you*?"

I look at him blankly. "I read."

He and everyone else in this nation would be surprised at what they could find if they simply went to the library and picked up a book. I supplemented my shitty education and lack of high school and college with Atlas Library books for years. Much of what I know was never digitalized or the digital versions were lost and corrupted during the national "recovery" in 2500. But unlike the burning of the Library at Alexandria, USA kept nearly all of its printed books intact at what was once the New York Public Library. Everything, save for religious texts, were preserved. Everything I know about the history of this nation and where it went wrong is in those books.

"I can't believe they're airing it," Jenner whispers this time.

I shake my head. "Of course they're airing it. It's too big a story to pass up. Even Atlans want to hear about it. Lieberman isn't going to ignore it, no matter how much Hamilton may want him to."

"Speak of the devil," Jenner mutters as Hamilton's face appears on screen.

The café customers around us start to jeer and boo when they see his face. I honestly can't think of a more hated man on Commons than Victor Hamilton. He knows it too, which is why he hasn't made a visit to this island since his second election twenty years ago. Atlas alone has enough electoral votes to carry any election - which is why most Commoners never vote and politicians never visit.

Hamilton takes his place at the podium and speaks. "For more than eight hundred years, USA has been a beacon of personal freedom, liberty, and the pursuit of happiness."

I can't believe it. He has the gall to pull from the Declaration of Independence.

He continues, "Over the centuries, as is the case with any powerful empire, changes to laws and amendments were made out of necessity for the continued flourishing of our society."

"Bullshit!" a customer jeers. The customers around us murmur in agreement. They quiet down in time to hear him continue.

"The USA government is utterly committed to the well-being and joy of its citizens and continues to work hard to protect this nation from the influence and tyranny of foreign powers that would threaten to displace its long-held beacon of life and liberty."

I shake my head in disgust. He's deflecting the issue to his warped foreign policies.

The threat isn't beyond our borders - it's right inside!

Jenner turns from the screen as the man continues to speak. He's clearly had enough.

"He's been in office twenty-eight years," I mutter. "Longer than any other president in this nation's history."

Another amendment overturned.

"What was the original presidential term?" Jenner asks.

"Two four-year terms *maximum*. George Washington himself set the precedence."

"He was the first one, right?"

I nod silently, keeping a passive expression. Sometimes it amazes me how little Jenner knows. Like me, he didn't receive a high school education, much less a college one, but most people - even Commoners - still know who the first president of the country was.

I look back at the screen in time to hear Hamilton announce, "The flyers distributed were an intentional invasion of privacy via digital hacking as well as a malicious attempt to undermine the nation's confidence in the USA government.

Too late buddy, I think. *Confidence was undermined* years *ago.*

"Due to the serious nature of this attack and the resulting unrest it has caused, we are offering a generous bounty for the apprehension of the originators of this flyer."

Jenner's eyes lock with mine.

Hamilton continues, "If anyone has useful information about the criminals behind this slanderous propaganda, they are encouraged to contact the police. Any information useful to the apprehension of these hackers will be rewarded four million dollars."

Several gasps erupt at the figure. Silence falls over the entire café as conversations cease and even the baristas stop what they're doing. My heart stutters. Four *million* dollars? It's a figure unheard of in Commons, where the average income is $10-$40,000 max.

If seeing what we've done on the news hasn't made this real, this bounty sure as hell wakes me up. I knew this would be dangerous. All three of us did. But a bounty of four million dollars means we've scared Hamilton and his cronies. We've scared them really bad. I tear my eyes away from the screen and look at Jenner. His expression is passive, thoughtful, as his eyes scan the room, taking in the reaction of our fellow Commoners. I follow suit and to my surprise, though shocked by the figure, many still sneer at the screen. The allure of money hasn't won them over. If anything, it's pissed them off.

At last, a customer breaks the silence. "Man, screw Hamilton and his bounty. Show me the person who told me the truth and I'll personally aid and abet them."

Surrounding customers murmur in agreement and the conversations pick back up in a rapid flurry. The baristas go back to work. We can hear bits and pieces of the conversations that have now drowned out the news.

"Whoever had the balls to do this has my support."

"I want in on what they're doing."

I quirk my brow at Jenner. We're surrounded by people openly expressing an interest in our cause. Isn't that what we made these flyers for?

He quickly shakes his head and nods towards the door. We get up and leave.

Outside, he quietly explains, "I wanted to as badly as you but we can't just go up to strangers and make ourselves known. One bad apple and we're done for. We need people we can trust."

I nod. "I agree. The question is," I lower my voice even further. So much so that he has to lean in to hear. "How do we surround ourselves with enough trustworthy people?"

How do we recruit and still stay under the radar? Is

that even possible?

Jenner looks around then back at me. "I'm already working on it. Meet me at the shed tomorrow night. I have some guys I *know* we can trust."

I'm back at the library. As I walk up the polished steps, I check my watch. As long as I'm back on the five o'clock train, I'm clear of police scrutiny. I go directly to the section I'm searching for. At this point, I've memorized the catalog numbers and go directly to the shelf where I know I'll find the best selection. To my surprise, the shelf is nearly bare. I've never seen so many gaps in it. What was once crammed tight with volumes and volumes of writing now has several book holders to keep the remaining books upright. I look around, almost expecting to find the party responsible for this. But I'm the only one here.

I sigh, reach up and pull down the remaining useful volumes. I grab anything related to the first Revolution, the one that separated us from the British nearly a millennium ago. I pull books on historical war tactics, the structure of the American economy, how the founding fathers centralized their new government and handled diplomatic affairs. Suddenly, I hear shuffling nearby. I look up from the books in my hands and see several feet scurrying back to my section, carts wheeled in front of them. They pause two rows away from me and I hear the thud of multiple books hitting the carts in quick succession.

It's the librarians.

They're the ones clearing the shelves.

Why?

The wheels squeak as the librarians move swiftly, clearing shelf after shelf in their row. I never knew they could work so quickly. They're clearly in a rush to get these books out of public access.

"Susan, did you get all the books on AM42? The American History section?"

They're referring to my section. The very shelf I'm standing by.

"There's a few left. I'm getting them now."

Shit.

I start scanning the shelf frantically, trying to find any volumes that might be useful to me. I can't carry them all. And something tells me that I need to leave now before I'm seen. Before the books already in my hands get taken away too. I'm about to turn and bolt when the spine of one book catches my eye. It's not even a book really. It's a slim, minuscule volume that looks more like a pamphlet but I examine it closer before my eyes widen.

George Washington's Farewell Address.

I've heard of the address. Have read portions referenced in other books. But I've never read the entire address in context. My hand whips out and grabs it before I turn and stride down the row and around the corner, pulling myself out of sight right in the nick of time.

"Wait a minute…" I hear the librarian say suspiciously.

I don't wait to hear the rest. I rush up the stairs, two at

ATLAS DIED

a time, and make my way up to a completely different area of the building. An hour later, I'm sitting in the biological sciences section two floors up, reading chapter after chapter on the Revolution, the Continental Congress, the Constitution and the reasoning behind it. I've managed to find a corner of the room not surrounded by cameras. The more I read, the more I'm convinced that we're doing the right thing. Every law established in the founding of this nation was meant to create a free republic for all, not just the elite. Not just those with the deepest pockets. As I read the works of James Madison, John Jay, and Alexander Hamilton, I'm struck by the absence of quarters, standardized aptitude tests, and limits on education. I briefly scanned Washington's *Farewell Address* but even he mentions the importance of a free society also being an enlightened society. Creating a fractious nation by roles and socioeconomic class has eroded the very ideals these founders fought for.

I'm snapped out of my thoughts at the sound of several feet running - *running* - up the stairs to my floor. The librarians disperse as soon as they reach the landing. Loud whispers reverberate as they search the shelves for something.

"How many are missing?" one whispers loudly.

"Ten," the other whispers back. "Including Washington's Address."

My heart drops at those words and I immediately kick myself for not reading faster. For not reading this Address first. I've gotten the gist of most of the books but I only

155

browsed Washington's. A surge of irrationality hits me. I take three of the ten books I had and go up another level. Eyes scanning for cameras, I go to an unmonitored row and do something I never thought I would. I start tearing sheets. Every page I earmarked, I systematically rip it out of the books, fold them and shove them in my jacket pocket. I close the remaining pages and put them in random spots on the shelf. I open Washington's *Address,* about to do the same when I realize, it's too small to rip out anything. I can't take the book without the alarms going off and I obviously can't check it out. Apparently it's made some sort of library black list. But something tells me I *need* to read what's inside, at length, not just a quick scan or two.

"Decker?"

I flip around at the sound of my name and blink in surprise.

"Hey, Nicole."

She looks at me, her long lashes fluttering over her brown eyes. "How have you been?"

She asks like she cares.

"I'm fine," I quickly answer. "Your folks okay?"

"Yeah." She nods. "We all miss you, though. Listen, I'm glad I ran into you here. I wanted to tell you this the last time, but you were in such a rush. My dad's been wanting to get in touch with you."

I frown. "Why?"

She blinks at my blunt response. "Well, he wanted to help you out. We all do. He has some connections for work you maybe could use."

I shake my head and quickly nix the offer. "Nicole, I really appreciate that. Please let him know I do. But I've already found work and I'm doing okay."

She's about to respond when we hear loud steps running up the nearby stairs. Loud whispers once again break out and I know it's them again. Searching for the last three books, one of which I'm holding in my hands. Crap. I didn't even get the chance to read it. But this is the last level and when I glance at my watch, I realize I don't even have the time to read this document if I wanted to. If I'd known what they were doing, I would have brought some change to make copies of the book in my hands. But I'm out of change, time, and options. I stick the book between two large volumes on the bottom shelf and turn back to Nicole.

"I've got to go. The five o'clock leaves soon."

She frowns, her eyes swinging from the shelf to my face. "The trains go 'till ten. Decker, are you okay? Why are you pulling back from me? From my family? We all still care about you. You may not work with us anymore but we still care."

It's the worst thing she could have said to me. I already feel a world of guilt for distancing myself from the only friend I've ever known on Atlas. Her family was good to me for so many years. But things have changed. I'm no longer working for them - *for* them, not "with" them like she graciously said. I'm no longer an officer and my allegiance has drastically changed. I can't tell her what's going on. Because as kind as she and her family have been to me, I have no idea how they would react if they *really* knew what I've been up to most recently. Would Nicole support what I'm doing or try to stop me? Would she help me or report me? I've only ever known her in the context of guarding her family. It's too big of a risk to try and find out.

She looks as if she can see the wrestling on my face. She reaches out as if to touch my arm. I pull back and sigh. "I'm sorry, Nicole. I know this is weird but...things have changed. *I've* changed. I wish you and your family well. Please thank them for being so good to us."

I walk around her and past the shelf.

"Take care," I say with a final glance back.

I leave the library, never expecting to see her again.

• • •

The next night, I arrive at the shed with no idea what to expect. Yards away from entering, I can see that it's dimly lit inside. Not too conspicuous but enough for someone too curious to see. We'll have to make it quick and probably find a better meeting place in the future.

When I open the door, there's already a group of about twenty men circled near Jenner, speaking in low tones. Several heads turn in my direction and the voices drop in five seconds flat. Though dim from outside, it's lit well enough inside that I can see everyone pretty clearly. And they're all wearing similar expressions. It's the same one I saw Bill wearing a few days earlier. Like they admire me for some reason. Like I'm important. Once again, I'm uncomfortable. I want to tell them I'm no different from any of them. I'm just one person. And I need a lot of help.

Jenner breaks from the crowd and gives me the breakdown.

"There are twenty new guys here. Most mine, a couple his."

I frown. "A couple *whose?*"

Before he answers, I see a familiar face just over his shoulder.

"Adams?"

He steps forward. "Hey, Decker."

"What are you doing here?"

He shrugs, an apprehensive look on his face. "Anything I can to help."

Jenner glances at Adams before turning back to me. "After everything that went down, Adams and I kept in touch. When they pulled you in for questioning, he got wind of it, got a hold of me and told me to zip it before I got us both in deeper shit."

"Was that before or after I hit you?" I ask.

Jenner rubs his nose, a mock wince crossing his face. "After. Minutes after, actually."

I smirk at him and he grins back. I'm glad we're past that. I forgave him for being an idiot. He forgave me for being a jerk. Adams looks between the two of us then turns to the two young men approaching him. They're both taller than him and almost half his age.

"These are my guys: Philip Donahue and Curtis

Jenkins. Former trainees. I'd trust them with my life."

I nod. They're to Adams what Jenner is to me: a former student I took under my wing. I immediately remember and catalogue their names and faces like I'm trained to. Donahue has the close-cropped brown hair with matching brown eyes and a playful look on his young face. Jenkins, same height and muscular build, has a head full of bright red hair and matching red freckles. More serious, he looks like he can crack a joke or two as well. Adams explains that they came on the Force right after I left.

And they're signing up for this? I think to myself. I'm not sure I would have taken such a risk so early into my career. They're risking a lot.

Adams adds, "They've been dying to meet you since Academy."

"Why?" I scoff.

Donahue answers, "You're a myth over there. The only trainee to ace your exit test. The first in your class on all five zones. Not to mention the greatest trainer the Academy's ever seen."

Jenkins nods. "I've never heard an officer's name as many times as I heard 'Officer Channing.' 'Officer Channing did this drill in one-fourth your time.' 'Officer Channing outlasted all his classmates in this fight.' 'Officer Channing designed this test.' I made myself survive Academy just so I could meet you one day."

I scratch my head as the praise goes in one ear and out the other.

It doesn't matter how much anyone excels in the Force or any other Commoner field. Unless you're an Atlan, hard work rarely yields a worthy reward. Besides - I was just doing my job. Anyone not half-assed could do the same.

Unsure of what to say, I nod and murmur, "Well, I'm glad you two are here. Thanks for coming."

I turn to Jenner. He immediately gestures to his guys.

"These are my friends." Though significantly larger than Adams' two recruits, I take the time to match and memorize names with faces.

One of them, a black man by the name of Holmes, apologizes about the interrogation incident. "We had no idea there were cameras where we were standing. We haven't said a word on Danielton since."

"I understand." I shake his proffered hand. "Thanks for coming."

Jenner shakes his head, a chagrined expression on his face. "It's my fault, man. I'm the one who forgot the camera coordinates on Danielton."

"Don't worry about it," Adams says. "He's been off the grid for a while now. Ever since that attack."

My eyes snap to Adams and he quickly nods. He knows about the shakedown that provoked me. He continues before anyone can ask about that night. "Out of sight, out of mind. All of Yang's energy is in finding the flyer culprit. He's so focused on it, he hasn't even put two and two together."

I breathe a sigh of relief that I'm really not a suspect so

far.

I had realized that it might all come crashing down on my head - even though Bill guaranteed the flyers were untraceable. But the police haven't needed substantial evidence in the past to do something to a labeled suspect. Released so soon after my interrogation, I'd been wondering for days if I would be able to defend myself against another "warning" from Yang. Or if I'd run out of all of them at this point.

"Okay," Jenner announces, bringing the room to near silence. "We don't have a lot of time. Every minute we stand here is a minute we can be booked for illegal assembly."

That statement adds an air of tension to the room. It's as if we all suddenly remember why we're here. We're plotting. Planning. And doing something very much against the corrupted law of a ruthless government. Jenner puts his hand on my shoulder and says without preamble, "Even though Decker just met you, he has memorized every single one of you standing here. I know this because it is one of the skills that set him apart in the Police Force for more than fourteen years. He's the author of the Bill of Rights flyer that you all got on your phones and he's the brilliant mind behind a declaration called *American Sense*. Some of you," he glances at his friends, "have already read this. Those of you who haven't, see me after this meeting and I will be sure to share it."

I look at him, surprised. He never burned it after all. I wonder if he knew I was going to change my mind.

"For the sake of time, this is what I will say: Decker is intelligent, self-educated and *well-educated.* Every time I talk to him, I learn something new about this country, its history, and the rights I had no idea I'd been robbed of as a citizen. But most importantly, Decker has integrity. You could not ask for a better leader. I know we can do this only because he's the one in charge."

My heart pounds at the weight of his words. I knew Jenner respected me but I had no idea the level of his esteem. Or his trust. And as I look at the faces of the men in front of me, the weight of their trust settles squarely on my shoulders. I barely hear the rest of what he says but the deafening silence and expectant eyes before me tell me it's time to speak.

I wasn't prepared to give a speech. So I say what comes to mind.

"I'm not much of a talker," I say, glancing at my shoes. "So I'll keep this short and to the point."

I raise my eyes and look at the twenty plus men, risking their lives. "I want to thank you for coming. I'm well aware of the risk you're taking just by being here. That said, you need to know this is just the start of many risks. I'm gonna be honest with you and tell you that I decided to join Jenner in this...revolt because I woke up in the middle of the night scared. I'd just lost my job and didn't know how I was going to pay my bills, care for my mom, and survive on an island notorious for letting those who can't make it die."

I barely see the several nodding heads as I continue.

"Over the course of the night, my fear turned to anger. And when I ran into authority issues *again*, my anger turned to rage. Eight-hundred years ago, this country was founded by a revolution. A war that determined the rights of every man to walk in freedom and pursue happiness. For more than six-hundred years, these rights have been eroded by the greed, selfishness, and ignorance of corrupted leaders and unscrupulous business men. I'm 32-years-old. For thirty-two years, I have lived in a society hell-bent on telling me what I cannot do, what I cannot learn, where I cannot go because of where I happened to be born. America wasn't always like that. USA stands for the United States of America - a country that used to be the land of opportunity."

I pause, scanning the eyes of men who may just die alongside me for what we're doing.

"For thirty-two years, I have not been living. I've been surviving. Breathing. But not living. Now I don't know about you, but I will not live another year of my life restricted by the pride of spoiled, selfish men. I'm not rich. I'm not educated. And I'm not particularly special. But I am a man. I have a life. And as long as I have life, I'll live it as I see fit: free."

That's it. That's all I can think to say. I shared more than what I thought I would but it's too late to take it back. And I'm not even sure I would.

At first the men are silent. They look at me with a mixture of expressions. Sober. Thoughtful. Determined. Even angry. But the one that overrides them all is wonder.

Wonder at what I said. Probably at how they feel. And wonder that after all these years, we're finally going to do something about it.

One of them, a man in his forties with five o' clock shadow - Ramsey - begins to clap; slowly...then rapidly, tears in the corner of his eyes. He looks like he's about to burst. It doesn't take long before the others join him. They all clap emphatically, several of them shouting their support. Jenner comes up, clearly moved as well. He looks around and quickly gestures to the men to quiet down. We could still be caught - especially if we raise enough noise.

"Okay," he says, his voice slightly shaky. He clears it and starts again. "Okay. We're grateful you came here tonight but this is the part where you decide. Decker has a plan for this to work but if you've decided not to commit, this is your chance to leave now, before we move forward."

Not a single man leaves.

"What's the plan?" Adams asks. He's calm but I can tell from his stance, he's eager. Locked and loaded, ready to go.

Jenner walks to the chalkboard and writes two words: "USA Government." Nothing underneath.

"A new slate," I explain.

I give the men the same rundown I gave Jenner days ago. And same as before, we reach the difficult conclusion he and I reached before.

"I don't want to take lives. I don't want to be responsible for someone's death-"

"But how many lives have Atlans taken before?" Donahue points out. The men around him murmur in agreement.

"Maybe not Atlans in particular but certainly their guards at their orders," Jenkins says. "And with that idiot planning on staying in office another term, it's open season for Commoners."

"Yeah!" the men murmur in agreement once more.

I'm surprised they're so comfortable being in the two young officers' presence. It gives me hope that my plan might actually work.

"So it's decided," Jenner says. "We knock 'em out."

"The only question is how," Adams says.

Jenner and I glance at each other. He nods and I speak. "There's only one event in which all these people are required to be in the same room."

"Wait," Adams says. "You're not thinking..."

I nod. "The President's Ball."

A hush falls over the room. Everyone has heard of the President's Annual Ball. In lieu of a State Address, Hamilton started holding extravagant annual balls to celebrate his power and address only the elite who keep him in office. He wines and dines them while the rest of us look on from our genetically modified poison we call food.

"I know it's close - less than two weeks away. But this is the best chance we have of eliminating them all and starting fresh."

I go to the chalkboard and start sketching the layout of

the ballroom. I draw a stick figure of Hamilton in the middle, at a podium. "I've only guarded it twice before but if it's the same, we'll have access to all the key players in one contained room. During Hamilton's address."

Jenner looks at Adams. "You know the layout for this year, don't you?"

He nods and approaches the board. He tells me, "Not much has changed since you last took the shift. The guest list is more exclusive since Hamilton is up for re-election. Only the government and his donors and lobbyists."

That's even better news. That means we eliminate the risk of innocent Atlan guests getting caught in the fray. The only people who might perish are the ones directly responsible for his totalitarian regime.

Reaching out, Adams grabs a piece of chalk and draws stick figure guards on the board. "A basic perimeter around the ballroom and of course, guards outside of it."

"So we infiltrate it?" Donahue asks.

I shake my head and take the chalk from Adams.

"We infect it," I answer. The men look at me questioningly. Adams and Jenner look confused too.

I lift the chalk to the board and start to draw a gun in each guards' hands, pointing away from the President in a protective stance. I point to the guards on the board. "This is what they are supposed to do," I explain. I erase the guns and re-draw them, this time pointing to President Hamilton. "This is what we convince them to do."

I look away from the board and at the faces of the men as the plan dawns on them.

"Now, that's brilliant." Donahue smirks.

"It's Channing," Jenkins murmurs beside him.

I look at Jenner and Adams. To my surprise, they look just as impressed. Jenner looks at Adams and asks, "Is it possible?"

Adams looks at me. "If it is…this just might work."

The meeting ends shortly after the game plan is discussed. We then disperse in groups of twos and fours, several minutes at a time, careful to go in separate directions. Many of the men stop to shake my hand and assure me of their support before they leave.

They speak with Jenner before they leave. Every last man. All have sworn to absolute secrecy and all have pledged to see who they can recruit without risking the operation. The Danielton guys agree to smuggle supplies from the island. Scrap metal, tossed aluminum. Anything we can use to render into weaponry and other materials we know we'll need. Donahue and Jenkins agree to keep their ears and eyes open for anything related to the President's Ball.

Adams pulls me aside when I bid a Factory man goodnight.

"It's been a while," he says quietly.

I nod. "Yeah, it has."

He comes right out with it. "Decker, I'm really sorry for what went down. If I'd taken the shift - if I didn't ask you to cover last minute, none of this would have happened."

"Exactly," I reply. Adams blinks, clearly hurt by my response. I shake my head, explaining.

"Exactly," I repeat. "None of this…" I gesture around the shed… "…would be happening. I know it wasn't your fault. And I'm sorry I didn't respond sooner. I never blamed you, I was just so consumed with finding new work."

He nods. "Of course."

"This is a huge risk, Adams." I say with sober regard. "Why are *you* doing this? You have everything to lose."

"We all do," he replies. "If we fail, we die. But something has to change." He looks around. "Maybe…maybe I'm tired of standing around watching other people get treated like shit. Maybe I'm tired of being *used* to treat other people like shit. I'm really starting to believe I'm just as guilty as Atlans for keeping Commoners down."

I frown and he continues. "Maybe I didn't do the oppressing or the brutalization. But I stood silent. And that's just as bad. I'm not standing silent anymore."

My respect for him skyrockets.

He adds with a smirk, "Besides, everything's a risk. I'd rather risk my neck for a friend I trust and a cause I care about than continue risking my neck for an egomaniac and the pretentious brats he serves."

We chuckle together. He extends his hand and I immediately grab it. We're good.

"What's that about brats, Boss?" Donahue sidles up

behind him.

"He can't be talking about us?" Jenkin adds beside him.

Adams frowns at the two friends. "I thought I told you to go without me."

"No dice, Daddy-o. Those streets are dangerous."

"We don't want an old man like you getting hurt."

Adams rolls his eyes while I laugh at their ribbing. The kids are pretty funny. Though serious about the cause, they've lightened up the mood of the night. I'm glad they're on our side.

Jenner joins us as the last of his men leave. Adams nods to him and tells us both. "I'm going to head out with these two knuckleheads."

"Hey!" they both exclaim.

"We'll look into getting some men but it may take a while. We have to be careful."

Donahue and Jenkins sober enough to nod in agreement.

Jenner nods too. "We wouldn't have it any other way."

I slap Adams on the arm and shake the other two's hands. "Thanks, guys."

He takes his leave.

Jenner turns to me, his eyes practically glowing.

"We did it! They're on board."

I nod, contemplative. Jenner notices my sober demeanor.

"What? Come on, you have to admit we did good! Two days ago, it was just you, me and Bill. We're a couple dozen strong now. And we'll only get stronger as they recruit."

I'm worried.

Jenner may be excited but all I can think of are the obstacles. Yeah, several men stepped up, passionate about this revolt but what if they unknowingly recruit a mole? What if one of them is already a mole?

Nah. I shook most of their hands and locked eyes with all of them at some point this evening. Nothing in my gut tells me these men are untrustworthy. And if Jenner and Adams trust them, I should too. But that doesn't eliminate the chance of *them* recruiting someone disloyal. And even if they're all loyal, Adams reminded me of the risk we're all taking. This is treason. These men are risking their lives and the livelihood of their families to join in this fight. If we fail, we will all be executed on the spot, or worse, thrown onto The Gauntlet as retribution. And I know this from history. The last attempt at rebellion took place in 2572. The leader, Nicholas Terranio, was tortured, treated, and then thrown onto The Gauntlet the minute he'd regained strength. He likely saw the rotting corpses of his followers, who were sent to the island two weeks earlier.

In the one-hundred years since the Atlas regime came to power, not one revolt has proved successful. Who's to say ours will be any different? How are we going to get supplies, mobilize teams and communicate without being discovered? How will we turn the Force against the very people they're paid to protect? What's in it for them?

Even worse, my mind starts to wonder what we'll do if we *are* successful. How will we set up the government? Who will fill what role? It would be the first fair election in over thirty years - how would we figure out the polls? What about the Constitution? How will we restore it and keep it from corruption this time around? The questions keep rolling in the more I think about the angles of this enormous task. It dawns on me that we have started something we are woefully ill-equipped and unprepared to do. I'm completely overwhelmed and acutely aware that everyone is looking to me for the answers. The same way they looked at me to break down the President's Ball strategy.

"Decker? Decker? *Hello?* Earth to Decker!" I look up and see Jenner's exasperated frown. "Man, what's wrong with you? Talk to me."

I sigh deeply and keep it simple. "This might not work."

His frown deepens. "What? Why not?"

"Jenner, we need more than numbers to succeed. We need more than men willing to fight." I tick the list off my fingers. "We need supplies, a tighter plan, a fail-safe communications system, and a safer way to recruit men."

"I agree."

We both whip around at the sound of a female voice. Sharp high heels click along the concrete floor as she walks into plain view.

My jaw drops. "Nicole?"

"Hey!" Jenner yells, starting to approach her. "Who are

you? What are you doing here?"

I grab his arm and hold him back. "It's okay," I tell him. "I know her."

He stops his approach but his stance is still stiff, his expression unwelcoming. I turn to her and ask, "Nicole, what on earth are you doing here? How did you find this place?"

She reaches into her purse and pulls out a slim book. "Recognize this?"

I do. *George Washington's Farewell Address.* She hands it to me while explaining, "This was an older edition. Instead of tampering with the binding, they only put a tracking page on the back. Which I ripped and stuffed in a biology book. As soon as I saw that title, I put two and two together and here I am."

Her words send a chill down my spine. That she could figure it out so easily...I wasn't being careful at all. That still doesn't answer something. "I saw you yesterday and was at work all day today. How did you find me on Commons?"

Her serious expression breaks into a brief smile. "Easy. I called your mom. She gave me your work address and I came around quitting time... Followed you here." She steps closer to me, her pretty smile fading. "Like I said, it was *easy*, Decker. And if it was easy for me, it'll be easy for Hamilton or anyone else who puts two and two together. You need to start covering your tracks and fast. I can help you-"

"Whoa, whoa, whoa - wait a minute!" Jenner's voice

cuts in, sharp and aggravated. "I still don't know who the hell you are."

Nicole's eyes flicker in annoyance. She turns to him and extends her hand. "I'm Nicole Washington. I'm part of the family Decker used to guard."

He takes longer than he should but slowly shakes her hand in return. "Your mom makes all those nice meals for him." He finally gets the association and his hostile expression slowly softens.

She nods quickly, pulling her hand from his. "We've known Decker since he first joined the Force."

Jenner blinks at that - as if he finds it hard to believe that anyone outside my family has known me longer than him. Nicole's chocolate brown eyes swing back to me.

"I want to help you," she repeats. "Meet me at my place tomorrow night. You can decide for yourselves if I'm genuine or not."

I blink at that, concerned that I hurt her for being so secretive. "Nicole-"

"It's not a good idea for us to stay here longer. Most of the lights are going out in this quarter."

She has a good point.

"Meet me at my place tomorrow."

"I can't," I tell her. "I can't be on Atlas past a certain time anymore."

"Oh…okay, then what about Mohanan Bridge? It's on your side of the river and Atlas vehicles aren't monitored. I'll pick you up."

Jenner is noticeably silent behind me. I don't know

what he's thinking but I'm sure he'll tell me outside of her presence. He may still have reservations about her trustworthiness. But for the first time, I feel like the heavy weight of this thing has been lifted off my shoulders and shared more evenly.

"Mohanan Bridge tomorrow night," I confirm. "We'll be there."

FINANCIAL RUIN IMMINENT FOR UNITED STATES

Clementine Ekeh
Nigerian Tribune
September 14, 2432

It has been exactly one year since the United States' stock market crashed on Wall Street. An unprecedented blow to their economy, the financial crisis has rendered the U.S. dollar virtually useless in the international market. Economic historians claim the collapse is far worse than the Great Depression ever was five hundred years prior. Stock that once sold at an average of $500 a share have plummeted to less than fifty cents a share. Every industry in the nation has been devastated by the ripple effect.

In the wake of the crisis, more than 70% of American citizens are now unemployed, the other 30% underemployed. In an effort to preserve financial resources, the U.S. government has ceased all international aid and is attempting to recover all international debts while stalling on the debt it owes. The cash-strapped government has also eliminated all domestic federal aid and financial assistance for its citizens. Millions of Americans have reportedly starved to death and homelessness has skyrocketed across the land.

Hospitals are dangerously understaffed, numerous patients are turned away. And those too sick to leave or quickly recover are euthanized. Circumstances have grown so dire that many have resorted to crime, particularly theft, to survive. Others, so desperate to receive consistent shelter, food, and healthcare, reportedly commit these crimes and then *wait* for officers to arrest them so that they will be sentenced to prison and taken care of there.

Hundreds of religious leaders and citizens have broken the Thirty Fourth Amendment by requesting calls for prayer and repentance. They have all been arrested and imprisoned.

"When the righteous rule, the people rejoice; when the wicked rule, the people groan."

-William Paterson

CHAPTER EIGHT

We're at the Mohanan Bridge. The largest bridge in USA, it is the only other way besides the Atlas Express to travel from Commons to Atlas on ground. It's past nine and dark. Jenner and I stand a few feet away from the harbor overlooking the Wellington River. I keep my eyes fixed on the toxic, murky water below but I can feel him pacing beside me.

"Will you calm down?" I tell him. "She'll be here soon. It'll be fine."

He keeps pacing. "I don't know, Decker. This is dangerous. I know you know her but are you positive she's someone we can trust? She's an Atlan, for Pete's sake!"

I frown at that. Ever since he found out about the Bill of Rights, Jenner's expressed more and more vitriol towards Atlans than he has the entire time I've known him. I know they're part of the problem but I also know there are Atlans like Nicole and her family who want the best for all, regardless of their status.

I tell him in a calm voice, "If it were any other person

on Atlas, I wouldn't think twice about shutting them out. But I know her. I've known her since she was fifteen-years-old. Since I joined the Force at eighteen. If I can't trust her, I can't trust anybody, save my own parents."

He stops pacing. I realize that in giving her that level of confidence, I may have inadvertently insulted him.

Oh well, I think. *He'll just have to get over it.* I'm not about to entertain a pissing match between Jenner and Nicole. They're both my friends. And they both want to help.

Bright headlights suddenly shine on the two of us as a sleek, four door black Atlas Cyrilliac rolls up to our side. The windows are fully tinted but they roll down to reveal her pretty face.

"Get in."

I sit beside her in the front and Jenner wordlessly slips in to the back.

"Hello, Jenner." Nicole greets him in a friendly tone.

"Hi," he replies, his eyes taking in the car. I guess he's never been in one of these. The Atlas Cyrilliac is known for its innovative technology.

The temperature adapts to every passenger's preference, based on their natural body heat. The front of the vehicle is like a small couch, the gear consul missing with only a lowered dashboard fit with a small fridge and counter top fit for food. There's no steering wheel, no speedometer, no radio. Everything is operated by voice command. The minute we're in, the doors automatically close and lock. We pull our seat belts on and Nicole simply says, "Drive home."

"Destination received," an automated voice responds.

The engine revs quietly and the Cyrilliac reverses. On its own.

"Holy shit!" Jenner exclaims.

The car stops, switches to forward drive and heads towards the bridge. It crosses onto Mohanan without security, without suspicion, and drives across the structure at top speed. Nicole hasn't lifted a finger the entire time. She turns to me, as if this is the most normal thing in the world for her. And I'm sure it is - she's had the car for nearly five years. She reaches into the mini fridge and pulls out a couple beers.

"Drinks?"

The drive doesn't take long. Within half an hour, we're at her place. We take the private elevator up to her home. When I walk in, I'm not prepared for the sting of nostalgia. I feel like I'm coming home from a really long trip. I hadn't realized how much I would miss this place.

And the people in it.

I glance at Jenner and see his watchful eyes take in every expensive, luxurious detail. He guarded Atlas homes for years but I guess he feels the same way I do when in an Atlas home and not on duty: out of our element. Nicole looks at the two of us and gestures with her hand.

"Follow me."

She leads us down the long hall, past two doors before

making a left. I know then where she's taking us.

"Hi, Dad." She walks in her father's office and greets him with a kiss to the cheek.

"Hey, sweetie." He stands, his eyes landing on us as we follow in behind. "Decker! Hi!"

Mr. Washington immediately walks around his desk, past his daughter, hand extended to me. "How have you been, son? We've been trying to get in touch with you."

I smile, touched. "I'm well, sir. Thank you."

"The station wouldn't tell me anything when I asked about you. I was about ready to head to Commons and search for you myself."

My eyes swing to Nicole in surprise. She raises an eyebrow at me. "I told you we were worried."

"Wow," is all I can say. "Thanks. I...I don't know what to say."

Mr. Washington's eyes travel past me and over to Jenner. Nicole makes the introduction.

"Dad, this is Caden Jenner, Decker's friend and former partner in the Force."

Mr. Washington shakes his hand. "Nice to meet you, young man. If you're a friend of Decker's, you're a friend of ours."

Jenner blinks in astonishment. Perhaps it'll take him a while to really get how kind these people are. And I understand. Like me, he has never encountered someone on Atlas who was warm or friendly. Right before my eyes, I see my friend start to relax under Mr. Washington's hospitable air. He glances at his watch before turning to

Nicole questioningly.

"I'm happy you've brought them, dear, but aren't we supposed to meet…?" He trails off with a hinting tone.

His daughter nods and looks at us. "Dad," she gestures to us, "meet the men behind the Bill of Rights scandal."

Her father's jaw drops. He swings his head back to us, mouth still gaping.

"Is it - is it true? Decker? You were behind this?"

I notice Jenner has gone rigid again. He's nervous about what this Atlas man might do.

I meet Mr. Washington's eyes and give a silent nod.

He gasps, his shoulders hunching over under the weight of surprise. "Wow…*wow*."

He turns and circles back around to his desk, running a hand over his face again and again. I can feel Jenner's eyes burrowing into the side of my face. He's nervous and he thinks we should leave. I don't look at him. We're already here and I want to know why Nicole brought us to her father. Still, I'm worried that even though she wants to help, she may have inadvertently ruined it all by bringing her dad in on this.

He surprises me when he suddenly looks at me and asks, "How did you know about the original rights in the first place?"

I sigh, hiding my exasperation, and give him the same answer I gave Jenner. "I read. I went to the Atlas Library and found it in an American History book."

He whistles. "You must have gone way back then. We don't even refer to this country as 'America' anymore."

I nod. "I know."

"How did you get the flyers out? You managed to hack into every phone and computer - mine and my wife's!"

Jenner clears his throat loudly, a not so subtle indication for me not to rat Bill out.

"A friend of ours. He's good with computers," I answer cautiously.

Mr. Washington looks between Jenner and me, as if finally registering our hesitation. He's asking us to put all our cards on the table and hasn't shown a single hand of his. He moves from his desk to a small vault in the corner of his office. He crouches down to the door, until he's at eye level. A scanner runs over his iris and unlocks the door. He opens it, shuffles some papers around before closing it up again and turning back to us with what looks like old newspapers and pamphlets in his hands. He gives me one of the pamphlets and Jenner one of the newspapers.

I can't help the gasp that comes out when I see the face on the front. It's Nicholas Terranio - the notorious revolutionary leader who failed and was tortured to death as a result.

Jenner mutters, "I've heard of this guy. He was the last one to try and…"

Mr. Washington nods, the most sober expression I've ever seen on his face.

"Why do you have these?" I ask. "*How* do you have these? I thought they burned every trace of his propaganda."

He glances at his daughter who gives him a

sympathetic smile.

"These were my father's copies." He straightens and clears his throat. "Nicholas Terranio was born Nicholas Justus Washington. My father's older brother. My uncle."

My eyes stretch wide.

"Holy shit!" Jenner exclaims. "Your uncle was Nicholas Terranio?"

Mr. Washington nods. "A good man. Or so my father and mother always said. He was sentenced to The Gauntlet a week after I was born. My father was never the same."

He hands me another item in his hand. It's an old photo. In it, stand two young men in their early twenties who look a lot like him, clearly brothers. His father and his late uncle, the revolutionary martyr. Finally I get it. All this time I wondered how Nicole and her family would react to what I was doing...when all along they were the secret family of the most notorious USA rebel in recent history.

"They never traced his origin to you or your parents?" I ask Mr. Washington.

He shakes his head. "He corrupted the Atlas birth registry and input his death two years before he started the movement. Had all of his documentation changed to his new name. Even had cosmetic surgery so family friends wouldn't recognize him."

He's right. As I compare the family photo to his image on the pamphlet, his face was changed just enough to be unrecognizable to most.

"The last time he saw my dad was a month before I was born. He covered his tracks really well. No one ever came knocking on Dad's door. Nicole is named in honor of him."

I glance at her and even though she's not crying, I can tell the story of her namesake still moves her.

Mr. Washington extends a hand for the papers and photos. Jenner and I give them back. He turns and puts them back in the vault.

Turning back to us, he tells us, "I didn't show you that to get nostalgic or to discourage you in any way. I want to help you. For years, my father agonized over how his brother got caught. How his movement failed. My uncle was a brilliant man and extremely passionate about restoring the middle class. When he was alive, it was hovering around ten percent. Now it's under one.

"The attempt failed for several reasons. There was a lack of resources, organization, intelligence on the enemy, and confidentiality. If my uncle had the money, if his team planned more carefully…if they could have found a way to communicate without alerting authorities and if one of their men wasn't a coward…maybe…maybe he could have succeeded. Maybe he'd still be alive."

An awkward silence hovers over the room as Mr. Washington's blue eyes see unknown memories. He blinks and focuses on us again. "My family has always been dedicated to seeing the middle class restored. But when my uncle took the leap, we could only give him so much in support. The lack of support among other things caused him to fail. I don't want this to fail again."

I level my eyes at Mr. Washington and ask him point blank, "What are you saying, sir?"

He goes back to his desk and pulls out a black tote bag from beneath it. Placing it on his desk, he unzips the bag and invites us forward. My breath gets trapped in my throat when I look inside. Wads upon wads of hundred dollar bills sit inside, neatly bound and stacked. Jenner and I gape at each other, astonished. Mr. Washington looks between us, strictly business.

"There's $100,000 here to start with. Will this tie you over until I can get more?"

Half an hour later, we're sitting in Nicole's office on her end of the wing. Her parents purchased the apartment next door to expand into it for their daughter. It allows her a degree of privacy from the rest of the family but still keeps them all connected. It's great how close they are to each other.

We're all sitting at the board room style table centered in her office. Jenner and I are still in slight shock. After he handed us the funds, Mr. Washington made it clear he wants no part of the planning. With his business and status as its owner very public, he doesn't want to draw attention to what we're doing or jeopardize his family's safety. He gave Nicole a very stern warning to be careful and discrete. I look over at her, seated at the head of the table, a white board behind her on the wall.

"You never told me why you're doing this." I ask her. "I get your dad helping but…Nicole, this is a huge risk for you too."

She turns to me, her long ponytail swinging slightly. Her chocolate brown eyes are thoughtful as she speaks.

"Decker, you didn't always know me. Growing up, I lived in a bubble. I thought everyone had the same rights, privileges and opportunities as me-"

"Seriously?" Jenner asks, laughing slightly. He's not being an ass but looks genuinely surprised that she believed that.

She gives a chagrined smile. "I know. I should have known better but I didn't. I was happy and I figured everyone else was too. I can't remember the exact moment but one day I just…woke up." She shrugs. "I actually stopped and looked at the faces of the maids working in our house, the doorman at the front, the gardeners tending our terrace. No one had a smile. At least not one that reached their eyes. I didn't know I was privileged until I observed how others lived.

"Finally I saw the little things. The way my mother would prepare extra food. How my dad would smuggle a tip to someone. And then…" To my surprise, she fixes her eyes on me. "You came. And…"

She blushes.

I frown. "What?"

She shakes her head. "Nothing. Just…I noticed even more how good we had it. How badly things needed to change so that everyone had at least the *chance* to have this." She gestures around her.

When I look away from her, I find Jenner's blue eyes bouncing between Nicole and I. He quirks a brow at me and I shrug. *What?* If I didn't know any better, he seems to think something's going on between us that isn't. He doesn't look convinced but turns to Nicole and gives her a friendly smile, the first one I've seen him offer since meeting her.

"Listen, I know I was a bit…abrasive when we first met. But I'm really glad you're helping us. Thanks."

She smiles, pleased by his words.

"Thank you," I voice my gratitude as well. "You're an invaluable part of what we're doing. I've never been so glad to be stalked in my entire life."

She tosses her head back and laughs freely, so much so that Jenner starts to chuckle too.

When she calms down, she's all business again. "Okay, let's talk game plan. I heard most of what you said in the shed. Annihilate and start fresh. President's Ball."

I nod. "What do you think?"

She tucks a stray strand behind her ear. "It's a good plan, provided the police actually do their part. Do you know when you'll hear back from your connection. What's his name?"

"Adams," Jenner replies. "He's working on it but he has to be careful."

She leans back in her seat, rocking back and forth. "Of course. But that's not all you need to consider."

"No?" I ask.

She shakes her head. "Have you considered what

happens if and when we do succeed? If you do this covert operation and get rid of USA's entire leadership - what then? Who will lead?"

I shake my head. "We'll have a new election - and a better election system for that matter-"

"Decker, you're not hearing me," Nicole cuts me off and sits up. "No revolution has ever succeeded without a known leader. Without a face behind the revolt. My great uncle did many things wrong when he led his movement but one thing he did right was put a name and face to the rebellion. Commoners need a leader to stand behind. Someone to rally and support. They need a hero."

I understand what she's saying, even though I don't want to. She looks at me intently. I look away from her searing eyes only to find Jenner staring at me too, nodding in agreement with her. I look between the two of them, attempting to hold off the inevitable.

"Wait a minute." I look at Jenner. "I said I was in. I never said I'd play some hero. You're just as passionate about it - in fact you're the one who suggested spreading revolutionary ideas. You do it."

He shakes his head. "It has to be you-"

"*Why?*" I ask. I hate how desperate my voice sounds but I can't hide it. It's just hitting me that the meeting with Bill, the meeting with the men in the shed, talking to Nicole's dad...every single time they looked to me like I was the leader. I've stepped into a role I had no intention of filling. I thought I was along for the ride only to find out, I've been the one driving.

Jenner must see my panic because he puts out a hand for me to hear him out. "Decker, it has to be you," he repeats. "You're the master mind behind the Bill of Rights scandal."

"I-"

"You *know* the history of this government and what it once was. Better than any other Commoner. Hell, better than any other Atlan." He looks at Nicole. "Am I right?"

She nods, leaning back in her seat again. "Most historians - all Atlas snobs - only focus on the past one hundred years of USA history. Their institutions and museums *pay* them to ignore history. So they propagate the same misinformation to the rest of Atlas and it trickles down to the poorly-written text books of Commoner children. Atlans are just as ill-informed about this nation's origins as Commoners. Decker, *you* know. You may not have realized it, but your twenty odd years of self-education has made you the most qualified leader of this movement. And quite frankly, of the country-"

I stand up at those words, hands up. I squeeze my eyes shut and turn to the other side of the room, my back facing both of them. I don't want to hear that shit. It's bad enough they want me to lead the revolt. I can't wrap my head around leading all of USA. I didn't sign up for that.

The truth is I don't know.

I don't know what I'm capable of. I don't know if I'd make a good leader - in any capacity really. The most I've led were a group of teenage boys in training to become officers - something I did well because someone once trained *me*. This is uncharted territory. All my life, my future has been outlined *for* me, by others more powerful than me. My education, my career, and my advancement. What will it look like to finally have a say? To finally lead the charge? Can I do it?

I can't look at either of them behind me right now. Because I know if I do, they'll see the naked fear written all over my face.

I'm scared.

I'm scared shitless.

Not of dying or losing this thing. But of letting other men and women down. Of endangering *other* people's lives. And even worse than that, I'm terrified of unseating one terrible government only to bring in something worse - an incompetent one. I'm just one man. I'm only *one* person. But these people are looking at me like I'm some sort of superhero from one of those ancient *Superman* comic books. I'm way in over my head and I don't know how to come up for air.

Suddenly, I feel a small hand on my shoulder blade.

"Decker." Nicole's voice is soft, gentle. It's a soothing balm to my erratic nerves. She speaks closely to my ear. "We need you. We *need* you. If not you, who else?"

The question rings in my ear. Who else? Who else can do this?

If she and Jenner are right…if no one else can lead this thing…then I either have to swallow my fear and *try*. Or let my fear consume me and fail. If I step up, I risk failure.

If I withdraw, I guarantee it.

And everyone else fails right along with me.

Nothing will change.

I can't live with that.

I think back to the morning I woke up - for the first time excited to be alive. I haven't woken up dreading life since. Every day, there's something new to look forward to. A hope I haven't had in so long. I can't go back to what was. I'll die before I do that. There's no turning back for me. I feel the weight of this thing settle firmly on my shoulders. It's heavy. Uncomfortable. And permanent. It's a burden I will not unload until I see this thing to the end, dead or alive.

Here goes nothing.

I turn to face them and slowly nod. I don't know what my face looks like but she and Jenner blink in surprise. Nicole pulls her hand away and a wide smile forms on her lips. She knows I'm in. I settle back in my seat and watch her return to hers.

"So like I was saying," she continues. "You need the people to be behind you. That will draw numbers, rally support, and establish loyalty to our cause. This is where I can help."

We look at her expectantly.

"Propaganda," she says.

"Propaganda?" Jenner frowns.

She nods. "What you guys did with the flyers was great. It started some discontent, some conversation…but we need to step it up a notch. People need to see our ideas, our desire for change, and link it to a specific cause. One group. One name. One face. Decker's face. The more content we pump out, the more our ideas will spread, and the greater influence we'll have over the people."

I agree. "Will we focus our efforts on Commons?"

She nods. "There's no point on Atlas."

Her response is so succinct, I almost want to laugh.

Jenner leans forward on the table in front of him. "Okay, so we have a dual agenda, then: spreading support for the cause publicly and working on the President's Ball covertly."

"Exactly," she says.

I look at my fingers on the table and frown. "Nicole? Exactly how is this going to work? There's already a four million dollar bounty on my head for the flyers. I know I have to take the credit but the minute my name becomes associated with it, Hamilton will have me killed." To my surprise, the words don't scare me. I state them like cold, clinical facts because they are. I'm in this, sink or swim. But I'm not about to sink without a fight.

Jenner nods, concerned. "How do we do this and keep him out of their hands? And how do we manage this entire operation without getting caught? There are millions of cameras all over USA. There are cameras even Atlas cops don't know about!"

She nods, completely unruffled. "I know. I've thought about it. That's where Dami comes in."

Jenner and I glance at each other before returning our gaze to Nicole.

"Who?"

TRAVEL BAN ON UNITED STATES IN WAKE OF DEADLY CYRIAN EPIDEMIC

Zachary Filmen
Irish Times
24 December 2450

The UN has instituted an international travel ban on the United States in the midst of the deadly epidemic plaguing the nation. A strange and aggressive virus now known as the **Cyrian Flu** has spread across the United States, killing 100% of its victims. Not much is known about the illness, aside from the fact that it initially produces the typical symptoms associated with a standard seasonal flu before rapidly disintegrating the vital organs of its carrier.

There is no known cure or vaccine to protect those infected and scientists have classified this disease as an airborne illness. Every city and state in the country has been infected except New York City. Remarkably, one of the most populous cities in the country, the Big Apple has not reported a single case of the virus. The United States Congress and President Elise Northington initiated a strict quarantine over the nation's capital within days of the virus's spread. So far the measure has proved effective.

The first case was discovered in Charlottesville, Virginia on June 8th. Since then, more than one billion people have died in the outbreak - more than half of the population. Doctors, nurses, and researchers across the globe initially flocked to the U.S. in a humanitarian effort to fight the epidemic. Within weeks, the surge of support dried up as every international doctor, nurse, and researcher, regardless of the protective gear they wore, died after coming in contact with the infected air. Scientists theorize that there must be a small percentage of people immune to the disease as there are survivors who live in cities ravaged by the disease.

According to President Northington, the number and rate of deaths have slowed down for the past two months. Scientists predict that by the time the worst of the contagion passes, nearly 85% of the population will have perished.

"We must go home to be happy, and our home is not in this world. Here we have nothing to do but our duty."

-John Jay

CHAPTER NINE

"Allow me to introduce you to my friend, Dami Aderele. Dami is a biological scientist and technological inventor." Nicole says. "Dami, this is Decker Channing and Caden Jenner."

Nothing's happened to me so I can't explain why it feels like someone threw a heavy brick directly at the center of my chest. I blink at the sight before me and it stays the same.

She stays the same.

Dami Aderele is the most beautiful woman I've ever seen. Tall and slender with sculpted cheeks and full soft lips, she looks around the same age as Nicole. Her skin is so dark, it's luminous. A straight slender nose, perfectly arched brows and a full soft afro makes her look as if she hearkens back from Africa itself. She probably does, with a name like that. If her parents immigrated before the steel wall rose, she may very well be a first generation citizen.

But what gets me are her eyes.

They're arresting. Deep, almost black, they tell a

thousand stories but reveal none. I'm dying to know what's on her mind and I've only just met her.

Snap out of it, Channing, I chide myself. I'm here to work. I'm here to overthrow a centuries-long regime, not salivate over a woman. No matter how stunning she is.

We shake hands quickly and I look away, forcing myself to ignore the pins and needles prickling me from the top of my head to the soles of my feet. *Damn, she's beautiful.* But when Jenner takes her hand, he holds it just a little longer than necessary.

"It's a pleasure to meet you," he says in the most syrupy tone I've ever heard him use.

Apparently I'm not the only one who finds her attractive.

I shove the sudden surge of irritation back down. If she senses our male preoccupation, she doesn't act like it. She gives us a slight smile, showing a stunning row of pearly white teeth and invites us into her home. Her place is tastefully modern with black and beige accents all around. Much smaller than Nicole's family home, her apartment looks like it has two rooms, a bathroom and a medium sized kitchen and living area. It's nowhere near as grand as Mrs. Washington's decorations but it still reeks of Atlas middle class money. Better than anything I've ever lived in. And it looks like she lives on her own.

We follow her into the simple living room adorned with suede black furnishings and I notice something in the corner of the room.

"Is that an elevator?" I ask.

She glances at it before looking at me. "Yes."

It's only one word but I'm surprised at how smooth and rich her voice is. It almost matches the smooth luster of her skin.

What the hell is wrong with me?

I look away from her mysterious dark eyes. We all sit down, Nicole and Dami on one side, Jenner and I on the other.

"Nicole has told me a little about you," she says. "Why don't you tell me the rest?"

Nicole nods at us and Jenner sits forward on his seat. "I'll explain."

He then gives her the full story. I hold back my frown. Just hours ago, he was giving me a hard time about trusting Nicole with this and now he's spilling everything to a woman he's just met - a woman neither of us know.

Jenner hands her a folded sheet that I immediately recognize as a copy of *American Sense*. Does he carry it everywhere with him? She glances at me before reading it. It takes her less than a minute to read the page. When she's done, she raises a slender brow. Her eyes land squarely on mine.

"It's impressive. No wonder you're leading this."

I give a slight smile and will myself not to flush under her gaze. I nod my appreciation before she hands the sheet back to Jenner. He folds it back into his pocket and continues to explain our plans and the obstacles we're running into.

Nicole sums it up. "Now the dilemma is Decker.

Making him visible while keeping him safe."

Dami's dark eyes hit me again and I try to ignore the impact. She stands and moves towards the elevator in the corner of the room. "Follow me."

It's a small space, not fit for the claustrophobic, but we all manage to squeeze in enough for it to take us down a level. She's standing in front of me, her floral perfume teasing my senses. Once again, I shove aside my irritation as I watch Jenner's eyes admire her from behind.

The elevator opens and we all step out. I blink in surprise as we step into what looks like a metal-lined, state of the art lab. There's a large metal table in the center with several rolling stools. Computers and various machines line the perimeter of the room and a large flat screen stands formidably over the advanced desktop filled with complicated, multi-colored keys. The automatic lights above bathe the surface area in bright, fluorescent light.

"My office," she says, unfazed by our expressions. She strides over to one end of the room and pulls out a small box. Bringing it to the table, she opens it and retrieves a small, slim, rectangular piece of transparent film, peeling the paper back off of it. I look at it closely and can see the faintest of wiring running throughout the material. But further away, the film is completely transparent. I wonder how something so intricate can disappear so seamlessly.

"What is it?" I ask.

She looks at me and waves me forward. I approach her and follow her lead. She has me stand directly in front of the large screen.

"Camera on," she says aloud. Within seconds, the screen changes from black and shows me standing, front and center. It's as if I'm looking in a mirror. She moves in front of me and wordlessly sticks the film to the side of my neck. Once again, I get a whiff of her perfume. I look at her hands. Smooth brown skin stretched over long, slender, agile fingers. Her nails are unpainted, her hands devoid of rings, but there's a glow to her dark skin that makes me ache to touch it. I've never been around a woman who's had such an unnerving effect on me. I'm so focused on her, I don't even register what the film does. It isn't until Nicole gasps and Jenner exclaims, "Holy shit!" that I look away.

I look from their shocked expressions back to the screen.

I'm not there anymore.

The camera is still on and Dami, who hasn't moved, is still in the shot. But I'm nowhere to be found on the camera. I wave a hand in front of it, move a little…nothing. I'm completely unseen.

"How did you do that?" I ask her.

She touches the film on my neck. "I call this the 'cloak film.' It's wired to place a holographic shield over you, only effective on cameras. It disrupts their ability to properly perceive images and also distorts your voice so that your words are unintelligible."

She looks up at nothing in particular and orders the camera, "Rewind thirty seconds!"

The screen automatically rewinds and plays once again.

I watch as I suddenly disappear on camera and Nicole and Jenner react.

"Holy shit!" Jenner's voice replays.

Suddenly a strange, squealing noise blasts through the speakers. It sounds like a drowning rat, followed by Dami's voice explaining the film.

The camera picked up everyone else's words but mine.

"Now you can walk around and meet others undetected by the cameras on Commons, or the few that are around Atlas," she adds.

"This is amazing," Jenner gasps. He leans against a nearby table and starts tossing his keys up and down, a look of sheer admiration on his face. We all watch her go back to the box and pull out another film, the exact same size and makeup of the other one. She lays it on my neck and quickly steps away.

Jenner's keys drop to the ground and his jaw drops to his chest.

"What now?" I ask. I still can't see myself in the screen with the "cloak film" on. I look at Dami, who's smiling mysteriously. She gestures to an actual wall mirror a couple feet away from a stupefied Nicole.

"Whoa," is all I can say as I look at my reflection. Instead of seeing the face I've been accustomed to for thirty-two years, I see a man with red hair and bright green eyes staring back at me. He's about twenty pounds heavier and looks a few years older than me. But he *looks real.* I feel like I'm looking at an actual person not just a...a...

"What is this one?" I ask.

"A holographic mask," she replies. "If you have to leave a safe location and get around unrecognizable, this will disguise you. It's water and weather resistant with a magnetic charge that allows you to use it an unlimited number of times. If you prefer a different look, I can design it. I don't know what you may need to do in plain sight, but this can easily hide you while you do it."

Jenner has recovered. "This is *amazing!*" He exclaims, his arms flailing in excitement. "We're set! You can go anywhere and do anything without getting caught!"

Nicole is more sedate in her praise. "I knew you were brilliant Dami, but this is incredible. You're a genius."

Her friend smiles ruefully. "Thanks. So what else do you need?"

Nicole starts to talk about her propaganda campaign. "The flyers were a great start. It was brilliant to put them on people's phones but now ADC has created a sky-high firewall. I don't know if their tech guy can break through it and even if he can, we need to find another way to get our message out."

Dami nods. "I have just the thing."

She goes to the gigantic keyboard below the large screen and types up something, each key lighting up under the touch of her fingers. Suddenly, a large machine stationed in the opposite corner of the room starts lasering out yet another film. This must be her favorite type of inventing material. She goes to the machine and retrieves the film. She sticks it on a bare patch of wall and goes back to the keyboard. After a few more strokes, a large, holographic poster emerges from the vicinity of the film. The only problem is…it's impossible to see the film now. It's disappeared into the wall.

Dami explains, "This is an untraceable holographic poster. I can make it as small as a paper-sized flyer or as large as a billboard. I can also change the dimensions of the poster; make it vertical or horizontal, depending on your needs. Most holographs have a round, metal chip, easy to trace the feed from. This film anchors the holograph and transmits the signal while camouflaging itself into the surface on which it rests." She points to the space between the wall where the now invisible film rests and the blank holograph floating in mid-air. "There's no holographic trace to show exactly where the poster comes from. So authorities will be looking around for a chip, not realizing an invisible, weather and water resistant film is actually responsible for the transmission. It'll be impossible to find."

And our message will be seen uninterrupted.

Of all her inventions, this one takes the cake for me. It does for Nicole and Jenner too, if their reaction is any indication.

"Listen," Dami adds. "I can provide the technology but someone will need to design the actual content."

Nicole looks between Jenner and I. "Is that something Bill can do?"

Jenner scoffs and I shake my head. "He tried his best with the Bill of Rights flyers. And you saw how those looked."

The only reason they were effective was because of the mind-blowing information they revealed. It had nothing to do with the aesthetics of the design…or lack thereof.

Nicole nods. "I know someone who can make it work."

"Sarah?" Dami asks her. She nods.

"Who's that?" Jenner asks.

"A graphic designer. She'll pretty everything up and make it visually appealing. That's incredibly important in campaigns like this."

I nod. It makes sense.

"We'll still need Bill, though. If he can load the content into the holographs-"

"That's another good thing about them," Dami adds. "Content can be loaded onto them from a remote site, even when they're up and running. So if you need to update anything or make a change, it can be done at anytime."

"Excellent," Nicole says. "I'm calling Sarah now."

Dami looks at us as Nicole makes the call. "What are you doing for weapons?"

Shit. Just when I think things are coming together, there's another major piece of the puzzle to solve.

"We haven't figured that out," Jenner answers. "I work on Danielton. Several factory guys are also in on this and we can pull out scrap material but none of us know how to design guns. Unless we find someone in Repair who can do it."

"Or get an in with a gun factory worker," I suggest.

Dami shakes her head. "Don't worry about that yet. I

know a guy who can help."

She turns to make a call just as Nicole finishes hers.

"Okay," Nicole says. "Sarah's on her way. How soon can Bill get over here?"

I glance at my watch. "He can't. The last train to and from Atlas left over an hour ago."

Nicole nods. "Then I'll get him."

Dami returns, sticking her phone in her pocket. "You shouldn't go by yourself. Jenner, can you escort her?"

Jenner nods, "Of course."

Two minutes later, we're all upstairs again. As soon as Nicole and Jenner leave, Dami shuts the door and turns to me.

"Are you okay?" she asks, her brows furrowing in concern.

Her question surprises me. "What do you mean?"

"You're exhausted and overwhelmed. You should take a nap before the others arrive."

"Do I look that out of it?" I ask. Did the others see my fatigue? My concerns?

She shakes her head. "You actually look calm and in control. Stoic. And you keep the other two calm by your demeanor. But you're exhausted. I can tell by how dilated your pupils are and how often you've held back a yawn."

Suddenly it all makes sense. Even though I've known Nicole much longer than Jenner, even though she'd probably feel more comfortable with me accompanying her to Bill's, Dami asked Jenner to go…so I would have a chance to rest.

"Thank you," I murmur. "You're right - I've been up since six and my head is fried."

No one's ever done this for me. Observed me then arranged for me to get what I needed right away. Now that I think about it, she's been doing this for the whole team all night.

"Thank you for your help," I add. "Before you, this whole thing seemed impossible. Insurmountable."

She shrugs and gives a slight smile. "Without you, none of this would be happening," she says. "I...I want you to succeed. Very badly."

The sincerity shines through her enigmatic dark eyes. I believe her. I don't know why but something in me gives over to trusting her. Maybe it's the same thing that got Jenner to trust her right off the bat but I doubt it is. While her beauty got him to spill it all, something else about her makes me feel like I can let my guard down. She glances at the couch and looks at me pointedly, making me smile.

I nod and take a seat. Just as I drift off completely, it hits me what it is.

She's serene.

"How long has he been asleep?"

"Just over an hour. He needed it."

"Okay, well we need him now. We've discussed everything that doesn't require his direct input-"

"And there's not much that doesn't."

"I think he's waking up."

I am. I don't know how long my mind was aware of the nervous whispers but my eyes open to find the small group standing around me in the small living room. Nicole and Jenner are back with Bill. Two unfamiliar faces are next to them. I stand and am once again the tallest in the room.

"Decker," Nicole says. "This is Sarah Williams, our graphic designer."

I turn to the young woman next to her. Sarah is a short, petite woman in her early twenties with platinum blond hair and bright brown eyes. She smiles shyly and shakes my hand. "Nice to meet you."

"Likewise," I reply.

Dami speaks next. "This is Sam Tate. He's my friend and pseudo-apprentice. He'll help with weapons development."

I shake the young man's hand. He's about the same age as Sarah, maybe twenty-four. With bright red hair and light blue eyes, he's the same height as Jenner with the same thin build as Bill.

He smiles brightly. "The Author awakes."

I frown at that. "What?"

Nicole says, "They've both read *American Sense*."

"How did you come up with that?" Sam asks, shaking his head in amazement.

I shake my head. "It's a long story."

Jenner murmurs, "I'll tell you all about it later."

I roll my eyes and they laugh.

We all migrate to the lab. Bill and Sarah, but especially

Bill, take a few moments to salivate over Dami's space and all the cool features surrounding it. Bill fires off questions about the design and technological capabilities, which Dami actually takes the time to answer. They soon carry off in a brief tech-heavy jargon exchange that might as well be Polish, none of us have any idea what they're talking about. Before long, other conversations erupt. When Dami shows the rest of the team the holograph posters, Sarah and Nicole start talking design. Sarah insists that the Bill of Rights needs to be featured, followed by *American Sense*.

"Only, I think it would be better for Decker to read it aloud to the people," she says.

"In a video?" Nicole asks. "That's brilliant. It'll break up the number of things they have to read."

"And it'll make them stop." Sarah says. "We see stagnant images all the time. But if they see holographs floating *along* with a video of the leader of this revolution? They'll stop and listen."

While they continue to chat about background, colors, and recording techniques, Bill and Dami seamlessly work on the technology behind the holographs.

"So this gives me a direct link to the holographs?" Bill asks her, holding up a thin micro chip.

She nods. "You have the same operating control as I do on the main board here. My only question is, can you keep the line secure?"

He nods. "Absolutely. My firewall blows ADC's out of the water. They don't even know I created an independent network. As long as I use that, we're undetectable."

Sam and Jenner are talking weapons, what will be most effective for the President's Ball. It's all coming together. Unbeknownst to the group, I quietly board the elevator and take it back up to the living room. Like Nicole's place, Dami's living room overlooks the city. The lights are off inside so that the lights from the cityscape outside shine brilliantly against the pitch black sky. Looking out at it, one would never guess the change that's about to sweep over this land if we succeed.

Everything is moving so fast. It's hard to believe that just days ago, my life was moving along in painful predictability. Now, everything has changed - in just *days;* and everything we hope to change will happen - in just *days.* It's the ultimate mental whiplash. I sigh heavily. Why is it that I just woke up and already want to go back to sleep?

I hear the elevator open behind me but don't turn to see who it is.

There's shuffling and movement in the kitchen. Minutes later, she appears by my side.

"Coffee?" Dami asks, holding out a piping hot mug to me.

"Thanks." I take it and enjoy the first fresh cup I've had in ages.

"They'll all go crazy in a few minutes when they realize you aren't there," she says.

"They'll all go crazy sooner because they'll notice you aren't there either."

She chuckles. "I normally don't stay up this late. Coffee was a necessity."

"Same here," I reply, taking a sip. The hot liquid rolls down my throat in soothing waves. "Why are you doing this?"

I see her look at me, surprised by the question. She shrugs. "I believe in what you're doing. What *we're* doing, I guess I should say now."

I smile. I like the sound of that.

"How do you know so much about the history of this nation? You didn't go to college, did you?"

I shake my head. Normally the first question would annoy me and the second one would offend me. But the way she asks them...I can't react adversely to either of them.

"No. I read. I've been inhaling books for as long as I can remember."

"And yet you never planned on starting a revolution. You just did it for fun? Why?"

I smile at her astute observation.

"When my parents split, I used books to escape. I found it fascinating that I could go to another part of the world or exist in a different dimension just from picking up a book and reading. And they had to be books. Hard copies. The literature of the past is much...*deeper* than the literature of today."

She nods silently, encouraging me to continue.

"When I was ten, my mom had to work on a weekend - the first weekend since she landed the job before I was born. Afraid to leave me home alone, she made me stay in the Atlas Library the whole day. I got bored of the section I usually stuck with and wandered to the area that was virtually empty. With a bunch of dusty ancient books labeled 'American History.' It was the first time I learned that USA was once called America. That there was once an 'American Revolution.'"

She nods.

"I never would have known about it had I not wandered over there. They don't teach USA history further than the past fifty years on Commons. It's awful."

"It's not much better on Atlas. They don't teach it further than a hundred years."

"The more I studied, the more I realized how little I'd been taught. So I started teaching myself." I started with history and moved into politics, legislation, and even economic affairs.

"So do you think it can really be restored?" she asks me. "The Constitution? This nation?"

"I don't know," I answer honestly. "I still can't trace what caused the breakdown in the Bill of Rights."

"You don't have to," she replies. "It's been five hundred years since it was first weakened. That's a lot of generations screwing it up and all it takes is one to drop the baton."

I smile at her. She really is brilliant.

"I personally think money destroyed it," I say, eyes focused on the skyline.

"Money?" she asks.

I nod. "All the lobbying. Corrupt politicians. Soch, Wartman and Lieberman have all but purchased that president. Money really is the root of all evil."

She makes a strange noise at the back of her throat. I look at her.

"You don't agree?"

She shakes her head, impressing me with her honesty. "No, I don't. I don't think money is the root of all evil. It's existed for thousands of years across countless cultures with perfectly functioning governments, including the original United States."

"Then where did that saying come from?" I ask.

"*Love* of money is the root of all evil," she amends. "Who loves money? Greedy people. What type of characters do greedy people have? Poor ones," she chuckles slightly at her pun. "Poor character results in poor leadership and empires fall to poor leadership every time."

I nod, speechless.

"Why did you come up here?" she finally asks.

It only takes me a second to grapple with whether or not to be honest. "I felt useless. Everyone has their role and I was just sitting there."

People keep saying I'm the leader of this thing and yet everyone is leading it but me. Which is fine. But I feel like a caricature of something, rather than a member of it.

"It's become this big moving machine with all the parts in place and I don't know where I fit. Much less if I'm driving it."

I can see her nodding out of the corner of my eye. The

top of her head reaches just beneath my shoulder. I love how tall she is.

"That's what happens when others come on board, Decker. But look on the bright side. You're no longer alone. The overwhelming feeling you felt earlier - is it still there?"

I think for a moment then shake my head, relieved and amazed.

"That's good, isn't it?" she asks. "And you've now started something that actually can work. They're running off with their ideas and planning because they *believe* this can work. We all do. All hands are on deck and yours were the first ones to appear. Yours are the most important."

The elevator opens behind us again. Nicole appears. "Oh! There you are! Decker, we're ready to shoot you."

I glance back and find Dami smiling at me. "See?"

I smile back, amazed at her insight. She extends her hand for the mug and I hand it back. I turn and follow Nicole, feeling fresh and revived to do my part in the campaign. But I honestly can't tell if it was the strong coffee that revived me or the woman who made it for me.

"And cut!" Nicole calls. "I think we got it. That's the take."

Four reads later and my speech for the poster is done.

Dami pulls us all in to talk communication.

"I know this is one of your biggest concerns." Her dark eyes graze over all of us. She once again opens the box that contains the treasure trove of technology she's developed. She pulls out yet another clear film. She looks at me and nods slightly. I know she's asking me to demonstrate.

The entire group stares at me as she takes the small square piece and fits it behind my ear, in the very crevice where it attaches to my skull.

"Okay, you're good." she says. She turns back to the box and pulls out another square film, this time placing it behind her ear. I glance down at the floor as she works.

"Can you hear me?" she asks.

"Yeah," I look up from the floor. "You're right here."

The group gives me a strange look. I look back at her and see her smiling.

"What?" I ask? What did I miss?

"Can you hear me?" she asks again.

"Yes, I can hear-"

That's when it hits me. She isn't talking. Her mouth isn't moving.

"What the hell-"

"Think the question - don't speak." I hear her voice but she still isn't talking.

"What is this?" I think in my head.

She smiles and nods, answering. "The world's first telepathic telephone. Instead of speaking, the film behind your ear picks up on the wavelengths in your brain and translates the signals into speech, matching your voice, your tone, and everything you're saying - just in your mind."

My mouth flies open but it's a good thing I don't have

to speak because words will not come out.

"What?" Jenner asks, looking between the two of us. "What is it?"

"This way," she continues telepathically, her eyes boring into mine, "you can hold conversations with anyone on the team unmonitored. You'll be able to communicate in full confidence, even if the enemy is standing right beside you."

"You *are* a genius." The words fall out of my mouth before I can even think of catching them.

She smiles, turns from me and looks at the rest of the group.

"What you just saw was Decker and I having a conversation telepathically."

The group responds much the same way I did.

"What?"

"How is that possible?"

"How can you-?"

She holds up her hands, staving off the questions. Reaching into the box, she pulls out several more pieces of film and instructs them to place it in the crevice behind their ear lobes. I watch as she communicates the same way to Nicole, then Jenner, then Bill and finally Sarah. Sam is the only one who seems familiar with the software. She audibly explains what the telepathic phone does.

"You can only use one line at a time so don't talk too long because someone could be trying to get a hold of you when they think your name."

"Wait," Bill says. "All you have to do is think

someone's name in order to call them?"

"Not exactly. You have to give the phone a specific command. Simply think, 'Dial Nicole' or 'Dial Jenner' and the phone will connect to that person's line to transmit a telepathic connection."

Sarah begins, "How did you-?"

Dami holds up a hand with a gentle smile. "You don't want me to get into the mechanics of this. It even makes *my* head hurt."

Sam smiles and nods. He must have seen her in the throes of designing this thing.

"This is incredible, Dami." Jenner says. "You had me sold on the first two films but *this*…" he trails off, at a loss for words. He finally just adds, "Thank you."

"Sure," she says. "The next thing we need to talk about is recruitment, right?"

Jenner nods, a serious look overtaking him.

"I have an idea on how to screen potential recruits."

She takes him to the side of the lab and they discuss some more.

Bill glances at his watch. "So when are we planting the holographs?"

UNITED STATES SHORTENS ITS NAME TO USA

Susan Lobache
New Zealand Inquiry
8 January 2515

A new year comes with a new name for the United States of America. For the first time since its inception, the U.S. is changing its name. In a recent vote, the nation's Congress decided to rename the United States to simply USA. This comes in the aftermath of the nation's recovery from economic and medical disaster in the last century.

The last known case of the Cyrian Flu was 4-year-old Mason Huckanwall who died on June 2, 2451. In the aftermath, the nation struggled to recover not only from the chaos and isolation the pandemic brought, but also the economic and social consequences of losing more than 95% of its population. What was once an issue of overpopulation quickly became an issue of under population. Despite the lift of the Population Control Act, it became impossible to replenish the number of citizens required to maintain fifty states and the vast land it covered.

In 2452, survivors of the Cyrian epidemic started flocking to New York City for supplies and work, leaving the majority of the land a desolate urbanized ghost town. Over time, the populace concentrated to the five boroughs of New York City and established a new social order determined by socioeconomic status. The nation abolished the concept of states in 2500 and now refers to its territories as quarters. All territory west of what was formerly New York City is abandoned, left to Native

Americans on reserves, the Amish, and anyone willing to brave the desolate and ravaged lands - much of which still contains the unburied bodies of Cyrian Flu victims.

"A watchful eye must be kept on ourselves lest, while we are building ideal monuments of renown and bliss here, we neglect to have our names enrolled in the Annals of Heaven."
-James Madison

CHAPTER TEN

It's almost one in the morning by the time we reach my place. Jenner has gone to Mechanics to warn my dad.

The lights are out when we arrive. I quickly turn them on and open Mom's door.

"Mom," I gently shake her shoulder. "Mom, wake up."

She rises slowly, her voice groggy. "Sweetheart? Honey, what is it?"

"Mom, you have to leave. Now."

My mother looks past me as she hears shuffling in the kitchen.

"Who's here? Is that Caden?"

"No. Mom, listen." I can tell she's starting to shake out of her grogginess. "You can't stay here anymore. It isn't safe."

Her eyes are fully alert now. "Why? What happened? Are you alright?"

I cut off the questions before they compile even more. "I'm fine. Everything's okay. Nicole will explain it all on your way to her place."

"Nicole?"

Nicole suddenly appears beside me. She smiles at my mother and greets her warmly. "Hi, Ms. Kim."

Mom smiles, always happy to greet a guest. "Oh, hello dear! How's your mother?"

Nicole nods. "She's well. She'll look forward to seeing you soon."

"I don't understand." Mom looks between the two of us. "What exactly is going on? I'm not doing anything until I understand."

I sigh heavily, knowing she's not exaggerating. Mom will sit put and keep asking questions until the next millennium if she doesn't understand something the first time around.

I blurt out, "I'm the one behind the Bill of Rights scandal."

Silence.

Then, "*What?!*"

I nod. "Mom, we're leading a revolt against President Hamilton and his regime and I'm going to be his number one target soon. We need to get you somewhere safe where Hamilton won't be able to use you to blackmail me."

"Or worse - hurt you." Nicole adds. The thought makes my stomach clench. It's bad enough friends and complete strangers are sticking their necks on the line for me but the thought of risking my mother's life brings an unwelcome surge of guilt I try my best to ignore. She didn't sign up for this.

Mom has been uncharacteristically silent for several

long moments. In the dark of the night, with the light from the kitchen barely touching her face, I can see a myriad of emotions raging war on her worn face. Fear. Outrage. Pride. And love. She battles through them all before looking at me with a resolved expression probably not unlike the one I wore that made Jenner and Nicole blink hours before.

She slowly stands and touches my cheek.

"Are you sure about this, Decker?"

It throws me that she uses my given name. She almost never addresses me with anything other than endearments. I look into her slanted dark eyes, the very ones that match my own.

"Yes," I reply, nodding slowly.

She takes a deep breath, her resolve now set in stone.

"Okay," is all she says before turning from me and getting into gear.

In just under an hour, my mother, Nicole, and I pack decades' worth of her belongings into several large suitcases. Many of the dusty luggage were owned by my grandparents when they were my age. She fills them to the brim with clothing, photos, papers, even dishes. Anything and everything she finds essential or sentimental, she packs away. Nicole helps me pack a few of my own belongings for storage. I won't be able to take much of anything with me as I move from quarter to quarter; but she promises to put them in safe keeping until the revolt is over.

Whenever that happens.

We give Mom a disguise film and a cloak film and

sneak her out of the apartment to the car with the cover of night on our side. I carry the suitcases close to me. Dami said the cloak holograph can extend up to a foot away from us, shielding the things we carry as well. Just in case, I hug the luggage close to my body. Nicole carries a large tote strapped across her shoulder. Mom walks quickly with her pocketbook in her hand. We walk down two and a half blocks to Nicole's car, hidden from view of the main road.

When the suitcases are stowed away, my mother squeezes me with a strength I didn't know she had. She whispers into my ear, "I love you. I love you with everything that's in me."

I push back the tears threatening to burn my eyes. I hate how my voice croaks as I reply, "I love you, too."

"Be careful. *Please*. Don't let me lose my only son."

Those words almost do me in as I find myself holding her just as tight, waiting just as long to let her go so she can climb into Nicole's car.

Nicole nods at me. "See you tomorrow."

I nod back. "Tomorrow." I glance at my mom, seated somewhere behind the tinted window. "And thank you."

Her folks didn't have to take Mom in. They offered without a second thought. She nods wordlessly before climbing back inside. Seconds later, the car starts up and the wheels take off, carrying my mother towards safer land.

• • •

The next morning, barely six hours later, I pack my most essential items into a backpack and eat the last of the food. For once, I'm glad the fridge is so empty. Not much will go to waste when I leave. It's strange to me that this is the last time I'll eat in this apartment. Sit in this ancient wooden chair, look out at the shitty view facing my window. The same view my parents saw when they were married. The view my grandparents saw when they first bought this place seventy years ago.

It already looks empty. Void of my mother's things. I didn't have much to begin with. I scarf down my toast and drink the last of the juice. Throwing everything away, I shower, change and give the empty, desolate apartment one last sweep with my eyes before closing the door behind me for the last time.

Cloak film on, I go to the shed and meet the team there.

My eyes land on Dami the minute I enter the building, but there's only one thing I need to know first so I turn to Nicole and ask, "How is she?"

She nods and smiles. "Fine. She and Mom have hit it off perfectly."

I sigh, relieved. I look at Dami again and she smiles before beginning.

"Okay," she says. "I have gifts for all of us today."

She holds out a panel of transparent film, the size of tickets and we all know what they are.

"The holographs," she confirms.

We split off into teams: Bill and Sarah hit the Repair

Quarter, his stomping ground; Sam and Jenner go to the Factory Quarter and Nicole opts to go to the Maids Quarter by herself.

"I've been there several times. Visits to employees with Mom," she explains.

That leaves Dami and I. Familiar with both Mechanics and Police quarters, I show her the most visible parts of both towns. We take a cab over to the Police District then ride into Mechanics when we're done there. Dami has given everyone ten holographs each so we take our time to get them in just the right locations, sticking them in the crevices of brick and stone, where they won't be seen unless someone is looking hard for a clear piece of film. Even then, it'll be next to impossible to find and extract. They fit onto the surface just like tape with a super adhesive. It still blows my mind that each razor thin slice holds the data and technology needed to display such powerful images.

She watches me as I apply yet another piece to a popular bar along a main street.

"How did you learn all this?" I ask her.

She looks surprised at the sudden conversation. "I went to school for it. Learned the basics of technological engineering in high school and chose Advanced Inventions as one of my majors in college."

College. Definitely an Atlan woman. I apply the film and then join her to move on to another building. Though we're both wearing our film disguises, I can envision her face in spite of her holographic cover. It helps that the eyes in her disguise are the same shade as her eyes in real life. I'm looking at a black woman with a completely different facial structure and hairstyle, but I know it's her underneath. The disguises don't affect our communication.

"Were you born on Atlas?" I ask.

I glance in time to see her shake her head with a slight laugh. "I was born in Lagos, Nigeria. My parents moved me here when I was an infant, right before the steel wall rose."

I was right. She is a first generation citizen. Rare for someone so young.

"How long ago was that?" I ask.

She smiles, her dark eyes fathomless. "I'm twenty-eight."

I grin at how easily she saw through my question. I'm about to ask her another one when this time she stops at another building and applies her last holograph, asking, "Do you know if your dad's okay?"

I nod. "Jenner called me when he landed on McKenzie Isle."

In addition to housing my mother, the Washingtons offered to have dad stay at their vacation home on McKenzie Isle, posing as a gamekeeper like many of the Commoner men and women lucky enough to land such a job. It's the only one Commoners seem to enjoy - and it's highly competitive.

"It'll be good for him," I remark. "The car work was wearing on him."

She nods as we move on. "It's one of the worst jobs for your back. My mother was a chiropractor. She always said the worst Commoner job was mechanical work because of all the bending and repetitive motions."

This is interesting info. Her mother was a doctor.

"When did your mother retire?" I ask. Nothing prepares me for the shadow that falls across her face. She looks stricken, caught off guard by the question.

"Dami, are you okay? What did I say?"

She shakes her head, continuing to walk, her eyes fixed in front of her. "It's nothing. You didn't say anything. My mom's been dead for fourteen years. She never retired from chiropractic work."

"I'm sorry," I say solemnly. I didn't know.

"Thanks," she says quickly.

"You were only a kid. Was she sick?"

She shakes her head, drawing a shaky breath. "They both died in a car crash. You might have heard of it - their car crashed over the Mohanan Bridge."

My heart nearly stops as two and two click together.

"Aderele," I say under my breath. She stops and looks back at me, confusion clouding her face. "Emmanuel Aderele. Was that your father's name?"

She straightens and nods, her eyes assessing me. I walk over to her and once again, our strides match.

"He was a good man," I comment. "A brilliant attorney."

"He made a costly mistake," she says. "So you can see I'm not just doing this to help Nicole or join a worthy cause. I have my own biases too."

She's more biased than anyone involved in this. Even more than Mr. Washington.

"What happened after they passed?" I ask.

"You mean after they were murdered?" She says it in such a casual tone, it almost startles me. "The government seized all of their possessions. My father's papers, documents, property and money. They allowed me a few sentimental items of my mom's but they re-possessed virtually everything, leaving me destitute."

"How did you-?"

"The week before their deaths, I received acceptance into Rockefeller Academy. It was a boarding school and my parents were debating between having me go there or having me commute between home and Solaris Academy. When they died, one of the board members at Rockefeller, an old friend of Dad's, arranged for me to receive a full scholarship given my academic performance and what they perceived to be my 'extraordinary potential' for scientific endeavors."

We're crossing into Factory but I barely notice the scenery around me. The more she speaks, the more I'm intrigued by Emmanuel Aderele's enigmatic daughter.

"It was the best option for me, with nowhere else to go. So I accepted, worked my way up and got a full ride to Columbia-"

I whistle, impressed. Even Commoners know about Columbia University. The only college standing that existed before the Cyrian epidemic.

"You said Advanced Inventions was one of your majors. What was the other one?" I ask her.

"Biology."

I blink at that. I've never heard of a scientist mastering both biological and technological disciplines. She guesses what I'm thinking. "I know. It's weird. But I leveraged the double major to be more competitive post-college. I landed my first job before I graduated and I haven't looked back since."

I nod. "Good for you. And you've known Nicole since-"

"High school. She commuted to Rockefeller and was a year ahead."

"She never invited you to dinners?" I ask. I never saw her when I was guarding the family.

She shakes her head. "After my parents died, I was very…careful about leaving the Academy. I didn't want to draw attention to myself or…I don't know."

I look down at her and can hear what she's not able to verbalize.

She was traumatized by the murder of her parents. Her only family in this country.

Who wouldn't be?

Her disguised face brightens. "But her family came to visit often. Her mother brought me gifts and food. Sometimes they would sleep over and we'd all have a girl's night in my dorm. Her family's amazing. They're really good people."

"You'll never hear me say otherwise."

I want to ask her more, keeping talking but we're just

yards away from the pier leading to the shed. Moments later, we join the rest of the team inside.

"How did it go?" I ask everyone.

"Good," Nicole replies. Everyone nods in agreement. No hiccups whatsoever. And even better, no suspicion.

Bill looks at Dami and holds his tablet up. She nods and steps to the center of the shed, reaching in her back pocket to pull out one more holograph. She looks around quickly before sticking it to the rotting wood on one of the walls. It's a test drive holograph; one, she explains, will represent what every holograph is expected to look like when they go live.

Like clockwork, Bill taps a couple keys on his touch screen and the holograph opens up into a life-sized poster. Seconds later, Sarah's stylized version of the Bill of Rights appear on the screen, followed quickly by my face, reciting *American Sense* as if I'm having a personal conversation with the viewer.

The display is only a few seconds long. But it's all we need.

"We can loop this endlessly or have it air every hour on the hour. When it's not playing, the revolution symbol will remain."

I have to give Sarah credit. The symbol is the American flag with the map of USA on the front. The islands are merged together and in large print, the logo simply says, "Liberty and Justice: FOR ALL!"

Jenner is grinning from ear to ear. I can feel the excitement radiating from him. We're all excited. And anxious.

"When does it go live?" I ask calmly.

Bill glances at his watch. "5:00 this evening, just in time for rush hour. We'll keep it on a continuous loop until 9:00 tonight and then switch it to an hourly rotation during the day time."

Nicole glances at her watch. "That gives us four hours to get you settled and hidden."

I nod and sling my bag over my shoulder. "Alright. See you guys soon."

"Hell yeah, you will!" Jenner exclaims, clapping me on the back, still excited.

I meet Dami's eyes briefly and nod. I wish we could spend more time talking. It means a lot to me that she shared so much during our time together. She gives me a slight smile and nods. She, Sam and Jenner will stay behind to meet with the recruiters, the men Jenner brought to this shed a few nights ago. They've come up with a system to recruit others and will use the men we have now to branch out throughout Commons. Sarah stays with Bill, making sure all the graphics are just as she wants them before they go live. Nicole and I head out to the main road. We manage to hail a taxi that takes us straight to Maids Quarter. For a town named after women who clean, Maids Quarter is just as filthy and depressing as all the other ones in Commons. Perhaps the residents here are so tired from cleaning the homes of others, they completely neglect their own environment.

We step out of the car and quickly walk into one of

only five hotels in the area. All of them Atlas owned.

"Dawson," Nicole gives as a last name. She made the reservation while planting holographs. The concierge doesn't ask for ID or any further information. Just takes the cash and hands us our keys. Two pairs. She looks between the two of us and seems to assume we're here to do what every other guest here does: make a kid by accident and leave the woman to care for him on her own. We don't bother to correct any assumptions. When we open the door to my room, it's surprisingly clean and neat. The queen sized bed has fitted white sheets without a spot or blemish. There is a desk, a small dining table and a kitchenette for me to work with.

"This was the nicest one I could find. It doesn't look too bad," Nicole says, her ponytail swinging as she looks about. She rips the disguise film off her neck but I keep mine on for now.

"It's good," I assure her. Better than most places on Commons. I lie on the bed and am thrilled to discover it's even more comfortable than the ancient mattress I used to call my bed.

"You should get some rest," she says, looking me over. "You deserve it."

In the quiet of the room, it finally hits me that there's no turning back. The plan is for me to lay low here for a couple of days. See what happens as the country responds to the holographs when they go live. After that, I'll change quarters and continue moving as the rest of the team pulls together the covert mission alongside the propaganda campaign. Yeah. I definitely need to take advantage of this time to rest. Something tells me I'm not going to get another opportunity anytime soon.

I look up to find Nicole watching me silently, her chocolate brown eyes soft.

"What?" I ask her.

"Nothing." She shrugs. "I'm just…I'm really proud of you. You've started an amazing thing."

"Nicole, it wouldn't be anything without you. You brought all the pieces of the puzzle together."

She gives me a warm smile, as though touched by my words. "So you trust me now?"

I know she's only half-joking.

"I'm sorry if I hurt you before," I reply. "I didn't know about your great uncle. I didn't know how you or your family would respond-"

"Decker, we love you-"

"I didn't know, Nicole." I repeat. I shrug and meet her eyes. "I didn't know. Now I do. And I'm grateful. Do you forgive me?"

Her chin starts to quiver and her eyes tear up. She quickly nods and gives me a hug. "Of course I do. I'm glad you finally got it through your thick skull."

I laugh against her shoulder as the smell of her Strawberry scented shampoo tickles my nose. It's a comforting scent. I pull back slightly and meet her eyes again. "Thank you. I mean it. Everything you've done…everything you're doing…thank you."

She takes a deep breath and pulls fully out of my arms,

sticking her disguise back on. "You're welcome, Decker. I'm really glad I'm here."

• • •

I wake up suddenly to the sound of a door getting broken a couple rooms down. Heavy footsteps march along the hall, feet rapidly approaching. I check my neck and sure enough both films are still on. I turn on the light, grab my backpack and shove it into the tiny space that passes for a closet. Thankfully Nicole took all my I.D. and stowed it with Mom. The only way anyone can know it's me is if -

My door flies open.

"Freeze! Atlas Police!"

I raise both my hands as two men storm into my room and search the premises. I recognize them - Tarek and Jones. Jones points his gun at me, even though I'm clearly nonthreatening. I raise my hands in compliance.

"Name!" he barks.

I rack my brain for the name Nicole gave.

"Uh, Dawson." I mercifully remember. "James Dawson."

I wonder what I'll tell him if he asks for I.D. but Tarek emerges from the bathroom. "He's not here."

Both men leave the room without a word. Seconds later, I hear them slam through the next door. I sit down on the bed, chest pounding in relief. I knew both of those men and one of them looked me dead in the eye without a clue as to who I really was. I glance at the clock and it all makes sense.

7:30PM.

It's already begun.

I wait until the heavy footsteps disappear from this floor. Until all that's left are the sounds of random men comforting their startled lovers. When I'm certain no one will reappear at my door, I turn on the small, outdated television and immediately go to ANN.

There they are, flashing and illuminating in all their glory on the news. Ground cameras pick them up and they can be seen from the news helicopters flying overhead. The holographic posters are larger than life and impossible to ignore, especially at night as our flyer, banner, and video glows throughout the streets and town squares of every Commons quarter.

"For those of you just joining us," the news announcer says. "You are looking at footage of an overnight propaganda campaign. At five o' clock this evening, holographic posters suddenly appeared as Commoners returned home. The poster once again shows the original Bill of Rights alongside the years those rights were modified. Most stunningly, a man by the name of Decker Channing has taken credit for both the flyer and the brief declaration *he* calls *American Sense*."

The footage cuts to a clip of me speaking into the camera as if I'm talking directly to the people.

"We hold these truths to be self-evident that all citizens born on this soil are Americans: not Atlans, not Commoners - but Americans. And all Americans, regardless of income, have the right to life, liberty and the pursuit of happiness. The

founding fathers of the United States of America - not USA - but the United States of America - once said that when a government actively interferes with these rights, it is the right of the governed to abolish it and institute a new government. I know I am in agreement with every Commoner watching this that the government of today has done just that. And it is time for their removal."

The clip cuts to the anchor, a young woman in her twenties. "Channing goes on to say that the National Recovery of 2500 did nothing to ensure the equality and protection of all citizens, regardless of their socioeconomic standing. He cites years of inflation, unfair tax, stagnant wages, lack of infrastructure, and the Educational Reform as heavy, government-instituted blows that have brought Commoners to the end of their rope financially, vocationally, and even physically."

Our video appears again. *"When a full-time working adult is unable to afford groceries of real non-genetically modified food, much less the other expenses made unaffordable by inflation, something has gone terribly wrong with the structure of a nation's economy. The rich flourish and get richer while the impoverished suffer and fall deeper into poverty. A poverty they can no longer work their way out of. American sense tells us it is time to end this oppression and establish justice for all."*

The footage cuts to real-time images of the streets in Factory Quarter. Scores and scores of highly armed uniformed officers pour through the streets and into buildings. It must be really bad if they have to wear uniforms. I can't remember ever wearing one in all my years of service.

"President Hamilton has ordered heightened security entail for all five quarters as officers and investigators attempt to find the holographic chips that are serving as projectors for the posters."

I smile at the footage of numerous groups huddling around the buildings that house the holographs. Their flashlights are on as they look around for round metal chips that typically display such images. If they haven't found the transparent, water-proof, super-glued films yet, they're never going to.

Those holographs are here to stay.

"After reviewing the cameras stationed at every building from which the holographs are airing, authorities still cannot determine who installed the chips to begin with or when they were installed. A special task force has been assembled to find Decker Channing, the leader of this propaganda. Channing is reportedly a former Atlas police officer. Once ranked first in his graduating Academy class, he served on the Police Force for fourteen years before he was dishonorably discharged by new Chief of Police, Stan Yang, two weeks ago. Atlans wonder if this rebellion is simply the result of a disgruntled former employee."

I roll my eyes at that.

Yang suddenly appears on screen, his beady eyes barely containing his rage. "The actions of a rogue former officer do not represent the integrity of the Atlas Police Force. At this time, we are employing every resource in our power to locate and apprehend *former* officer Channing before his divisive rhetoric tears even further at the fabric of this great nation."

Footage cuts to my apartment building as the anchor speaks. "So far, authorities have been unable to trace the former officer. His apartment was found mostly empty and has since been quarantined and sealed pending police investigation. Channing lived there with his mother, 53-year-old Eloise Kim. Despite searches, authorities have been unable to find her or her ex-husband, Channing's father, 58-year-old Walker Channing."

Pictures of Mom and Dad appear on screen and while I know Mom is safe with the Washingtons, I can only hope Jenner stressed to my father how important it is for him to keep his film disguise on at all times, especially if he even thinks of stepping outside of their McKenzie Isle vacation home.

I pick up the remote and lower the volume. With all of this going on, I need to check in with the team.

I pull my bag from the closet and retrieve my phone film. When I stick it back on, a flood of voices ring in my ear.

"Decker?"

"Decker, are you there?"

"Did they apprehend you?"

"Decker, pick up!"

I wonder how long they've been calling.

I think to the phone, *Dial everyone.*

"Guys are you there?" I ask.

"Decker!" I recognize Jenner's voice. *"Finally, man! We were worried about you!"*

"I think we're all here. Is everyone on the line?" Nicole asks.

Everyone answers yes.

"We did it, guys." I tell them. *"We're live."*

There's a momentous silence…until Jenner starts howling, *"Hell, yeah, we did! Did you see Yang's reaction?"*

The voices overlap and descend into a flurried rush of excitement. We reiterate the plan - for me to lay low the next two days. I tell them all how the film disguise worked.

"Saved my ass, too." Jenner says. *"I was walking out of my place as the cops were storming it. When I got to Bill's place, no one recognized me."*

"So Jenner and I are the only ones on their radar, right? Jenner, did Adams mention anyone else who needs to hide?"

"Everyone's good." To my surprise, it's Adams' voice.

"Adams, when the hell'd you get a phone?" Jenner asks.

"Nicole got me one," he answers. *"Figured it's a good idea to keep you guys as many steps ahead."*

He's right. We need all the intelligence we can get.

Adams says, or more accurately, thinks, *"Decker, Yang has just about lost his shit looking for you. Hamilton is breathing down his neck every ten minutes trying to bring this thing to a quick end. They can't figure out how any of it started. How you got the money, the technology - even the ability to disappear."*

"Do any of them suspect the Washingtons?" I ask.

"No. They haven't said a word about anyone on Atlas possibly helping this cause. They somehow think you've been planning this for years, squirreling away money on the side."

Jenner scoffs. *"How the hell could he have done that?"*

Adams replies, *"It doesn't matter how stupid their theory is - whatever keeps them from guessing we have Atlas help, I'm all for it. They plan on doubling the search effort tomorrow. You said they swept your hotel?"*

"Yep."

"Then you're good for another two days at least. That's when they'll start re-trying places they already looked. Just stay off the street for now and let this thing sink in a bit. I'm keeping my eye out for sympathizers here. Donahue and Jenkins are too. Oh! And they asked me to tell you you're very 'hologenic.'"

I inwardly groan at the pun while everyone else laughs. When are those two *not* attempting to make a joke?

"We're on our way, guys." Jenner says. *"Hamilton and his cronies are already scared shitless."*

"Get ready guys," I say, my calm against his exuberance. *"We've only just begun."*

• • •

Two Days Later:

Commons is a war zone.

I'm scrambling around to pack my bag and get out of this place. A large crash and several bullets erupt outside. I can feel the vibration of the crash below. It's been this way non-stop for days. Commoners fighting Atlas cops. Rebellion breaking out unchecked. Atlas has never sent so many officers to Commons before. And as more cops flood in, more Commoners rebel. Our posters have done exactly what we wanted them to - they've created dissent, inflamed anger, and have given Commoners hope that things can change.

Film disguise on, I check out of the hotel and make my way to the abandoned subway south of town. The streets are flooded with people. No one is working. Everyone, men and women, march along the streets, protesting against the Atlas Police Force

"Return to your homes now!" a voice says over a loud speaker. "Detained criminals will be punished to the full extent of the law."

The warning angers the crowd.

"Then detain us, assholes!" someone yells back.

The noise of the crowd is deafening. My shoulder bumps into people left and right as the crowd marches on and I move in the opposite direction of traffic. They're throwing cans, scraps of metal, anything they can get their hands on towards the fully armed and shielded cops. I make my way to the perimeter of the march, continuing to move in the opposite direction.

Our holographs are bold and bright over every major street corner. On it, the logo and banner of our movement shines.

"Liberty and justice for all!" someone starts to chant.

"Liberty and justice for all!"

The crowd picks up the chant and their voices carry across the block.

"No justice, no peace!" someone yells.

The new chant gets even louder. More and more people start throwing things. I need to get out of this crowd and fast. I pick up my pace, reach the turn I'm looking for, and slip out of sight, down an empty alley. I find the boarded up entrance to the abandoned subway and pull the wood aside. It's dark, wet, and smells dank below. I light my flashlight and make my way down. When I reach the landing, I hear them.

Voices. Grunts. Fists hitting leather and bodies slamming on mats.

A loud crash explodes above, followed by the peal of several bullets. I made it here just in time. I follow the noise until I see the light. On what were once subway platforms, men and women assemble in the abandoned, open space. To my surprise, what I thought would be a small gathering is actually a large encampment of scores upon scores of men and women. Some look young enough to be my kids, others old enough to be my parents. Either way, there are a ton of people training.

"Hey!"

Amongst the crowd, Jenner yells and starts to approach me, his stance aggressive and threatening. I quickly realize my film is still on. I rip it off and grin. "What?"

"Decker! Hey!" His face immediately breaks into a smile and he pulls me into a gruff hug. I look past his shoulder as Nicole and Bill emerge from the group too.

"You made it," she murmurs, pulling me into a hug. "Isn't it crazy out there?"

"Insane," I agree.

I'm about to ask her how she gets to and from Atlas safely when I notice the volume has suddenly dropped. I look past my friends and into the crowd. Everyone is staring at us. They've gone dead silent. A couple of the men jab each other in the side and point to me.

Jenner glances at me and steps up to them. "Yes, this is Decker Channing. We told you guys he would be with us soon and he's arrived."

The crowd erupts in a deafening applause.

It quickly breaks, though, at the sound of another loud crash above. The impact causes dust to fall from the low ceilings above us.

I step forward and cut to the chase. "Thank you all for being here. When Jenner said we had new recruits, I had no idea he meant this many people. You guys are joining an amazing movement and we have the chance to bring change that hasn't happened to this nation in hundreds of years. I look forward to working with you, getting to know you, and preparing you for the battle ahead. We're all risking our lives doing this. And I'm honored to risk mine beside you."

They clap in response, several of them shouting in support. I realize this is a lot like the meeting at the shed, only with a ton more people. I walk right into the crowd and start shaking hands, introducing myself personally to the men and women pledging their support. They cross all ages, all ethnicities, all quarters. I thought I was good with names and faces but at this point, so many have joined that I can only do my best to memorize faces and focus on the names of those working closest to me.

"Alright!" Jenner yells out, "Let's get back to training."

The subway station, though rudimentary and bare, is a pretty decent space for training new recruits. There are old mattresses lined across the floor for safe impact. Punching bags hang from the steel rafters.

Jenner gives me the layout of the land and explains that for the past two days, they've been gaining in number, getting vetted by him and Sam before learning how to fight. I jump right in and start teaching alongside Jenner. Once they get over the shock of seeing me in person, the recruits fall right back into what they were doing, listening to Jenner and I instruct them on shooting, patrol patterns, and hand-to-hand combat. We show them the basics, demonstrate on each other, practice with them, and then watch as they practice on each other. So far, we've been limited to my personal unpermitted handgun for firearm training.

At night, though, Donahue and Jenkins come by and bring their patrol weapons and help train. Just five minutes into watching them teach recruits various offensive moves, I know they're excellent officers. They cut our training workload in half and I especially appreciate them helping us out at night, after a long shift on Atlas during the day. Though jokesters at heart, they take the cause very seriously.

That night, several of us, circle around Bill's small tablet. The news plays, giving an overview of things above.

"Authorities are still unable to trace, much less remove, the holographic posters that have been streaming the propaganda of rebel leader, Decker Channing non-stop for two days. Attempts to shield the propaganda have proved null and void as the holographic posters elevate or shift in order to avoid being obstructed. Holographic experts can't yet determine why the hidden chips have not lost their battery power yet."

Nicole smirks at the screen. "The posters haven't lost their power because the holographic film strips are solar powered. Every day they remain on the walls, they absorb light and charge."

"Commoners in the Factory Quarter and Mechanics Quarter have already started walking out on strikes, assembling illegally and risking both arrest and police discipline. Thousands of rebels on Maids Quarter were arrested throughout the day for vandalism, disturbing the peace, and assaulting Atlas officers."

"Oh, please!" Bill rolls his eyes and turns off the device.

"Ugh!" Jenkins grunts as he slams Donahue's heavy body into the mattress on the ground. They're demonstrating a technique for a group of recruits and there's no other way to do it but make noise.

Several times, the volume has elevated to a level that concerns me.

I turn to Nicole. "Are you sure no one can hear us

down here?"

She nods. "No one uses underground transit anymore. And there aren't any homeless people to occupy it since Eilenwich's crusade against the homeless thirty years ago. But just in case, Dami gave us a sound-proofing spray. We coated the perimeter in it so the place is now sound-proof from the outside."

A sound-proofing spray.

"Is there anything she *can't* do?" I ask in astonishment.

"Sing," she says behind me. I whip around as she and Sam walk in, several brief cases in their hands. They walk over to the table where Bill is stationed with his laptop and monitoring equipment. Somehow, he rigged the old electrical lines to give his computers juice so that he can continue tracking the holographs and other communication lines from this location.

Sam and Dami stack the cases on the table. They snap them open and inside are two opaque white guns, the same color and style of Atlas police guns. She hands me one and to my surprise, it's half the weight of a standard glock.

Sam gives me the run down. "Lighter for easier transportation, less detection, and equipped with self-generating bullets that fall into the chamber when your finger touches the trigger. Auto-locking and steadying technology makes human aim unnecessary for an accurate shot. I figured that feature would help since we can only train so many people so quickly."

"It's perfect," I say, blown away. Yang would kill to

give his officers these.

"I'm producing Sam's design at my facility. How many do you need?" she asks me, her dark eyes pensive.

"Five hundred to start with. Can you do it?" I ask.

"I can do anything."

"Except sing," I remind her.

She laughs at that.

Sam gives Jenner the rundown on the weapon options. With Donahue and Jenkins' help, we decide which recruits get which ones, depending on their skill and ability.

I look at Donahue and Jenkins. "What's the status on the officers? Any sympathizers since the posters have gone out?"

Donahue straightens, a sober expression coloring his normally youthful face. He shakes his head. "So far, no dice. At least not for me." He turns to Jenkins. "You?"

Jenkins shakes his head, his face reddening to match his freckles. "It's so frustrating. Because officers aren't like the rest of Commoners. And we don't want to say anything that could remotely tip us off and lead to you all."

I nod.

"Adams might have had more luck," Donahue says. "I've been working around the clock lately so I haven't caught up with him yet. Have you heard from him?"

I shake my head. "I'm sure I will soon."

The two men nod and head back to do more drills with the recruits.

I turn right as Dami approaches me. She reaches into her pocket and hands me three more small films. "An extra cloak film and two more disguises."

I stuff them in my pocket. "Thanks."

"No problem." She looks around, nodding at the surroundings. "They're getting better."

I know she's referring to the recruits.

"They're deadly now. And once we put one of Sam's guns in their hands, they'll be unstoppable."

She smiles. "Good. How are you doing?"

She asks me the question but every time she does, I know she can already tell how I'm doing. Outside of my mother's ultra-perceptive moments, I've never had someone read me so quickly. So easily. I shrug and reply, "There's a lot to figure out. Not just this 'revolution,'" I quirk my fingers into quotation marks, "But also the aftermath. If we succeed, then what?"

"What do you mean?"

"I mean…what will we do to fix the economy, give Commoners a chance to recover, keep the peace between them and Atlans? What about foreign policy and social justice reform? Which laws need to be reversed and overturned?"

"Everything," she says calmly. We both know that's an exaggeration but not by much. A lot of things need to be rectified - much more than preserved.

I sigh, the weight too heavy for me to bear. "If we win, there's a mountain of changes that need to be made."

"*If* we win," she says. "Which means you should

concern yourself with these *after* the war's been won."

I look at her in amazement. She just took the concerns that have been walloping me over the head and neatly folded them away for later.

"Not to mention," she adds. "The good thing about this campaign is that you're informing the people at the same time you're liberating them. When the time comes to introduce change, they'll likely be on board because they'll already know it needs to happen."

I nod.

"The Bill of Rights is just the start of what you're showing them. The majority of society doesn't know about the founding fathers or their original ideas. By exposing them to the truth, you're ensuring that they'll want it for themselves. A wise man once said, 'You shall know the truth and the truth shall set you free.'"

"I like that quote," I reply. Before I can ask her who said it, she smiles and turns away from me.

"Wait," I say, startled by her abrupt turn. I scramble for a way to keep talking. "Is Dami your full name?"

She blinks at the random question and shakes her head. "It's short for Damilola."

"Which means?"

"'God gave me wealth.'"

I'm surprised. Not many people have religious names in USA.

"And did he?" I ask with a smirk.

She smirks back. "You tell me."

Suddenly a voice behind me asks, "So does that mean

we can call you Lola for short?"

We both look up to see Jenner approaching. I can't put my finger on it but I feel annoyed at the sudden intrusion. We're in a public place but I felt like I was having a moment with her. No one else. I try to shake off his random remark, as well as the fact that he must have been listening several yards away.

She looks slightly jarred by the interruption as well and quickly shakes her head. "Not if you expect me to answer."

He laughs louder than necessary and I refrain from rolling my eyes. He's still attracted to her. This is nothing new. I just can't figure out why my irritation with him skyrockets whenever he expresses it. I tell myself to snap out of it. Jenner is my best friend and Dami and I have nothing going on. If he wants to flirt with her, as clumsily as he's doing it, I have no business getting annoyed by it.

An hour later, I settle in Repair Quarter. Bill offers to let me stay at his place, but I decline, not wanting to crowd his already-cramped space. Or draw suspicion to him in any way. There's already heightened security in all the apartments and hotels. Dami manages to fabricate some I.D. to match the film disguises I wear and I check in without a hitch.

I sit on the bed and turn on the news.

"New propaganda was loaded into the holographic posters authorities are *still* trying to remove on Commons. In the recent video, rebel leader Decker Channing calls for President Hamilton's removal from office."

The footage cuts to the message we recorded hours

earlier. In it, I look at an unseen audience and clearly say, *"Things can never be better with the status quo. A president who should have only been in office for eight years, a precedence started by the country's first president, has been running things into the ground for twenty-eight years. That's not a democratic president. That's a tyrant."*

"I don't know what all the fuss is about," a pretentious voice says over the footage. The screen cuts to an Atlan woman being interviewed near Atlas Park. "These people live in one of the wealthiest nations in the world and they're protesting. For what?"

Is she serious?

"I find the whole thing rather barbaric." The screen cuts to an Atlan man. "With Hamilton in office, the unemployment rate is at zero. That has never happened in the history of this nation."

What the idiot fails to mention is what happens to the homeless, disabled, or injured who are unable to work and don't have wealthy or decent families to support them. When a Commoner is unable to work, for whatever reason, they are at the mercy of their relatives' provision. There's no such thing as government aid for the poorest of the poor. And if the poor person happens to have no family or friends to take them in, the individual is given two options: either check in at the Atlas Hospital to be *released* of the cares of this world or be sent to The Gauntlet to face a much slower, excruciating *release*. The release is inevitable - the mode of release is up to them.

When my mother injured her back and was unable to

work, I had just joined the Force. By some miracle, I started earning an income right as hers went out the window. I shudder to think what would have happened if she'd injured herself just a year earlier. All of our extended family is dead. My thoughts snap out of the rabbit trail in time to hear the anchor say, "President Hamilton insists that the annual President's Ball will still occur in the same place at the same time."

Music to my ears.

Hamilton appears on screen, answering reporters, "We will not be intimidated by a bunch of self-righteous terrorists."

I turn off the TV. It's just like Atlans to deny the plight of the people working for them. And it's just like Hamilton to let his hubris get in the way of common sense. Yang is probably pleading with him to change the venue, style, format, *anything* regarding the President's Ball. And he won't. Because it's more important to him to send us a message that he will not be intimidated or moved by our revolt.

And that suits me just fine.

I leave the room an hour later and meet Jenner at the training site for the Repair recruits. It's late. I've only had a quick nap and I'm tired from working with the recruits on Maids but we have to keep moving and we have to keep training. Donahue and Jenkins are staying behind to give them some last tips but Jenner and I are starting on new blood.

Something tells me Jenner and Bill must have had a

talk with them because when I walk in, though slightly unnerved, the men don't waste too much time gawking at me. They get in their formations and start doing drills. We train them like we did the others on Maids Quarter, this time using some of the guns Dami and Sam managed to produce in such a short time.

I can do anything she told me. She's proving herself right.

"They're really good," I murmur to Jenner, voice low. He looks at me and nods, smiling. I don't have to say anything else - he knows I'm very happy with the progress.

"They catch on quick. Quicker than the guys - and gals - in Maids. But the recruits in Maids can handle themselves now. They're also armed. Half the men here are armed and the weapons for Mechanics and Factory should be done tomorrow evening in time for their training."

"Excellent," I reply. "Have you heard from Adams yet?"

Jenner shakes his head, worry clouding his blue eyes. They widen at something he sees behind me and he quickly shouts, "Decker, look out!"

I turn in time to see a man bee-line straight to me. Before I can get in any sort of defensive position, he reaches up and rips the film off his neck, revealing his true identity.

"Adams!" I'm so relieved to see him, I don't hesitate to give him a friendly hug.

Jenner greets him next. "We've been waiting to hear

from you."

He nods. "I'm sorry. I've been waiting in the hopes I could give you good news." He glances at the recruits behind us and pulls us further aside. "Hamilton and Yang have been working overtime to mind trip the Force. Convince them that it's us against them."

I nod. "There was already that mentality building while I was there. You know that."

Jenner nods. "Same here. It wasn't as bad when Stanton was around but now it's out of control."

Adams nods. "Well, it's only gotten worse. I've been trying to get a feel for who could join without giving myself or the whole cause away. I have yet to find any sympathizers. It's strange…" His face twists in confusion. "They live on Commons but don't see themselves completely as Commoners."

"Atlas ass-kissing shits," Jenner curses. He looks like he's about to pop a vein, he's so pissed.

I'm already over it. "If there's no one to join, there's no one to join. The question is what do we do now? Because our whole plan hinged on those guards turning against Hamilton. On the Force taking our side."

And we have less than three days until the ball.

• • •

The next morning, the same question is still pulsing through my mind.

I pace the hotel room, mulling over the issue and trying to find a solution. I'm so focused on the problem, I can't eat my breakfast. Jenner, who meets with the recruits in a few minutes, has no problem eating it for me.

"What if we attacked the Police Quarter?" he suggests. "A preemptive strike."

I get his logic: wipe them out before they can interfere with the operation. But I shake my head.

"Hamilton would be forced to cancel the President's Ball. If that happens, he and the entire government scatter to safer ground, far away from us and our ability to get rid of them."

And we *have* to get rid of them.

"But what happens if we succeed and a highly trained, highly armed contingent is after us?" Jenner counters. "You can start packing for The Gauntlet now because that's where we'll all wind up if Yang gets his way."

I swipe a heavy hand across my face, feeling overwhelmed yet again.

What I wouldn't give to have Dami next me, figuring this out. I frown at that. When did *she* become my go-to solution for issues with the cause? Or simply issues with my nerves.

"Atlas shits," Jenner mutters around his food. "The most selfish, ruthless, despicable people to walk this earth. All they care about is money. Wave a dollar bill over their carcass and they'll rise from the dead."

I shake my head. "They're not *all* that bad. Look at the Washingtons. And Dami."

He shakes his head. "Exceptions. I don't trust Atlans as far as I can throw them." His voice lowers. "It's us against them."

I frown at that, unsure of what to say.

I walk to the window overlooking the street below. Officers line the streets like dominoes ready to fall atop each other. They're all dressed in white with conspicuous guns fastened in front of their hands like unwanted presents for the Commoners who live here. My eyes drift to a young family walking along the dirt-crusted sidewalk. The mother lifts a young boy, only a toddler, onto her hip and laughs as his father tickles the boy, sending him into a fit of giggles against his mother's chest. All three of them are laughing - a rare sight for anyone on Commons.

What would it be like for everyone to experience that joy? That breath of fresh air?

I want that for Commoners and Atlans alike.

The family walks to the end of the block and makes a turn, eclipsing themselves from my sight. My eyes shift and catch the sight of the guarding officers moving from their posts.

All of them.

Their cadence and stride quickly turn into a full on run.

"Jenner, look at this."

All of them are picking up speed, so much so that the civilians notice too. I look beyond the horizon and see several Atlas Police helicopter wings spinning on the tops of buildings, ready for takeoff. The cops are running into those helicopters.

Jenner joins me at the window. "They're retreating?"

"Looks like it," I mutter, looking beyond the helicopters. I look at the sky and see other helicopters coming in - these ones different in shape and scale.

"What are *those*?" Jenner asks, mystified.

They look familiar to me but I don't know why. I rack my brain trying to remember where I saw these types of helicopters before. A book? A movie? No… TV. On the news when…

"Oh my God." Fear paralyzes me. "Oh my God…"

But not for long.

I back away from the window, glance at Jenner, and grab him by the arms.

"We have to go! *Now*!"

He looks at me, alarmed. "What is it?"

"They're bombing us," I reply, booking it for the door, shoving him out into the hall.

"*What?*" Jenner asks in disbelief. He runs down the stairwell behind me, past the lobby and into the street. The cops are all gone. Only civilians wander about the streets.

"Those are bomber helicopters," I explain. "I saw them on the news when there was a skirmish with Iran."

USA wiped the country off the map. Nuked them completely.

"We have to get underground, Jenner." It's our only shot.

"Training is six blocks south," he replies.

I shake my head. "No time."

I look around frantically, searching for another

abandoned subway entrance.

Suddenly Jenner yells, "There!"

He points to a boarded up entrance two blocks ahead, across the street. I follow him as he hightails it to the entrance. Suddenly, something blinks from the corner of my eye. I immediately zero in on it: it's a small round device latched onto the brick face of the building Jenner is about to run in front of. A red dot flashes in the center of it and suddenly turns green.

"Jenner, look out!" I don't even think about it. Just run over to him, over to the triggered device, and throw myself into his body, knocking the both of us down as the thing goes off. A loud, mind-numbing explosion accompanies the earth shattering vibration that knocks us clear off of the road.

My head hits something hard and the last thing I can recall is Jenner screaming.

"Decker! Decker!"

Everything fades to black.

THE STEEL WALL IS RISING
Jennifer Womack
Daily Mail UK
26 January 2600

People worldwide have just thirty days left to either enter or exit USA. In one of his first measures as the nation's new leader, President Victor Hamilton, alongside Congress, has announced that USA will permanently seal its borders and end immigration to or from the nation starting February 25 of this year.

The measure comes as no surprise to foreign diplomats. Hamilton has been very vocal about his plans to continue the agenda of his predecessor, former President Richard Rudolph Eilenwich. Eilenwich announced USA's withdrawal of foreign aid and diplomatic representatives exactly two years ago, breaking away from the UN acrimoniously. Having left the world stage of politics and economy in favor of domestic priorities, China has since stepped forth as the world's latest super power nation - though it has yet to challenge its lethal predecessor militarily.

Those considering a permanent move to USA should know the recent state of the nation, far removed from what it was known for centuries ago. Divided into two major territories, Atlas and Commons, a symbiotic economy exists on USA where the skilled workers of Commons serve the extremely wealthy on Atlas.

Though making up more than 90% of the population, Commoners buy all of their resources: food, clothing, shelter, utilities, and basic supplies from wealthy, and some say overpriced, Atlan monopolies. Prices increase to accommodate Atlan wealth while wages stay the same to the detriment of Commoner income. The extractive economic cycle is enough to fund Atlan prosperity without the assistance of foreign trade - something President Eilenwich realized when he announced USA's diplomatic withdrawal.

The UN cautions people worldwide: immigration into USA is not advised - not unless one can guarantee they will live and work on Atlas.

"He who neglects his duty to his Maker may well be expected to be deficient and insincere in his duty towards the public."

-Abigail Adams

CHAPTER ELEVEN

I wake up in a dark unfamiliar bedroom, soft pillows plush against my head.

There's a dull throbbing pain on the back of my head. I look around and to remember where I am, how I got here. I sit up suddenly and pain explodes through my skull, turning the room a dizzying white right before my eyes. I gasp against the pain and close my eyes, hoping it'll abate the rising nausea.

"Shh," I hear as two soft but firm hands push me down by my shoulders back onto the pillow. "Breathe."

I immediately recognize the voice. I open my eyes and see Dami sitting beside me with a gentle, nurturing smile. I'm almost embarrassed at the sudden rush of relief I feel.

"Shh," she repeats. "You're alright. You're safe."

Even if I wasn't, something tells me her presence would calm me anyway. I'm finding it more and more disturbing how she does that. How being around her immediately soothes me. How I long for her presence when I'm stressed and she's not around. Even when I'm in a good mood, I want her there. I try to remember the last thing I was doing before I ended up here. As soon as it comes to me, I open my mouth to ask but she cuts me off with-

"Jenner is fine. He's in the next room with Nicole and everyone else. He pulled you underground after that planted bomb near your hotel went off. I don't know how you did it, but you managed to get both yourself and Jenner out of direct reach of the blast. Otherwise, neither of you would have survived."

Something in her voice changes when she says that but the room is so dark, I can't see her face clearly. I reach up and feel the heavy pad of gauze wrapped around my head.

"Do I still have hair?" I ask her.

She laughs, as if pleasantly surprised by my joke. Well, I'm only half-joking.

She nods. "I only cleaned and dressed the wound, Decker. I didn't perform surgery."

"Good." I smile and stretch stiffly.

I keep feeling the gauze until she finally reaches up and gently moves my hand. "The MRI and x-rays I took show no broken bones. Just a couple fractured ribs and you had heavy bleeding on the back of your head. You have a hard skull. Most would have cracked open at the impact."

A shudder goes through me at the reminder of how close I came to dying.

"They attacked us, didn't they?" I ask her. "Atlas."

She nods, the shadows of the room hiding her expression. But I can hear the turmoil in her voice.

"A lot of people died, Decker. The hotel you were

staying in collapsed. You could have..." her voice trails off. She doesn't say anything else. I don't say anything either.

I just look at her.

Because the more I look, the calmer I feel. I can barely make out her dark eyes in this dark room but I'm glad I'm here with her. Just the two of us.

She starts to shift uncomfortably under my silent stare. "Say something. How are you feeling?"

"Like shit." I tell her honestly. "But I'm alive. Thanks to you."

She smiles and shakes her head, her pretty afro moving just slightly. "It was Jenner who managed to drag you underground before the helicopter released their bombs. He saved you, not me. Then again, you saved him earlier."

"It doesn't matter who saved who. I'd be dead if I didn't get the right treatment."

"I'm not the Healer," she says quietly.

I frown at that. What does she mean by that? Something tells me not to ask and she doesn't offer to explain.

"Where am I?" I finally ask.

"Danielton. My second office and facility."

"You *own* property on Danielton?" I almost sit up in astonishment but she catches me by the shoulders again.

I've never heard of such a thing. Not even the wealthiest of Atlans can purchase acreage on Danielton, USA's factory island - and they *have* tried - going so far as to take it to the Supreme Court for their "right" to purchase whatever they want. It was one of the few rulings that gave this Commoner satisfaction. Rarely do Atlans get told they can't buy everything.

"How the hell did you get property on this island?" I ask her, still reeling.

"I inherited it…"she trails off. "I'll tell you about it later."

She turns to the side table and pours something in a cup. She gives it to me when she's done and I drink a syrup that tastes sweet and fruity. "What is it?"

"Atlas Serum."

"I've never heard of it."

"You wouldn't," she replies. "Only Atlans have access to it. It'll help increase the speed of your healing. I thought of giving it to you intravenously but I figured you could wake up and just drink it."

I grunt my appreciation. "I hate needles."

She smiles. "Who would have thought? Big Bad Decker does have fears."

"You know most of them by now."

I hold her gaze and she holds mine. My eyes have adjusted to the dark and I can see hers clearly now. She looks nervous. Scared. Not at the situation but at the way I'm looking at her. And I know why. I'm communicating something to her I myself am scared to put into words. Maybe because they're words I've never spoken to another woman. Words I never thought I'd say to *any* woman, much less one I just met days ago.

I guess I'm scared too.

Because I've never had all of my spare thoughts go to a

person who wasn't in the same room. I've never been intrigued, excited, and bowled over with respect for anyone all at the same time. I've never felt my heart race to the point where it feels like it's about to explode just because that person entered the room. And I've never felt like someone took a torch to my chest by simply leaving my presence and going about her business.

While everyone else has been climbing down my neck with mission concerns and tactical strategies, she's been here, providing solutions, giving support, easing burdens, and preserving my sanity. But I don't want her for all that she does for me - all that she brings to me without even trying. I want her because *she's her*. I want to somehow inhale her into myself, keep her safe and never let her go. I thought my greatest achievement in life would be succeeding in this mission. But it completely pales in comparison to having the woman in front of me be *mine*.

That's how much she means to me.

How is this possible in just a few short days? Is it the revolution? Is everything else that's going on causing my feelings to heighten irrationally?

I don't think it is.

Something tells me that if we happened to meet in any other context, any humdrum circumstance...I would still find her as enchanting as I do now and just as soon. I want her. And I'm pretty sure she wants me.

When she looks away from my silent regard, I can tell she isn't ready.

I try anyway. "Dami-"

"The rest of the team is eager to see you," she says. "Are you up for it or do you want to rest some more?"

What I want to do is tell her the truth. But I can see the fear in her eyes.

What is she so afraid of?

My desire to tell her is now burning inside of me but I will myself to wait.

I sigh and slowly nod. "I'm up for it."

This time she helps me rise, but not before cautioning me to go as *slowly* as possible. That's not too hard for me to do. It turns out I'm sore all over - not just on my head - but I can move stiffly. I rise to my feet and follow her to the next room. Not there yet, I can already hear everyone talking over each other in a panic. I almost want to turn and go back to bed but I push myself to stay and take in all of my surroundings. When we walk in, we're in another state of the art lab, even more elaborate than the one she has on Atlas.

"Dim lights," she says to the computerized room. The lights immediately dim to a level my pounding head can handle. Everyone falls silent when we enter.

Not as dim as the bedroom, I can still see everyone clearly. Nicole rushes up to me and hugs me gingerly. "Thank goodness you're alright!"

Jenner's next. He sighs in relief and gives me a gruff hug. If he notices my sharp inhale at the less than careful move, he doesn't say anything. Instead he tells me, "You scared me for a second."

I look him over. He has several cuts all over his face

and his clothes are torn, dirty and tattered but he looks better than I feel. "I heard you saved me," I tell him. "Thanks."

"You saved us both. Good looking out."

"Is Adams alright?" I ask.

He nods. "He called us an hour ago. Said he'd tried to warn us on our phones but-"

"I didn't have mine on this morning."

"Neither did I."

He pauses, struggling for words. I feel a sense of premonition as I wait for him to speak.

"Donahue and Jenkins are missing. Adams and some officers are searching for them as we speak."

The words hit me like a blow to the jaw.

Silence washes over the room. My heart races at the thought of something happening to those two. I can still envision Donahue's impish grin and Jenkins' shock of red hair. Of all the people Jenner and Adams brought to the shed that night, why do those two have to be missing? They've only been on the Force a few weeks. They're not even twenty-years-old yet. It was foolish of me to think everyone on our side would make it out unscathed but these two...they have their whole lives ahead of them. They're too young to die.

I sigh. "All we can do is hope that they find them."

Alive.

I look past him at Sam, Sarah and Bill. They all look very rattled. Bill especially.

"You okay?" I ask him.

He looks at me, his dark blue eyes troubled. "They bombed my apartment." His voice doesn't even sound like his voice. "I'm normally there most days. If Nicole hadn't asked me to check some stuff at her office…"

Sarah goes to him, laying a soothing hand on his shoulder. "But she did. And you're alright."

She then pulls him into a tight hug, one he returns rather intimately. I look at Jenner and Nicole in surprise. The pair shrugs. Apparently I'm the only one who didn't know about their budding relationship. For some reason my eyes swing to Dami, who glances at me before looking at the rest of them.

"You need to show him what Hamilton said."

The hairs rise on the back of my neck as the room falls silent again. Dark expressions shadow them all. Nicole nods and walks over to the consul, pulling up a video on the massive lab screen. It's a recording of the news.

Immediately, footage shows what was once an overcrowded town, now completely desolate and burning. I can't even tell with quarter it is, it's so disfigured. Large buildings that stood strong now look like melting molds of wax, charred inside out. Smoke rises from every block and not a single person can be seen on the ground. They've either all been killed, are dying under the rubble, or somehow managed to escape. I hope Donahue and Jenkins are in the last category.

"Authorities haven't been able to secure a toll on the amount of deaths since the attack on Commons. At 9:42 this morning, Atlas Police, under the order of President

Hamilton, released several overhead explosives on four of the five quarters. A number of explosives were already planted by guarding officers on field before their sudden retreat. The scale of the destruction is massive in the majority of quarters, but the Police Quarter remains untouched."

President Hamilton's face suddenly appears. His expression is grim, his green eyes calm, as he stands at the presidential podium and speaks to the media. "In light of today's events, I realize that many citizens watching this are reeling in shock, horror, and possibly even disgust that I would order our very own Police Force to carry out such aggressive acts. I want all USA citizens to ponder the meaning of the name *Atlas*."

I frown at that and step closer to the screen.

"Atlas was a mythological god who carried the world on his shoulders. It was a heavy, daunting task that was actually given to him by Zeus as punishment for his rebellion against the other gods of Olympus."

"What the hell is he talking about?" Jenner sneers.

He may not get it, but I immediately know where this man is going.

"We on Atlas function very much the same way for USA. In fact you could say we *are* the Atlas of USA. We start businesses, fund enterprises, and employee all the citizens who live on Commons. Without the Atlans of this nation, there wouldn't be any Commoners alive."

I hear the small outburst of my team around me but keep looking, keep my eyes focused on the screen. They've seen this before and yet it seems to agitate them all over again. I remain calm.

"Commons needs Atlas in order to survive. And like a parent swatting a child's hand before they *really* get burned, what happened this morning is what I'm determined to call 'Atlas Discipline.'"

The protests of those around me grow so loud I have to shush my team. "Quiet. Let me hear."

He continues, "I do not relish the idea of hurting, and even killing, so many people. Most Commoners are peaceful, hardworking, respectful citizens. Unfortunately, some Commoners, in various quarters, are aiding and abetting a known criminal, Decker Channing. And far too many are supporting his treasonous rebellion, opting to riot in favor of him rather than working in the jobs Atlas has so graciously provided this nation. It is the rash actions of a few that have so poisoned Commons relationship with Atlas. And we want to see that relationship restored."

"Yeah," Nicole murmurs sarcastically. "Like a master to his slave."

"In light of the rebellion of Decker Channing and his followers, all wages will be reduced by half until further notice." My stomach drops. "No aid will be sent to help Commons recover so long as there is an active rebellion afloat. I strongly encourage Commons to surrender Decker Channing over to the police so that no more will have to suffer."

I shake my head in disbelief. He's cutting them off at the knees. He's cutting the wages just to send the people into starvation or even homelessness once more.

"Atlas," Hamilton concludes, "is very close to shrugging. While we value the hard work of Commoners, we ultimately don't need the labor in the long run. Computerized assistance can work wonders. But I want Commoners to think long and hard about allowing Atlas to shrug it. This punishment is a taste of what will happen if we do."

His eyes move from scanning the media around him, to landing on the camera dead in front of him. His green eyes bore into the screen.

"If Decker Channing is watching, I implore you: turn yourself in before anyone else has to die for your rebellion. I will give you forty-eight hours."

I have no doubt that he's serious.

The screen shuts off and I immediately look away. As disturbing as his words were, I find it more disturbing how he delivered them. Calm. Napalm. Completely cold and unfeeling about what he's just done to millions of innocent people. If those forty-eight hours pass without him getting what he wants, he *will* retaliate. And he'll follow through on every one of his threats, possibly sinking us the way USA did Iran only years ago. I remember that young family I saw just minutes before the attack. Did the little boy survive? Did his parents?

"I have to go in." The words fly out of my mouth and are quickly drowned by a sea of protests.

"What?" Bill exclaims.

"You're not going anywhere," Nicole says.

"Over my dead body!" Jenner challenges.

I hold up my hands to silence their pleas. "If that was just a warning strike, do you know how bad it will be if they launch a full-scale attack?"

They all fall silent, unable to fight my logic.

"I have to go in. If I don't, more people will die."

There's a moment of silence.

"'The tree of liberty must be refreshed from time to time with the blood of patriots and tyrants. It is its natural manure.'"

I turn to Dami and find her dark pensive eyes anchoring mine.

"Thomas Jefferson," I say.

She nods. "Not once did Washington, Adams, Jefferson, or any other revolutionary throw up their hands and quit because their soldiers and civilians died. They pushed through. If you turn yourself in now, Decker, you *will* die. And this cause will die right alongside you. And all of the deaths that have already happened will have been in vain. Do you want that?"

"Of course not!" I reply, heat flooding my face.

"Then stay the course," she tells me, her eyes smoldering with something I can't identify. "All hands are on deck. Don't you dare jump ship."

We hold each other's gaze for several tense moments. Her words steady me and I'm calm again. She's right. The only way to honor the dead is to push through and make their sacrifice worth it. I can't fold now. Because if I fold, that leaves USA the same as it was before - actually, it leaves it worse off. Commoners will forever fear maniacal, ruthless leaders like Hamilton, who carelessly try to crush their spirit under his heel. I'll be damned if I contribute to his tyranny.

"Okay," I turn to the team. "This is what we're going to do..."

The plan forms in my mind as I say it aloud to them. We need to set up provisions and protection for the surviving Commoners. I decide that we'll create barracks in the underground training facilities at each quarter. The trained recruits will shield the barracks while some care for the injured inside.

"That means we need to get the rest of the weapons to them *now*." I conclude.

Dami, Sam, and Jenner start packing guns in crates. I haven't had a chance to look at the rest of the facility but I can already tell it's large. The three of them go down an elevator to the area of the lab where Sam manufactured the guns. While they attend to the weapons, Nicole, Sarah and Bill set up for filming my rebuttal.

"This is a critical time," Nicole says. "Revolutions can be invigorated or annihilated by attacks like this. If you wield what happened properly, you'll have all of Commons and maybe even some of Atlas on your side. The people want to know what you'll do."

I sit down and start to write, the pressure of the moment weighing heavily on my shoulders. As well as the guilt.

I had no idea that two little words to Jenner - *"I'm in"* -

would result in so much carnage and loss. I'm horrified by Hamilton's actions, shocked by his ruthlessness. And angry. Angry that Commoner lives mean so little to him. So little to Atlas.

The rest of the team comes back up with crates upon crates of guns.

"How are you going to get it to them?" I ask.

Sam explains. "Dami's hover car. It's the same one we used to get you off Commons. Dami installed a holographic chip that can render the vehicle invisible to cameras and live sight."

I look at her and shake my head. Nothing should surprise me at this point.

"How are you not working for the government?" I ask.

"Long story," she replies.

I want to hear it.

Jenner says, "Sam and I will fly into Factory then cross into Mechanics and deliver as many as we can. There's a second batch downstairs - we'll come and get it when we're done."

They take off.

"Hey." I look up and find Dami standing over me. "How you feeling?"

I pause and realize that the pain is gone. It's been gone for a while now, I've just been too busy answering questions and focusing on the Commoners.

"Better," I say. I still as she reaches over and checks the wound on the back of my head. She starts to remove the gauze when Nicole stops her.

"Don't. We need them to see that he's injured. That he took a hit and was in the thick of it."

Dami nods and refolds the material over my head. She looks at me and smiles slightly. "You can take it off when you're done filming. The wounds have healed."

"Already?" I ask, highly doubtful.

"I told you that serum would speed up your healing."

I hand Nicole my speech.

"This is brilliant!" I hear her exclaim. Hear because I can't detach myself from the other woman's deep dark eyes. I hear Nicole pass the speech to Bill and Sarah, who talk about graphics.

"What is it?" Dami finally asks. "You're still discouraged. Why?"

I marvel at her ability to perceive what's going on in others even when they don't speak - even when they try to *hide* their feelings from others. Like I am.

"I'm worried," I admit to her. "Adams said the cops weren't on board for the President's Ball and based on their attack, I doubt they ever will be. I'm worried we won't get the weapons out to recruits in time and that they'll be unable to secure the barracks. And even if they do manage all this, the survivors need to eat. Many of them are also injured. How are we going to get enough food and medical supplies to care for them?"

She smiles.

"What?"

"Don't you see? That's the type of leader USA needs. A leader who thinks of his people."

"That doesn't solve the problem-"

"So the cops aren't joining. So what? You have four quarters' worth of men and women trained and willing to fight. Storm the hall if you have to and execute your plan. Yes, more people will die and yes, it'll be a lot more complicated than having an 'in' with the guards...but do what you have to. You have enough manpower to succeed."

I watch her, admiring the fierce determination that overtakes her normally gentle features.

She continues, "Don't worry about the weapons. Jenner and Sam are stocking up Factory with them and will be back to deliver the goods to Mechanics soon. I packed several first aid kits with the weapons and several bottles of the Atlas Serum I gave you. That should help with even the most severe of injuries. You'll have to trust the recruits you trained to do their best. Hopefully it will be good enough."

"And the food?" I ask. She's ticked off everything but that major concern.

"Don't worry about the food," she replies. "I know where we can get some."

I frown. "*How*? What - are you a farmer too?"

She smiles cryptically just as Bill announces, "You guys are going to have to give me time. More than eighty percent of the holographs are damaged or destroyed. And everyone is underground now thanks to Hamilton's attack."

"How are we going to reach them?" Nicole asks.

"I've been studying ADC's new firewall since our first flyer. There's a way to get around their security and reach people's personal devices again but it would mean Decker giving his speech live. It doesn't allow for pre-recorded content."

All eyes turn to me. I probably should be nervous. All the correspondence I've done to the public has been through well-prepared, pre-recorded messages with a professional PR expert and graphic designer to help me look good. But for some reason, the prospect of me speaking to Commoners and Atlans live doesn't scare me. In fact, the more I think about it, the more I want to do something entirely different…but I'm not sure it would be the wisest or safest decision. I decide to stick with their plan.

"I'm ready when you are," I tell him.

He nods. "Give me thirty."

Nicole and Sarah break into yet another conversation about how to set up the shot without giving our location away. Dami nudges me with her elbow. "Hungry?"

She leads me up the elevator to the main floor of the compound. It's even larger than I expected, grander than Mrs. Washington's Atlas apartment. Light floods the open living space, reminding me that it's only the afternoon. So much has happened, it feels like it should be night. I follow her to her kitchen and sit on the barstool while she makes us both some sandwiches. All with fresh ingredients.

"Let's eat out back," she says. "You could use some

fresh air."

Her backyard is even more magnificent than the compound. It must be seated on the edge of Danielton, tucked behind the only remaining forested region of the island. A small clean stream runs along jagged rocks that line the base of the home...office...whatever she calls it. It's peaceful here. Beautiful.

I start in on my sandwich, relishing the savory delicious taste. "I could live here, you know. Just forget everything and stay put."

She nods, an understanding look on her face. She looks even more beautiful in natural light than the harsh bright fluorescents of her lab.

"I tried doing that. It only works for so long."

"How did you get this place, Dami?" I ask bluntly.

She meets my eyes and replies, "I inherited it. While I was attending Columbia, I started interning for a man named Gerald Petre. He created-"

"Petre Automations."

She nods. Everyone knows the name Petre. Petre Automations single-handedly transformed the hover car industry, merging the outdated fuel-run technology with solar power engine panels to make the vehicles permanently reliant on nothing but the sun to run. The panels preserve enough of the energy to keep the cars running, even at night. Petre also single-handedly eliminated the need for gas and much of the oil USA was paying through the nose for. Many give him partial credit for the independence from oil that spurred Eilenwich's decision to withdraw USA from the diplomatic scene.

I watch Dami closely as she explains, "Mr. Petre took me under his wing. He saw potential that I couldn't see and pushed me to keep inventing, keep trying, keep working on the ideas I had buzzing around in my head. He gave me full access to his labs on Atlas and brought me out here on occasion for day trips."

I frown slightly, not wanting to let my mind go there but...

She notices the look on my face and immediately adds, "Nothing inappropriate happened. He genuinely wanted to mentor me and teach me everything he knew. I didn't know why at first...until a year after Sam joined us."

I wait.

"He informed me that he had terminal stage four lymphoma and would be out of time in a matter of weeks. For three years, he'd kept this from me, fighting the disease in secret, training me when he felt well. He liked Sam but he made it clear that he'd invested all those years training *me* so that I would one day inherit Petre Automations, his labs, and all of his wealth."

"Why you?" I ask gently. I can see her starting to tear up at her loss. He sounds more like a father figure to her than a mentor.

"I asked him the same thing. That's when he revealed that he used to know my mother. He was her patient for a number of years. She talked about me all the time and even introduced us when I was little but I don't remember. He said that when he learned who I was and the field I moved in to, he couldn't resist helping Dr. Aderele's daughter. In time, he started to view me as his own. He died two years ago."

"I'm sorry," I say plainly. She swipes at her tears with the back of her hands.

"Gerald Petre was the great-great grandson of Daniel Sorronto. As the founder of Danielton, Sorronto maintained the right to keep this property private for him and future descendants. That's how this place became mine."

I nod and we both fall silent for several long minutes.

"Thanks for telling me," I finally say.

She gives a weak chuckle. "I'm always telling you things."

Our eyes meet and don't move. It's the first time she's acknowledged that I affect her too.

I'm glad.

She stands and gestures back to the compound. "Let me show you the food solution."

Minutes later, we're in another wing of the estate, underground in what feels like an enormous freezer. Dami turns on the lights and my eyes round to saucers. Rows upon rows of food - *fresh* food - line the room in neat succession. Lettuce, tomatoes, fruits, and flour.

"Shortly after Mr. Petre died, Sam and I discovered a small greenhouse on the western wing of this compound. We had no idea Mr. Petre liked to produce his own food. The place was overgrown and messy but Sam cleaned it up, started cultivating it and in time, the produce started growing beyond our ability to eat it on our own. Sam would give the Washingtons, Sarah, and others the extra but even they couldn't consume the full batch. I didn't want the food to go to waste so I created this cryogenic vault for the excess. Now Sam stores whatever's left over from what he can't give away. It's supposed to last for up to five years. This might be enough to feed them."

It is enough. My eyes take in what has to be thousands of pounds worth of fresh, perfectly preserved food, and I know this will be enough to feed all of the people in the barracks, so long as they ration it out. When I take my eyes off the food, I find her looking at me, her expression indiscernible. Her beautiful dark eyes gazing into mine.

"You're incredible," I whisper. Because I can't think of anything else to say.

She shrugs and looks away from me. I wonder what she sees that makes her turn self-conscious. "That's what I'm here for. To be useful."

I frown at that and quickly shake my head. "Dami, I don't see you as some resource."

I need her to understand this.

"An asset, yes. Essential to this cause? Absolutely. But I hope you realize that you mean much *more* to me than anything relating to what we're doing here. I value you *for you*."

I tip her chin and force her to make eye contact with me. "I was drawn to you long before I ever knew what you could do."

There. I said it.

I want her.

She looks into my eyes and shakes her head. "This is *crazy*. I've only known you-"

"A few days. I know."

"This can't be happening."

I stroke her chin softly. "It already has."

I can't explain why or how but it has.

I can feel her chin start to tremble under my finger.

"Decker…" her words break off but her eyes remain locked with mine, pleading for me to do something she seems too afraid to ask for. We gravitate closer together, two magnets unable to pull any other direction. I don't know when my eyes close but shortly after, I give in to the intoxicating sensation of her full soft lips against mine. I pull her fully into my arms and pour everything I feel into our kiss. Her floral scent floods my senses and sends me reeling as I hold her tighter. She reaches up and caresses my cheek, her fingers soft and gentle - just like her.

Desire explodes from the very center of my being. I pull her closer to me, trying to eliminate any inch of space between us. I want her so badly, I physically ache with longing. I stroke the length of her slender back and explore the crevice of her mouth with my tongue. Her lips are so soft, she tastes so good. It's like a bucket of cold water thrown on me when she suddenly pulls back.

"Please stop," she pants, struggling for control. She yanks herself out of my arms with a strength that surprises us both.

I look at her, confused, my heart pounding out of my

chest. "What is it? What's wrong?"

"I can't do this," she says, shaking her head adamantly. She refuses to meet my eyes but as she regains control, I see a very clear emotion on her face. Fear.

"Hey," I say gently, approaching her slowly. She moves back, out of my reach and I stop. "Dami, what is it? Was I coming on too strong? What did I do wrong?"

She shakes her head. "It's not you. It's me. I shouldn't have done that. I don't want to lead you on."

I straighten, feeling burned.

"I thought you felt what I-"

"I do." Her words give me hope again.

"Then why-?"

"Because I can't give you what you'd want."

I look at her for a moment, surprised by this side of her. She still won't look me in the eye and she seems afraid to come out and say what's really on her mind. It occurs to me that this is the first time I'm seeing a flaw in Dami. Up until this point, she was perfect in my eyes. But she's not perfect. She's real, with fears and insecurities and communication issues to match. Who knows what other quirks and issues she has that I have yet to discover. And yet the realization that she's human, just like the rest of us, doesn't disappoint me in the slightest. If anything, it makes me want her even more.

"What do you mean you can't give me what I'd want?" I ask her. "Do you mean sex?"

Her eyes snap up to mine and a look of terror crosses her face.

I think I understand. "Dami," I clear the air right away. "I wasn't trying to have sex with you. I hope I didn't communicate that from a kiss. I would *never* try to force myself on you."

We've only known each other a few days, for goodness sake!

She nods, looking slightly relieved. "I didn't think you were."

"Then why did you pull away from my kiss? You want me. I want you. What happened?"

She shakes her head, the fear returning to her eyes. "I can't…I'm sorry. I can't tell you."

I look at her for a moment, trying to make sense of what she simply won't say. She's kind. She always considers other people. I'm not used to having to read between the lines but the only guess I can come up with is that she can't think of a way to tell me the truth.

She doesn't want me - regardless of her claims otherwise.

It's not fair for me to keep pushing. I look away from her just as she manages to meet my eyes. "I didn't mean to push myself on you."

"What?" she exclaims, looking surprised. "You didn't! Decker, I want you."

I shake my head, convinced of the opposite. "I don't think you do."

"Wait! Decker-"

But I don't wait to hear anything else. I should but I don't. I can't bear the thought of her inadvertently saying yet another thing that confirms her rejection. I read her all wrong. And in the process made a fool of myself. I find my own way back to the lab, where the Nicole, Bill and Sarah wait with the camera ready. Somehow I'm able to hide all the turmoil I feel. I cut off the hurt and focus on the task at hand.

"Change of plans," I tell them, finally deciding on the idea I've been toying with.

"What do you mean?" Nicole asks warily. "Decker, the people need to see you speak."

"You're right," I reply. "They do need to see me. But not through a tiny phone. I'm going to Commons. I'm going to deliver the speech in person."

"Are you insane?" Jenner bellows through the phone. It's telepathic but he still somehow manages to scream into all our ears.

"It's too late to argue," Nicole replies. *"We're already packing the second hover car. We're bringing the rest of the weapons and medicine, too. Most of the survivors are in Factory, right?"*

We can all hear him huffing and puffing mentally before he bites out, *"Yeah. We just finished assigning the weapons. We treated the most severe injuries."*

"Good." I add, *"We're bringing some food for the barracks. We'll divvy up supplies when we get there. See you soon."*

I disconnect the conference call before he can think of

something smarmy to say. Jenner hates surprises.

It takes us just under an hour to get everything together for the trip into Commons. The plan is simple. We'll fly in, deliver some goods, I'll say my speech and then book it right back to Danielton before I'm apprehended. It's a huge risk but one I *need* to take. After several attempts to convince me to stay on Danielton, Nicole, Sarah and Bill gave up pretty quickly and followed the new plan - especially after Nicole conceded that I had a very good point.

"It's one thing to see your leader on video. But to *see* him face to face? To know that he cared enough to risk his safety and speak to you? That's priceless."

Bill, to his credit, adapted immediately and has figured out a way for my speech to be heard at the other barracks live. Sarah agreed that it would be best not to do a video but solely audio, for the sake of protecting the barrack where I'll be speaking. We decide to send a recording of my speech to Atlas when I'm back on Danielton, out of reach.

"And we have to leave for Danielton *immediately after*," Nicole stresses for the thousandth time.

We talk and move, eager to get everything done as quickly as possible. Every minute I'm silent is another minute the Commoners have to give over to Hamilton's fear-inducing terrorism. I can't let that happen. But even in the midst of my busyness, I'm still completely aware of *her*. Dami is quick, efficient, and resourceful as always but there's a stifling tension between the two of us that threatens to choke us all. Her conversation with the others flows out easily. It's just the silence between the two of us that's making things unbearable. She didn't say anything when I announced the change of plans. I want to know if she thinks it's a good idea or not but I'll admit it, I'm too damn proud to ask her. Several times I've felt her eyes on me but I've refused to look at her.

Multiple times, the rest of the group looks between the two of us, as though they can tell something is off. But no one is about to ask.

We ship out ten minutes after the call with Jenner. Unlike the Cyrilliac, Dami's hover car requires a skilled driver to fly the vehicle over a significant amount of water and terrain. She calmly navigates it over Danielton, across the channel, and onto the Factory Quarter, landing directly on the coordinates Jenner gave her.

Factory looks worse than anything they've shown on the news. Most of the buildings are leveled. Everything is charred and melted, with rubble piled half as high as the buildings they once were. There are bodies too, strewn about the ground - some intact, others blown apart. I wonder if Atlas intends to clean up the decay or if they'll leave the corpses to the loved ones of the dead. It's hard to believe this was once a town. Less than a week ago, our entire team met by the quarter's pier. Our little shed is probably blown to bits. When we arrive, the only thing veiling us is the heavy smog of dust, debris, and ashes. I step out and immediately cover my mouth and nose with my shirt. The burning stench chokes me. I figure it's better than the stench of charred corpses. A man runs toward us with the sleeve of his sweater covering his mouth and nose. Though disguised, I know exactly who he is by his gait.

"You're a freakin' idiot, Decker." Jenner says by way of greeting. He grabs a couple crates from the trunk and leads us to the barrack below.

It never ceases to amaze me how quickly a room can fall silent.

We enter what was once Factory's training facility; now lined, wall to wall, with men, women, and children initially talking, playing, sleeping, crying. Everyone's dirty. Many are injured. Most are just frightened. After a while, the blood, dirt, and despair all mesh into one miserable blob and silence overtakes the room as more and more eyes land on my undisguised face. Scores of people whisper to each other as I pass, wondering aloud if I am who they think I am. We quickly unload the carts and Jenner rushes me to the focal point of the room. He takes an empty cart and flips it on its head. Standing on top of it, he yells out to the already-silent crowd.

"Ladies and gentlemen, may I have your attention please! Those of you whispering and wondering - you're right. This is Decker Channing, the leader of our movement. He's risked his life and safety after waking up from an explosive, to speak to you in person and meet you face-to-face. This is our response to Hamilton and Atlas."

He steps down and I immediately step up. I see several eyes drift to the gauze I still have wrapped around my head. Several children point at it and whisper to their parents. I feel perfectly fine but I remember what Nicole said about appearances. They already seem to identify with me through my injuries.

Bill stands a few feet away, a simple recorder in his hand. He nods, ready to record and I begin:

"My fellow Americans," I look around and see their surprised expressions. No one has used that term in centuries. "None of us could have imagined the ruthless cruelty of the man we once called 'President.' I speak to you this evening with a broken heart, a heavy burden, and a piercing anger. My heart is broken because of the countless lives that were lost in today's bombings: innocent men, women and children were attacked for no reason other than living on the wrong side of the river."

Already, people start wiping falling tears from their eyes.

"I feel a heavy burden because in all that we've lost, we have much more to gain: freedom, equality, and justice for those who were killed. And I feel anger: a hot, pulsing, growing anger that will not die until justice has been won for every single death on this island."

"Yes!" a man cries out fervently. Scattered applause breaks out.

"I realize in starting this revolution that I have inadvertently dragged you into the fray. I know there may be some of you who are very angry with me for speaking out against Hamilton and his regime. Perhaps you believe that if it wasn't for me, your loved ones would still be alive. You wouldn't be injured and your wages wouldn't be slashed-"

"No!" another man cries out. I don't know if he's saying no to that statement or to me but I continue.

"I urge you to remember, though, the life you had before this revolution broke out. And I urge you to seriously consider if you can stand to live that way for another fifty years. Because that is what Hamilton is proposing. And after what he has done to you, me, and your loved ones - how can we possibly go on under the reign of a man evil enough to bring such catastrophe?"

"We can't!" someone cries back. Others cheer in agreement.

"Many of you were surprised when I called you Americans. I say this because we are no longer Commoners. Our days of working for the wealthy and suffering in poverty are over." I continue through the powerful cheers. "If you stand by us, by this cause, *we* will have your backs. *We* will provide you with food, medicine, ammunition, and supplies. *We* will protect you and we will defend your *American* rights. This country is no longer split into Atlas against Commons. I propose a new government: one this country hasn't seen since the founding of this once great nation. I propose a country where my rights and your rights are just as equal, honored, and protected as any other person's rights - regardless of their money. I propose a land of the free and a home of the brave that gives every citizen an equal chance to live their lives the way they choose to. I propose a country that does not fear the differing opinions of its people but fights to protect their right to express those opinions. And I propose a nation that will not tolerate the terrorism that took place this morning - especially from the people we're supposed to consider our leaders!"

"*Yes!*" they cry out in agreement, the cheers and applause overwhelmingly loud.

When they quiet down, I continue, "With this in mind, I stand and declare that I reject the regime of Victor Hamilton and the government that only serves Atlas. I declare our independence from his tyranny, their injustice, and our oppression. On behalf of those fighting for change, I declare that we are no longer Commoners and they are no longer Atlans. But we are all *Americans* and *that* is the country I am fighting to restore!"

The crowd goes insane. All who are able rise to their feet and applaud. Even those who are injured struggle to rise and cheer as well. I move into the crowd and shake hands, looking into faces. I'll never remember them all and I quickly lose count of how many I encounter after the first hundred, but I'll never forget the way these people look back at me. The tears flow freely down the cheeks of these men and women but they're no longer tears of despair or hopelessness. They're tears of fire and determination.

"Thank you," they repeatedly say to me.

"Thank you for standing up."

"Thank you for speaking out."

"Thank you for fighting for us."

"We need you. Don't give up."

They're tears that will not let me fail.

We rush back to Danielton and I'm surprised we make it with little fanfare. The deafening applause in the barracks alone should have tipped the authorities off that I was there. But we managed to lift off without any detection. When we enter the lab, it's almost as if the five of us never left in the first place.

Bill stations himself at his computer, trying to find a way around ADC's new firewall so that he can at least stream the audio onto the phones and personal devices of citizens. The women all head back to the freezer and start packing the rest of the food. On Commons, Jenner and Sam had a good system to divvy up the resources. At the rate they were going, they'll be back very soon for the rest. I join the women in the freezer and start packing crates alongside them. Once again, Dami and I say nothing to one another. Once again, Sarah and Nicole look between the two of us curiously.

I reach for a perfectly preserved squash right as her slender dark hand lands on it. I can't help it when a feeling of hot lava fills my stomach at the sensation of touching her again.

I can feel her eyes on me as I pull back my hand.

"Sorry," she says.

"Go for it," I murmur, turning to the pile of lettuce closest to me.

"Decker-"

Suddenly Bill runs through the open door. "You guys need to see this!"

Back in the lab, the news appears on screen. "Minutes after Decker Channing all but declared war on President Hamilton and Atlas, Hamilton has responded with an invitation to speak peaceably."

The screen cuts to Hamilton in front of a podium. "There has been enough bloodshed and destruction-"

"Since when?" Nicole says snidely.

"I would like to explore a way to bring this conflict to an end without any more lives being lost. If Decker Channing is watching this, I invite you to call me at the number on the screen below. We can talk 'face-to-face' and explore an end that both Atlas and Commons can abide by."

"Bullshit," Sarah says as the screen cuts to black. I blink at her unusual swearing. "He's probably just saving face."

"He is," Nicole nods. "Probably realizes he looks bad even to Atlans right now. No one wants to hear that their employees have been attacked or killed over what they perceive as a small rebellion they don't even understand."

I look at Dami but she remains silent. Still too stubborn to ask her thoughts, I turn to Bill.

"Can this be done without him tracing us?"

"Absolutely."

I nod and remove the gauze from around my head. "Then put him on. I want to see what he has to say."

The three of them scramble to set up the background and hide the details of the lab. Bill secures our feed and lets us know when he's ready. My nerves start to spike again. They go completely haywire when, out of the corner of my eye, I see her leave the room. She'd tried to speak to me earlier, before Bill interrupted. And now, in spite of everything going on, I want nothing more than to follow her and hear what it was she wanted to say.

But I can't now. He's about to come on. The screen lifts from black and comes into subtle focus. And here we are.

Hamilton and I.

Face to virtual face for the first time.

He's a lot older than he seems on TV. I wonder if they airbrush him when he telecasts. He gives a stilted smile that clashes against his glittering green eyes. "Still alive, are you, Officer Channing?"

"Call me Decker, Hamilton." I have no intentions of calling him president.

His cold green eyes flicker maliciously. "You've caused USA a world of trouble, young man. And for what? Your delusional fantasies of ancient revolutionary change?"

"I'm not the one who bombed most of Commons," I bite back, anger rising. "You are."

"And I will bomb the rest of it into the Atlantic if you don't stop this at once."

I hear Sarah gasp beside Bill. He clearly couldn't care

less about the lives of those who survived.

"I thought you wanted to talk. If you don't have anything new to say, why are you wasting my time?"

His face crumples into a ferocious scowl. "Listen, you little no-name prick!"

"Ah, ah, ah!" I cut him off. "Your temper is showing, Hamilton. What happened to 'we will not be intimidated'?"

I'm egging him on but I can't help it. It thrills me to see him lose control, to have a taste of the frustration every Commoner has lived with their entire lives. He's not used to things not going his way. He's not used to having no control, no immediate solution. He throws a tantrum like a two-year-old because he's never had to deal with someone saying "no."

Hamilton barely reels it in enough to spit out. "You won't win. You just promised ammunition, resources, *and food* to people who can't access it anywhere outside of Atlas. You've shot yourself in the foot with those idiotic promises. Now do us all a favor and shoot yourself in the head."

Out of the corner of my eye, I see Nicole lift a hand to her mouth in horror. Disgust mars the pretty lines of her face. Bill scowls fiercely at the screen, his fist balling at the keyboard on his lap.

"The only person I'm shooting in the head is you."

Hamilton's mouth twists into a mocking laugh. "You and what army, my friend? You do realize that all of your former comrades work for me, don't you? I just killed most of *your* supporters but the Force is on my side."

I ignore the dig, though a part of me hates to acknowledge he's right. Even my plan of storming the ball with the recruits is up in the air. All of them are needed to protect and defend the surviving Commoners now.

"How can you be so cruel?" I ask him, genuinely wanting to know.

He leans back, his eyes the cool political mask he shows so often on screen. "Ahh, there he is. The self-righteous hero who looks sanctimoniously at us money-hungry Atlans. You know Commons hasn't had one of you in say, fifty odd years." I can see Nicole stiffen nearby. "Nicholas Terranio had a handsome mug too. Too bad Chief Richard Nystrom smashed it to a pulp before sending him to The Gauntlet."

Nicole quietly leaves the room before he can torture her with any more of his cruel words.

"This is a waste of time." I gesture to Bill to shut it off.

Hamilton won't be dismissed.

"Surrender yourself, Decker. Surrender and I may just grant you a swift, public execution and put this to rest. Surrender yourself so that others don't have to die. There are children on Commons."

I blink at that. "Did you think of that before you killed so many of them?"

His green eyes are flat. Everything I say seems to bounce off of them as he prattles on, ignoring his role in the attack. "You were an officer. You know how well these men are trained. You're fighting a battle you cannot win.

What on earth makes you think you can come up against my men?"

"I'm not after them," I reply. "I'm after *you*."

I can't believe I ever wrestled with any guilt in getting rid of this man. Keeping him alive would be a punishment to humanity.

"You will lose, Decker." Hamilton threatens once more. "And it won't just be your life."

The screen cuts to black.

"Such a monster," Sarah murmurs. Bill wraps an arm around her waist, stroking her back in comfort. I look away from the intimate gesture as the doors in the back suddenly open and Nicole walks in with Dami's arm around her shoulder. The sight of her makes my heart career against my chest. We avoid each other's eyes and I keep my gaze on Nicole.

"Are you okay?" I ask gently. She nods, a weak smile on her face. Her eyes are red but it looks like she cried it all out minutes ago.

"Okay, we need to keep working." I tell everyone. "Jenner and Sam will be back soon."

We spend the next hour and a half packing the food and labeling the inventory. By the time the guys arrive, the cryogenic vault is almost bare and the weapons are stowed away. To our surprise, Jenner and Sam return with an additional man.

"Adams?" I ask in astonishment. "What are you doing here? How did you-?"

"I have some news," he cuts me off soberly.

I take a second look at him. His usually bright blue eyes are somber and his voice is dark.

"What is it?" I ask. Behind him, Jenner and Sam are visibly upset.

"What happened?" Nicole asks.

"Donahue and Jenkins are dead."

"No," I whisper.

My stomach wrenches at the news I had hoped against hope I wouldn't hear.

Adams nods. "They were helping several families find shelter in Maids Quarter. Managed to get a group of kids under right before an explosive landed a yard away from them. They were buried under the rubble."

Nicole shakes her head quietly while Bill comforts Sarah, her soft cries filling the room.

I take another look at Adams and can see he's damn near broken. His tears are barely in check. "Adams, I'm so sorry."

My heart feels so heavy with their loss.

"I'm not," he says. We all look at him, shocked. "They died with more honor than any Atlas Police Officer ever has." His voice breaks as his tears fall. "And as long as I have breath in my body, I *will not* let their deaths be in vain. They were *great* kids. *Great* men. Their deaths are not in vain."

"He's right," Jenner nods. "The tide is turning. When the officers found out what happened to Donahue and Jenkins, they petitioned for a special officer's burial. Yang refused. Refused to even acknowledge their deaths."

"He called them traitors," Adams spits out the words in disgust. I've never seen him so upset. "He refused to honor their memory or their sacrifice because they lost their lives in service to *Commoner* children not *Atlan* children."

"The officers are pissed," Sam adds. "Adams has already recruited much of their support."

"What?" I exclaim. It's like the first break of sun after weeks of dreary rain. A wave of relief washes over me.

Adams nods. "The Force is broken, Decker. It's not just their deaths…it's the attack period. The men who planted the bombs were told they were quarter surveillance cameras."

"Wait." I blink at him in shock. "Do you mean Yang *lied* to them? He had them plant bombs without their knowledge or consent?"

"Yes! You know there are officers with family outside of Police Quarter. It was the only way Yang could ensure the bombs would be planted without obstruction. Most of the men are wracked with guilt - others, disgust. They didn't sign up for this. It's one thing to hurt someone who isn't where they should be or is being a prick to you at Atlas Express. It's another thing to kill innocent men, women, and children. Decker, they've had enough."

A silver lining. A silver lining around the worst possible circumstances anyone could have asked for. In his hubris, Hamilton has failed to see that his cruelty has repelled the hearts of his most needed allies. His officers.

"What now?" Nicole asks.

"We equip the officers and prepare for the ball in two

days." I answer.

Jenner claps me on the back. "Bill says you threatened the crap out of Hamilton. Is that true?"

I nod. "He will pay for what he's done."

Adams looks at me, confusion clouding his face. "I appreciate the sentiment but exactly how do you plan on killing him when you'll be here?"

"I won't be here," I reply. "I'm going in."

"What?" Nicole exclaims.

"You're serious?" Bill asks.

"That's a bad idea," Dami mutters. It's the first time she's said anything in over an hour.

I look at her. "Why is it a bad idea?"

Her eyes meet mine and I hate what I see in them. Fear. Again. Like she's scared to say anything to me. How did we dissolve to this?

"You're the leader of this revolution," she says cautiously.

"I know that," I reply.

"If you fall, this revolution falls."

I try to keep my cool. "Who says I'm going to fall?"

"Don't do it, Decker!" she snaps. "This could cost you your life!"

I frown at that and snap back, "Since when did you care about my life, Damilola?"

Silence.

We stand opposite each other, challenging one another with our eyes. It takes us a second to realize that the whole group is looking at us in stunned silence. Aware of our surroundings, but too heated to be embarrassed, I take Dami firmly by her arm and lead her into the bedroom I woke up in hours earlier. I can't do this anymore. I can't stand the silent treatment. I'd rather we be verbally acrimonious to each other than continue in painful silence.

The new environment, low-lit and soothing, helps assuage my frustration but not by much. And what frustrates me more is that despite the confusion, despite the miscommunication, despite the rejection I feel, I still want to grab her and kiss the hell out of those soft, full lips. I speak before I follow through on the desire.

"I made you uncomfortable," I start. "I shouldn't have kissed you. I was wrong. But don't pretend you care about me. I'm a grown man. I can take your rejection. Just be honest."

Maybe *I* should be honest. Because the truth is, I'm not handling her rejection well at all.

She shakes her head. "You've got it all wrong"

"Then enlighten me."

"I wasn't trying to reject you."

"You pushed me away, Dami."

"Because I was scared."

"Of what?" I don't understand. "A kiss? We were only kissing."

"I'm not as experienced as you, Decker."

I blink at that. "What do you mean-?"

I stop mid-sentence as it clicks. I look at her incredulously.

"You've never been kissed?" I ask her. "*Ever?*"

Was that really her first time?

I don't know how I must look to her but she suddenly stiffens her spine and withdraws from me. She hasn't physically moved back but she now feels miles away. If I have any sense, I should know to tread carefully. But my mind is spinning with the implications of what she's saying. If she's never been kissed, that must also mean…

"You're a virgin."

That I cannot wrap my mind around. *No one* waits to have sex in USA. The minute puberty hits, virginities fall out the window.

She looks at me silently, watching me react.

"I…I don't…I don't get it." I stammer. "You're kind, stunning, and brilliant. You're 28-years-old. Why haven't you…? What…?" I sigh in frustration and finally blurt out, "*What's wrong with you?*"

The words fly out of my mouth before I can even think of editing them. I cringe inside the minute they fall out. I didn't mean it like that. I just want to know what would possess her to wait to kiss a man, let alone have sex with one. Nothing prepares me for the shocked hurt that fills her eyes at my reckless words.

I scramble, trying to rectify what I've said.

"Dami, I didn't mean that. I just meant…"

It's too late.

The hurt in her eyes morphs into anger right in front of me. She's visibly shaking with it.

"Dami, I'm sorry."

She holds up a hand and closes her eyes, taking deep breaths, willing herself to calm down. When she opens her eyes again, it's as if someone completely foreign is looking at me. Her dark pensive eyes are guarded. Completely closed and blocked off.

Her voice is as cool as ice. "Well, I'm glad we figured out the problem was me."

I've never seen this side of her and it scares me.

"Dami, let me explain. Please."

She shakes her head and moves to the door. When I try to pull her back, she violently yanks her arm out of my grasp.

"Screw you, Decker. We're done."

"Give me liberty or give me death."

-Patrick Henry

CHAPTER TWELVE

We're on Atlas.

It's been two days since the attack on Commons and it's hard to believe that only forty-eight hours ago I was rallying men and women while threatening the most powerful man in this country. Hamilton has been deathly silent since the line was drawn in the sand. According to Nicole, he's working overtime to redeem his image to his Atlas constituents. The middle class, he was surprised to learn, were horrified by his attack on so many people. The wealthier of the population don't care as much about the carnage as they do about his mental stability. What leader attacks and obliterates half of his populace unprovoked? He sent bombs to squash a rebellion but has inadvertently bombed his own reputation.

He hopes to get it back tonight.

And I hope to bring him to an end.

Nicole and I leave her place, dressed to the nines with our disguise films on. It's a shame she has to put hers on. She's stunning in a floor-length sleek magenta silk dress.

I've only ever worn a tuxedo twice - both times when guarding the ball. It feels strange to go to the old opera house as a guest and not a hire. Adams managed to secure us last minute tickets just in the nick of time. We're posing as wealthy Hamilton donors. We slide into the sleek limousine and speak in low tones.

"You're sure this is okay?" she asks me. "They've all been screened?"

I nod and whisper, "Sam went with Jenner and Adams last night and ran the voice detection test on every officer through the same phones used to screen the recruits. He also gave them their weapons. Eighty-five percent of the men assigned to that room are on board. The rest were switched to exterior security by Adams himself."

She nods, her hands fidgeting in her lap. I can tell by the tense outline of her disguised jaw that she's nervous. I am too. Everything is riding on this night. We're the only two civilians infiltrating the ball. Jenner wanted to come but there weren't enough tickets. Besides, he's needed in the barracks.

"It'll be okay," I tell her, though I'm also trying to assure myself. I've never been this scared in my life.

She looks at me and reaches out to squeeze my hand. "You're right. One way or another, this will end at last. Let's make sure it ends our way."

I nod, grateful to see her suck it up for both of us.

Her expression alters slightly. "Have you spoken to Dami since...?"

I shake my head stiffly, removing my hand from hers.

I'm almost grateful for the distracting thought because as nervous as I am about tonight, I'm somehow more upset about things with *her*. I miss her. I miss her voice. Her smart solutions. The way I feel whenever she's around.

I've never screwed up with someone so badly - and worse, with someone who means so much to me. I can still remember how hurt she was. How her hands and voice shook with emotion when she called me out for being such a dick. She wouldn't even look at me when I left Danielton for Nicole's place last night. And I was so upset about the tension, I couldn't fully enjoy seeing my mother again. Well fed and nourished by Mrs. Washington's company, Mom looks eons better than she ever did living in Commons. I could barely hold back the tears when she squeezed me close to her in reunion. Still, I longed to feel Dami's arms around me. I longed to smell her floral scent again.

"We're here," Nicole whispers. To her credit, she allowed me to mull over the whole thing in peace the entire ride. But without saying anything, I can tell she's asking me to snap out of it. And I do. Tonight, I can't afford to get distracted. Putting thoughts of Dami aside, I step out of the limo and extend an arm to her.

The President's Annual Ball takes place at what was once known as The Met, a world famous art museum. Unfortunately, most of its content was sold and distributed to the wealthiest on Atlas during Eilenwich's tenure. The lavish architecture dates back to the late 19th century with the interior re-designed to seat several hundred in a gala-style dinner. Nicole and I walk the plush red carpet leading up the stairs to the entrance. There are three security lines with guards scanning invitations, ID, and the guests themselves.

I feel Nicole tense on my arm. "You didn't mention the scanners."

"They didn't have them when I guarded," I whisper back.

Our line moves forward quickly.

"What do we do?" she asks, her eyes circling around us in a panic.

"I don't know."

Right as we reach the guard with the scanner, Adams steps forward and pulls the device from the man's hand. "Dr. Havanov, good to see you."

"Likewise," I reply, relieved that he memorized my alias. He scans us himself and blinks in surprise. "Mind if I have a word with you and your lovely wife?"

He hands the scanner back to the oblivious guard and pulls us aside.

"It went through," he whispers to us, still surprised. "Dami's film actually passed the scanner."

"I told you she's a genius." Nicole replies, as if she wasn't panicking just seconds ago.

I take a deep breath, half admiring Dami's work, half kicking myself for screwing things up with her. I don't want to think about her now. Not when I need to focus on this night.

Adams seems to read my thoughts. "Okay. You're

assigned to table C4. I'll tell all my guys where you are, but rip off those films when the time comes so there's no confusion or crossfire, got it?"

We nod and start to head in but he pulls me back by the arm again. "Southeast wing," he whispers in my ear. "The group concentrated there are not with us and I couldn't get them reassigned. Be careful."

I nod.

Nicole's heels click along the marble floor as we both take in the magnificent ball room. We quickly find our table and sit, unsure of what to do. Nicole looks at me and smiles. "Breathe. Just chat with me and ignore everyone else. They'll not want to interrupt two 'lovebirds.'"

"Great," I nod. "'Blah blah blah. How's that?"

She chuckles while I scan the room for all our guys. Within seconds, I lock eyes with several of them. Adams must have managed to inform them of our alias and seating arrangement. Along with the guns we supplied them, they also have their own telepathic phones. My eyes drift to the southeast end of the hall. Congregated are the men Adams referred to. I lean in to Nicole.

"See the guys near the warship painting?" I whisper in her ear. She smiles like I said something charming but nods slightly, eyes drifting there.

"What about them?"

"They're not with us. Stay alert."

She nods.

Minutes later, the remaining guests pour into the ball room. Our table fills with people drenched in diamonds, silk, and expensive perfume. Stylish, cool, and richer than gold, they greet Nicole and I warmly, figuring we're one of them. *So this is how they treat their own.*

The program starts and servers pass out appetizers. There are noticeably fewer servers working at this ball. Most of them were probably killed in Maids two days ago.

"This is so lovely," an older woman with stylish white hair says. "So nice to get away from all the dreadful business of those Commoners."

A low murmur travels across the table. Nicole and I keep silent, though I can feel her tense beside me.

"Did you see the footage of those areas - what are they called? Quarters? Yes, did you see the footage of what remains? It's terrible. Like another world."

They once again murmur in agreement.

I can't help myself. I speak up. "Have any of you ever visited Commons before?"

They look shocked at the question.

An older gentleman with an immaculate mustache laughs. "Heavens no! Why on earth would I do such a thing?"

The table laughs.

"It looks terrible now but it's not that different from how it looked before, if the pictures are at all accurate," another Atlan quips.

The blood boils in my veins as they laugh and joke about the impoverished conditions of my home. Not once do they mention the numerous people killed or injured. All they seem to care about is how it *looks*. My fist tenses around my fork and just as the man opposite me is about to ask a question, a question I'm not prepared to answer politely, Nicole leans in and whispers in my ear.

"Pretend I said something romantic and laugh."

I laugh. I turn to her and whisper in her ear. "I can't take this much longer."

She giggles and looks at me through her lowered lashes. I glance at the man opposite me and he's bought it hook, line and sinker. He strikes up a conversation with a man closer to him and she and I continue our pretend banter until the speakers go on stage.

"Good evening," a polished Atlan man says. "Welcome to the twenty-fifth annual Presidential Ball, honoring and featuring President Victor Hamilton."

We join the audience in its applause, though it pains me to do so.

"We are aware that this ball falls on the most unorthodox of nights, where active terrorism threatens to destroy the safety and prosperity of so many in this nation."

"You cannot be serious," I whisper to her.

"Shh," she responds. She's right. I have to hold my tongue. It won't be much longer until I can finally reveal who I am. The speaker goes on to give announcements, honorable mentions, and a brief rundown of the evening's itinerary. As he speaks, the servers reappear with plates carrying our main dish and hands ready to retrieve our finished appetizers. Various speakers come to the stage in between musical selections and they drone on and on about the greatness of USA, namely Atlas, while giving regular and thinly veiled jabs to our revolution. I tune out the nonsense two speakers in and scan the tables, identifying the key players near the stage. As predicted, every member of the Senate, the House, and the Supreme Court is present. Hamilton wines and dines with his constituents, jovial and charming as ever. He almost looks likeable. His entire cabinet sits with him at the table on stage, in full view of the audience.

And my team.

I briefly touch the film behind my ear and try to dial Adams. *"Who's assigned to which group?"*

Adams replies, *"Wing one to the justices; wing two to the Senate; wing three to the House and wing four to the executive. I'll get Soch, Wartman and Lieberman myself."*

"On my shot?" I confirm.

"Roger that," he replies.

Moments later, Hamilton is introduced. The night full of brainwashing must have gotten to the guests - either that or the champagne because the minute he stands to take the podium, every guest stands to their feet, applauding. We sit down as his glittering green eyes sweep the room.

"Good evening. Thank you so much for taking the time to attend our annual gathering. Every year, it never ceases to amaze me how much we have to celebrate as a nation. And though this year has introduced many challenges, particularly one that came out of nowhere in recent days, I am confident that we as a people will continue to flourish under the leadership and guidance of the men and women elected to steward this great nation."

More applause as he looks down at the podium then back up to the men and women seated here.

"When I ran for president…several terms ago…" The audience chuckles. "I ran with the full intention of serving my nation. We were still recovering from the devastation of the Cyrian Flu and most citizens were existing - not living. I watched my predecessor work tirelessly to restore the nation to what it once was and to become even better by standing on our own two feet, without the assistance of, or reliance on, foreign powers that could dictate us. Two years after coming to office, my mentor and friend, former President Eilenwich died. And I promised myself to spend the rest of my years honoring his memory, his legacy, and his plans for this nation. We are on the edge of a rebellion. A treasonous rebellion that seeks to destroy everything we've worked tirelessly to achieve. I want to promise you tonight that any action I take seeks only to prevent that destruction - to preserve what we have accomplished."

My fist balls in my lap as I look around and watch the men and women here continue to drink and ingest this delusional garbage.

"My desire," Hamilton continues, "is to see Atlas flourish above all else. We are essential to the well being of the Commoners." The audience nods with faux sympathetic expressions on their smug faces. "I ask my fellow Atlans to be firm but merciful on Commoners when they surrender. It's not their fault they're entrenched in a rebellion but it is the fault of a reckless and narcissistic young man."

Adams voice explodes in my mind. *"If you want that shot, this is the clearest one you'll ever get."*

I stand.

Initially, no one notices but Hamilton's eyes catch mine and then widen as I tear the film off the side of my neck. "If I'm narcissistic Hamilton, I can only imagine what that makes you."

Gasps fill the hall as the audience looks on in shock.

Whispers abound asking how I got in, if it's really me, what they will do, why I even came. The house lights turn on and the whispers only get louder when everyone sees that it really is me. Decker Channing - leader of the Commoner rebellion.

"How did you get in here?" Hamilton asks, his eyes a steely green.

"I promised you we would meet again."

"You've made a very foolish mistake, Decker."

Suddenly, an officer breaks from the fold and raises a gun to my right temple. My heart races because I don't remember seeing him before this very moment. Is he a part of the Southeast team or one of our guys?

Hamilton lifts a hand and tells him. "Let him speak first. Every man deserves one last word, no matter how deplorable the man."

I look around the hall, at the men and women seated. Some stand to get a better look at me, others sit with arms crossed and eyes narrowed. To them, I'm enemy number one. I speak up and speak loudly.

"I don't have much to say to you. For fourteen years I guarded multiple families on Atlas, watching you live your lives carefree. I only ever encountered one family that treated me like an equal - like a fellow citizen - the rest of Atlas treated me like trash. You all have labeled us terrorists, criminals, and troublemakers but have you ever stopped to consider what it is like to be a Commoner in this country? As much as our rights have been stripped as a whole, Commoners live on less, have no protection, and next to zero opportunity to rise up and work their way to a semblance of the prosperity you enjoy. Some of you have wondered what this whole movement is about. The fact that you have to ask alarms me greatly. We don't want to hurt you or harm your families. All we want is a chance to live as well as you do. Is that too much to ask?"

The expressions don't change one iota.

If I didn't know better, I would say they've actually hardened into angry masks.

And I should have known they would. These are all staunch, long-time Hamilton supporters. Any Atlan sympathizers are outside of this building.

"See?" Hamilton says. "This is an example of benevolence. Allowing the man his say. But this next act is one of firm resolve." He looks at the officer next to me, gun still levied to my head. "Kill him."

The crowd gasps at the order.

I turn to face the man, the barrel of his gun now

between my eyes. Various voices whisper in shock as I face off with the man poised to kill me.

"Decker," I hear Nicole gasp in my phone. *"I can't get Adams. I don't know if he's one of us or not."*

"What are you waiting for?" Hamilton exclaims. "Shoot him!"

I meet the officer's clear blue eyes and see them dart to the Southeast then back at me. Immediately I understand. The barrel disappears from my line of vision when he suddenly hands me the gun and pulls out another. I turn to the stage in time to see Hamilton's horrified expression. It's the last look he'll ever make. I pull the trigger and shoot him square in the head. He's dead before he hits the ground.

All hell breaks loose.

Half the men and women duck under their tables while the other half make a dash for the doors. It's all a blur as I duck and dash to Nicole, who has removed her disguise film. We both crouch at the now-empty table as gunfire breaks out all around us. The other guards spring into action, half barricading the entrance, the other half taking down their assigned tables. The officer who covered me shoots two of the four men on Southeast. We duck as the remaining two fire back. One of them runs towards the executive table, determined to protect the Cabinet. I shoot and he falls like lead.

"Look out!" Nicole screams. I turn and see the other one aiming at me. I throw us both under the table and the clothe gives way as food and plates shatter around us, the bullet narrowly missing me and hitting an Atlan man nearby.

I duck back out and aim but when I do, he's already down.

"You okay?" the blue-eyed officer asks me, crouching near our table.

"Yeah," I reply. "What's your name?"

"Deluger. I joined last minute, before the doors shut. I didn't get one of the phones or I would have found a way to tell you."

I shake my head. "You found a way. Good job."

He probably saved my life. Neither Adams nor I thought of what to do to keep the Southeast men from shooting me dead immediately. Had he not stepped up under the guise of killing me, one of them might have actually done it.

"Thank you," I yell over the screams of the guests around us.

Nicole emerges from under the table, her hair a messy halo around her head. Her brown eyes are focused, her hands pressed to her ears. "Adams called. The other officers are trying to break in. They won't be able to hold the barricades much longer."

The loud thumping on the other end of the doors confirms it.

I pull us all into conference mode. "Focus on your assignments. Tell me who's down."

Immediately, the men respond.

"Justices down."

"Senate down."

"House down."

"Vice President Flemmel down."

"Secretary Former down."

Adams voice rings, *"Soch, Wartman and Lieberman are down!"*

"Secretary Selo down."

"Galvin down."

"Is that everyone?" Nicole asks me.

"Attorney General Stuart," I ask. *"Did you get Stuart? He's the last in line."*

"There!" Nicole's actual voice breaks out. She points to a man crawling near the door. I aim but the man is shot down before I even pull my trigger.

"Attorney General down," a voice confirms.

"That's everyone," I tell them.

"It's fallen," Adams voice comes on. *"The government's fallen. Everyone to Wing Eight. We have ten seconds before they open the main door."*

I grab Nicole's hand and make a dash for the exit closest to the stage. Bodies lay strewn about the marble floor and the remaining guests scream in terror. We make it to the exit, surrounded by other officers right as the doors to the main hall break open and a sea of opposing officers flood the ballroom.

A rope hangs down the center of the winding stairwell and the men slide down, one after another. Nicole and I follow suit, bypassing the stairs and going straight to the bottom of the multi-leveled floors in mere seconds. I ignore the burn of the rope against my palms.

"Last down, cut the rope!"

"Got it!"

At the bottom, we follow the men climbing down a ladder beneath the floor. It leads to an old sewer system. Too much adrenaline pumps through me to notice the putrid smell of the dank, dark passage.

Seconds after we enter, someone yells down the tunnel, "Is Channing in?"

"He's clear!" Deluger calls back.

"Then seal the door!"

"Come on!" Nicole pulls my hand, leaving the two men behind us to wield the door shut above us before the opposing officers can follow.

"Go! Go! Go!" the men around us yell. We run with all our might, following the line of feet in front of us, flashlights bouncing off the dark, wet walls. Finally, after what seems like a small eternity, we reach another ladder, climbing up behind the officers and into the fresh night air above. I hold the train of Nicole's dress as she breaks through. A strong hand grabs mine and lifts me past the sewer entrance.

It's Adams.

I look around and to my amazement, we're on the opposite end of the street, outside, facing the ancient building. It takes me mere seconds to see Yang in person, pacing back and forth on the balcony of the building. Adams doesn't have to tell me what they've done. I already know the standard drill. He's called every loyal Atlas

Police officer to the hall, barricading the entrance so that none can go in and none can come out.

Suddenly, Yang looks out and sees us standing just yards away. He immediately speaks into his ear piece but he's too late.

"Everyone get in!" Adams yells. We all run inside the building facing the street. He's far but I can just make out Yang's expression enough to know he's frowning in confusion. From the safety of our position, Adams looks at his watch and counts. "Three...two...one."

The building detonates.

It bursts into flames before falling and caving in on itself. Yang, the opposing officers, and all the corrupt Hamilton supporters inside are gone.

We did it.

Atlas is dead.

"The distinctions between Virginians, Pennsylvanians, New Yorkers, and New Englanders are no more. I am not a Virginian, but an American!"

-Patrick Henry

CHAPTER THIRTEEN

It's a madhouse here.

We're all assembled in front of the Capitol: men, women and children from all quarters flood the streets of Atlas unhindered. News of Hamilton's fall has spread like wildfire throughout the land. ADC's firewall has been torn and ANN has no choice but to report the truth.

I stand on the makeshift podium. Seas of joyous faces look up at me, cheering half in victory, half in shock. It doesn't escape me that many Atlans have evacuated their homes. Others have remained shut inside, probably fearful. I use this moment to lay my cards on the table.

A country divided will not stand.

"My fellow Americans," I speak into the microphone. "The days of 'Atlas' and 'Commons' have died."

Deafening cheers fill the open air, electrifying the crystal clear night.

I speak again as the noise dies down. "We are no longer a people divided by class, money, or education. We are a people united by the founding ideals of this nation. Ideals of life, liberty, and *justice* for all!"

Cheers erupt again, streamers fly into the air, and confetti flies across the sky as people celebrate and listen at the same time.

"We have done the impossible. We have torn down more than five hundred years' worth of systematic oppression and revisionism. We have cried out that enough is enough and we have destroyed the feet that sought to tread on us!"

I pause, allowing for more jubilant cheers.

"Like our forefathers eight hundred years ago, we are at the precipice of a brand new nation. It has been so long since this country operated on the ideals with which it was founded. We are starting over. Starting fresh. And may the tree of liberty we've planted this night never be uprooted again!"

"We all want to live in safety, peace, and joy. With this in mind, *former* Commoners I urge you: seek peace with *all* Americans. Yes, even those we once called Atlans."

A suspended silence falls over the crowd.

"Prove to them and the rest of the world that we are not the ruthless animals Hamilton tried to paint us out to be. Never again will we live under the tyranny of the system that favored the rich and impoverished the poor. Work with me to restore the middle class, rectify the errors of our lopsided economy, and set the path for a better, brighter, freedom-giving future for our children!"

When the applause dies down, I go on to explain what will happen in the next few days. Teams are already in place to provide food, clothing, and shelter to those who have lost their homes. Mr. Washington has already arranged a middle class coalition to bring about a peaceful fusion between former Commoners and former Atlans. I give my word that they will receive regular updates every day through their personal devices. Bill now has complete command of ADC.

"This nation was once called the *United* States of America. Work with me to bring unity. It is the only way we can stand."

Two hours later, I'm at the Washingtons. Former Atlans and former Commoners already mingle and celebrate together as the night wears on. His coalition is coming to a great start by the look of things. My mother pulls me into her arms, trembling slightly as I hold her.

"What's wrong?" I ask her.

"Nothing," she smiles tremulously. "I'm just…grateful. You could have been…"

I nod. "But I wasn't. We won."

Her smile is brilliant and her small dark eyes light up. "*You* won. I'm so proud of you, sweetheart."

"Are you proud of me too?" a voice asks beside us.

"Caden! Oh, sweetheart!" Mom pulls Jenner into a tight hug as well. I stand and watch as she lavishes him with almost the same amount of praise she's given me. When she's done talking, he thanks her and glances at me.

We excuse ourselves from Mom and head to the

hallway, near the elevators. Immediately the noise level drops.

"We did it," I tell him, my eyes bugging in near disbelief.

He nods, a contemplative look on his face.

I frown at him. "You alright?"

His blue eyes lock with mine. "That was quite a speech you gave earlier."

"Thanks."

"Did you…uh…did you mean it all?"

I frown. "Yeah. I meant every word. Why would I lie?"

He takes a deep breath and looks around the hall. No one's out here. It's just the two of us.

"Even the part about Atlans and Commoners merging?"

I cock my head to the side and look at him. "Jenner, what are you getting at?"

He finally meets my eyes again. "I'm just trying to understand your thoughts on Atlans. I mean…I thought we were of the same mind. That they've ruined this nation."

"Hamilton ruined this nation. And so did all of the presidents and elected officials before him all the way to the 21st century."

Not to mention the scores of biased and irresponsible Supreme Court justices.

"But Atlans were a huge part of the problem."

I nod. "Absolutely."

"They should be punished," he says.

"Punished how?"

We stand, at opposite ends of the walls, and look at each other.

Several long moments pass until, finally, Jenner speaks again. "I just want what's best for USA - *America*."

I nod and give him a reassuring smile. "Of course you do. You always have."

We head back in as countless people eat, drink, and enjoy the night for what it is: one of hope. But as much as I want to join them, as happy as I am that we've succeeded, I can't give myself over to the excitement everyone else is feeling. The conversation with Jenner reminds me of the planning and recovery that's ahead and the thought of it alone overwhelms me. There's so much work to do. Deposing Hamilton was one thing. But starting an entirely new government is another. Sure, we have the blueprints of our founding fathers but the prospect of repairing and rebuilding Commons alone fills me with trepidation. Jenner just expressed legitimate resentment against the Atlans. How much of Commons feels the same way? I called us all Americans tonight but saying something and living it out are two entirely different things. Within minutes, I have to pull away from the crowd. I'm drowning in my anxiety and I don't want anyone to see it.

I leave and go to the quietest wing of the apartment. I knock on one of the doors and open it. "Nicole, do you mind if I hang here for a min-?"

To my surprise, Nicole's not there. It's Dami. On her

knees at the side of the bed, hands folded and eyes closed. She must not have heard my knock because I find her speaking silently to something unseen. Within seconds, though, the hall light behind me seems to alert her and she looks up at me in surprise, her eyes squinting to make out who it is. I step in and close the door behind me.

"Decker," she says, able to see me with the door shut.

I stare at her, astounded. It finally makes sense. Her purity, her chastity, even her ability to keep calm. She's religious. She's been hiding it this whole time.

"You were praying," I say. It isn't a question.

She looks at me, remaining silent.

"What are you?" I ask. "A Buddhist? Muslim? Hindu?"

"I'm a Christian." Her voice is so quiet, I almost miss what she says.

My jaw drops. Just when I think she couldn't surprise me further, she does.

I exhale in disbelief. "Of all the religions you could have chosen, you pick the one most reviled in USA."

"It wasn't always reviled," she replies. "And my faith has nothing to do with popularity. It's the truth."

I blink at that, unwilling to challenge the conviction in her voice.

"Why didn't you tell me?" I ask her. "You pushed me away. It was because of your religion, wasn't it?"

"I was saving my first kiss," she replies. "For my husband. No one else."

Her words rock me.

I gave her, her first kiss when she'd planned on saving

it for her spouse. It all makes sense now. I don't know much about Christianity but I know historically religious people didn't have sex before marriage and intimate gestures like kisses were held in higher regard. My heart soars as I finally realize she wasn't rejecting me when she pushed me away. She was standing by a religious code I didn't know she had. All this time, I had no idea about her faith. I can almost understand why she kept it under wraps. Before Hamilton's death, any open expression of religion was punishable by death. Any expression of Christianity warranted a one-way ticket to The Gauntlet. The thought of her dying there for her religion makes me shudder.

But still.

"You could have trusted me," I whisper. "You could have told me."

"Could I?" she finally challenges me. "Look how you responded when I pulled away."

I look down, ashamed. She told me the truth about her inexperience and I made her feel like a freak. Why would she trust something so dangerous to me when I couldn't even respond properly to the first bit of information?

"I'm sorry," I murmur. I meet her eyes and shrug, void of any excuse. "You didn't deserve that. You've been a safe place for me this entire time. Dami, I want to be that for you."

I step closer to her, finally baring it all. I'm done wrapping everything I feel in my cloak of pride. After two days of being at odds with her, after days of keeping my feelings at bay, I can't do this anymore. I know how much

I need her. Now I need her to know.

"Dami, I want you." I tell her bluntly. "I want to be with you. Your religion, your beliefs...I'm willing to wait for you. I don't need to be intimate to be serious about you or to stick around."

She's worth it to me. More than worth it.

My heart plummets when she shakes her head, her dark eyes next to impossible to see. "You were right to be mad at me, Decker. I had no business responding to you the way I did."

"So what you felt for me wasn't genuine?" I ask, already knowing the answer. I can tell by the way she's trembling that my nearness affects her as much as she affects me. She wants me too.

"Of course it was," she whispers.

"Then why can't you give us a chance?"

She sighs. "It's not enough for you to want me or be willing to wait. I will not bind myself to someone who isn't a believer."

I'm astounded.

"Are you saying you expect me to buy into your religion?" I ask in disbelief.

It's not enough for me to tolerate it?

She bristles at that and quickly replies, "I don't expect anything from you, Decker. Let's just focus on the work at hand."

She steps around me and leaves me in the room, the same way I was when I entered.

Alone.

"I do not believe that the Constitution was the offspring of inspiration, but I am as satisfied that it is as much the work of a Divine Providence as any of the miracles recorded in the Old and New Testament."

-Benjamin Rush

CHAPTER FOURTEEN

Life post-revolution is surreal.

We're going on a trip. To Martha's Vineyard. It's the only American land outside of New York City that remained habitable after the Cyrian Flu. Few citizens, even Atlans, have visited or explored the land that was once a part of the state called Massachusetts. Shortly after the party ended last night, the eight of us reconvened in Nicole's boardroom style office. I laid my cards on the table again, reiterating what I said to the people at the Capitol.

"I made it clear in my speech that I want us to have as peaceful a transition as possible in merging both classes. Both islands. I meant what I said."

"That was good," Nicole replied. "You set the tone immediately for civility and friendship. Former Atlans won't be threatened by former Commoners and former Commoners can celebrate without retribution."

"Thank you for that," Sarah murmured, her hand enfolded in Bill's.

I reminded them of the work ahead of us.

"We'll have to talk about the economy. Infrastructure. What to do about Danielton and McKenzie Isles. Foreign affairs. And leadership. With a new government to start from scratch, we need to hold an election as soon as possible, especially the presidential one."

They looked at me like I grew horns in my head.

"What election?" Sam asked. "You're the new president."

Everyone murmured in agreement, shaking their heads at my suggestion. Everyone that night was vocal except Jenner. He'd been silent ever since our discussion outside the apartment. I was tempted to pull him aside, ask if we were cool, but I shrugged it off, figuring it was stress. Like me, he probably realizes now how varied people's opinions are regarding the new society ahead of us - and how to merge Atlas and Commons. He's also been my right-hand man for weeks, coming up with several key strategies and training hundreds of men in the span of days. He's probably just exhausted like the rest of us - maybe even more so.

By the end of the meeting that night, it was clear to us all that we needed to find the original Constitution and Declaration of Independence as well as draft a revised one with which to govern the nation.

"And the sooner the better," Adams said. "We don't want this nation to descend into anarchy. We have to establish order immediately."

His eyes locked with mine and I nodded, backing him

up.

"We can't claim we're starting fresh on the basis of our founding fathers' ideals if we don't even have the documents they left behind to help us guide this nation."

After Washington D.C.'s fall, Congress motioned to move the documents to storage on Martha's Vineyard for safe keeping while the new capital was being arranged. And there they stayed for several generations, unseen and untouched. Eventually forgotten.

Now we're getting them back.

Sarah, Sam and Dami are going with me to the island. We're giving ourselves three days to find the originals and work a rough draft of the new Constitution. We'll be back the day after tomorrow. I've left Jenner and Adams in charge of the transitioning while I'm away. When I asked them to stay, they immediately knew what I needed them to do. There are numerous resources that need to be distributed equitably for the citizens to profit. Instead of having a free-for-all descend into looting, Jenner and Adams will work with the recruits that assisted with the barracks to allot various resources - food, clothing, and even shelter - to those who need it most while the officers Adams recruited will guard and keep order during the process. Nicole and her father will continue to work on measures to merge the two classes together and build a stronger middle class while Bill stays behind to work on the communication lines with ANN and ADC so that all the citizens can remain informed.

I hate to leave at such a critical time but Adams is

right: there's no point in me stepping up to lead if I don't even have a constitution to work from. And while I haven't told the others, I'm still determined to hold an election - including a presidential one. I will not claim to start a new democracy only to lead it unelected.

I sling my backpack over my shoulder as I walk into the living room. Sam and Sarah are packing the last of their things while my mother and Mrs. Washington sit at the kitchen bar next to Dami. I pause when I see her. Her hair is pulled back into a simple ponytail that looks more like a puff ball than a ponytail but it exposes her long sleek neck and gives an unobstructed view of her stunning face.

She's so damn beautiful.

"Hi, honey." Mom gets up and pulls me into a warm hug. I kiss the top of her head and smile down at her.

"You sleep well?" I ask.

Somehow her smile gets even brighter as she stretches and nods. "Oh, yes! Your lovely friend here, Dami, helped me with my back."

I risk a glance at her and am met with a closed, guarded expression. I quickly look away and ask, "How so?"

"She cracked it," Mom replies.

"Adjusted it," Dami amends. "I'm glad I remember a few of the techniques my mom taught me. You had several vertebrae out of place, Ms. Kim."

Mom goes to Dami and lays a motherly hand on her cheek. "Such a lovely girl. And quite brilliant too, I hear. All those inventions! I don't know how you would have won without her help."

Dami keeps her eyes averted from me, allowing me to admire her openly and say, "I don't know either. She was invaluable. She still is."

Her eyes snap back to mine and we look, unable to break contact. Out of the corner of my eye, I can see my mother looking between the two of us. As sharp as she is, I know she can tell something is up. Dami looks away first, glancing at her watch then looking around the corner at Sarah and Sam.

"We should be heading out now."

I nod. "I'm ready."

She joins the other two in the living room and grabs her bag. I turn back to find my mother *and* Mrs. Washington grinning at me. I look between the two of them.

"What?"

Mom smiles. "I think you found your girl."

"Mom!" I exclaim, shocked. Mrs. Washington starts to laugh. I look at her. "Not you too! What's so funny?"

"Oh, come on, Decker!" Mrs. Washington exclaims. "We *do* have eyes! I've never seen you look at a young lady that way."

Mom nods. "Neither have I. She's the one for you, sweetie. I can feel it."

I refrain from pointing out how quickly she's jumped shipped. Just days ago, she was saying Nicole was the one for me. Still, I can't help but feel glad that she likes Dami so much.

"We haven't even known each other a month."

"When you know, you know." Mom says stubbornly.

Mrs. Washington agrees. "Tobias and I got married three weeks after meeting each other. Best decision we ever made."

I ignore the chill that runs down my spine. All this time, I've secretly battled with my feelings for her - wondering if I was manic for feeling something so strong when I've only known her for such a short time. Their words are liberating and validating. But also really scary. Because as much as I want to run with what they're saying, I'm reminded of just how uncertain things are between Dami and me. She wants nothing to do with me now and I don't know how to change that. I pull my mother into a hug then hug Mrs. Washington goodbye as well. While I love them both, I have no desire to discuss my love life with either of them again.

Ever again.

For convenience sake, we take one of the hover cars and make the trip to Martha's Vineyard in under an hour. I'm instantly in awe of the small, historical island. I've never seen so many trees, cobbled streets, and quaint Colonial homes. It feels like I'm stepping back into time. Before we land, Sam, who grew up on the island with grounds keeping parents, gives us an aerial tour. Many of the homes and sites that were once overcrowded are now unoccupied or simply torn down. We eventually land on an area of the island called Edgartown. More like a ghost town, it is the most populated part of the vineyard during the summer but is practically empty this time of year. As a part of her inheritance, Dami owns a property here several miles away from the main shore. We make the trek through the woods to a spacious, wood-stacked home overlooking a small river.

Fully furnished, the home looks like something in one of the vacation magazines Atlas used to print for its residents on a yearly basis. Rustic yet comfortable, Gerald Petre obviously spared no expense to deck out this vacation home. But we have no time to enjoy it now. We drop off our bags and immediately head into the empty town to start exploring the various county buildings. We walk along the worn but clean sidewalks, taking in the abandoned cityscape.

"Adams checked the archival registry on Capitol Base," Sarah says. "The log said the documents were stored in the basement of the Sheriff's office."

"But didn't he also say there was a sticky note on top of it? With some scribbling about the old Federated Church?" Sam asks.

"I think so," she replies.

"Well, we can't ask him now," Dami says. "The phones I designed don't work at this distance and there are no ADC lines out here either."

We're unable to correspond with anyone on the mainland until we come back the day after tomorrow.

"Then let's split," I suggest. "Half of us go to the

church. The other half to the Sheriff's Office."

"Okay," Dami agrees. To my disappointment, she immediately teams up with Sarah and they head in the direction of the ancient church. If the documents are there, that's probably the only reason it's still standing, considering how many churches were burned and torn down in the 23rd century.

"Hey!" I look and see Sam further down the sidewalk. "You coming?"

The Sheriff's Office is covered with dust. It hasn't been used in at least a hundred years, not when every Atlan family started using officers as personal guards during vacations. Sam and I walk right through the unlocked double doors and make our way down the dry rotted wooden stairs to the basement below. We use flashlights to illuminate the place, the old electric system of the building useless to us now.

"There." Sam points. A room with a dusty gold sign that says "Storage." The key to it hangs right next to the door on a hook and we're met with the lovely smell of aged, unattended papers, stacked from floor to ceiling, left and right. File cabinets are lined all over the room and free sheets are strewn about on every available surface. It's a mess.

"Don't panic," Sam says. "Something this historically important wouldn't just be thrown around. They're probably filed away in one of these cabinets."

I'm still panicking.

We get to work, pulling out drawer after drawer,

identifying and inadvertently cataloging every document but the ones we're looking for. Two hours in, we've only touched a quarter of the room.

"It may just be in the old Federated Church," Sam murmurs, head bent over yet another file.

I grunt but say nothing in reply.

"If it is there, Dami will find it. She knows that building like the back of her hand."

That gets my attention. "She spends a lot of time there?"

He nods. "We've had Bible studies there too."

I look at him in surprise. *No way.*

"You're a Christian too?"

He smiles and gives a slight nod. "It feels good to finally be able to say it. She told me you know about her so…"

"Who else in the group?" I ask. "Sarah?"

He nods again and it suddenly makes sense to me why she was so eager to go with Dami to the church.

"This is so strange." I mutter mostly to myself. "It feels like people are finally revealing who they are."

Sam replies anyway, "Yeah, I guess so. Now that we have the freedom to, why hold anything back? It's nice to live without fear for a change."

It suddenly occurs to me that Atlans have had their share of oppression too. Not nearly as much as Commoners but they weren't immune to the government's strict prohibition of religious or even political expression. Anything that went against the grain of Hamilton or Eilenwich's agenda was considered a threat, punishable by death.

A slight shudder goes through me as I look down at the papers in my hand. Thankfully those days are gone.

We continue looking in silence. A few more hours roll by as we look and look and look. Dust rises and swirls in the air like smoke as papers that haven't been moved in over a century get shifted left and right. I search through all the file cabinets on my side before moving to an old, rickety desk in the corner of the room. The papers strewn on top are of little significance. I try to open the drawers but they're locked. After a couple seconds of running my fingers under the surface of the desk, I get lucky and land on the key. I cough when another puff of dust unexpectedly flies up at me as I open the drawer. Once more, several papers, documents, IDs, now insignificant, are hidden inside.

I pull the last drawer open and underneath another useless pile, I'm surprised to see a metal case below. I pull it out and swipe the cover. Written in very faded marker is the word "Heritage." I open it and blink. At the very top is a perfectly folded American flag. Underneath it are several printed articles. I look at the bottom corner and see they were printed from the Library of Congress's now-defunct website on May 17, 2147, just one year before the U.S. renounced all claims as a Judeo-Christian nation. The article reads, "Religion and the Founding of the American Republic." Behind it are several other articles on the same topic - religion and how it influenced the founding of the nation. Another article on separation of church and state and Thomas Jefferson's intended meaning. I flip past the various papers and find one more item at the very bottom.

It's an ancient, thick and tattered book.

I carefully lift the delicate hardcover and gasp in surprise. Inside it reads: "The Holy Bible Containing the Old and New Testaments Newly translated out of the Original Tongues." At the very bottom, it reads: "Philadelphia - Printed and Sold by R. Aitken."

"No way…" I mutter, shocked but ridiculously excited. "Sam, look at this."

"What is it?" he asks, making his way to me. He looks over my shoulder, eyes fixed on the volume in my hand.

"I didn't think any more of these existed," I reply. "It's an Aitken Bible - endorsed and approved by Congress." I'd read about these in my research. "Congress approved them for the citizens to read in the 1780s. They're so ancient, I didn't think a single copy survived, especially after the burnings."

I don't know what makes me more excited: the fact that I'm holding such an ancient volume in my hands or the fact that I'm actually holding a Bible. After the country's war on religion in the 22nd century, the government started burning religious texts in the 23rd century. The most popular book selected for burning was the Bible.

"Wait," Sam looks from me to the tome in my hands, frowning. "You mean to tell me Congress actually endorsed Bibles for the people?"

I nod and look back at it. "The endorsement should be in there."

I flip the delicate page, scared to tear it. But two pages in, I see it. Three paragraphs down: "RESOLVED that the United States in Congress assembled highly approve the pious and laudable undertaking of Mr. Aitken, as subservient to the interest of religion, as well as an instance of the progress of arts in this country…"

My eyes scan the words and read aloud, "…they recommend the edition of this Bible to the inhabitants of the United States…"

Sam gasps, clearly struggling to understand. "The government *hates* religion. Why would it-?"

"Only in the past three centuries, Sam." I tell him. "Most of the founding fathers were religious. Separation of church and state was meant to protect the church from the tyranny of the state, not exclude people with sincere religious beliefs from letting those beliefs influence the government. If that were the case, the majority of the Continental Congress would have been excluded from the founding of the nation. Many of its members had theological degrees."

I can tell when the information sinks in and registers with him because his eyes light up and he smiles as if relieved. I glance at his end of the room and ask him, "No luck?"

He shakes his head. "Let's hope the girls have better news."

The sun has set by the time I follow him back out onto

the cobbled street, metal case in hand. We don't even make it two blocks before we see the girls bouncing on the balls of their feet running over to us excitedly.

"We found them!" they yell simultaneously.

Sam and I run over to see.

"I don't get it," Sarah says back at the house. "All these years, I thought the founding fathers were Deists only mildly interested in religion and that separation of church and state was essential for the government."

"Well, who taught you that?" Dami asks.

"And how did that work out for the country?" Sam asks pointedly.

We're gathered around the living room table, on the floor, eating sandwiches as a quick dinner. The Constitution and Declaration are carefully laid out in the dark guest room, ready to be transported back to the mainland tomorrow morning when we leave. The faded ink is impossible to read on the ancient parchment. Even the titles of the documents are illegible. But Dami and Sarah found commercially printed copies of what the originals would have looked like as well as a transcript of the documents alongside the originals. We'll display them on the Capitol, never to be hidden again.

"Do you want to know when this nation started falling apart?" Sam asks. "When it turned its back on God."

There's a moment of silence as we all ponder those words.

I think back to all I know about the nation's history and slowly nod. "You're right."

They all look at me, surprised that I agree.

"What?" I shrug. "I'm not religious but I do have a brain. In the first two centuries, this nation flourished - when the majority of citizens were Christians and the nation stood under the banner of God. Yes, there were severe issues like slavery and women's rights to name a few. But for the most part, the nation stood strong. Then things started to change in the late 20th century and early 21st century."

Sam nods excitedly. "And what happened shortly after the country renounced its claims as a Judeo-Christian nation?"

"The Cyrian Flu," Dami mutters. "The worst epidemic since the Black Plague."

"*Concentrated* in the United States alone. Even traveling Americans didn't infect foreign nations with it. It stayed in this country."

Sarah shudders at that, clearly spooked by the idea.

I stand and retrieve something from my room.

When I return, Sam points to the book in my hand with a querying brow.

"George Washington's *Farewell Address*." I flip to the page I earmarked earlier. I'd had a chance to read it during the release of the holographs. "Listen to this: 'Of all the dispositions and habits which lead to political prosperity, religion and morality are indispensable supports.'"

"*He said that?*" Sarah asks in astonishment. "The first

president said that?"

I nod and read another part, "'...let us with caution indulge the supposition that morality can be maintained without religion. Whatever may be conceded to the influence of refined education on minds of peculiar structure, reason and experience both forbid us to expect that national morality can prevail in exclusion of religious principle.'" I close the book and look up. "I was shocked when I read that. I knew the founding fathers were religious men but I didn't know they considered religion *that* essential to society."

"See?" Sam exclaims. "We can't ignore all of this and continue the status quo."

"We're *not* continuing status quo," I object. "But what you're suggesting would set the tone for the entire nation. Do we really want to go religious? Is that really what the founding fathers intended?"

To my surprise, Dami gives an exasperated exhale. "Why are we making this so complicated? Just look at the verbiage used in the Declaration and the Constitution. The Declaration alone makes reference to God at least four times. The original first amendment protected religious rights immediately. The majority of the citizens at the time of the revolution were Christians even if the founding fathers weren't. And we have sitting right here," she gestures to the Aitken Bible I found, "proof that the founding fathers believed Christianity was essential for the nation's flourishing. Some may have been Deists. Others owned slaves. Obviously we can't idolize them - they were all flawed men. But the question is, even if they *weren't* Christians intent on building a Christian nation, we're here now. What do *we* do?"

Her words rock us.

And she has a point.

All this time we've been focused on what the founding fathers had in mind, we didn't even stop to consider that this is *our* nation now. Maybe they got some things wrong that we can rectify. Or improve. It sounds almost blasphemous but maybe we're facing the very same opportunity they had eight hundred years ago, at the end of another revolution: to create something new and keep it from devolving into the disaster it did the first time around.

I speak slowly. Cautiously. "How would we do it? There aren't many believers in this nation, guys. How would we do it and not be yet another regime forcing our beliefs down other people's throats?"

Sam replies, "We can be a nation welcoming of all faiths but loyal to one."

Sarah nods. "People aren't as antagonistic about religion as they once were. That Bible burning generation is gone, thank God. We can start something new."

Welcoming of all but loyal to one.

But what warrants us being loyal to *this* one?

We all finish our food in silence and head to bed, exhausted from the day. But the minute my head hits the pillow, the exhaustion I *thought* I was feeling takes flight. My mind is restless. I toss and turn on what is the most comfortable bed I've ever had the chance to sleep on but no matter what position I take, I simply cannot fall asleep. I get back up, walk to the living room and turn on one of the lamps near the sofa. Sitting down, I grab the heavy, ancient text, and carefully flip the pages that were once forbidden reading. I turn to the New Testament and read the first portion. The heading on the page says "Matthew."

It's morning. I'm elevated hundreds of feet in the air and am looking down at what looks like a farm. I've never seen one of these in person. I can only guess what it is from what I've seen in picture books and TV shows. There's a big red barn in the middle of an open field with rows upon rows of crops. The sun is shining, its rays of light hitting the barn and illuminating the house several yards away from it. The sky is a clear bright blue. The clouds, puffy and white. I look closely at the house and see the lone flag. Stars and stripes: red, white and blue. Waving proudly on the front porch.

"Decker."

I turn away from the house and see a man standing next to me. Elevated beside me. His eyes are warm. His face friendly.

He smiles at me and I ask, "What is this?"

"This is what you never knew. What once was. What could be again."

I look around once more. There's grass everywhere. I hear the laughter of children and see two little boys bound headlong out of the house, running into the sprawling field, their overalls smudged with dirt. Their faces flush with joy.

"This was America?" I ask. But it's not really a question. I look back at him and he nods, a sad smile on his face.

"'One nation under God, indivisible, with liberty and justice for all.' If you remove the first part, none of the rest can stand."

His words hit me and I take a deep breath. "So they're right? Sam and Dami? God blessed this country?"

"God blesses any nation that honors Him. Do you want to know why He first blessed America? It wasn't on behalf of the founding fathers. It was on behalf of the Puritans."

"The Puritans?" I frown.

He nods, unruffled by my reaction. "The Puritans crossed dangerous waters to live for God in peace. They dedicated the land they inhabited to Him and He honored the land for their sake. He blessed the nation for its people's faith, if not the men of the Continental Congress. The revolution wasn't fought by a small group of educated men. The war was one by an entire nation of godly men and women.

"But over the years, this nation turned its back on Him. Not just the leaders but the people themselves."

Suddenly the setting beneath us disappears and changes. We're in a courtroom. Several robes assemble around a table but I can't see their faces or make out their names.

He speaks again, "The Lord removed His lamp stand from this nation in 1973."

Understanding dawns on me as only one landmark case could have evoked such a response.

"Roe v. Wade," I mutter.

"The blood of millions of children cry out to me from this ground."

I look at him closely and finally ask, "Who are you?"

He meets my eyes again and smiles. And when he does, I can barely stand to look at him. He's radiant. Glowing. Something powerful radiates from him and robs me of my speech.

"I am the Son of Man, seated at the right hand of the power of God. All authority has been given unto me. Every knee shall bow and every tongue will confess that I am Lord."

My heart thunders at those words. I realize immediately who He is. I'm looking in the face of God. I sink to my knees and lower my head to His feet. Within seconds I feel a gentle hand on my head.

"I know you, Decker. I have chosen you since before you were born. I am giving this nation one more chance. And I am giving you one as well. Follow me and you will see my wonders."

"Ah!" I jolt awake with a gasp, the heavy book nearly sliding off my lap. I look around the room and realize there's enough natural light filtering in for me to turn off the lamp. My body is sore. My eyes are blurry. But my mind is buzzing with the dream I just had. I look down at the open tome in my lap. The heading of the page reads "Romans." I don't remember turning to this part of the book. I'm on chapter ten. Like magnets, my eyes are immediately drawn to the ninth verse in the text: *That if thou shalt confess with thy mouth the Lord Jesus, and shalt believe in thine heart that God hath raised him from the dead, thou shalt be saved."*

"I believe." I say it aloud. Quietly. To no one around me. I say it again, cementing it to myself. "I believe."

I hear padded feet shuffle into the room. Sarah walks in, eyes half closed with her blond bed hair a frizzy mess.

"Morning," she yawns.

"Morning," I reply, unsure of what to say. What do you say when someone walks in on the most important, earth shattering moment of your existence?

"How'd you sleep?" she asks around a yawn, digging in the pantry for some cereal.

"I didn't," I reply. Not really.

Sam enters next, his red hair sticking up on all ends.

"What do you mean you didn't?" Sarah asks, pulling a box out of the cupboard.

"Didn't what?" he asks, also yawning from a good night's rest.

"Sleep," Sarah answers him. "Decker said he didn't sleep."

He looks at me and frowns. "What were you doing all night? Reading?"

Dami walks in next, the only one fully dressed. "Morning."

"Hi." I look at her, openly admiring her bright white outfit. It makes her dark skin even more luminous. Her clothing reminds me of what He wore in my dream. All white. Spotless.

"Guys, I need to talk to you. Now."

They all grow silent and look at me in concern. I

gesture to the chairs near me and ask them in a very serious tone, "Please sit."

I don't waste time with preambles or explanations or theories about what I saw. I just tell them - from beginning to end. And while I'm sitting half in shock, I can tell they believe every word I say. Even more so, they seem to understand what I don't.

"You really think it was Him?" I ask them. "Jesus?"

Sarah nods. "Who else could it be? I doubt the devil would say what you heard in your dream."

Sam glances at her, nodding too. "It makes perfect sense. He's chosen to reveal Himself to you at this time. I know He speaks through dreams but I've never met a person who's experienced it himself!"

I look at Dami. "What do you think?"

Her dark eyes are fathomless. Thoughtful. I can tell she's working through a million different equations in her brilliant head. Finally she looks at me and simply replies, "It's not about what *I* think. What do you think? What do you believe?"

I look around at the three of them and add the last part of the story. How my eyes landed on a single verse open on my lap. How I was in John when I fell asleep but woke up to Romans.

"That isn't a coincidence," I tell them. "I believe."

There. I said it aloud.

For a second, we all just sit as the weight of my words sink in.

Then, suddenly, Sarah and Sam fly off their seats and

start jumping up and down. They rush over to me and pull me into fierce hugs, welcoming me to "the family." Dami is more reserved but her smile is as radiant as theirs. She refrains from hugging me but I can tell she's barely containing what she feels.

"Let's baptize you now!" Sam takes me by the arm and marches me out to the stream passing behind the yard. I follow him and wade into the cool but refreshing water. I turn back just as Dami and Sarah reach the edge of the water. I lock eyes with Dami.

"Will you do it?" I ask.

She blinks and folds her arms across her chest, an alarmed look in her eyes. "*Me?* Why would you want me to baptize you?"

"You know why," I reply. She blinks at that and for the first time in ages, I catch a glimpse of the woman who was once open to me. And vulnerable. I've missed her so much.

I walk back to her and pull one of her hands free, leading her into the water.

She scans my eyes nervously before a look of peace breaks over her. She nods and walks out to where Sam is standing, waist deep in the shallow water. Sam joins Sarah and watches. A gentle hand at my back, Dami looks me in the eyes and asks, "Decker, do you believe that Jesus is the son of God, that he is God and that He died for your sins and rose again?"

"I do."

"Do you accept Jesus as your Lord and Savior?"

"I do."

She smiles, tears welling in her dark eyes. She places a hand over my chest and lowers me into the water. It covers my face and my ears but I still hear her say, "I baptize you in the name of the Father, the Son, and the Holy Spirit."

I break through the surface, a watershed of peace washing over me as I rise.

Overwhelmed, I pull her into my arms and laugh. The most important thing has happened to me this very moment. And God used the most important woman in my life to bring it about.

Thank you, I tell Him inside and I realize this is my first prayer.

With what He told me hours earlier, I know this is the first of many.

"Being a Christian… is a character which I prize far above all this world has or can boast."

-Patrick Henry

CHAPTER FIFTEEN

It's close to seven at night when we finish the first draft of the Constitution - our renewed one. I made my stance known the minute we started working on it. That even though we'll never truly know if the founding fathers wanted this nation founded on Christian principles, their intention isn't really the point anymore. This is *our* nation now. *We* fought this second revolution. And *we* will decide how we need to move forward. One nation under God.

We propose to reinstate every right that was stripped from the Bill of Rights but strengthen the language to specify that *all* citizens regardless of race, gender, religion or creed are entitled to these rights. We also alter the language to protect these rights from future nullification. We add a preamble to this Constitution, clearly stating that the new republic, though open to all faiths and tolerant of all differences, is a nation restored on the basis of Judeo-Christian ideals. A new amendment is added forbidding the Supreme Court from making rulings that subsequently change or alter the laws of the nation, given that justices are not elected government officials.

It takes us hours upon hours to fine tune the details of the new republic, the bicameral legislature and the three branches that we will continue to lead. We talk briefly about the economy and how to restore equity between former Commoners and former Atlans.

"We should probably focus more on helping former Commoners get to a place of middle class living." Sarah says.

"Raise pay," Sam suggests.

"Provide education," Dami adds.

"We also need to repair the infrastructure. Taxes will have to rise and the national budget will have to be altered."

"You're getting ahead of yourself," Dami says gently. I meet her calm eyes and immediately relax. "We'll figure out the finer details when we get back. I'm sure Nicole's dad will have a suggestion or two and there are supportive former Atlans who know the ins and outs of a national fiscal system."

I nod, the weight lifted off my shoulders for now. As usual, she reminds me that I'm not on my own. I'll see the rest of the group tomorrow and we'll work on this together. I don't have to figure an entire nation out when there's an entire nation full of people to help do it.

Sarah stands. "Who's hungry?"

Rapid banging erupts downstairs. We all stand, alarmed at the sudden noise.

The banging escalates but this time a familiar voice is

muffled behind the wooden door. "Decker! Open up! It's me!"

I run down the stairs and immediately let him in. Adams rushes through, panting and very alarmed. His blue eyes scream urgency and his cheeks and neck are bright red. The rest of the group race down and look at him, startled and concerned.

"Adams, what is it?"

"What happened?"

He catches his breath just enough to gasp, "It's Jenner. Jenner's snapped."

My mind is spinning.

Ten years.

Ten years I've known Caden Jenner. And the man I know - or thought I knew - would never do everything Adams says he's doing. We're in the hover car, halfway to the main land. On the way, Adams explains how Jenner, with a small contingent of men, have been killing Atlans unprovoked, terrorizing them across town.

"His team is still small but they're growing in number and they've been working systematically," Adams says.

"How many has he killed?" Sam asks.

"Dozens of families. At least a hundred now. Nicole and I started hiding some in underground areas on Atlan, sending others to Commons... Mr. Washington was glued to the phone, warning families until Jenner forced Bill to cut off ANN and ADC's communication lines. We've been able to use the telepathic phones but we couldn't get you because of the distance. Deluger's standing in for me. I would have come earlier but none of us knew how to operate the second hover car at a long distance. I drove then took a boat to find you guys."

I nod. "You did what you could."

Had he waited for our scheduled return tomorrow, there might not be any former Atlans left.

"Several teams are out searching for him. There was a skirmish earlier but he managed to get away. What worries me is that he's getting more and more Commoners to follow him."

"How does he have any men in the first place?" I ask.

"He recruited them. First the Commoners. Then he tried to start poaching off my men. That's when I found out something was off. I went to meet him at Capitol Base but he had already started the rampage by the time I got there. He's lost it, Decker. I don't know what happened to him."

"What the-?" Dami's voice breaks off as she steers the hover car over the Wellington River. All of us stare out of the passenger windows. Several feet below, an enormous mob has gathered on the Mohanan Bridge. Bright lights illuminate Jenner standing on a podium, giving some sort of speech to the crowd. By some miracle, Dami manages to land the vehicle safely, on the edge of the pier.

Adams must have called Deluger because within seconds, the officers meet us at the car.

"Decker!" Nicole runs up behind them and pulls me

into a quick hug. "Thank God you guys are back. We need to get him off that stage."

We turn and run straight into the crowd. Nicole wastes no time in catching us up. "He started speaking five minutes ago. Is rambling on about a moneyless society and how money is the root of all evil. He's trying to incite the rest of the Commoners to wage war on the Atlans."

The longer he talks, the higher chance he has of swaying them. I push through crowds and crowds of men and women, trying to reach the bridge as quickly as possible. The people are initially testy until they turn and see my face. Suddenly, they start to part like the Red Sea and within seconds, I'm on the bridge.

"You know that I respect Decker Channing and what he's done for our nation. He wrote *American Sense*, which propelled me to start this revolution."

Jenner is still speaking on his makeshift stage when I break through the crowd. There's about three yards of space between his stage and the audience he's addressing. I step forward.

"Freeze!" one of his men yells before registering who I am. He and the men around him lower their weapons hesitantly. Jenner is so caught up in the sound of his voice, he doesn't even realize what's happened.

"I believed that Channing would be the leader we all needed to restore this country to the liberty and justice Commoners so richly deserve. But did you hear that speech he gave before he left? The talk about a peaceful transition? Peaceful merging... Why should Commoners be respectful to Atlans? These are the men and women who lorded over us with their wealth and greed and unfair taxes for *years* and *years*. They twisted the political system to have a nation that worked for *their* interests - not ours! Money is the root of all evil," he says again. "If we kill everyone with the money - *Atlans* - we will be on the path to a brighter, equal future."

Adams is right. He is insane.

"Jenner!" I yell.

He freezes mid-sentence. His eyes stretch wide, shocked to see me in front of him.

"What the hell are you doing, Jenner?" I yell out to him. My anger rages within me but the fear warns me to try and talk him down. I'm not scared of him. I'm scared of the damage he may continue to inflict if I don't convince him to cease fire.

"How did you-?"

"What are you doing, Jenner?" I repeat, my voice loud enough to be heard by the people behind me. The crowd falls to a dead silence as Jenner meets my eyes. And right before me, I see my friend disappear for good. His light blue eyes, once filled with laughter, encouragement and respect...they darken with an unmistakable self-righteousness. Anger. Bitterness. And even jealousy.

"I'm doing what's right for our people, Decker. Something I can no longer say about you."

"You're killing innocent men, women and *children*!" I yell. The crowd gasps at the accusation and I see his eyes dart to them, nervously.

"Only the wealthy," he corrects me. "Only those who would ensure the return of the Atlas regime." He points an accusatory finger at Nicole, two yards to my left. "Why don't you ask your little friend what she's been doing all this time? Watching *their* backs while I try to bring them to justice!"

I shake my head, horrified to see how far gone he really is. "What happened to you, man?" I ask helplessly. "What happened to you?"

"This isn't personal, Decker-"

"Like hell it isn't! How can you turn on us like this?"

We were all a team. We were all on the same side.

"Don't you see, Decker? I'm preventing another Atlas from forming. I didn't give up everything to have another Hamilton in office. Atlas must die!"

"Atlas *did* die!" I bellow. "It died the minute Hamilton died! You're talking about *murdering* innocent people."

"No," he shakes his head. "As long as Atlans are alive, Atlas is alive. Atlans alive, Atlas alive."

My heart breaks in two watching the man I once considered my closest friend, completely morph into the picture definition of insanity.

"End this now, Jenner. Please."

His eyes snap up defiantly. "No! I will not end this until every last Atlan roach is dead."

Out of nowhere, he lifts his hand and levels a gun directly at Nicole.

"What are you doing?" I move to help her but his men point their guns and I pause. Deluger and our guys draw

377

their weapons in response and the crowd behind us begins to break, scared to get caught in the crossfire.

"We're outnumbered," Adams tells me. *"Our other officers are in Atlas, fighting the rebels. And we can only correspond one-on-one. Jenner still has his phone."*

Shit.

Jenner narrows his eyes at Nicole. "Where are they?"

She shakes her head silently.

"Where *are* they, Nicole?"

"Who?" I ask her. "Who is he looking for?"

"The kids!" he yells. "The thirty-five children of the delegates, politicians and businessmen killed at Hamilton's Ball. All of whom can rise up in revenge one day and kill this new nation before it even has a chance to stand!"

"They will do no such thing…" Nicole says calmly.

"Where are they?"

"I'm not telling you."

"I'll kill you if you don't!"

"Jenner, don't!" Dami screams behind us.

"Tell me!" Spittle flies out of his mouth as his face contorts with rage.

"No!" she yells back.

His gun fires.

"No!" I bellow. My heart stops but time doesn't. Everything is instant: the bullet hitting her square in the chest, the way she falls back, crumbling to the ground, the blood spreading across her blouse. In shock, I respond automatically and immediately fire at Jenner. Panic erupts as the crowd behind us runs back to Commons, terrified they might be next. Adams and Deluger flank my sides, firing at him as well. It's no use. Jenner and his men retreat into their cars, parked only yards away from the podium, and drive off into Atlas, cloaked by the night.

"Stay with me. Stay with me, Nicole!"

I turn back and see them. Dami crouched over Nicole's body. The blood pooling on the ground beneath her. Her Mediterranean skin already a chalky white. I crouch on her other side.

"The serum!" I tell Dami. "The Atlas Serum!"

"I don't have any!" she cries hysterically. "Not on me!"

"Shh," Nicole whispers to Dami. "You know I'll be okay."

I frown at that. She's clearly dying. She doesn't have a lot of time. Her chocolate brown eyes - eyes I've looked into and smiled at for more than a decade - turn to me, struggling to keep focus. She rasps out, "Protect...the kids. You'll know...where to find them."

I frown at that. "What do you mean I'll know? How could I possibly know where to...Nicole? Nicole?"

"No!" Dami cries out. She pulls Nicole's lifeless body to her chest. Her eyes are still open but the chocolate brown is hollow. I swipe my hand over them, knowing I'll never see them again. I shrug off my jacket and coax Dami to lay her back down. Covering the upper half of her body with it, I silently say goodbye to the friend I should have trusted all along. Grasping Dami's arms, I force her to rise with me.

"We've got an aerial," Adams says behind me. "They're

going to her place."

Fear grips my sides.

My mother is there.

She's not in Commons.

"Go!" I yell. "*Now!*"

We all start running to the hover car.

"Sarah!"

Out of the Atlas darkness, Bill comes running across the bridge. There's blood streaked across his face and he's limping as he moves. Sarah runs to him and pulls him into an embrace. We pull the car up beside them and they climb in.

"I escaped," he gasps at us. "They tied me up at ANN before killing the entire staff."

"Dear God," Sam mutters. Sarah tucks her head into Bill's shoulder, crying silently.

Sam drives and we follow the officer escort to the Washingtons while Deluger gets a team of men to safely take Nicole's body to the Atlas morgue. I pull Dami closer to me. She's sobbing silently against my chest, her soft hair brushing the bottom of my chin, unable to speak. I can't either. I'm sitting, on my way to a home where I can only hope my mother and the other people I love haven't been slaughtered. My greatest fear is unfolding right before my eyes. Not only are innocent people dying in the wake of this movement, the people I love most could die. One of them already has. I look out the window at the pitch black buildings. Eerie with no light. I can only imagine the countless men, women and children hiding in those buildings. I close my eyes, hoping the guilt will somehow disappear behind my lids.

I've created a revolutionary monster.

I trusted someone I never thought would do such a thing. I think back to all the vitriolic comments he made about Atlans. How they were awful. How he didn't trust them. What I thought was normal Commoner frustration was really a deep, abiding, premeditated hatred of an entire segment of society. All the times I shrugged off those comments, the conversation we had before I left for Martha's Vineyard...

"How could I have been so blind?"

"We all trusted him." Dami sniffles beside me. I turn to her as she lifts her head from my chest. Eyes red and puffy, she looks me dead in the eye and croaks out, "Don't you dare blame yourself for what that lunatic is doing. This blood is on *his* shoulders. No one else's."

Easier said than done.

"I've reversed all of ADC and ANN's systems." Bill and Sarah work from the tablet he managed to take with him. "We can get in touch with the people through ADC at least."

"Good." I call the Washingtons' home number on my cell and tell him while it rings, "Make an announcement warning that Jenner and his men are in direct opposition to this movement. They are armed, dangerous, and criminally insane. Warn the people to stay inside their homes and barricade themselves from his men. Call all loyal recruits to assist in guarding Atlans until we apprehend Jenner and his men. And warn all Atlans to hide. There may be some who still don't know."

The phone rings and rings relentlessly. Finally, it sounds like someone is picking up.

"Hello?" I ask hopefully.

"Hello! You've reached the Washingtons. Sorry we're unable to-"

I turn off the phone with a desperate growl of frustration. I try again. And again. And again.

"Dammit!" I curse, allowing the anger to try and mask my fear. It's not succeeding.

Dami briefly squeezes my hand before turning to Bill and the tablet he's just finished typing on. "Let me see that."

She makes several keystrokes, accessing a part of her lab from the tablet.

"What are you doing?" I ask.

"Cutting off the telepathic phones. The less they're able to communicate, the better. We don't have to worry about detection anymore. Use your cells."

We race to the Washingtons and somehow arrive in less than fifteen minutes, half the time it would normally take. We all climb out and rush into the building.

"It's not good," Adams murmurs. "His men aren't here."

He wouldn't hurt her, I try to tell myself. But a terrifying premonition fills my core as I race up the stairs to their floor, two stairs at a time, ahead of everyone else. The sight that awaits me feels like an eight inch knife thrust into my chest.

Bodies are slumped all over the place. Mrs. Washington on the kitchen floor. Mr. Washington at the threshold. His son, Tobias Jr., dead just a few feet away from...

"Mom!" *This* is my greatest fear. A nightmare I truly believed wouldn't happen. She's on the ground, crumpled against the heavy Persian rug. Her gun - the gun I gave her for protection - lies several feet away from her, far out of reach. I turn her towards me. Her face swims behind my tears. I look down and shake my head. "No, no, no, no!" A wide circle of blood fans out across her torso.

Her small dark eyes look up at me. "Decky!" My heart shatters at the use of the nickname. A name she hasn't used since I was eight and told her to stop. "Decky, you're here. I knew you'd get here," she gasps.

But I'm not here in time.

"Mom, please." I beg her. "Please don't die-"

"Shh." Her response is eerie. It reminds me of Nicole's last words to Dami. "It's okay. I got to see you one last time before I...I..." she coughs and blood spurts up from her mouth.

"Mom!" I hug her close to my chest.

"The kids..." she gasps for air. "The kids...we hid them. You know where they are."

"How do I know where they are?" I ask her, frustrated tears spilling over. I really want to yell who cares about the damn kids? My mother's been shot.

She makes a faint gesture with her hand and I'm worried the loss of blood is making her delusional.

"Everything," she coughs up more blood.

"No!" I look up and see the group, standing there helplessly as I hold her.

"Don't just look at me!" I scream at them. "Help me! Help *her*!"

Dami breaks through the fold and kneels beside us, coming into my mother's focus. Mom's face lights up immediately. She reaches for Dami's hand and smiles. "Thank you. Thank Nicole for me too."

Dami's eyes flood again. "Nicole…Nicole…"

Mom nods, her expression somber. "Then I'll be seeing her soon."

I frown at that. "What do you mean? What do you-?"

"Take…care of my son, Dami…You'll tell him, please? Promise me you'll…make sure he knows."

"He already knows, Ms. Kim. He got baptized this morning."

I look from Dami's face to my mother's, her eyes on me, glowing once more. "You *know*! You know! Oh, thank God."

I frown in confusion. She sounds like Sarah and Sam. "I don't-"

"The Washingtons were Christians," Dami quickly explains. "Mrs. Washington witnessed to your mother shortly after she moved in."

It all makes sense now. The bowed heads, the moving lips in the kitchen. Even the uncharacteristic kindness of an entire family. The Washingtons were Christians. And they converted my mother before they died. Before she…

I stare at the woman who gave birth to me. The

woman who has always been by my side. Her eyes are drifting more and more to something unseen.

"Mom, *no*!" I shake her. "No, don't leave me!"

I don't care if I'll see her again when I die. I don't want to lose her now. Not yet.

Her eyes drift back to me one last time. She reaches up, a weak hand touching my tear-stained cheek. "I...lo...I love...you...Decker..." she gasps. "You're...the best...thing I ever did."

Her eyes close and her hand falls back down like lead. Her body falls slack in my arms.

She's gone.

I hug her body close to my chest and pour out all of my grief, tears falling into her silky, soft hair. Her body is still warm. She still smells like herself. But it's a lie. A lie that will quickly give way to the truth.

She's dead. Gone forever.

Several hands touch my back in an attempt to comfort me. Nothing can comfort me but for the sake of my mother, I force myself to push forward. I suddenly stand and carry her small light body to a nearby room. I lay her on the bed and close the door behind me, knowing if I look back, I'll break down all over again and won't get up.

Adams, Sam, Sarah, Bill and Dami are still looking around the house.

"They're not there," I call out to them. I go back to the living room, ignoring the streak of my mother's blood. I move the coffee table off of the rug and lift back the rug from the wooden floors. The five of them come back to the living room.

"What are you doing?" Sarah asks.

"Get me a knife," I tell her. I look at Adams and Sam as she runs into the kitchen. "Put their bodies in a bedroom and lock the door."

They scramble to remove the bodies from sight.

I knock on various parts of the wood, testing the spots to find the weakest point. It all makes sense to me now.

"You'll know where they are."

"Everything's under the floorboard. Ever since you were a child, everything important. Under the floorboard."

She wasn't making a random gesture as she died. I now realize my mother was trying to make a cupping gesture. She and the Washingtons hid the kids where I always go to hide important things. Sarah hands me the knife and I stick it in the crease. Several tugs and pulls later, the wooden plank pops up. The first face I see has wide, terrified blue eyes.

"Decker?" Karen says, her voice trembling.

"Bill, help me!"

Together, we lift the remaining wooden planks and down below find dozens of children, various ages, curled into terrified balls on the base floor below.

We quickly come up with a plan. Sarah and Bill are to stay and guard the kids. Sam will go to Maids Quarter to get reinforcements and care. With so many women who once cared for these kids, we reason they'll defend them as if they were their own. At least we hope they will. I can't stand to be here any longer. My mother's dead body is in one room and I'm surrounded by children whose parents I helped kill just days ago. Though for vastly different reasons, I did to them what Jenner has just done to me and I can't bear to meet any of their eyes.

"We need to split," Dami says. "The guns can only be disarmed directly from my lab. If I can disarm their guns, they won't be able to kill anymore kids."

"Not necessarily," Adams reminds her. "Some of the rebel cops have their own weapons."

"Which means we need to go after them," I say.

"Then let's split," Dami repeats. "You guys check the Capitol. I'll go to my place and disarm the guns."

"Be careful," I tell her. The thought of her going anywhere by herself fills me with dread. I can't lose her too. She meets my eyes and gives a slight nod.

"You too," she says quietly. Our eyes hold another brief second before she turns and leaves the apartment.

"Come on," Adams says. "They're several minutes ahead of us."

We reach the Capitol and immediately take in the ornate building. We glance at the small contingent of men near us. "Okay," Adams says. "Our plan is simple. Run and shoot."

We burst through the doors of the grand hall and are immediately met with a hail of fire.

"Take cover!" I yell, ducking and tumbling to the nearest marble column. We break off in groups, bunching at opposite ends of the hall. Adams starts the retaliation, firing at the opposing men wherever we see them: on the ground, on the level above.

"Move forward!" I yell. The lights are off and it's difficult to make out who is who. I focus on the sounds as much as the sight and shoot anyone in front of me or above. The guys behind me crouch low and look about, guarding my back. We surge on, firing at any moving man to the front of us. There's a break in the hailstorm, at which point Adams and I scream, "Run!"

We surge forward, completely elevated and rush to the back of the hall, near the office corridors. A team of men await us there.

"Down!" I shout, pulling a guy out of the line of fire.

Adams crouches on the opposite end of the hall, near an antiquated A/C unit.

"Decker, we've got this! Go!"

I take my opening and run, headlong, into the Presidential office. Gun drawn I shoot as I step in, unwilling to get hit first. I close the door behind me and crouch low, pacing the room and looking for movement. The firing outside continues for another minute or so but by the end of it, I realize there's no one in this room.

The door opens behind me and Adams walks in. "They're all down. We got them all."

"He's not here." I tell him.

Adams looks around, confusion marring his face.

"Why would he have his men guard this place and not be here himself?"

Behind the door, we hear muffled calls. "*Adams! Channing! We need to leave now!*"

Our guys rush into the office.

"It's a trap! They planted a bomb!"

One of the men shoots open the window overlooking the lawn. Rough hands grab my shoulders as we all jump through our closest exit. Seconds later, a wave of heat, noise, and debris fly out behind us. My ears are ringing and my chest heaves. I cough and choke desperately for a fresh gust of air. Unable to ask, I look around and count. To my relief, everyone's out. Everyone's alive.

We look back at the building. It's in flames, the bomb localized to the Presidential office suite, nowhere else in the building. He did set a trap. He had every intention of us going here.

"Now what?" Adams coughs, his face a sweaty, dirty mess.

I force myself to stand. "Go back to the Washingtons. I know where he is."

"I'm not going to hurt you. You don't have to be afraid of me."

Jenner took it for granted that his trap would work. That we wouldn't be alive. There are no men guarding the building when I walk right in, up the stairs to her floor and through the open door. I hear voices on the floor below. They're in her lab.

"Dami, you know me. You know that I would never hurt you."

"I don't know who you are at all. The Jenner I knew would have never hurt Nicole, much less killed her! She was my best friend!" Her voice is filled with rage, but it doesn't stop it from cracking in fear.

"I'm sorry about Nicole. But she was part of Atlas. If she and Decker survived, the whole regime would come alive again."

I scramble, trying to find a way to enter the lab without alerting him through the elevator.

"What do you mean *if* Decker survived? What have you done now?" I can hear the panic in her voice.

"Forget about him!" he says savagely. "I know I'm not him but don't you see how much you mean to me? You're the only Atlan I will spare. I love you that much. Couldn't you find it in your heart to love me?"

I blink at that. He's really gone off the deep end. What I thought was a passing attraction, he's warped into a twisted confession of love.

"Marry me, Dami. Be my co-regent. We can lead Commoners to a better future."

"Get out, Jenner."

"Please, if you'll just give me a chance-"

Something crashes to the ground as feet quickly shuffle.

"Get *away* from me Jenner! *Ouch!*"

The alarm in her voice shocks me into action. I run

and take the elevator, this time *hoping* the noise will get him to stop whatever he's doing. I tuck myself in the corner, as far away from the door as possible and crouch. Before the lift even settles, bullets rain over it, covering it in a hailstorm of gunfire.

The door somehow opens and I wait.

"Whoever is there - show yourself now!" Jenner shouts. I keep still but push the button to hold the door open.

"Show yourself *now*!" he repeats. I look at the reflective, bright white floor of the lab, willing him to step a little closer. If I can pinpoint him, I can get a shot. But things don't go as I plan.

"What are you-? What are you doing?!"

Out of nowhere Dami runs to the massive keyboard and quickly types a code. The computer suddenly responds: "Password confirmed. All firearms aborted."

"No!" Jenner shouts. I exit the lift right as he runs to her and yanks her back roughly by her arm. The momentum of his shove throws her into the side of the metal table. The edge makes contact with her head and she slumps to the floor. A rage unlike anything I've ever known fills me.

Our eyes lock - his surprised to see me alive. We lunge for each other. He swings but I duck and plant my fist into the center of his diaphragm. His breath rushes out of him and he stumbles back, clutching his chest. I go for another blow but he manages to roll and twist, snatching my arm into a lock behind my back. I jump and flip, pulling my arm free of his hold - but not in time to miss his punch. He hits the center of my jaw and sends me reeling, the pain exploding across the side of my face.

He lunges again but I duck.

I lunge again but he turns.

We go back and forth like this until finally…we crash. Bodies collide and fists connect to face as we roll and wrestle each other into submission. He's above me - pummeling me with his fist over and over again. I block the next blow and jerk my head up, connecting my forehead with his nose. It sends him flying back, onto his back, clutching his face. I stand and kick him across the torso again and again until finally I hear one of his ribs crack near his chest.

"Ahh!" he cries, blood spilling from his mouth. He looks up at me. "You don't understand. I did what I had to do."

"You killed my mother!" I spit out at him. "She fed you. She cared for you. She *loved* you like a second son. How could you hurt *her*? Of all people - *her*?"

Tears fill my eyes as the rage evaporates. He's broken something in me that I can never get back. And rage won't fill the void.

His eyes shutter close.

"I did what I had to do," he pants again, eyes squeezed shut in stubborn insistence. Completely unapologetic. "I did what I had to do."

I look at him, chanting to himself on the ground. Pathetic. Broken. Snapped.

With no gun to work with, I grab him by the head and

give his neck a clean, hard twisting pull. His vertebra snaps loudly and instantly his body falls limp. He's dead. It's the most merciful death he'd get having done what he's done.

God help me.

I've just killed the man I once considered my closest friend.

The sound of groaning on the other side of the lab snaps me out of my spiraling thoughts. I rush to the metal table as Dami begins to come to. She moves gingerly, wincing at the pain in her head, and I can only imagine where else. A small rivulet of blood flows down the side of her face, past her ear. I help her up slowly, rubbing the length of her arms in comfort. Her eyes connect with mine and a watershed of emotion breaks out across her features. Disbelief that she's seeing me. Relief that I'm alive.

"Decker." She looks at me with disoriented, tear-filled eyes. "He said you were dead-"

"Shh. It's okay. You're okay. It's over now," I whisper, pulling her close to my chest. "He's gone now. It's over."

I kiss the top of her head as her arms wrap around my middle. She tucks her face into my neck and breathes a sigh of relief.

The worst is over.

The final enemy has died.

USA ONCE MORE "UNITED STATES OF AMERICA" WITH NEWLY ELECTED PRESIDENT DECKER CHANNING

Natalie Rummel
South African Times
October 24, 2628

Nations around the world rejoice as revolutionary hero and leader, Decker Channing, prepares to give his inaugural address on the heels of his landslide electoral victory following the deaths of USA Dictator Victor Hamilton and his corrupt regime. Channing, and a small band of citizens, successfully planned and executed a nearly impossible insurrection against one of the most lethal leaders in the world.

For the first time in twenty eight years, correspondence has been received from the world's most isolated nation. Disturbing reports continue to emerge, recalling the classist, elitist, and oppressive society the former government championed. Citizens report that for nearly three decades, Hamilton ruled USA, now renamed the United States of America, with an iron fist, promptly ridding the country of any citizens who dared speak dissention.

Reporters are still learning precisely what took place on the night of October 14, when Channing and a small contingent of officers unseated the government. Prior to the insurrection, Hamilton ruthlessly bombed the majority of what was formerly known as Commons, killing millions of men, women and children.

In light of this atrocity, and other destructive measures

endorsed by Hamilton's regime, foreign powers are calling this new development a "triumphant victory" of good versus evil, equality versus oppression. The nation has a very long way to go in recovery but with the inauguration of a trusted leader, many are hopeful that the United States can once again be the "land of the free and the home of the brave."

"Posterity! you will never know how much it cost the present generation to preserve your freedom! I hope you will make a good use of it."

-John Adams

EPILOGUE

Ten Years Later:

"And there's the nation's flag waving proudly as it enters New York City's Time Square, a float right behind it prominently displaying scrolls representing the Constitution."

The headline on the screen reads: **"CELEBRATING 10 YEAR ANNIVERSARY OF 2ND AMERICAN REVOLUTION."**

We all watch the screen as ANN gives play-by-play details of the day's celebration. It's the first time we're not there live, preferring instead to watch it from our home in the comfort of our bed. Two of our kids, Emmanuel and Kim, bounce up and down on the bed, jostling all of us in their play. I wave to my eldest.

"Emmanuel, sit. I want to see."

He sits down and scoots over, as Dami turns up the volume, the news anchor continuing. "Americans attending the parade are all saying the same thing: that it's hard to believe it's been only ten years since the old regime of Victor Hamilton crumbled. Two days after Caden Jenner was killed, Decker Channing was elected the new president of USA, quickly renamed the United States of America. Since his election, the country has doubled in population and geographic range with the re-annexation of four states so far. President Channing created a cabinet of former Commoners *and* Atlans and worked tirelessly to merge the two classes that had been so divided culturally and socioeconomically for more than a century.

"The surviving leaders of the 2nd Revolution joined his core government and helped reinstate the democracy of the founding fathers with a strict ban on lobbying, the only exception to the free speech amendment immediately restored. Recent polls show that ninety-two percent of citizens now consider the government incorruptible. There is no lobbying, there are no pensions for Congressmen, all elected officials can only serve two terms, and the United States is now the only nation that conducts elections purely on the basis of presidential debates and a basic statement of beliefs on the part of the candidates. No campaigning and no opportunity for politicians to be bought by special interest persons or groups."

The footage cuts to people cheering on the streets, waving flags of their own as they cheer and celebrate, many with small children. Our son, Walker, is on the floor in front of our bed, practicing cartwheels on the safety of the carpeted floor.

"Six," Emmanuel rates him.

His sister is more generous. "Seven and a half."

"Elected officials are also held accountable by the people through Bill 249, a measure that allows citizens to signify every six months if their elected official is fulfilling his or her duties to the people's satisfaction. If a majority vote concludes otherwise three times in a row, the elected official is removed without pay and the seat is given to the individual with the next highest vote. Since the 2nd Revolution, infrastructure on what was once Commons has been restored and renewed. Education reform provides free education all the way through college and includes a thorough curriculum on biblical and theological studies alongside domestic and world history. Many cite this as the reason for the overwhelming number of citizens who self-identify as Christians, a number that has more than quadrupled in the last decade alone. All constitutional rights have been restored, including the freedom of religious expression."

I reach over and squeeze Dami's hand. She squeezes back and leans into my shoulder.

"Mommy," Kim asks her, "When are Joey and Cara coming?"

"The Humphreys will be here in about an hour."

My wife rolls her eyes and I smile. Our kids are obsessed with Sarah and Bill's two kids. And the feeling is mutual. It's a good thing they only live a couple neighborhoods away or we'd have to take the hover car for play dates every few days.

"You'd think they'd be tired after seeing your father,"

Dami murmurs.

I shake my head. "The only one tired after that visit is him."

The ANN anchor continues, "Diplomatic relations are cautiously picking up again. Channing's successor, President Samuel Tate met with Great Britain's Prime Minister, Harry Waldwell, two weeks ago - the first time an American president has met with a foreign dignitary in nearly half a century. The move is seen as a positive sign that the steel wall that was torn down ten years ago will remain lowered. President Tate has repeatedly stated that he maintains regular contact with former President Channing as he navigates leading the nation in his first term."

I smile at that comment. Sam has steadily transformed from a nervous wreck to a confident leader. He calls me regularly for advice but I can tell he's coming into his own. He has all the support he needs with Adams as his VP.

"And what about President Channing? The leader of the 2nd revolution and founding president of a revived America, served as president for two terms, insisting that George Washington's example be continued. It's been two years since he handed over the reins to President Tate and he has since spent his years out of public service, earning his bachelor's degree in history with plans to study his way to a PhD. He has been married to his wife, Damilola Channing, daughter of slain Commoner rights attorney Emmanuel Aderele, for ten years. They married shortly after his election and have four children together ages eight to two…"

"Hey! That's us!" Walker points to the screen excitedly.

The kids scramble off the bed and run over to the TV, enamored with the sight of our family photo on air.

Dami laughs. "You guys have been on TV your entire lives. What's the big deal about it now?"

"Not all of us," Emmanuel shakes his head. "Nikki wasn't born when we left the White House."

"He's right, you know?" I murmur to my wife in a low voice. "We were busy making her right before we left."

"Decker!" She slaps my arm as if scandalized. I laugh and lean in for a long, deep kiss. I'll never get enough of her full soft lips. Leaning back, I smile into her happy dark eyes. "I love you."

"I love you, too."

We stare at each other like idiots while the news plays on. My eyes shift up to her beautiful, tightly coiled curls. Over her shoulder, something catches my eye and I frown. Leaning across my wife, I gently but quickly pull the book from our two-year-old's chubby dimpled hand. Her bright red crayon is poised in the other hand. Our youngest daughter, Nicole, looks up at me with confused brown eyes. It never ceases to amaze me they're the same shade as her namesake's.

I hand her a scrap piece of paper and put the Bible on much higher ground. "That's not a coloring book, honey."

Dami lifts her up and kisses her soft cheeks before she has the chance to get upset. "You'll know all about it when you're older, pumpkin."

I nod in full agreement, grateful we have the freedom to tell her one day.

Author's Note

Dear Reader:

I want to thank you for taking the time to read *Atlas Died*. This story is unlike anything I have ever written before and I hope you found it entertaining, regardless of your political, religious, or cultural philosophies. I was inspired to write this book after watching *Park Avenue: Money, Power and the American Dream,* a documentary on the socioeconomic disparity of New York City. In addition to numerous problematic trends I've seen in America over recent years, I was inspired to write a dystopian novel exploring the themes of socioeconomic injustice, classism, religious freedom, and liberty.

I want to thank you for having an open mind and taking the time to escape into Decker, Dami and Nicole's world, regardless of your spiritual background. If I could rank the number one critique I often get as a writer, it is for my references to Christ in a novel that is available on the secular market (despite the clear disclaimer I include in the description). Certainly, some may find spiritual references offensive – especially if they are not ambiguous but I am a believer and I am a writer; I will check neither aspects of my identity at the storytelling door.

If you enjoyed the story, **please take the time to write a review and let me and other readers know what you thought of the book.** I do read the positive reviews and it warms my heart to see the encouragement! Also, spread the word about the story. I'm still processing much of what took place in the book and am sure that, if anything, this story is a great conversation starter about government, society and differing ideologies at large.

Please also stay in touch. Join my Facebook page to stay in the loop (www.facebook.com/authormichelleonuorah). If you want to be notified of new releases, go to http://tinyletter.com/mnomedia. And feel free to explore my other work via my website: www.mnomedia.com.

Also, if you aren't a believer and are curious to learn more about Christ, please feel free to visit my website or contact me directly. I am more than willing to share.

Sincerely,
Michelle

MNO|MEDIA

The MNO Media Challenge

Stories are powerful. If you liked this novel and think that others would benefit from reading it, regardless of their background, please consider the MNO Media Challenge by:

1.) Writing a review on Amazon, Goodreads, and Barnes & Noble.
2.) Recommending it to people in your inner circle – family and friends.
3.) Purchasing copies of this book and other MNO Media titles as a gift for others.

Stories can impact lives and with your help, a bigger impact can be made. Thanks!

Excerpt: Type N

CHAPTER ONE

Nicolette:

I run. I run as hard as I can in the middle of the forest, cell phone pasted to my ear. I run so hard my chest feels like an inferno. I ignore the burn.

It's the dead of night, and I can hear shouting in the distance pierced every now and then by the dogs barking.

"Information. How can I help you?" the operator asks.

"I need the address for 206-555-6484. Hurry, please!"

Flashlights circle behind me, and I try to run even faster. Suddenly, I lose my footing and trip over an unseen root, cell phone flying out of my hand. I gasp in pain but get back up and scramble to find the phone. There is no time for pain, barely time for running. I find it just as the operator pulls the address.

"1504 Menlee Drive," she rattles off. I shut the phone and take off again.

My race leads me to a residential area. I squint at the little numbers on the street curbs until I find the house I'm looking for and bang on the door. A tall, very young, blonde hair, blue-eyed man opens it. He takes one look at me and wordlessly lets me in.

One Year, Four Months Earlier:

If I, Nicolette Talloway, could sum up my day-to-day existence in one word, it would be isolated. At school, I go through my day surrounded by people yet entirely alone. Sometimes I feel like if it weren't for the numerous records of my existence, I would literally vaporize from the consciousness of those around me. How do I begin to describe myself to you?

Let's start with the basics: I am a seventeen-year-old junior at Bellmont High School. I make good grades, go to school every day, and always sit in the corner of class. I'm the kid who was just *too something*: too weird, too skinny, too tall, too pale. Never cool enough to be noticed, but not strange enough to be picked on. Growing up, sometimes I envied the kids that got bullied.

At least they were seen.

Nothing is out of the norm today. I wake up, get on the bus, and go to school. I go through classes taking notes, watching the idiotic behavior of my clown classmates, virtually invisible. It's quite entertaining actually. Some of my classmates are straight jackasses but some of them really could have a career in comedy. I walk down the hallways, into the bathroom, into the cafeteria… alone, alone, alone. My favorite place to be is the library.

During lunch, I sit in the almost-empty room of books and switch between reading my book, drawing in my sketchpad and observing the people who pass by outside.

People-watching has always been one of my favorite hobbies. By watching the habits and outlines of others, I'm better able to mimic them in my art. Not that I'm a real "artist" but I'm a hell of a doodler, always drawing stuff on scraps of paper and convincing myself that I know what I'm doing. It also helps being inconsequential to others because they never notice me watching them.

People tend to look over me, past me, or right through me. And making friends is easier said than done. Sometimes I feel like friendship is a train that everyone hopped on and for some reason I missed it and am still standing on the platform.

At home, life isn't that different. My family has gotten used to my withdrawn nature and stopped trying to draw and include me in their conversations years ago. As long as I'm not pregnant or doing drugs, my parents aren't concerned. If I were carved out of the picture, my family would be the embodiment of 1950s Americana.

My parents are an average-attractive couple in their forties; my father an accountant, my mother an interior designer. Our house was built from scratch with an open floor plan and practically reeks of upper-middle class money. It is both modern and warm with beige, bronze, and orange hues. We sit around the dark oak table in the dining room adjoining the kitchen. Conversation swirls around me like normal.

"How are classes, Nat?" Mom asks.

"So far so good," she replies. "I'm on the weekly rotation now. No more reporting about dances and crap. My team got assigned to the elections."

My older sister, Natalia, is a blonde bombshell who blows every dumb blonde stereotype out of the water. A junior at the University of Washington, she is at the top of her class and is on the fast track to a promising career in journalism.

"All right!" Dad exclaims.

"Congratulations, sis." Nate winks at her.

My younger brother, Nathaniel, is an equally attractive, amiable guy. He's just a year younger than me and my parents have strong hopes for him, their only son. I guess you could say he is the poster child for courage and strength and the only family member who ever sees me on occasion. Every now and then, I catch him watching me with half concern, half curiosity. Sometimes he'll even ask me how I'm doing. That's just him…he's…nice.

"Thanks," Natalia replies. "Call it the benefits of being an upperclassman at UW. *Finally* we get to-"

My brother starts coughing incessantly. He looks at my sister apologetically but we all know that he can't help it. He can never anticipate when it's going to come. Mom rushes to the kitchen. Dad clasps my brother by the back of the neck, as if to brace him for the coughs racking his body.

Growing up, Nate has always had a string of illnesses, combined with chronic asthma. Between my parents' constant praise and adoration of Natalia and their pride mingled with concern for Nathaniel, I know they have nothing left in the emotional bank for me. Middle-child syndrome, I guess.

"How bad this time?" Natalia asks Nate.

He holds up seven digits.

"I'll get his medicine." She takes off without another word. Mom returns with an inhaler and pops it in his mouth.

"Top shelf in the pantry," she calls out to my sister.

Nate deeply inhales and his cough begins to subside.

"Does this have anything to do with…?" Dad asks.

"I guess we'll find out next week," Mom replies.

"What if she doesn't know?"

"Tom, she's the top oncologist in the country. Of course she'll know."

"But is melanoma her specialty?"

"She'll know, Tom!"

Yeah.

His latest challenge has been his recent bout with melanoma. I look at Nate, my worries stamped all over my face. He catches my eye and winks in assurance as if to say, *"I'll be fine."*

Two Weeks Later

"Hello?"

"Nikki, it's Mom. We need you to get to the Wakefield ER as soon as possible."

I glance at the clock which reads 8:35. My whole family is usually home by six at the latest.

"Why? What happened? Are you okay?"

"It's not me," Mom explains. "It's Nate. He's been in a car accident, and he needs blood. We've all been tested but none of us are O negative. Rebecca Jensen is but she's too anemic to donate. We need you to get tested right away."

My mother hangs up before I can get another word in.

The deluge of shock, worry, and anger hits me like a wave against the shore. Of all the people to get in an accident, did it really have to be my brother? Mom mentioned the Jensens. How could she and Dad have contacted them before calling me? I'm his sister. I'm seventeen. I'm not in college or grad school or some other state, married with two kids. I'm still a member of the nuclear family unit. Why didn't my family contact me earlier? How is it that I am just getting this news now?

As I drive to the hospital, the questions don't cease and as the questions mount, my anger rises. I can't help but stack my family's offenses the way a miser stacks his coins. I'm furious with them, and I'm beginning to wonder if my family would show nearly the same amount of concern if it were me in that hospital bed. I also wonder how many people already know. Who else have they called?

When I arrive at the hospital, my premonition is validated. Teachers, students, neighbors, and distant relatives crowd the hospital waiting room. The whole town knew of my brother's accident before I did. I approach the mob, fully aware that I am the last person anyone thought to call in this emergency.

I gaze around the room and catch my older sister's eye.

"Nikki!" Natalia exclaims. My parents' heads snap in my direction, and they rush over to me.

"Thank God you're finally here. What took you so long?" Mom says. She kisses my cheek absentmindedly and takes my bag out of my hand.

I squelch my urge to ask her, *"Are you kidding me? What took **you** so long?"*

I turn to my father. "Dad, how is he?"

He kisses my forehead but doesn't answer my question.

"You're here now, that's all that matters." Dad pulls off my coat and flings it on a chair. They usher me to the nearby nurse and I suddenly realize that they just tag-teamed me! The nurse's station is a mess. Telephones keep ringing, women and men in scrubs rush all around us. My dad singles out one of them.

"Nurse," Dad says. "This is our other daughter. Please test her too."

He waits a moment.

"Now," he clarifies.

The nurse looks like someone wrung her through an old fashioned washing machine. My parents aren't difficult people but they can be demanding when they are stressed.

"Mr. Talloway, I will test your daughter as soon as possible-"

"Why can't you do it now?"

"Mr. Talloway, there are other patients in this hospital-"

"Are there other patients with melanoma who have just

been in a serious wreck? Test her blood now, please!"

The nurse opens her mouth to respond, but my father gives her such a searing look of warning that she begins to look around for help.

"Don't worry, Jan. Jason will test her."

An average-looking, middle-aged man with brown hair gestures to a tall blonde guy in a white lab coat. The blonde guy extends his hand to me.

"Dr. Jason Monroe. I'm assisting Dr. McGrath," he gestures to the older gentleman, "in treating your brother."

Okay, I know I'm in the ER and this is a total emergency but I can't help but notice how good-looking this guy is. His eyes are a deep blue. Not sky blue or baby blue, but ice glazier water blue. He has a straight nose, sharp jaw line, and a full head of silky blonde hair. Even worse, as I lean in to take his hand, I'm met with a cool, refreshing scent that must be his cologne. His presence is so disarming, I have to look away. *Please don't let him see how nervous I am.* This is too much. My brother's in the hospital, my family didn't have the decency to call me until just now – and now I have to deal with a ridiculously attractive man.

"Please follow me."

"Thank you, Doctor." Dad says appreciatively.

This man looks *way* too young to be a doctor. If I could guess, I would say he's only a couple years older than me, but I silently follow him to a nearby lab room. They already have my file on hand and my thoughts switch back to my parents and the situation at hand. My anger begins to surge through me to the point where I can barely hold my arm still for the needle. As Dr. Sex-on-a-Stick draws my blood, I can only think of how my family has slighted me. Is it irrational to be upset? When an emergency takes place, aren't you supposed to contact loved ones? Or am I not a loved one even in my own family?

CHAPTER TWO

Jason:

Nicolette Talloway. She's upset. I mean, why wouldn't she be? Her brother is in the hospital, having suffered a serious accident. The kid is lucky to be alive. She seems more angry than distraught though. I'm running the test for her blood but all I can think about is how she had remained completely silent when I drew it, taking deep breaths to stay composed. The test will take almost an hour to complete so I decide to do some rounds in the meantime.

I take the long route and stop at the nurse's station near the waiting room to pick up my charts. I don't know why – okay that's bull, I do know why. I want to see her. I try my best to be inconspicuous as I observe her. She sits completely removed from her family. There is a huge crowd surrounding her, yet no one seems to notice her. Her arms are crossed and her head is down like it was in the phlebotomy room.

She has long, jet black hair that curls at the edges. Her skin is really pale – but it suits her. Long dark lashes shield her eyes from the outside world, and I wish I could have gotten her attention, if only to see her eyes for a second. *So this is what Snow White looks like.* Snow White could use a cheeseburger.

Or five.

When I first saw her in her black attire, I thought she

was trying to make a statement and stand out from her American pie family, but on second thought, I don't think so. Most Goth chicks would go for combat boots to finish off their look; instead she's wearing plain black running shoes. I can't see her eyes, but her straight nose, full lips, and high cheek bones indicate that she's just as beautiful as her sister if not more. Frankly, she's stunning, and she's not even trying. I feel like a pedophile watching her but I remind myself that I'm twenty and only three years ago, it was totally legal for me to dig a chick her age.

But that was three years ago.

Why is she sitting by herself? Why is no one in the room even acknowledging her? Her mother, father, and sister are all huddled together, giving each other hugs and words of encouragement. Did she get in a fight with them? Shouldn't an emergency like this squash any petty family dispute? And if she did get in a fight with them, what of the others in the room? She can't have alienated herself from the *entire town*. Watching her, I can't help but feel a deep sense of empathy. I feel a burning in my chest that is much akin to anger. What the hell is wrong with these people?

"Jason!"

I jump when I feel a meaty hand clap me hard on my back. I *hate* it when people do that. Hurts my back and scares the crap out of me at the same time. I turn to my supervisor and mentor, Dr. Greg McGrath. His brown eyes are crinkled in amusement and I can already feel the heat rising to my face. He caught me.

"No time to be in la-la-land, son. Even when there is a pretty girl."

He winks at me good-naturedly. I glance over his shoulder at Nicolette and to my surprise, and relief, her mother gets up, walks over to her daughter and crouches before her. They start talking. I can almost see the gratitude on the girl's face, and I'm glad.

I give Greg a curt nod. Staring stops now.

I force myself to take my chart and keep walking. I try, and fail, to stifle a yawn. I chalk it up to fatigue. I'm working a double shift. I'm exhausted and irritated; therefore my head isn't screwed on right. I stop at a water fountain and splash my face to wake up but my mind won't leave the waiting room. *How is this any of my business?* When an hour has passed, I stride over to the lab and look over the results. What the-?

This can't be right.

I turn to a nearby nurse.

"Carla, please page Dr. McGrath for me."

I turn back to the results. This can't be right.

Nicolette:

I wish I brought a book with me. Or my sketchpad. This is like school all over again except more stressful. Everyone won't stop talking and talking and talking to each other. I suppose mindless chatter eases some people's nerves but it just puts mine on edge. I think about my brother. Lying in a bed somewhere in this building but we have no access to him. All we know is that he's alive.

For now.

They say his blood is O negative, that he can only receive the same blood type. I find it ironic that he can give his blood to any human being but is the most exclusive in terms of accepting blood. I've picked up a lot from overhearing several conversations at once. Apparently my brother was heading to the mall with some friends and got t-boned by a red-light runner. He took most of the impact and his friends had minor injuries. The idiot who hit him is sitting in a jail cell and good riddance.

I've also learned that the latest stock of O negative ran out earlier this morning. Another shipment is on the way. I wish I could see him. I wish he didn't climb into that car or cross that intersection at the very second he did. I wish it were me in the driver's seat. To my surprise, I see a pair of feet walking in my direction. My mother crouches before me and rubs my lap absentmindedly. I was really beginning to think I was invisible.

She wonders aloud, "What's taking them so long? They should have the results by now. I can't stand this waiting."

So that's what she's approached me for? To air out her frustrations?

"Speaking of waiting," I venture. "Why did it take you and Dad so long to contact me about Nate?"

My mom looks up at me in surprise. I don't mean to sound so accusatory. In fact, I've been restraining myself from broaching the topic for the past hour. I couldn't look at, much less, talk to my family without feeling the anger gnaw at my gut and I know my question has a bit of a bite in its delivery. My mom is still pondering my question, her frown pinching even harder. She stops frowning after a while and looks me in the eye with all sincerity.

"Nicolette, I am so sorry. I won't even begin to add insult to injury by trying to explain what we were thinking. We weren't. We just..." she trails off, trying to find the right words.

"You just forgot about me."

It's not a question.

I guess my mother can see the hurt on my face even though I'm doing my best to hide it. She grabs my hands.

"Nikki-"

"Mrs. Talloway? Mr. Talloway?" Dr. McGrath and his intern approach us with strange looks on their faces. *Great timing, Doc.* My mother's attention immediately shifts to him and the whole room hushes in rapt attention.

"Mr. and Mrs. Talloway," he begins. "We are sorry for the wait. After testing your daughter's blood we discovered some unusual results."

"Nothing to worry about," he says at their worried expressions. "We were just wondering if it would be possible to get another sample of her blood and cross-check the results."

My parents immediately acquiesce to the request without even glancing in my direction. I'm about to look back down when I notice the doctor standing slightly behind Dr. McGrath. A slight look of annoyance crosses his face at my parents' automatic permission. Why would he be annoyed? Aren't they giving him what he and his supervisor wants? It's as if he feels indignant on my behalf. His eyes snap to mine and I quickly look down, too nervous to look back up as I stand to follow them into the lab room. My brother is running out of time. The sooner they discover a match, the better.

Jason:

Hazel. Her eyes are hazel. She looked at me. It was only for a brief second but I can still feel the rush of excitement at catching her gaze. The three of us: Greg, Nicolette, and I walk down the hall to the phlebotomy room. This time Greg draws the blood himself. I'm not offended. I need to know if I made a mistake the first time or if her blood really is as strange as I'm thinking. Greg tries to make small talk with her but quickly gives up after a string of softly-spoken one word answers. She keeps her eyes focused on her arm the entire time and refuses to make eye contact with either of us when it's over. She finds her own way back to the waiting room.

"Strange girl," he mutters. I bristle at the comment.

"Her brother's in critical condition. How can she be normal right now?" I respond in a sharp tone. He puts his hands up in mock defense and takes the blood to the lab. I decide to make my rounds without stopping by the waiting room this time. By the time I round the corner from my last check in, Greg is hot on my heels. He practically yanks me into the lab and lays out the results.

"Come again?" Mr. Talloway responds in disbelief. His wife puts her hand on his shoulder with the same look of incredulity.

"I said your daughter doesn't have a blood type. Or at least not a blood type known to medical record," Greg explains. "She's not A, B, AB, or O and her Rh results are inconclusive."

"So…you don't even know if her blood is positive or negative?" Natalia asked.

"Correct," I respond. "We tested Miss Talloway's blood on several different machines and even forwarded her blood at our own expense to a nearby hematologist. Your daughter has a blood type. Just not one previously recorded."

I watch her family take it in. Nicolette does not look pleased. She's not panicked or shocked like I would expect her to be but looks more annoyed at her medical anomaly. She's so different. Her parents and sister are flailing about like nervous rats in a maze but she remains steady. Calm. Her brows are stitched together in a thoughtful frown and to everyone's surprise she speaks.

"What now?" she asks softly. "Nate is still in critical condition and he needs blood. What now?"

She looks at us imploringly. Her parents turn to us.

"Your daughter's right," Greg says. "Your son is

running out of time. I don't know anything about your daughter's blood except that it comes from a healthy donor and a blood relative of your son. We can't use any of your or your eldest daughter's blood. You have three options. You can have your neighbor's highly anemic daughter donate her blood – which could kill him because of its iron levels; you could risk waiting until an O negative shipment comes through. Or you can take a risk and see if your daughter's blood may help her brother."

Mrs. Talloway looks like she's on the verge of an emotional breakdown. She tucks her head into her husband's shoulders and softly cries. Mr. Talloway holds his wife and looks at his youngest daughter.

He then asks Greg, "What are the chances of Jenny Jensens' blood killing our son?"

My supervisor's eyes widen in surprise.

"If she were mildly anemic or even moderately anemic, I would say around forty-five percent," he answers. "But this girl is on the verge of acute anemia and has around a seventy percent chance of adding toxicity to your son's blood –"

"Let alone risking her own health in donating," I add.

"No amount of iron tablets can turn her iron levels around in time. You daughter's blood on the other hand has a-"

"Fifty-fify shot," Mr. Talloway interrupts. "Use her blood," he says decisively. His wife jerks her head up from his shoulder and stares at him.

"Are you sure?" she asks.

"Nate has a better chance with Nikki's blood than Jenny's. Fifty is better than thirty."

Wow. What a mechanical, pragmatic way to look at things. For a second, it looks like his wife is about to slap him but she takes a deep breath, lowers her eyes, and nods her head in agreement. Once again, I notice that neither of them thinks to ask Nicolette about the decision. She stands and looks me in the eye for the second time.

"Let's do it."

CHAPTER THREE

Nicolette:

It worked. Or at least I think it did. One pint, two hours and a bunch of gauze later – my brother is still alive. The first rays of dawn hit his face which barely has any scratches. Looking at him, no one would have guessed he had just survived a near-fatal wreck. The worry lines on my parents' faces have diminished and my sister has felt confident enough of the situation to finally grab us all some food from the cafeteria.

My parents and I are in his room with him and there is a constant flurry of scrubs and white coats coming in and out. As long as he is still alive, I'm satisfied. The sun is beginning to rise and though my hips and bottom ache from sitting in this cold metal chair all night, I feel the lightness in my spirit matches the light pouring into the room.

It feels like the calm after the storm or the light at the end of the tunnel or all those other clichéd analogies used to describe things finally getting better. I actually want things to go back to normal even if it means returning to the dull reality of my desolation. I can bear my emotional torment but not the physical ones of my family. My parents finally nod off and I decide to stretch my legs and walk around. I quietly leave the room and go exploring. This hospital is like one giant maze. I'm pretty good at maintaining my orientation and make visits everywhere from the maternity ward to the psychiatric wing. I should have known there would be ample content for people-watching in a hospital. I'm about to make my way back to Nate's room when I hear a rush of voices in a nearby lounge. I recognize a couple of them.

"His level and speed of recovery is unprecedented. His vitals started stabilizing within thirty minutes of the transfusion and there was no trace of internal bleeding after forty-five minutes. McGrath, what did you give that kid?"

"I told you," Dr. McGrath responds. *"It was his other sister's blood. We still don't know what type it is or how to categorize it. I'm just glad he's recovering. Can you imagine if his reaction had been the opposite?"*

"Class action malpractice suit."

"I thought you got the parents to sign a liability waiver."

"Please, do you know how many loopholes a malpractice attorney can use to maneuver around that?"

"Hey!"

I whip around, surprised. My eyes snap up to a pair of cobalt blue peekers. It's him. Nate's other doctor. I feel flustered all over again. Not only is this guy incredibly good-looking, he just caught me eavesdropping into a conversation that was totally not my business. I look down on impulse and begin to walk away.

"Sorry," I mutter, hoping to escape. *Leave me alone, leave me alone, leave me alone…*I feel his strong hand grasp my arm.

"Whoa, hold on," he says in a voice light with laughter.

I turn. He lets go of my arm. "You're not in trouble or anything. I listen in all the time."

"But you're their colleague." I study the dated patterns on the tile floor.

"I know. That makes it even worse."

I look up at him. He's grinning a careless smile like something is tickling him. I can't imagine what it is. Is he enjoying my discomfort?

"Doctor –"

"Please," he holds his hand up. "Call me Jason."

I frown at him. Most doctors don't go by a first-name basis.

"Jason, how old are you?"

He grins again.

"Why?"

"You look-"

"Too young?" he guesses.

I nod. He smiles again and walks around me.

"See you around, Nicolette."

As I make my way back to the room, I hear voices much more familiar than Dr. McGrath's.

"Nate!" I exclaim and rush into the room. My brother is sitting up in his bed, his eyes alert, with a welcoming smile on his face. I scurry over to the bed and gently give him a hug. I'm surprised at how strong his embrace is in return. I take a second look at him. He doesn't just look good. He looks amazing. It's like seeing a before and after picture spaced out by only a few minutes.

He and my parents continue their conversation but I

can't even jump in – not that I normally would – because I'm too busy observing him. Not only are his eyes alert, the color has returned to his face and his bruises seem to have faded into a much lighter shade of purple. I can't seem to put my finger on the biggest change I notice until it hits me.

"You're not wheezing," I interrupt the conversation. My parents and brother look confused at first but the realization soon dawns on them as they listen harder for my brother's patented wheeze. Nathaniel himself looks amazed.

"You're right, sis." He closes his eyes and takes a deep breath. "So this is what it feels like to breathe without any effort." My mother's eyes well with tears as she rises to give him another hug. My dad, though happy, looks a little perplexed and I know what he's thinking. How is it that my brother is healing so well, so rapidly?

"Hello, Nathaniel," Dr. McGrath greets us warmly. "It's good to see you recovering so well."

And so quickly, I might add. After a series of tests, the doctor gives my brother the green light.

He's free to go home.

"Just make sure you take him to his oncologist as soon as possible."

"He's actually scheduled to see her in a couple of weeks. Is that soon enough?" my father asks.

"I would try to get him in sooner after what he's gone

through but," Dr. McGrath pauses, "something tells me your son will be okay either way."

He leaves the room without further instruction.

When my parents aren't gushing over me for donating or Dr. McGrath for administering care, they're busy fawning over Jason.

"Thank you so much for everything," Mom says softly.

"You're very welcome, Mrs. Talloway," Jason replies.

"Is there some way we can reach you if we have any other questions?" Dad asks.

"Yes, of course. Here's my card. My office and personal number are on there."

I think it will stop here. I've given my blood, and Nate will get better so he can continue with life as normal, recover from the accident and focus on fighting his cancer.

But I can't shake this feeling that nothing is going back to normal.

Jason:

"It's her blood," Norris insists. "There is no medicine, surgery, or apothecary miracle that can otherwise explain the boy's healing." I try to speak but Dr. Montgomery Norris, the state's top hematologist, continues.

"I would concede *if* his injuries alone were staunched and his medical condition returned to that previous of the accident. But he's not just healing. He's *thriving*! Maladies that he suffered *prior to the accident* are healing! His chronic asthma has vanished, his ribs are healed, and his left leg no longer needs a cast! Even his damn bruises are fading fast!"

"Montgom –"

"No – you give me an explanation. Any explanation. Hell, I might even start believing in that witchcraft, voodoo shit if it in some way explains this kid's one-eighty."

He pauses in all sincerity, waiting for Greg's reply. Just as he opens his mouth to respond, Norris continues with, "How much do you want to bet his cancer is gone?"

"What?"

We both look at him in shock.

"Why not? All of his other maladies have disappeared. Has he seen his oncologist?"

"Not yet," I reply. Greg looks captive in thought.

"Okay," he murmurs. "You're right. It is her blood. But you're going to have to do a hell of a lot more research to prove that it is her blood and not some other factor. The medical community will turn you out on your ear if you don't have some solid proof stacked up."

"Wait a minute," I speak up. "Medical community? Just how many people are going to know about Nicolette – I mean Miss Talloway's – blood?"

I can't put my finger on it but something just doesn't sit right with me about Norris's enthusiasm regarding her blood. I'm thrilled that her brother is getting better and that her blood turned out to be the best choice. But every milestone in his recovery further distinguishes the capabilities of her blood. What will this mean for her moving forward?

"What are we going to do now?" Greg ignores my question. "This is out of our jurisdiction. The kid is completely fine now and there's no reason to keep him here any longer."

"You're releasing him today?" Norris asks, alarmed.

"We have to."

There is a pregnant pause in the room.

"Let me talk to her then. The girl and her parents," Norris suggests.

Nicolette:

We're not going home...not yet. A new doc has entered the picture...something Norris. He's a few inches shorter than McGrath and over a head beneath Jason in stature. A balding, eager beaver in his late forties, this man has way too much energy for his age.

"Mr. and Mrs. Talloway, I recognize that this is the last place you want to be but please hear me out." the doctor pleads with an almost desperate smile.

"I have practiced medicine – specialized in hematology – for more than twenty years. I have never seen any blood sample like that of your daughter's."

He looks over at me with an expression I can't quite describe. Like he wants to consume me or something. I remind myself that he wants what's in my veins, not necessarily me but that doesn't comfort me at all.

Dr. McGrath speaks up, "This is somewhat unorthodox but Dr. Norris was wondering if we could contact your oncologist and have him—"

"Her," Natalia corrects.

"—her, come in and run some tests on Nathaniel. He would also like to continue examining your daughter's blood sample for further research," he finishes.

I look over his shoulder at Jason, who stands with a blank, professional expression. He catches me staring and his lips curve the slightest bit.

My dad looks at my mom with querying eyes. Mom shrugs her shoulders. I'm not surprised when they answer with:

"We'll be happy to help in any way we can. The oncologist coming over would save us the trip and we would like to find out how Nate is doing in that department sooner than later. As long as this doesn't disrupt Nikki and Nate's school work, you have our permission."

"Thank you, Mr. and Mrs. Talloway," Dr. Norris gushes. He's grinning a wide face-splitting smile, with enough excitement to cover both Jason and Dr. McGrath beside him.

They're just tests. Just blood samples. Besides me feeling the pain of more needles, there shouldn't be any major sacrifices on my part. Yet for some reason, I can't shake this feeling of foreboding.

Something tells me Dr. Norris did a little arm wrestling to get the oncologist in this morning. Dr. White, an attractive brunette in her mid-fifties, has "hassled" written all over her face. Though polite, she's very short with Nate and my parents, initially asking questions in a brief, succinct voice, almost as if she doesn't want to waste an unnecessary breath on any unnecessary syllables. To be fair, she probably has numerous patients in her own clinic, waiting to be seen. The more she observes my brother, however, the more she slows down.

I can see it in her face.

I had the same expression only hours ago. Her eyes widen in amazement as she tests his strength and dexterity. She takes care to personally draw his blood. We have yet to hear from her.

My sister stretches in visible irritation.

"What's taking her so long?"

I shrug. "She's probably running several tests at once."

"No, Nat's right," Mom says. "Even when we're at her clinic, the tests take a fraction of the amount of time she's spent. I hope there's nothing wrong," she says in a worried tone.

"Mom, I feel great," Nate tells her in assurance. "I've never felt this good in my life. Whatever the result, I'll take it over feeling the way I felt two days ago."

The door swings open.

Dr. White, Dr. Norris, Dr. McGrath, and Jason all stride in to Nate's little hospital room. I have never seen so many white lab coats congregated at one time. Dr. Norris has a wild look of happiness in his eyes. He keeps looking at me and it's really starting to get on my nerves. I ignore him. Dr. McGrath has a more controlled expression but I can still see something is up. Jason can certainly keep a poker face. It's Dr. White's expression that has us all waiting with bated breath.

Her eyes circle wildly in her head.

"I don't know how this happened," she says. "I've run the tests over and over and over again."

"We *know*," Natalia quips sarcastically.

"Natalia!" Mom admonishes.

"What's the news, doctor?" Dad asks, frowning in concern.

"There is no trace of his cancer."

"What?" My sister straightens in her seat. My parents' jaws hang ajar. Nate leans closer to the doctor and says:

"Can you say that again, please?"

"There is no trace of your cancer," Dr. White repeats. She looks at all of us. "I reviewed the results of his samples numerous times and then couriered the sample to a most trusted colleague. Never in my thirty years as an oncologist have I seen this type of turn-around. I've reviewed his charts. Nathaniel's blood count is better than it was prior to his diagnosis."

My dad sits back in his chair at a loss for words. Natalia seems completely out of it and Mom looks like she's about to cry.

"Nathaniel, how do you feel?" Dr. McGrath asks.

"*Great* now!" he replies. The doctors chuckle in amusement.

"Thank you for your patience and your willingness to stay a few more hours. I've given the nurses notice. You are free to go home."

"And I will be in touch with you shortly," Dr. Norris interjects, eyes darting from my parents to me. The last thing I want to do is see this creep again. But something tells me it's no longer an option.

Like the sample?
Find out what happens next by purchasing *Type N*.

Check out these other titles by Michelle N. Onuorah

Remember Me
Type N
Taking Names
Jane
Wanna Be on Top?

Acknowledgements

I want to thank Dr. Victoria Oshodi for undertaking the daunting task of editing this novel. I would also like to thank Karla Henderson, Sandy Lewis, Dorothy Scharer, Judy Campbell-Smith and Irma Alarcon for serving as my beta readers. All of you were invaluable to the development of this novel.

About the Author

Michelle N. Onuorah is the bestselling author of *Type N, Taking Names, Remember Me,* and *Jane.* The daughter of Nigerian immigrants, Michelle grew up with a love of storytelling. At the tender age of thirteen, she wrote her first book, *Double Identity,* and got it published the next year. For three years, she ran an independent magazine, *MNO,* and served as the main writer and editor-in-chief. In 2009, Michelle won the *Captured Moments Creativity Award* for her poem entitled *Encounter.* Her writing has appeared in *Vestiges Literary Magazine, Avalon Literary Review,* and *Medium.com* among others. In August of 2013, she broke several Amazon Kindle Bestsellers lists for her debut novel, *Type*

N. Since then, she has written and released three more novels, all of them reaching various bestseller lists. A graduate of Biola University, Michelle continues to write and publish under her company, MNO Media, LLC (www.mnomedia.com). You can learn more about Michelle at the website as well as like her page at www.facebook.com/authormichelleonuorah. Those interested in being notified of her new releases can go to www.tinyletter.com/mnomedia.